P9-BYV-133

everyone knows this
cowboy's business . . .
especially when
it's love!

The naked cowboy in the gold-plated horse trough presented a conundrum.

How had he come to be naked and still have his boots on?

A black Stetson lay cocked down over his face, hiding all his features, save for his strong, masculine jaw studded with at least a day's worth of ebony beard. The murky green water hit him midthigh and camouflaged his other naked bits.

"Hey, mister."

No response. Clearly it was going to take cannon fire to get through his stupor.

You've got to do something more to get his attention. Hanging back and being shy has always put you in hot water. Take the bull by the horns and be bold, do something about this.

Bolstered by her internal pep talk, she stepped up to flick his Stetson with a thump of her middle finger. "Yo, Cowboy, snap out of it."

One sinewy arm snapped up and his steely hand manacled her wrist. The tequila bottle made a dull pinging sound as it fell against the ground. Big fingers imprinted into her skin.

"Never thump a man's Stetson," he drawled, his voice as rich and luxurious as polished mahogany, "unless you've got a death wish . . ."

By Lori Wilde

THE COWBOY TAKES A BRIDE
THE WELCOME HOME GARDEN CLUB
THE FIRST LOVE COOKIE CLUB
THE TRUE LOVE QUILTING CLUB
THE SWEETHEARTS' KNITTING CLUB

THE CHRISTMAS COOKIE CHRONICLES
CARRIE
RAYLENE
CHRISTINE

Forthcoming
THE COWBOY AND THE PRINCESS

LORI WILDE

THE
COWBOY
Takes a
BRIDE

AVON
An Imprint of HarperCollinsPublishers

AVON BOOKS
An Imprint of HarperCollins*Publishers*
10 East 53rd Street
New York, New York 10022-5299

First Avon Books mass market printing: April 2012

Avon Trademark Reg. U.S. Pat. Off. and in Other Countries, Marca Registrada, Hecho en U.S.A.
HarperCollins® is a registered trademark of HarperCollins Publishers.

Printed in the U.S.A.

10 9 8 7 6 5 4 3 2 1

*To Carolyn Greene. A gifted storyteller.
Thank you so much for your friendship.
You'll never know how much you mean to me.*

ACKNOWLEDGMENTS

I grew up in cowboy country, not far from Fort Worth. I live in the cutting-horse capital of the world, and Jubilee is loosely based on my hometown. I've been observing cowboys my whole life. So writing about them wasn't much of a stretch. All I had to do was walk outside my front door and look around.

A big thank you to the folks at the Cutting Horse Association, who so graciously answered my questions. Also, many thanks to my brother-in-law, Michael Rountree, who is a true cowboy through and through. Stalwart, honest, brave, he epitomizes the cowboy spirit and is an example of what a real cowboy hero should be.

THE
COWBOY
Takes a
BRIDE

CHAPTER ONE

Good sense comes from experience, and a lotta
that comes from actin' like a damn fool.
—Dutch Callahan

The naked cowboy in the gold-plated horse
trough presented a conundrum.

In the purple-orange light of breaking dawn,
Mariah Callahan snared her bottom lip between her
teeth, curled her fingernails into her palms, and tried
not to panic. It had been a long drive down from
Chicago, and jacked up on espresso, she hadn't slept
in thirty-six hours. There was a very good chance she
was hallucinating.

She reached to ratchet her glasses up higher on her
nose for a better look, but then remembered she was
wearing contact lenses. She wasn't seeing things. He
was for real. No figment of her fertile imagination.

Who was he?

Better question, what was she going to do about him?

His bare forearms, tanned and lean, angled from
the edges of the trough; an empty bottle of Jose
Cuervo Gold dangled from the fingertips of his right
hand. Even in a relaxed pose, his muscular biceps

were tightly coiled, making Mariah think of hard, driving piston engines.

Like his arms, his legs lay slung over each side of the trough. He wore expensive eelskin cowboy boots. She canted her head, studying his feet.

Size thirteen at least.

Hmm, was it true what they said about the size of a man's feet?

She raised her palms to her heated cheeks, surprised to find she made herself blush.

Question number three. How had he come to be naked and still have his boots on?

Curiosity bested embarrassment as she tracked her gaze up the length of his honed, sinewy legs that were humorously pale in contrast to his tanned arms. No doubt, like most cowboys, he dressed in blue jeans ninety percent of the time.

She perched on tiptoes to peek over the edge of the horse trough. The murky green water hit him midthigh and camouflaged his other naked bits. Robbed of the view, she didn't know if she was grateful or disappointed.

But nothing could hide that chest.

Washboard abs indeed. Rippled and flat. Not an ounce of fat. Pecs of Atlas.

A rough, jagged scar, gone silvery with age, ambled a staggered path from his left nipple down to his armpit, marring nature's work of art. The scar lent him a wicked air.

Mariah gulped, as captivated as a cat in front of an aquarium.

A black Stetson lay cocked down over his face, hiding all his features, save for his strong, masculine jaw studded with at least a day's worth of ebony beard. His eyes had to be as black as the Stetson and that stubble.

Mesmerized, she felt her body heat up in places she had no business heating up. She didn't know who this man was, or how he'd gotten here, although she supposed that drunken ranch hands came with the territory. If she was going to be a rancher, she'd have to learn to deal with it.

A rancher? Her? Ha! Big cosmic joke and she was the punch line.

Less than twenty-four hours ago she had been standing in line at the downtown Chicago unemployment office—having just come from a job interview where once again, she had *not* gotten the job—her hands chafed from the cold October wind blowing off the lake, when she'd gotten word that Dutch had died and left her a horse ranch in Jubilee, Texas.

She didn't call him Dad, because he hadn't been much of a father. The last time she'd seen Dutch, he'd been hovering outside her ninth grade algebra class, battered Stetson in his hands, his sandy blond hair threaded through with gray, his blue eyes full of nervousness, remorse, and hope. Horse poop clung to his boots and he wore spurs—*yes, spurs*—against the polished maple hardwood floors of her Hyde Park high school. His Wrangler jeans had been stained and tattered, his legs bowed, his belt buckle big. He'd smelled of hay, leather, and horses.

The other students had stared, snickered, pointed.

"Where's the rodeo?"

"Who's the hick?"

"How'd the cowboy pass security?"

"He smells like horseshit."

"Hillbilly freak."

Dutch had stretched out a hand nicked with numerous scars, beseeching Mariah to come closer. "Flaxey? It's me. Your pa."

How many times had she fantasized that he would come back to her? Be a real dad? Love her the way she'd always loved him? But now that he was here, she didn't want him. Not in her high school. Not among her friends. Not dressed like that.

Shame flushed through her. She'd walked right past Dutch as if she hadn't seen him, and when he called her name, she started running in the opposite direction as fast as she could, schoolbooks clutched tight to her chest, heart pounding.

Not only was she ashamed of him, but also she was still mad because he had disappeared a week before her seventh birthday. He told Mariah's mother, Cassie, he was going to see a man about a horse, and he just never came back.

They'd been living in Ruidoso, New Mexico, at the time, and Cassie waited three months for him to return while she cleaned rooms at the Holiday Inn and cried herself to sleep every night. When one of the wealthy Thoroughbred owners in town for a race offered Cassie a job as his family's live-in housekeeper, her mother snatched the opportunity with desperate hands. They packed up their meager belongings, moved to Illinois, and didn't look back.

Dutch never missed a child support payment and he phoned a few times over the years, usually when he was drunk and feeling maudlin; the conversation generally ended with Cassie hanging up on him. Once in a while he sent Mariah gifts at Christmas or for her birthday, but they were always inappropriate. One year, a lasso. The next year, a lucky horseshoe engraved with the words "Make Your Own Luck." Another year, a pair of purple Justin boots, two sizes too small, as if he thought she stayed forever seven.

As she waited in line, Mariah's cell phone rang playing Wagner's Bridal Chorus. She fished it from her purse at the unemployment line and checked the caller ID.

Randolph Callahan.

A strange mix of anxiety, hostility, and gratitude lumped up in her throat. Why was Dutch calling her after all these years? If he was broke and looking for money, he'd certainly picked the wrong time to call. On the other hand, it would be good to hear his voice again.

The weary woman in line behind her, holding a runny-nosed kid cocked on her hip, nudged Mariah, and then pointed at the poster on the wall. It was a symbol of a cell phone with a heavy red line drawn through it.

"Hang on a minute," Mariah said into the phone, and then smiled beseechingly to the woman, "This'll just take a sec."

The woman shook her head, pointed toward the door.

"Fine." She sighed, never one to ruffle feathers, and got out of line.

A blast of cold air hit her in the face and sucked her lungs dry as she stepped outside. It was the first of October, but already cold as a Popsicle. She liked Chicago in the spring and summer, but the other six months of the year she could do without.

"Hello?" Head down, hand held over her other ear, she scuttled around the side of the building to escape the relentless wind.

No answer.

"Dutch?"

He must have hung up. Great. She'd gotten out of line for nothing. Huddling deeper into the warmth of her coat, she hit the call back button.

"Hello?" a man answered in a curt Texas accent. It didn't sound like her father.

"Dutch?"

"Who's this?" he asked contentiously.

"Who is this?" she echoed on the defensive.

"You called me."

"I was calling my father."

A hostile silence filled the airwaves between them.

"Mariah?" the man asked, an edge of uncertainty creeping in.

"You have the upper hand. You know my name, but I don't know yours. Why are you answering Dutch's cell phone?"

He hauled in a breath so heavy it sounded as if he was standing right beside her. "My name's Joe Daniels."

"Hello, Joe," she said, completely devoid of warmth. "May I speak to Dutch please?"

"I wish—" His voice cracked. "I wish I could let you do that."

A sudden chill that had nothing to do with the wind rushed over her. She leaned hard against the side of the building, the bricks poking into her back. "Has something happened?"

"Are you sitting down?"

"No."

"Sit down," Joe commanded.

"Just tell me," Mariah said, bracing for the worst.

"Dutch is dead," he blurted.

Mariah blinked, nibbled on her bottom lip, felt . . . *hollow.* Hollow as a chocolate Easter bunny.

"Did you hear me?"

"I heard you."

Joe's breathing was harsh in her ear.

So her father was dead. She should feel *something,* shouldn't she? Her heartbeat was steady. A strange calmness settled over her, but she didn't realize that she'd slowly been sliding down the brick wall until her butt hit the cold cement sidewalk.

All she could think of was how she'd cruelly run away from Dutch that afternoon fourteen years ago.

"Mariah?" A whisper of sympathy tinged Joe's voice.

"Yeah?"

"You okay?"

"I'm fine. It's not like my life is going to change," she said quickly.

"I know you weren't close. But he *was* your father." Joe's tone shifted, barely masking anger.

Oh, who was Mr. High-and-Mighty Joe Daniels to judge her? He didn't know her. "How did it happen?" she asked, ignoring her own shove of anger.

"He'd had pneumonia for weeks. We tried to get him—"

Jealousy ambushed her. "We?" she interrupted.

"The cutters in Jubilee."

Cutters.

She'd almost forgotten the slang term for people involved in the training and raising of cutting horses.

"We tried to get him to go to the doctor, but you know Dutch, mule stubborn and set in his ways," Joe continued.

No, she didn't know Dutch. Not really.

"He just kept working. Workaholic, your dad."

That Mariah knew. Dutch lived and breathed horses.

"We were at an event, Dutch swung off his horse, staggered, coughed. I could tell he was suffering. His face was pale and sweaty. He looked me in the eyes and said, 'Don't call Mariah until after the funeral.' Then he just dropped dead." Joe's voice cracked again. "He died with his boots on, doin' what he loved."

A long pause stretched out between them. Chicago and Texas in an uneasy marriage over the airwaves.

"Joe," she murmured, "Are *you* okay?"

"No," he said. "Dutch was my closest friend."

Joe's words finally hit her, a hard punch to the gut. Her head throbbed, and she felt as if a full-grown quarter horse had squatted on her chest. Dutch was dead, and the last thing he said was *Don't call Mariah until after the funeral.* Her father hadn't wanted her there.

"You've already buried him?" A soft whimper escaped her lips.

"At Oak Hill Cemetery in Jubilee. It's what he wanted."

She turned to stone inside. Iced up. Shut down completely. "I see. Well then, thank you for calling to let me know."

"Wait," he said. "Don't hang up."

Her hand tensed around the cell phone. "What is it?"

"Dutch left you his ranch."

Dutch left you his ranch.

The words echoed in her head, breaking the thin thread of memory and bringing Mariah back to the present.

The morning sun pushed free of the horizon, bathing the ranch in a butter-and-egg-yolk glow. The joyous twitter of birds greeting the dawn, filling the air with song. How long had it been since she actually paid attention to birds singing? She blinked, seeing Stone Creek Ranch clearly for the first time in full daylight.

It was a country-and-western palace.

The main house sprawled over acres and acres of rolling grassland. On the drive up in the predawn, it had looked like a fat dragon sleeping peacefully after a heavy meal of virgins and villagers. In the daylight, it appeared more like a lazy but handsome king lounging on his throne. Not unlike the lazy cowboy draped insouciantly over the horse trough.

Constructed from limestone and accented with wood finishes, the cowboy mansion boasted a Ludowici clay tile roof, an elevated stone porch, and an accepting veranda. It had to have at least five bedrooms, but probably more like six or seven. A circular flagstone driveway swept impulsively up to the house.

Mariah had parked just short of the main entrance, pulling her rental sedan to a stop by a planter box filled with rusty red chrysanthemums. Numerous other buildings flanked the house. Horse barns, sheds, garages, all well maintained.

Dutch owned this?

She now owned this?

All these years her father had been living in luxury while she and her mother scrimped every penny. The emotions she kept dammed up flooded her—hurt, anger, sorrow, regret, frustration.

Yes, frustration. She had no idea how to run a ranch. She was a wedding planner's assistant, for crying out loud.

Correction. She used to be a wedding planner's assistant. "Used to" being the operative phrase.

What was she going to do with the place? And on a more immediate note, what was she going to do with the man in the horse trough?

Tentatively, she inched closer.

He didn't move.

The shy part of her held back, but the part of her that had learned how to slip into the role of whatever she needed to be in order to get the job done—and right now that was assertive—cleared her throat. "Hey, mister."

No response. Clearly, it was going to take cannon fire to get through his stupor.

You've got to do something more to get his attention. Hanging back and being shy has always put you in hot water. Take the bull by the horns and—

Okay, okay stop nagging.

She reached out and poked his bare shoulder with a finger. Solid as granite.

No response.

Come on. Put some muscle into it.

She poked again. Harder this time.

Not a whisper, not a flinch.

What if he was dead?

Alarmed, Mariah gasped, jumped back, and plastered a palm across her mouth. Dread swamped her. She peered at his chest. Was he breathing? She thought he was breathing, but the movements were so shallow she couldn't really tell.

Please don't be dead.

In that moment, the possibly deceased naked cowboy was the cherry on top of the dung cake that was her life. Three months ago, she'd lost her dream job working for the number one wedding planner in Chicago, and then her vindictive boss had black-balled her in the industry. And now Dutch was gone too and she'd been left a ranch complete with a dead naked cowboy.

Be rational. He's probably not dead.

Maybe not, but clearly he was trespassing, and she couldn't have him thinking that it was okay for him to go around stripping off his clothes and falling into other people's horse troughs during his drunken stupors.

Be bold, do something about this.

Bolstered by her internal pep talk, she stepped up to flick his Stetson with a thump of her middle finger. "Yo, cowboy, snap out of it."

She was just about to thump the Stetson again when one of those sinewy arms snapped up and his steely hand manacled her wrist. The tequila bottle made a dull pinging sound as it fell against the ground. Big fingers imprinted into her skin.

"Eep!" Oxygen fled her lungs. Panic mushroomed inside her. So much for being bold.

"Never thump a man's Stetson," he drawled without moving another muscle, his voice as rich and luxurious as polished mahogany. "Unless you've got a death wish. You got a death wish?"

"N-n-no." Mariah stammered.

She tried to pull away from the Clint Eastwood clone, but pushing against his grip was like trying to bully marble. In fact, struggling only seemed to ensnare her more tightly.

With a lazy index finger, he slowly tipped the brim of his cowboy hat upward, revealing eyes as black as obsidian, and he studied her with a speculative scowl, like he was the big bad wolf just aching for a reason to eat her alive.

Oh man, oh wow, oh just kill me now.

He was one hundred percent alpha male, the kind who staked a claim on a woman with one hard sultry stare and who would fight to the death to hold on to her. The kind of man whose self-confident arrogance had always unsettled her.

She shivered.

His gaze lasered into her as if he could see exactly what she looked like with no clothes on, his intelligent eyes full of mysterious secrets. He didn't seem embarrassed in the least. In fact, he had an air of entitlement about him. As if he had every right to sleep off a berserk bender in her fancy horse trough.

Strangely enough, he made her feel as if *she* were the naked one.

Who was this man? Did he live here? Was he one of Dutch's cowhands?

Even though he was sitting up and she was standing, he seemed to tower over her. He would tower over her when he was on his feet. Of that she was certain. Almost everyone towered over her.

The steady pressure from his strong fingers stirred a bizarre fluttering inside her. Her stomach quivered. Unnerved, Mariah marshaled her courage, gritted her teeth. "Please let go."

His smile exploded, exposing straight white teeth. This cowboy possessed serious star quality. "What if I don't?"

"I'll dunk your Stetson in the water."

His devilish eyes narrowed. "You wouldn't dare."

Her knees wobbled. She was scared witless, but she learned a long time ago to hide her fears behind

bluff and bravado and act brave whether she felt it
or not. Ignoring her sprinting pulse, she swept the
cowboy hat off his head with her free hand. A thick
tumble of inky black hair, two months past the point
of needing a trim, spilled out.

"Try me," she said as tough as she could, hoping
her voice belied her trembling legs.

His hard laugh clubbed her ears as he slowly released her. Mariah slapped his hat down on his head
and snatched her arm back, held it across her chest.
He hadn't hurt her at all, but his sizzling body heat
had branded her.

"What's the deal?" She glared. "You don't have
indoor plumbing?"

"You're funny," he said. "And I don't mean ha-ha.
Who are you?"

His ebony voice unnerved her. That and his big,
lean, bare body. It occurred to Mariah that she was
completely alone here with this stranger. If this were
a slasher flick, she'd be in deep trouble.

She swallowed hard, notched up her chin, and si-
lently repeated the mantra her mentor and former
boss, Destiny Simon, had taught her. *Never let 'em
see you sweat*. Then again, Destiny had been the one
to put her in the sweatbox, so what did she know? "I
should be asking you that question."

"Oh yeah?" An amused smile played at the corner
of his mouth. "Why's that?"

She drew herself up to her full five-foot-one. "Because my name is Mariah Callahan and this"—she
swept a hand at the land around them—"is my
ranch."

"Oh yeah?" he repeated.

"Yes, and you're trespassing."

"Am I?" He lowered his eyes half-mast. Bedroom eyes the exact color of the cup of strong coffee she'd snagged at the Starbucks drive-through in the last big town she'd passed.

"You are."

He studied her as if she was the most comical thing he'd ever seen. As if he wasn't lying naked in a gold-plated horse trough looking as sexy as three kinds of misdemeanors.

Not that she cared. Not really. She had no room in her life for men—especially those of the cowboy persuasion. She knew just enough about cowboys to know she never wanted one.

"You sure about that?"

His words gave her pause, but, determined not to let him intimidate her, she plunged ahead. "I just inherited this ranch from my father, Dutch Callahan, and I'd appreciate it if you'd remove yourself from the premises immediately."

"Okay." He made a move to hoist himself up.

"No wait." She shielded her eyes with her hands. "I don't need to see that."

He chuckled, clearly finding her amusing, and sank back in the trough. But beneath the incongruous smile, she spotted the shadows that dug into the hollows beneath the angular blades of his cheekbones.

"Your father, huh?" he said.

"Yes."

"That's funny. I don't ever recall you coming to visit him."

Was that an intentional dig? Or just an innocent observation? Mariah glanced over at him. There was nothing innocent about this guy. "You knew my father?"

He crossed his middle finger over his index finger. "We were like that."

She felt envious, melancholy, and irritated. "We were estranged."

"And yet he left you this impressive ranch. I wonder why?"

Sarcasm. From a naked cowboy. The guy was cocky. Mariah shifted her weight, feeling like she was being indicted or mocked. "I didn't say it made any sense."

"That's because it doesn't."

"Look," she said. "Could you just go?"

He shook his head. "I'm just not buying it."

"Buying what?"

"That you own this ranch. Perfect hair. Perfect makeup. Perfect fingernails." He waved a hand at her. "You look like a Barbie doll."

"I'm not tall enough to be Barbie."

"Barbie's sidekick then."

"Sidekick?"

"I don't know what they call Barbie's sidekick. Tonto Barbie. Doc Holliday Barbie. Sundance Barbie. Pick one."

"Are all your references movie cowboys?"

"Pretty much. Except the Barbie one. I could call you Calamity Jane instead if you prefer symmetry."

Seriously annoyed, Mariah sank her hands on her hips. "Do I have to call the cops?"

"Do you?"

What a jerk. "I'm calling the cops," she threatened, pulling her cell phone from her purse.

"Are you always this friendly?"

"Whenever I find a naked cowboy in my gold-plated horse trough I am. I'm pretty sure there's laws against public nudity, even in this backwater place."

"First off, I'm not naked," he said.

She couldn't stop herself from raking a gaze over his amazing body. "You look naked."

"Appearance can be deceiving. For instance, you look stuck-up."

"Sometimes appearance can be deceiving, but on the whole, I've found that generally what you see is what you get."

"So you're saying you *are* stuck-up?"

"I'm saying you look like a drunken derelict."

"Hungover derelict," he corrected. "I'm not drunk anymore."

"Excuse me for missing the distinction. I'm sure your mother is so proud."

"I have underwear on," he offered.

"How comforting." As if a little strip of soaking wet cotton cloth hid anything. Why she should find that even more tantalizing than full nudity, she had no clue, but she did.

And that bothered her. A lot.

"Secondly, this isn't public," the cowboy continued. "It's private property."

"I know," she said. She couldn't believe this conversation was happening. Had she driven down a rabbit hole when she wasn't looking and ended up in Wonderland? She half expected to see the White Rabbit pop up at any moment, muttering about being late. "*My* property."

"Thirdly, it's not your horse trough."

Her finger hovered over the keypad. Should she call the cops? By challenging him, was she making things worse? Maybe she should just walk away and let him get out of the horse trough at his own pace. She was thirty-six hours without sleep and hungry and sad and strung out from the road and she wanted to find a place to curl up and take a nap, but first she had to set things straight with this cretin.

Before she could make up her mind whether to call the cops, a sheriff's cruiser motored up the road.

"Ha! Apparently someone else has already reported you," she said. "Nice of them to save me the trouble."

"I wouldn't gloat too hard," he observed. "The deputy will be on my side."

"Why's that? Just because you know each other? The good old boy network in action?" Mariah clenched her teeth. She'd had enough of cronyism in Chicago.

"Nope. The deputy is a woman."

"Then why are you so sure she'll side with you? Did you sleep with her?"

"Does that bother you?"

"Why should it bother me? I don't care who you sleep with. Why would I care about who you slept with?"

"You tell me."

"Tell you what?"

"Why you're upset at the idea that I slept with a lady deputy."

"I'm not!" She snorted.

"You look upset."

"I'm upset because you're naked in my horse trough."

"This conversation is going around in circles."

"No kidding."

"It's not your horse trough."

"It is."

"Nope, because it's not your ranch."

"It is and I can prove it."

"It's not and here's the reason why. My name's Joe Daniels, this here is Green Ridge Ranch, and I have a sneaking suspicion you're looking for Stone Creek."

CHAPTER TWO

Don't judge people by their kinfolk.
—Dutch Callahan

At first glance the woman looked so much like Becca that for one heart-splitting second when he first opened his eyes, Joe thought his dead wife had come back to life and the last two years had been nothing but a terrible nightmare.

For one brief moment he'd felt it. *Magic*. Followed by a quick breath of utter joy.

But now that he'd gotten a good look at the woman in the early morning light, and saw past his throbbing headache, she didn't resemble Becca nearly as much as he'd initially thought.

Different personalities too. He could tell that right from the get-go. Becca enjoyed being the center of attention. She'd been an outrageous flirt, gregarious, naturally bold, never met a stranger. Much as he'd been once upon a time.

Mariah Callahan had more of a shy kitten-with-claws thing going on. Like she was scared, but desperate not to show it.

His wife's eyes had been stark blue, this woman

possessed eyes the color and quality of a melted Hershey bar; her hair a different texture and hue. Thick and golden, whereas Becca's hair had been baby fine and sandy. Becca had been lean and wiry. This woman's body curved softly in all the appropriate places. Becca had been a stunning beauty, whereas this one shone in a girl-next-door kind of way.

She was shorter than Becca as well. By at least two inches. Becca had favored tight-fitting Wranglers, cowboy boots, a Stetson, and Western-cut shirts. Mariah wore black slacks, a fluffy light blue sweater, and skimpy black shoes that looked like something ballerinas wore.

No ghost at all, but another woman entirely. Disappointment squeezed his throat.

"Y-you? You're Joe Daniels?" she stammered, her cheeks flushing a high pink, her fingers clutching the strap of the purse dangling from her shoulder.

"In the flesh," he said, appreciating how his pun made her color burn even hotter. This tough little kitten riled easy.

"This isn't my father's ranch?"

"Nope." He shook his head. It had been contrary not to tell her his name right off the bat, but he'd been unable to resist the tease. She looked at once defiant, yet gullible.

Plus, no matter how cool he acted, it shamed him to admit he couldn't quite recall exactly how he'd ended up in his BVDs in the horse trough, and he didn't know how to get out of it gracefully with her standing there.

The police cruiser pulled to a stop. His sister-in-law, Ila Brackeen, was behind the wheel, no doubt puzzling out what was going on.

"So . . . um . . . where's Stone Creek?" Mariah asked.

Joe waved at the one-lane dirt road running on the far side of his property. "Keep followin' that road another mile. Once you cross the cattle guard, you'll see Dutch's cabin off to the right."

"Thanks. Sorry to bother you. I'm just going to"— she jerked her thumb in the direction of her car, her cheeks still the color of bubble gum—"go."

She spun on her heels and scurried across the grass toward the car, nodding to Ila as she got out of the cruiser. Ila shot her the stink eye. His sister-in-law was suspicious of everyone not born and raised in Jubilee.

Mariah jumped into the Malibu and revved the engine. Joe could feel her humiliation all the way from where he was. She drove away, but not before she turned to glance over her shoulder at him.

One last time.

For no good reason, he had an overwhelming urge to call her back. Ask her to stay a spell. See if he could get her to smile. Stupid impulse, but there it was.

She's not Becca.

'Course she wasn't. He knew that. Joe rested his head back against the trough; every muscle in his body ached.

Ila walked up. His sister-in-law was the opposite of her half sister, Becca. Tall and dark and tomboyish, with a husky voice and a tendency toward klutziness, she put him in mind of the actress Angie Harmon. He and Ila had been friends since first grade. Long before he married her younger sister.

"Who's the misfit?" she asked.

"Dutch's daughter."

"Aw, the princess bitch."

"Aren't you being a bit hard on her?"

"After how she treated, Dutch? No way." Ila raised an eyebrow and peered down at him. "How in the hell did you get in this predicament?"

"Mornin', Il. You're looking bright-eyed and bushy-tailed."

"Don't try to sweet-talk me, Joe Daniels. What in the hell happened? When I left last night you promised me you were going to bed. Looks to me like you spent the night in the horse trough again."

"Jose Cuervo." He winced against the pain shooting through his skull. He turned his head, letting his eyes stray for a lingering glance in the direction of the car disappearing in a dusty cloud toward Stone Creek.

"One hundred percent city girl," Ila said, following his gaze. "She'll have the ranch up for sale and be gone in a New York minute. Nothing to worry about."

"What if she sells the place to some Dallas land developer. Can't have that."

"Good point. Better head her off at the pass."

"I've got to convince her to sell the acreage back to me," he grumbled. "I had no idea Dutch was going to drop dead three weeks after we signed the papers or I never would have traded him the land for Some Kind of Miracle."

"What if she demands more than the land is worth? She seems like the money-hungry type to me." Ila snorted.

He loved Ila like a sister—hell, like a brother; she could match any man in the saddle or with a gun or a fishing pole or her knowledge of football—but she had zero tolerance for girlie-girls or big-city ways. "I'd pay it."

"With what? All your cash is tied up in the ranch and cutting horses."

True enough. Joe was a millionaire a couple of times over, but it was all on the books. Nothing liquid he could readily get his hands on. "Why'd Dutch leave the ranch to her? Why didn't he just will it back to me?"

"Maybe he felt guilty for running out on her when she was a kid," Ila said.

Joe glared, but that made his head hurt worse so he stopped. "It wasn't Dutch's fault. He tried. Mariah didn't want anything to do with him. Dutch finally figured it was best if he just kept his distance."

"You suppose a child might see things differently?"

"Now you're taking her side? A minute ago you were giving her the back side of your tongue."

Ila spread her palms. "You know how I like to play devil's advocate."

Joe tried to lever himself from the horse trough, but he was so stiff he was having trouble pushing up.

"Here," Ila said, and stuck out her palm.

He grabbed hold of her big, solid hand and she tugged him from the trough. His boxer briefs clung to his skin, but he wasn't self-conscious. Ila was like one of the guys. He didn't have to worry about the usual male/female sexual tension stuff with her.

"This may seem like a dumb question," she said, "but how is it you ended up with your pants off, but your boots on?"

"Long story," he said.

"Let me guess. You'd been into the Jose Cuervo be-cause you buried your best friend two years to the day

after you buried your bride. You were getting ready
for bed, thought of Becca, and slipped on your boots
to come out here to kick the horse trough and yell at
her for dying, lost your balance, and fell in. It was too
much trouble to get out, so you just stayed there."

Ila knew him too damn well. Becca had bought
the garish horse trough at an estate auction a few
months before her accident. They'd disagreed about
the appropriateness of horses drinking from a gold-
plated trough, but Becca had won the argument and
the trough stood as a symbol of her triumph. When
it came down to it, Joe had never been able to refuse
his wife anything.

"Amazing powers of deduction, Deputy."

"You're an uncomplicated guy, Joe-Joe."

She had a point. He'd gotten so drunk he spent
the night in his underwear in Becca's horse trough.
Simpleton behavior, true enough. "I miss her something fierce, Il."

"I know you do." Ila's tone softened. "I do too."

Joe pulled a palm down his face. "And now Dutch."

"You gotta move on. Jose ain't the answer."

"I know," he said morosely, and bent to pick up
the tequila bottle. The morning breeze was cold on
his wet skin, and his teeth chattered. Perversely, he
liked the discomfort. He had the privilege of being
uncomfortable. Becca and Dutch did not. "But for
about half an hour last night, I managed to drink
every nerve ending into submission."

"Becca wouldn't want you grieving so hard."

"Sure she would. Becca loved attention."

"I'll give you that," Ila conceded. "But we're talking about your mental health here. Just accept that

there's a bigger plan for your life, even though you can't see it yet. You'll love again someday."

"I've had my shot at my one true love. It's why I've thrown my heart and soul into cutting. I was lucky to have Becca for what time I had her. Lightning doesn't strike twice."

"Tell that to Cooter Johnston. He's been hit by lightning three times."

"Because the man doesn't have sense enough to come in out of a thunderstorm.

Ila cleared her throat, eyed the tequila bottle in his hand. "That's a bit like Fort Knox calling the horse trough gold."

"I suppose it is."

"I'm just saying it's narrow-minded to assume you only get one shot at this love business," Ila said. "You might find something even better than what you and Becca had."

"What do you know?" he groused, his feelings still too raw. "You've never been in love."

A strange expression crossed Ila's face. "Clueless," she muttered.

"What?"

"I said maybe you should stand closer to Cooter."

"You want me to get struck by lightning?"

"Maybe a lightning bolt would get through your thick skull."

"Tell me again, how come you're here?" Joe asked, irritated and a bit confused. Outspoken Ila wasn't normally cryptic.

"Excuse me for being worried about you. I know how close you and Dutch were. I just wanted to make sure you were all right."

He did value her friendship and he had no business taking things out on her simply because she was here and Becca wasn't. "Sorry," he mumbled. "I'm being a tool."

"Not disagreeing with you."

Joe folded his arms over his chest, nodded toward Dutch's ranch. "Wanna bet on how long it takes Little Bit to turn tail and run?"

"You're on." Her grin forgave him. "A Benjamin says one look at the inside of Dutch's cabin, and she's outta there before noon."

"I don't know about that. She might be feistier than she looks. I'll give her till Monday."

"You think she'll spend even one night in that cabin? Did you not see her? Designer sweater, trendy yoga pants, fake nails, expensive haircut? Horseshoe to a doughnut, at the very least, she'll hightail it back to Jubilee to the Motel 6."

"If she spends one night in the cabin I win," he said.

"Deal. Now go put some pants on before I run you in for indecent exposure."

Ila left Green Ridge feeling down in the dumps. Was she going to have to club Joe over the head to get him to notice her as a woman? She flipped on the radio, and Garth Brooks was singing "Unanswered Prayers."

She drummed her fingers on the steering wheel in time to the music. She and Joe were kindred spirits, cut from the same cloth. When would he finally realize that they were meant to be?

All her life Ila lived in the brilliant glow of her beautiful younger half sister. Death canonized Becca.

No matter what Ila did, she could never measure up. She'd forever be that klutzy, skinny, tomboy cop, uncomfortable in her own skin.

She'd been accepted into the police academy at eighteen, but no one had noticed because that was the same day Becca had been crowned homecoming queen. Then during the same week that she'd become the youngest female ever hired by the sheriff's department, Becca had won the Professional Rodeo Cowboys Association barrel-racing championship. And the month Ila got shot in the line of duty, Becca had been killed.

Upstaged by her baby sister one last time.

It was petty to hold on to her disappointments, Ila knew that. She didn't like feeling this way. She wanted to be magnanimous and loving and forgiving. Instead, she felt as if she was always drawing the short straw. It had taken every bit of strength she had to smile happily at Joe and Becca's wedding. To stand there as the maid of honor while her sister married the man she loved.

Memories of Joe tumbled through her head. Sitting next to him in Miss Coltrane's first grade class, playing hooky together in fifth grade to go fishing at Solider Springs Park, the time she'd kissed him under the bleachers at the Fourth of July rodeo when they were sixteen.

Shame shot through her at the old memories that the years seemed to sharpen instead of fade. She'd thrown her arms around him and plastered her lips against his and . . .

He hadn't kissed her back.

Joe had waited patiently for her to finish, and then he'd given her a funny look that knotted her up inside. "You're my best friend, Il," he said. "Let's not mess it up with that mushy stuff."

"Of course," she'd blathered. "You're right." She shrugged like the kiss hadn't meant a damn thing to her.

But she'd never stopped loving him. Not even when five years later he started dating Becca. It stung, but she forgave him. She forgave Joe everything.

She'd been shattered by Becca's death too. Her entire family crippled by the blow. But as she and Joe comforted each other, she secretly started thinking, *What if?*

This morning, she'd woken up with a strange premonition that something wasn't right. Joe didn't drink often—he cared too much about his horses to let anything get in the way of that—but when he celebrated or mourned, well, Katy bar the door. And he was mourning Dutch something fierce.

He buried his grief after Becca's passing by partnering up with Dutch and throwing himself into training Dutch's prize-winning stallion, Some Kind of Miracle.

Ila had been Joe's friend, his crying shoulder. She'd hung around, and just when she was beginning to hope that maybe, just maybe, she had a shot with Joe, here comes Dutch's daughter strutting into the picture.

Ila hadn't missed the way Joe looked at Mariah Callahan. With hot eyes and lusty intent. The way she wished he'd look at *her*. What was the big deal about Mariah? She was blond. Whoop-de-do. And yes, she was all cute and cuddly small while at the same time managing to look chic and stylish. Even so, she wasn't nearly as pretty as Becca had been, but the minute Ila spotted the interloper, she'd thought, *Uh-oh*, and her stomach had gone queasy.

Face it, Joe has a type and it isn't you. Stop pining for a guy who doesn't want you.

That would be the smart thing to do, but Ila's heart wanted what it wanted.

Joe.

And she knew she couldn't win his love if there was a Becca look-alike within spitting distance.

Chicago Barbie had to go.

The second Mariah saw the cabin, her heart started a slow, hard pounding.

She felt stupid for having mistaken Joe Daniels's ranch for Dutch's place. Darn GPS. They could be so inaccurate.

Honestly, she should have known better. Her mother had warned her not to expect too much when Mariah had called her in Argentina and told her about Dutch's bequest.

Last year, Cassie had found true love at long last. Her soul mate. She married a retired Argentinean jockey-turned-horse-trainer named Ignacio Rodrigo, who was a shorter but more successful version of Dutch. Mariah was happy for her, but she did miss the anchor of her mother's presence in her daily life. The distance between them had made the last few months that much harder to bear.

The cabin leaned like a drunken cowboy. A tin smokestack poked up from a roof that was missing more than a few shingles. A rusted old plow lumped up against the side of the house. Paint peeled off the sun-baked structure in long, gray, weathered strips. A derelict barbwire fence encircled the place, but at the back of the erratic enclosure sat an expansive barn, gleaming bright with fresh metal and surrounded by a solid rail horse fence.

Mariah parked beside the decrepit house and stepped out into knee-high Johnson grass. She stood eyeing the cabin, working up the courage to go inside, when a horse's whinny drew her attention.

She turned to see a woman riding up on horseback wearing faded jeans, a turquoise Western-style shirt, dusty boots, and a battered straw cowboy hat, with the brim curled up like a tunnel, gracing silvery curls that sprang out from her head like bedsprings. The lines on her face said she was closer to seventy than sixty, but her body was as athletic as that of someone twenty years younger.

"You look like you took a wrong turn off the freeway," the woman said in a whiskey voice. "Where do you belong?"

The question startled her, because it was one Mariah had been asking herself her whole life. She did her best to fit, blending in with whatever landscape she found herself inhabiting, but she never felt like she truly belonged anywhere. She'd grown up with rich kids, but because her mother had been a housekeeper, she hadn't been accepted into their cliques. What she never admitted out loud to anyone was her darkest fear of being utterly alone. She had a recurring nightmare where she was an astronaut walking outside her spaceship and fell into an endless black hole. Her fate, for the rest of eternity, was to drift alone in space, no contact with anyone, completely abandoned. She always woke from the dream in a cold sweat, breathing hard and clinging to her pillow like a lifeline.

"I . . . I'm from Chicago," she said, not really answering the woman's question because she didn't know how.

The woman loped closer, and then stopped the horse just a few feet from where Mariah stood. She loosened the reins so the horse could lower its head and graze on the Johnson grass. The woman lifted white eyebrows arched into a perfect V and studied her for a long moment. "You're Dutch's girl."

"I am."

The woman nodded. "You've got his mouth and his forehead. Eyes like your mama though. Welcome to Jubilee. Name's Clover Dempsey. I'm the president of the Jubilee Cutters Co-op and owner of the Silver Horseshoe."

"Okay." Mariah still didn't know why the woman was here.

"Dutch talked about you all the time. He was real proud of you and he was sorry about the way things were between you."

"Yeah," she said, unable to keep the sarcasm from her voice. "Me too."

"Don't be that way, hon. It don't pay to hold on to anger. Makes you all sick inside."

Mariah kneaded her brow with two fingers, trying to smooth out the tension. The last twenty-four hours had extracted a toll.

"So here you are. Dutch's Flaxey."

Flaxey.

Dutch's childhood nickname for her because she had blond hair.

Mariah forced a smile. It wasn't this woman's fault she and her father barely had a relationship.

"You don't remember me, do you?" the woman asked.

"Should I?"

A faraway look came into her blue eyes. "My husband, Carl, and I used to babysit you for Dutch and Cassie. We couldn't have kids of our own so we spoiled you something rotten."

"When was this?" Mariah asked, remembering none of it.

Clover waved as if shooing off a fly. "Oh, years and years ago. You were just a little thing, barely walking."

"Where was this?"

"All over. Texas, Oklahoma, New Mexico, California. We followed the cutting horse circuit together. Your daddy, he had a real gift for training cutting horses. Best I ever saw."

"Is this a cutting horse?" Mariah indicated Clover's mount.

"Nah, Juliet is just an old broomtail like me." Clover reached out a hand to pat the mare's neck. "So I hear you own some highfalutin wedding planning business in the Windy City?"

"I didn't own it. I was just an assistant." She was more pleased than she should be to realize Dutch had followed her career. Had known what she was doing, even if, apparently, he exaggerated her role.

So what? It was easy to follow someone from afar. Much harder to get intimate with them in person.

He tried. You turned him away.

Once. He'd tried once. And she'd been a kid. Still, she couldn't tamp down the guilt.

"Ha," Clover said. "Assistants are the ones who really rule the world. Where would those CEOs be without 'em? Lost, that's where." Clover eyed Mariah. "So why wedding planning?"

Mariah shrugged. "From the time I was a little

girl, I was attracted to weddings. Mom said I was besotted with brides. When it came to dolls, I didn't want infants. I wanted bride dolls."

"Your parents got hitched at the city hall in Jackson Hole, Wyoming. Carl and I were witnesses."

Mariah knew her parents had gotten married by the justice of the peace and only because Cassie had been pregnant. Her mother told her that while she'd been attracted to Dutch and found him exciting, she'd always known he wasn't the love of her life. She'd said it over the years with a wistful sigh of longing, often after she read Cinderella stories about happily-ever-after to Mariah.

Cassie told her never to settle, to wait for lightning to strike before giving away her heart. Otherwise, she could find herself stranded high and dry by a man who loved something more than he loved her. In Cassie's case, that something had been cutting horses.

"How is your mother these days?"

Mariah smiled. "She finally found true love." Then she told Clover about Cassie and Ignacio. "They had a lavish wedding. Two hundred guests. They got married at the Chicago Botanical Gardens last June. Her colors were pink and white. My boss said Mom was one of the happiest brides she'd ever seen, and she's seen a lot of brides."

"I'm glad to hear Cassie finally got her happy ending." Clover's eyes darkened. "Sounds like things haven't yet turned out so well for you. I see there's no ring on your finger."

Mariah put her hand behind her back, and then for no explicable reason she said, "I . . . I lost my job."

"I hate to hear that. It's tough losing any job, but

when you lose one that you really loved, well, that's a tragedy. But you're young. You'll find where you're supposed to be if you keep your mind open."

She thought about Destiny, who'd given Mariah her big break and had just as easily taken it all away.

"Well, I gotta get going. Co-op duties. On my way to check in on the Marin place, feed and water their stock, collect their mail while they're out of town." Clover tipped her hat, clicked her tongue to Juliet, and rode away.

Mariah watched the unexpected woman until she disappeared over the rise. All her life, loneliness had weighed against her like a heavy coin tucked into a breast pocket, small but constant. A child raised without siblings, in the households of families where she didn't belong. The remoteness of a girl longing to be accepted but unable to lower the mask that separated her from others.

She turned and regarded the ramshackle cabin once more.

Her destiny?

Optimistic, that thought.

The truth was that coming here had been her last option, and she couldn't shake the feeling that it was a very poor one indeed.

CHAPTER THREE

Cast your hook in the stream where you least expect to get a bite; if you hook a fish, then you'll know you're truly lucky.

—Dutch Callahan

After Ila drove away, Joe tromped inside the house, took a shower, and got dressed. Then he slumped into the kitchen, found the aspirin, thumbed the cap off the bottle, dumped three pills into his mouth, chewed them up, and winced as he swallowed them down. Hell, even his teeth ached.

Barefooted, he padded to the pantry and got out the Froot Loops. He poured up a bowl and ate them standing up over the sink in front of the back window that looked out over the corral, but the sound of his own crunching made his eye sockets hurt.

His gaze drifted over to the hutch sitting in the corner. Becca's hutch. Given to her by her grandmother. They'd painted it avocado green to complement the terra-cotta floor tiles. He remembered how they'd gotten paint all over each other from all the smooching and tickling they'd done during the painting process.

He'd been skeptical about the color at first, but it turned out real pretty, especially once they'd added the copper hardware shaped like horseshoes. On the top shelf of the hutch sat a framed picture of him and Becca on their honeymoon in San Antonio. They were standing in front of the Alamo, arms flung around each other, bright smiles on their faces as if they'd be young and carefree forever.

Stupid fools.

Joe dropped the bowl of soggy Froot Loops into the sink, leaned against the counter, and closed his eyes. He let out a long, slow breath of pain. Pastor Penney had told him about the five stages of grief.

Denial, that numb, no-way-this-can-be-happening-to-me phase. In his case, anger had quickly followed denial. The blind rage and self-pity dogged him for three hellish months of flayed sorrow. He'd done some damn dumb things during those three months. Things he wasn't proud of.

Compared to the anger, bargaining had been short-lived. At that point, not knowing what else to do, he'd gone to Pastor Penney, begging for help, asking what he could do to set things straight with God. He'd known Becca was lost to him forever, but he bargained for the pain to end, promised to be a better man if the suffering could just stop for a day or two.

After that depression gutted him with a round-house kick to the teeth. Knocking him down for the count. Joe was certain he'd never crawl from that black pit.

But the unexpected happened and Dutch found Miracle.

The young stallion had belonged to an old cutter in another county who'd gotten Alzheimer's and his family had been forced to put him in a home. Miracle had been skin and bones, his eyes haunted, his trust nonexistent. But Dutch had taken one look at the two-year-old quarter horse and he'd just *known*.

Dutch had an uncanny horse sense. He'd been more than a horse whisperer. The man was downright horse clairvoyant. He'd given the old cutter's kin five hundred dollars for the stallion. They'd been happy to have it. Dutch ecstatic.

That's when Joe's obsession truly began.

Dutch had brought Miracle back to life, but Miracle and Dutch had yanked Joe from the dark depths of despair. He'd thrown himself headlong into cutting, and it saved his life.

Just when he'd finally accepted that Becca was gone. When he'd stopped fighting the pain and let go. When he'd finally put away all her pictures in the trophy room, except this one on the hutch when they'd been at their happiest. He lost Dutch.

And damn if the awful cycle hadn't started all over again.

Now, he hung on by a thread. Dangling. The only thing keeping him sewed together was that stallion and the certainty that together, they could take the top spot in the Fort Worth Triple Crown Futurity. At this point, his only goal was to honor Dutch's memory.

Now there was a fly in the ointment.

Mariah Callahan.

Joe paced the kitchen floor, hands clasped behind his back, the thought of Mariah suddenly making him restless, impatient. He didn't want her here. He hoped Ila was right. That she would win their bet. He wanted Mariah gone because the woman stirred something in him, something more than irritation and inconvenience, something he didn't want to think about too hard in case he found he liked it. He didn't want to like her. Didn't want to have any feelings for her beyond indifference. Because feelings just led to pain.

On his sixth pass in front of the window, Joe caught sight of something from his peripheral vision. Something that stalled him in midstep.

The two top boards on the back side of the corral fence had been knocked down. No Miracle in sight.

The ornery stallion had broken out again, and Joe knew exactly where he was headed.

Memories pummeled Mariah as she climbed up the precarious wooden porch riddled with termite holes. She, Dutch, and Cassie had lived in similar hovels just like this, one after another, quick as the turn of a radio dial. The location changed, but the houses were all the same—dinky, desperate, and dilapidated.

A horseshoe hung over the front door. The ends pointed upward so all the luck wouldn't run out.

"Didn't help, did it, Dutch?" she mumbled past the lump clogging her throat.

The only thing that had changed from her childhood was that her father owned the property instead of renting it.

She knew without even entering it that the horse barn would be stocked with the finest equestrian equipment that money could buy. Dutch had been the kind of man who'd buy a new blanket for his horse before buying new shoes for his child. She recalled the vicious fights he and Cassie had over money. Dutch arguing that he had to spend money to make money. Whereas Cassie would point out he cared more about his damn horses than he did his family. Dutch would counter that the horses were what put food on the table.

That had been his delusion. His self-defense. That his constant chasing of a dream would eventually end in success. Clearly it had not.

Mariah sighed, braced herself for what she would find inside, and opened the door.

Her ballet slippers made a shuffling sound against the worn hardwood. Newspapers, horse magazines, and old clothing littered the floor—faded jeans, stained Western shirts, scuffed boots, athletic socks, battered cowboy hats, red bandanas.

A brand new cutting saddle sat on the stained, floral-print, 1970s-era sofa like a crown on the head of a rag doll. It surprised Mariah that she could identify a cutting saddle. More memories flashed through her.

"Look here, Flaxey," she recalled Dutch saying to her one day when he'd taken her with him to pick out a saddle. He took her little hand in his and ran it over the saddle's seat. "A good cutting saddle allows you to 'sit the stop.' Do you know what that means?"

She'd shaken her head. She didn't understand, but it seemed to matter to her daddy, so she listened real hard.

"It means the seat should lie close to the horse's back. You want as close as you can get. The pocket should be in the middle of the seat. See here." He pointed to another saddle. "This one sits too far back. It'll force the rider against the cantle and put him up on the swells."

Mariah hadn't known what he'd been talking about, but she made note of the lesson and now, twenty years later, it came rushing back. All this time she thought she'd forgotten her father's early lessons on horse care, but they weren't gone. They were still there lurking, hiding just below the surface, waiting to be unearthed.

The coffee table lay buried under horse tack—a German martingale, snaffle bits, headstalls, and reins. The smell of leather and horses rose up from the table, a scent that stroked the past and lit a fire in Mariah's brain.

The kitchen was no different from the living area. It was cramped and cluttered. More horse gear. A small dormitory-sized refrigerator held a six-pack of Coors beer, half a stick of summer sausage, and a block of rattrap cheese. The floor was a quarter-inch deep in sand, and dust covered everything. In the pantry sat a box of saltine crackers, a bag of beef jerky, a can of sardines, and a sack of horse feed. In the tiny laundry room she found an apartment-sized washer/dryer combo and an unusually large number of metal feed buckets.

She paced the kitchen, kicking up sand, trying to shuck off the feelings tightening around her throat. Anxiety bathed her back. She felt sweaty and claustrophobic. The creak of the floorboards echoed in her ears, old and cranky. The melody of "Camptown Races"—as solid as if someone was singing it—riffled through her head. A song Dutch used to whistle while he worked.

The photographs on the wall were all of Dutch and horses and various other cowboys. In one close-up, Dutch and Joe Daniels grinned at the camera, holding a trophy between them, but in Joe's eyes, beneath the smile, she saw pain. What haunted him?

Joe Daniels.

Everything about the man radiated dark, dangerous energy. Brooding, rugged, cocky. The worst kind of trouble. She should stay far away from him. She couldn't wait to sell this dump and leave Jubilee in her rearview mirror.

The neglected house was only about eight hundred square feet and covered with years of grime. Any rational person would throw her hands up in despair and have the property condemned.

Another thing that struck her was what was missing. No television set, no computer, no Internet service. The house echoed what she already knew about her father. Dutch cared about one thing and one thing only.

Horses.

The single bedroom had one twin bed with a thin mattress and a chair covered with more horse supplies. The bedside table was laden with books on the care and training of cutting horses and entry forms for upcoming cutting events. The lamp was made from deer horns. The shabby, discolored curtains were adorned with galloping horses.

He was here. Her father. She could feel him. Could almost hear his voice, a deep, rolling bass that sounded like thunder mumbling behind a cloud.

His home. Such as it was. He'd left it to her.

Mariah sank down on the end of her bed, felt an involuntary smile curl her lips. She drew her knees to her chest, wrapped her arms around her legs, took a deep breath, and inhaled the stale, horsey scent of the bed linens.

She felt Dutch around her, like a flash of lightning. Hot and close.

A strange fissure of joy cleaved her. Against all common sense, she felt a strange skip of inexplicable homecoming.

And that's when she saw the rattlesnake.

Joe stopped his Ford F–150 King Ranch, which was pulling a horse trailer, beside Dutch's battered old Dodge Ram dually.

His friend had been dead only a few days and Joe hadn't had the heart to step foot into the cabin. He had no idea what kind of mess Mariah had walked into. Actually, he didn't care. All he wanted was for her to go away.

Right now, he was here to retrieve his horse.

He wasn't about to let Mariah sidetrack him, no matter how much she reminded him of Becca.

He thought of the way she'd treated Dutch. Never calling him or coming to see him. Thought about how the last thing Dutch had asked of him was not to contact Mariah until after the funeral.

Joe clenched his jaw, hardened his heart against her.

Just go get your horse.

The morning sun was bright now and it had started burning off the dew. His head throbbed as if someone had buzzed a chain saw through it. So much for aspirin. No more tequila. Ever.

He opened the door of his truck and swung to the ground, but just as he did, Mariah came tumbling from the cabin screaming at the top of her lungs.

Immediately, Joe reacted. He ran toward her, grabbed her up in his arms.

The second his hands touched her, he knew it was

a mistake. The top of her sweet-smelling head grazed his shoulder and the earth shifted beneath his feet.

"Whoa there," he said, alarmed to hear his voice come out thready. He was speaking as much to himself as he was to her. "Whoa."

"Oh," she exclaimed, and pulled back as if she just now realized whose arms she ran into. "Oh, it's *you*."

She said "you" like it was a dirty word.

He grinned, tipped his hat back on his head, slammed a firm grip on himself, and drawled, "Joe Daniels at your service, ma'am."

She pulled herself up to the full extent of her five-foot-nothing and flashed him a haughty expression. "Good to see you finally managed to find your pants."

"How long are you planning to keep throwing that in my face?"

"Every time I see you."

"You're relentless."

"You don't like it? Don't come around."

"This wasn't voluntary."

"And yet, look, here you are."

Her smart brown eyes peered into him as if she knew every thought that passed through his head. The woman didn't miss a trick. Smart-mouthed and sassy. Paradoxically, she was cute in the way of baby chicks. Innocent bit of fluff.

He didn't like baby chicks. They were too cute, fluffy, and you had to make them a pen so things wouldn't eat them, and, well, they were just a pain in the ass.

Her pink cherubic cheeks gave her an angelic appearance. Like those wide-eyed kids in the Christmas figurines his mother collected. Her complexion was the color of cream, with a slight dusting of freckles over the bridge of her nose. Cinnamon sprinkled on eggnog. Her lush lips were full, but not wide.

Angels and baby chicks. Who needed that kind of hassle? Especially with the daughter of his best friend. A friend she'd treated like dirt.

But what rattled him to the center of his soul was the aura of loneliness radiating off her in waves. She was as isolated as Joe.

Startled by that realization, involuntarily he tightened his arms around her. "What's wrong, what has you running and screaming from the cabin like demons are on your tail?"

"Sn-sn-snake," she stammered, and trembled. "There's a rattlesnake in the cabin. I'm terrified of snakes."

But of course, snakes and baby chicks were sworn enemies. "In the bedroom?"

"How did you know?"

Joe laughed in relief.

"You're laughing at me." She glowered and swatted at his chest, a soft, girlie blow. "Why are you laughing at me?"

"The snake in the bedroom? That's just Stuffy."

Mariah narrowed her eyes. "Who's Stuffy?"

She aroused something in him, something illogical, improbable, impossible; something beyond the sexual attraction that instantly hardened him below the waist. Briefly, he closed his eyes, swallowed hard, struggled to gain self-control.

Frankly, his body's reaction shocked him. He'd grown accustomed to feeling nothing. Here was living proof that his libido hadn't died with Becca, and he wasn't sure how he felt about that.

Scratch that. He was sure. He didn't like it at all and he didn't like her. He wasn't going to let some cute little thing unhinge him simply because he hadn't had sex in two years.

But that was easier said than done when her well-rounded breasts were smashed snugly against his chest. Get away from her. Move now.

Joe stepped back and immediately felt better. "Stuffy is a taxidermied rattlesnake mounted on a shellacked tree stump. Dutch told me he won Stuffy as a trophy at his first amateur cutting exhibition."

"Oh yeah." Mariah sounded dumbfounded. "I remember that snake now. Dutch used to keep it on the bureau in the bedroom. He was so proud of Stuffy. My mom hated it and she kept throwing clothes over the atrocious thing to hide it."

"Ah, sentimental memories."

"Are you making fun of me?"

"Never." He put on a serious face.

"That damn snake really scared me." Her smart brown eyes flashed with spunk. Her scent—a combination of flowers and cookies—clung to him.

Before he'd married Becca, he'd been something of a scoundrel. He'd be the first to admit it. He'd been one helluva bull rider and that wasn't all ego talking. Eight solid seconds on the backs of critters named Terminator and Satan's Son and Buzz Saw earned a man his pick of buckle bunnies. He made enough money on the PRCA to purchase Green Ridge Ranch after a knee injury had knocked him out of the bullpen. But he hadn't minded. He had his day in the sun. He'd married Becca and he'd been faithful, and once he lost her, he lost all interest in sex.

Until now.

And he hated himself for it. Hated her.

"What are you doing here? Don't you have a bottle of tequila to kill or something?" she snapped.

"I'm not a drunk," he said lightly, suddenly wanting her to know that he didn't make a habit out of getting blitzed and falling into horse troughs. Why did he give a good damn what she thought of him?

Last night had been a rare lapse. He was over it now. Well, except for the pounding headache.

Mariah reached up to touch her neck in a self-conscious gesture. He tracked her movements, and that's when he saw that a couple of buttons on her sweater were undone, giving him a helluva glimpse at a pink lace bra.

Ah, hell. He did not want to stare but he couldn't look away.

"Stop ogling my breast."

"Yes, ma'am." His gaze stayed glued to her chest.

"Yo, buddy." Mariah snapped her fingers near her face. "Eyes up here."

"Kind of hard to do," he said. "When you're flaunting it."

"What?" She glanced down, her mouth formed an alarmed, silent O, then she instantly started buttoning up. "The buttons must have come undone while I tried to take a nap in the backseat."

Joe shifted his attention toward the white sedan, relieved to have something else to look at. "You slept in your car?"

"It's a long drive from Chicago."

"Why didn't you get a motel room?"

"I couldn't afford a rental car and a motel room. And since I couldn't drive a hotel room, the vehicle won out."

She had a fine sense of the absurd. Unexpected.

"You're broke?"

"In a word, yes."

"Dutch told me you were a wedding planner. What happened with that?"

"Dutch talked about me to you?" Her suspicious eyes instantly softened and her voice sounded hopeful. In that moment, she looked so starkly vulnerable it hurt Joe's head.

"Every day," he admitted, wanting for some perverse reason to hurt her.

Her teeth sank into her bottom lip and her eyes clouded.

"How come you never came to see him?" Joe murmured, knowing how much it had hurt Dutch to have so little contact with his only child. He never talked about his regret, but it was in his voice every time he spoke Mariah's name.

She tossed her head, struggled to control the tiny quiver in her chin. "That was his choice, not mine. He's the one who left me and my mother for horses."

Joe rubbed a hand over the nape of his neck, ashamed of his cruel impulse. Ila was right. He didn't know Mariah's side of the story. "I'm sorry about your father's passing."

"I should be giving you condolences since you knew him so much better than I did," she said.

"You're jealous?"

"That my own father preferred the company of strangers and horses to mine? Why would you think I'm jealous? 'Resentful' just might be the word you're looking for."

Ouch. He was strolling in a field strewn with land mines of emotions between Mariah and her father. One wrong move and he'd blow himself up.

She crossed her arms over her chest, knitted her brow in a scowl, tough as the South Side of Chicago, but she couldn't mask the quick glimmer of sadness in her brown eyes. "Why are you here?"

"Miracle."

She startled. "What?"

"Some Kind of Miracle."

"Is that supposed to mean something?"

"It's a horse. A quarter horse stallion to be precise and the best cutting horse I've ever had the pleasure to clamp eyes on."

"What does that have to do with me?"

"Miracle was Dutch's horse. When Miracle won several cutting events in a row, we knew we had something special on our hands."

"If he's Dutch's horse, what do you have to do with it?"

"He trained Miracle. I rode him. We knew we stood a good chance at winning the Fort Worth Triple Crown Futurity this season. The purse is four hundred thousand dollars. Dutch told me Miracle was his last chance."

"Last chance for what?"

"To settle down," Joe said. "Make amends. Redemption. Hell, I don't know. We didn't talk about stuff like that. He just offered me the stallion in exchange for this old cabin he'd been renting, the horse barn, and four hundred acres of land a few weeks before he died. I took him up on it."

"I see." She turned to run a scathing gaze over the ramshackle house. "Looks like you got the best end of that deal. Want to trade back?"

"What would you do with a cutting horse?"

"Sell it."

"You can't sell Miracle!" What in the hell was wrong with this woman? She had some screwed-up values. "That stallion is the best cutting horse to ever draw breath."

"Oops, forgive me for blasphemy." Mariah rolled her eyes. "I had no idea you were one of *those*."

"One of what?" he drawled lethally, not liking her tone.

"Pie-in-the-sky dreamers just like my father."

"You don't know what you're talking about. Miracle *is* going to win the futurity."

"You sound just like Dutch in the throes of his get-rich-quick schemes."

"Anyone who thinks you can get rich quick training cutting horses has no idea what they're talking about. It takes time, hard work, skill, and lots of luck just to make a passing living."

"And yet you're certain this horse is going to win."

"He's not named Some Kind of Miracle for nothing."

They fell silent, warily watching each other.

"Does that pickup truck belong to Dutch?" she asked, nodding at the dually.

"It does."

"Do you know if he left it to anyone?"

"I believe it's yours. You need to go see your father's lawyer, Art Bunting, for the details of his estate."

"Thank you," she said. "I'll do that."

Joe never intended on saying the next words out of his mouth, but somehow they just slipped out. Probably guilt over being mean to her a few minutes ago. Or maybe some damn misguided sense of chivalry. "You need someone to follow you to turn in the rental car and give you a ride back?"

"Would you do that?" She sounded astonished.

Every instinct was telling him to leave her to her own devices, but Joe wasn't built that way. He saw a damsel in distress and he broke out in Sir Galahad. Bad habit, but there it was. "Sure."

"That's very kind of you, considering I thumped your hat."

"I won't hold it against you." He grinned. "I was sort of asking for it."

She raised a palm to hide a yawn. "And could you give me just a couple of hours to get some sleep? I've been awake for over thirty-six hours."

"Tell you what," he said. "We'll do it tomorrow after you've had a good night's sleep. In the meantime, I'll just go round up Miracle from your barn and take him back home."

CHAPTER FOUR

At some point, home is a strange land.
—Dutch Callahan

Mariah left Joe to retrieve his horse and went back inside the house. One more look at the mess and she heaved a deep sigh. If she had any money, she'd drive to a motel. As it was, she had to make do. At least the house was hers and she wouldn't have to sleep in her car.

A place to call her own. In Jubilee, Texas. Cowboy country. The last place she ever wanted to wind up.

It was just temporary. Until she could sell the ranch, move back to Chicago, and start her own wedding planning business with a nice nest egg.

Retracing her steps, she walked to the car, wrestled her two suitcases—holding everything she owned in the world—from the backseat, and dragged them up the precarious front steps. Joe was nowhere in sight.

Good. She didn't need him running over here trying to help. Coming inside. Looming over her. She could take care of herself. No cowboy chivalry needed.

You sure accepted his offer of a ride into town quickly enough.

Yeah, well, that was different. She didn't have much choice in that. Jubilee was fifteen miles away and she didn't know anyone else in town.

She lugged the suitcases inside and dumped them in the middle of the living room floor. Later. She'd unpack later. For now, she needed sleep and lots of it.

Her cell phone rang. She hunted for her purse, found it on the sofa, and answered her phone on the third ring. The caller ID flashed Cassie's number. "Hi, Mom."

"Sweetheart, just calling to see if you made it to Jubilee. I worried about you taking that long drive alone."

"I'm here. I made it."

"Are you okay?"

"Sure, why wouldn't I be?" She didn't want to complain and worry her mother.

"I worry it hasn't quite sunk in yet that your father is gone."

"Mom, it's not like he was a presence in my life." Mariah ran a hand along the bar separating the small kitchen from the living room area, and her fingers came away dusty.

"You two never reconciled. You didn't get to say good-bye. You need closure."

"It's too late for that."

"Maybe not."

"How can I get closure, Mom? Dutch is dead."

"He had his faults but he wasn't a bad man, Mariah."

"I never thought he was."

"I wish your father and I could have loved each

other the way we should have," Cassie said wistfully. "But we just weren't meant to be, and if Dutch hadn't left us, I would never have met Ignacio. Other than having you, Iggy is the best thing that ever happened to me."

In the background came the sound of pans rattling.

"Iggy's making lunch, Mariah. He treats me like a queen. I still can't get over it. I wish . . ." She trailed off.

"What?"

"I wish you could find this kind of happiness."

"I'm happy," she said defensively.

"So, the ranch your father left you," Cassie said, wisely changing the subject. "Is it—"

"A hovel, just like you said it would be."

"I'm sorry."

"Hey, it's someplace to live." Mariah looked around the cramped space. Was that light coming through the ceiling over the sink?

"You know you could come to Argentina. We'd love to have you."

"You've got your life, Mom, and I'm trying to figure mine out. I'm fine. This'll do for now." She frowned, stepped to the kitchen, squinted up. Yep. Sunlight. Drifting down through a hole in the roof. Lovely. Well, as long as it didn't rain, she was good to go. And if it did rain, at least the hole was over the sink.

She glanced out the window and saw Joe leading a horse into the back of his trailer. The stallion was handsome, fit and toned. She could see why Joe had such confidence in the animal. There was something about him. Something special.

And then in a flash she found herself evaluating the

horse through Dutch's eyes. The stallion was just the right build for cutting. How she knew it, she couldn't say. Probably something that had soaked into her brain from when she was a kid. Something she hadn't even known she'd forgotten.

Joe looked up.

And caught her watching him.

Mariah jerked her gaze away, went back to studying the sunlight bleeding through the ceiling.

"Honey, are you still there?"

"I'm here."

"You went quiet for so long I thought we got cut off. Is something else the matter?" Cassie made a noise of pleasure. "Oh, that is delicious."

"What?"

"Iggy just gave me a bite of chicken empanada. It's to die for. I wish you could taste it."

"Me too."

"So anyway, sorry to interrupt, what were you saying?"

"I'm fine. Everything's fine."

"But . . . ?"

"No but."

"There's a but. I hear it in your voice. You can't fool your mother."

"It's not a big deal."

"Mariah, talk to me."

"There's this guy—"

"A guy? That's great."

"He's not that kind of a guy."

"Ugly, huh?"

"No, no, he's very good-looking." Mariah risked peeking out the window again. Joe had finished loading Miracle into the trailer. He shut the trailer door, and then leaned over to pick up a work glove he'd dropped, giving her a glimpse of his backside. Mariah tilted her head, tracking his movements, hung up on the way those snug-fitting jeans cupped his butt.

"So what's the problem?"

"He's a cowboy, for one thing."

"But of course, you're in Jubilee."

"And he lives right next door. In fact, he traded Dutch this chunk of land for a cutting horse."

"Hmm, that's interesting."

"What is?"

"Dutch was always trading away things for a horse, not the other way around."

"It's how he got the place he left me."

"What's this guy's name?"

"Joe Daniels."

"*The* Joe Daniels?" her mother asked, sounding impressed.

"Um . . . I guess so. Who is *the* Joe Daniels?"

"He was a bull rider. One of the best. Until he got injured a few years back and had to give up the sport. I know you've seen him on commercials. He used to endorse a brand of cowboy boots."

"I can't say I've ever paid much attention to the advertising of cowboy boots. Apparently, now he's a cutter."

"I'm not surprised. Jubilee is the heart and soul of cutting horse country. So what's the matter with him? Is he married?"

"I don't know and I don't care. I'm not interested." She stood up on tiptoes for a better look as she watched Joe slide behind the wheel of the pickup truck.

"So why did you bring him up?"

"Because I found him passed out naked in a gold-plated horse trough."

Cassie laughed. "That sounds like an auspicious beginning."

"To what? A comedy of errors?"

Joe circled his truck in the tall grass and drove away.

"Don't dismiss him out of hand. Remember how I met Ignacio?"

"You went in to clean the Willowbrands' guesthouse and he was stepping out of the shower. Nothing between you and Iggy but a bath towel."

"He took one look at me. I took one look at him." Her mother sighed happily. "And we both just *knew*. Fate has a way of putting us in the right circumstances at the right time."

"Believe me, Joe Daniels and I are *not* fated."

"You never know."

"I know. He was hungover in a horse trough. So not the man for me."

Cassie giggled, whispered something to Ignacio. Then Mariah heard the sounds of a prolonged kiss. "Um, it sounds like your lunch is ready."

"You're just trying to worm your way out of this conversation," Cassie said.

"Guilty. Bye, Mom. Go take care of Iggy."

Her mother started humming "This Thing Called Love."

"I know you're humming that for Ignacio, not me."

"Keep your mind and heart open, Mariah. Love may hit you when you least expect it."

"Sort of like the flu, huh?"

"You'll see. One day. Don't run away from love."

"I'm glad you're happy, Mom. Tell Iggy hello for

me. Gotta go." Mariah hung up feeling weary to the bone.

She loved her mother and was very happy for her, but ever since she'd fallen in love with Ignacio, she'd been like a teenager with her first head-over-heels crush. Because of it, Mariah had kept a lot of things from her. Like the dire financial straits she'd been in since Destiny blackballed her in Chicago.

Exhausted from the drive and the roller coaster emotions of the last twenty-four hours, she searched the house and found two mismatched but clean sheets in the hall closet and went into the bedroom to exchange them for the old ones. How she wished she had money for a motel.

Fighting back the self-pity, she stripped the old sheets from the bed, tossed them on a rocking chair, realizing no man had ever really loved her. Her own father had left her. She'd never felt any kind of magic with the guys she dated. Unlucky in love. That was her. But she stupidly kept hoping. Wasn't that the real reason she loved weddings? The hope? The dream? If other women could find love, why not her?

"Stop feeling sorry for yourself," she muttered. "At least you don't have to sleep in the car."

She rounded the corner of the mattress, tucking in the sheets as she went, and stumbled over the coiled rattlesnake.

Her heart vaulted into her throat. "Eep!" She bit off the scream, reminding herself the snake was dead. Damn vile thing.

Nose curled with repugnance, Mariah picked up the taxidermied rattlesnake and held it as far away from her body as she could get it. What was she going to do with it?

Immediately, she thought of the trash can, but didn't have the heart to dispose of Dutch's first cutting horse trophy. She ended up stowing it in the hall closet where she'd found the sheets, flinging it inside and then slamming the door closed.

Barely able to keep her eyelids open, she shuffled into the bedroom, kicked off her shoes, collapsed onto the bed in her clothes, and slid beneath the covers.

Sleep.

She craved the blissful oblivion of sleep. No worries. No ceilings with holes in them. No naked cowboys in horse troughs. Just sleep.

But surprisingly, sleep didn't come. Sleep escaped her in the way it often did if you went too long without it, too wired, too amped up to settle down.

She struggled to shove the worry from her stomach. Stress always lodged in her tummy, rumbling and disagreeable.

Breathe. Just breathe.

She curled up underneath the clean sheet that smelled of soap and fabric softener. The fragrance comforted her a little. But sweet-smelling covers were no defense against the loneliness twining around her heart. Her father had lived here. Slept in this bed. He was gone and she'd never had the chance to say good-bye.

Tears burned the backs of her eyes, but she couldn't cry. Loneliness turned to guilt, and then to regret. How had she gotten here—broke, jobless, no man in her life, with nothing more than a stuffed rattlesnake for company?

Once upon a time she'd had dreams, big dreams of owning a wedding planning business in Chicago high society. She'd worked so hard for so long, eschewing dating and relationships in her drive to get ahead, and what did she have to show for her sacrifices?

Nothing. No one.

For years, she'd believed that success would give her everything that was missing from her life—money, respect, a father. She cradled the pillow, brought her knees up, and crushed it to her chest. "Dutch," she whispered. "Why did you leave this place to me?"

Why was she asking why? If he hadn't left it to her, she'd very possibly be homeless. In all honesty, his bequest had come just in the nick of time.

Why, Dutch, why?

Her nose burned along with her eyes, but still the tears didn't flow. Why couldn't she cry for her father? She'd loved him once. Still loved him in a place deep inside where she couldn't touch.

What was she doing here? She didn't belong in this place. Didn't belong in Texas. Never mind that she'd been born in Brady, in the very heart of the state.

There was no opportunity for her here. A wedding planner in Jubilee?

Too bad she was all out of options.

She should sell the place. Selling the ranch was the only smart thing to do. Her heart twinged, resisting the idea, but not really knowing why. What else could she do?

In this economy? It might take months—maybe even years—to sell the property. Right now, she had two hundred and seventy-five dollars left in her bank account. She had to find a job ASAP and she couldn't afford to be choosy.

Finally, she drifted off and a dream came to her

immediately, unfurling like a package ribbon from a wedding present rolling down the aisle of a well-appointed church.

The dream was familiar, comforting. All around her were flowers of every shade and hue—red roses, purple orchids, white daisies, pink tulips, yellow jonquils. They were everywhere. In bouquets and boutonnieres, in vases, mounted on the ends of pew rows. Her nose twitched with the smell of them, sweet and velvet, civet and amber. It smelled like luxury and bliss. Beneath the flowers were other scents as well; the mustiness of hymnals, the creaminess of hand lotion, the crispness of spray starch.

Sounds of arriving guests filled her ears. Murmured conversation. The hollow squeak of new shoes against hardwood. The repeated creak of the front door hinges. Mariah could feel the chapel filling up. The room grew warmer. Goose bumps rose on her forearms. Her stomach clenched. Excitement spilled into her mouth. It tasted like Jordan almonds and butter mints.

She stood at the front of the room, off to the side, making sure everything was perfect. The bride was getting ready. The groom had arrived. No mistakes. Nothing wrong. In her dreams, she was in charge and all was right in the world.

And then she realized all the people in the room were dressed in cowboy clothes.

How strange was that?

Mariah awoke with a jolt sometime later. Sun spilled in through the west window. Resentment at being pulled from the bucolic dream nibbled at her. It was late afternoon. She'd been asleep for several hours.

Hunger drove her from the bed. She couldn't remember the last time she'd eaten, and a vague headache dogged her.

She threw back the covers and, yawning, stumbled to the bathroom to wash her face and brush her hair. She'd forgotten to take her contacts out before she'd taken a nap and now her eyes felt raw and achy. She plucked out the contacts and rummaged in her purse for her glasses.

Feeling fuzzy, she padded to the refrigerator and checked it again. Same unappetizing fare as before. She longed for a salad.

"To heck with it," she mumbled, grabbed her purse, and headed for the car. Already she felt claustrophobic in the confines of the small house crammed with the bits and pieces of her father's life.

At the end of the road, she turned left and headed for Jubilee. The drive was solitary. Trees and hills. Cattle and horses. Big rounds of hay rolled up in the fields. She passed several pickup trucks, some SUVs, and a car or two. The drivers invariably waved. To be polite, Mariah waved back. She missed the city already where no one waved unless they knew you and oftentimes not even then.

It seemed she drove for hours, but it was really about fifteen minutes. She rounded a bend in the road and passed a billboard sign with a cowboy in full riding regalia on the back of a quarter horse.

The sign said: "Welcome to Jubilee, Cutting Horse Capital of the World."

She hadn't noticed the sign when she'd arrived in the dark, tired and looking for a soft place to land. Nor had she really been able to see the details of the slumbering town. This time around, she took it all in, realizing she just might be stuck here for a while.

The main drag carried her past a feed store, an equine vet, and a mercantile that sold black pot-bellied woodstoves, stock tanks, and metal wind-mills. Deer feeders were set up in the parking lot of an independently owned hardware store, along with dog kennels and chain-link fencing. In the window of an old, rambling, limestone building, a sign out front declared: "Best Handmade Furniture in Texas." There was a boot and Western wear shop dubbed Western Wear Palooza, a tractor supply, and a place that sold horse trailers. She motored by the First Horseman's Bank of Jubilee, Farmers' Insurance, and a newspaper office called the Daily Cutter.

She'd never lived in a small town—well, not that she could remember. With her hands clutched on the steering wheel, she contemplated the dimensions of where she found herself. This place pushed against every boundary of the lifestyle she'd always lived.

And not in a good way.

Anxiety secreted a knot in her stomach and she thought of the way oysters made pearls, building a protective layer inside against an invading grain of sand.

What in the hell was she doing here?

You had nowhere else to go.

That wasn't entirely true. She could have moved to Argentina, started a new life in a new country, close to her mother and Ignacio. But that seemed even more foreign and faraway than Jubilee. Besides, she felt like a third thumb around her mother and her new husband.

What if no one here liked her? What if she didn't like them? Maybe she should turn north and just keep on driving until she reached the safety of the Chicago city limits.

And then do what? She'd already spent three months pounding the pavement, looking for a job she knew she was not going to get. Destiny had friends in high places. She had nowhere to stay. She'd already worn out her welcome on her friend Abby's couch after she'd been forced to give up her apartment because she couldn't make rent. This was it. Her new life.

Ugh.

She shook her head and let her gaze drift over her surroundings once more. Up ahead lay a restaurant called the Mesquite Spit. She could smell steaks grilling even through the rolled-up window of her car. Pickup trucks and SUVs jammed the parking lot, but it didn't look like the kind of place that put a high premium on quality lettuce, so she kept driving.

And then she saw the sign.

"Oak Hill Cemetery ½ Mile."

Oak Hill was where they'd buried Dutch.

Impulsively, she turned, following where the sign pointed, and took the road running up the hill behind the Mesquite Spit.

A wispy bank of gray clouds played across a sky glazed with the purple-pearl sheen of impending twilight. The temperature was sluggish, neither hot nor cold, midrange and noncommittal. Sixty-five, Mariah guessed, until she parked the car beside a maintenance shed and got out. The wind tickled her hair. Sixty, she recalculated, and the dampish air carried the musky smell of composting leaves mingling with the sharp, smoky scent of burning mesquite.

The cemetery wasn't big, but it was old. Oaks,

pecans, and elm trees so large that two people joining hands couldn't reach around them, sheltered the
plots. The burial ground was laid out in a simple grid
pattern on the flat of the hilltop.

Where to start her search?

Look for a freshly turned grave.

A prickling sensation tickled the back of her neck
as her feet processed the rows.

She found it with surprising ease, the rich scent of
loam leading her to the spot. No headstone yet. Too
soon for that. But there was a cardboard placard attached to a stake and numerous flower arrangements.

RANDOLPH "DUTCH" CALLAHAN
THE GREATEST CUTTER WHO EVER LIVED.

As she stood there, in the waning sunlight, looking
at her estranged father's grave, Mariah's emotions
formed a mosaic snapshot. Crystal clear. A fractured
monochrome of bands and circles, dots and triangles.
Black. White. Gray. The primary sensation was one
of deep, unabated loss.

"Dutch," she whispered. "I hardly knew you. Why
does it hurt so damn much?" It wasn't so much the
pain of losing him, but of never having him. An unrequited love, if you will. Loving someone who couldn't
love you back.

One of the few memories she had of her father was
when he'd taken her riding. She'd been quite small,
three or four at most, and the main thing she recalled about the day was sitting in the saddle with
him. Her back pressed against his strong chest, his
ropy arms around her, his tanned hands competently
holding the leather reins, guiding the horse. In that

moment, she remembered feeling utterly safe and protected. As if nothing bad could ever happen as long as her daddy had her back. She'd lost that feeling when Dutch left, and she'd never experienced it again.

She turned to go back to her car, but as she did, a brown pickup climbed the hill to the cemetery. It looked like Joe's truck.

Mariah didn't know why she did what she did next. She just reacted without thinking, slipping behind the maintenance building, holding her breath, spying on Joe as he pulled to a stop on the opposite side of the cemetery from where she hid.

He stepped from the truck, tall and lanky and easy-gaited. In his hand, he carried a wicker basket of yellow chrysanthemums. She assumed he was coming to pay his respects to Dutch, but instead of turning down the row where her father's grave was located, he walked closer to the maintenance shed.

Had he seen her?

Her heart galloped. Why was she hiding from him? Why did she find the thought that he was coming after her so compelling? Twisted. She'd always known she wasn't quite right.

But no. He wasn't coming for her. He walked on past the maintenance shed.

Twin ghosts, relief and disappointment, hovered around her. Mariah edged to the other side of the building and peeked around the corner so she could follow where he went.

He stopped at a grave, knelt down, and placed the basket of flowers near the headstone. He stood up, took off his Stetson, and bowed his head.

Joe was praying.

A lump formed in her throat. Feeling like the worst kind of voyeur, Mariah stepped back, glanced away, and gave the man his privacy. She stood with her spine pressed against the side door of the locked building, arms splayed against the wood.

The sun dipped to the horizon. The air thickened. In the distance, she heard a dog bark.

A minute passed.

Then five.

Whose grave was it? How long was he going to stay there?

Her stomach rumbled. She couldn't really come out now. He would know she'd hidden from him and she'd look stupid. Why had she hidden from him?

She heard a car door slam. Was it he? Had he gone?

The crunch of footsteps on fallen leaves echoed across the cemetery. Close.

Very close.

She shut her eyes. Prayed that Joe did not look behind the shed. Scrambled to come up with an excuse in case he did.

"Hey, lady."

Mariah jumped and her eyes flew open.

A middle-aged man dressed in blue jeans coveralls and rubber knee boots stood at the far corner of the building. He had a face like a glacier, flat, cold, and big. His salt and pepper hair thinned around his temples. He possessed eyes the size and color of watermelon seeds and an elongated, plankish mouth. "Hey, lady."

"Y-yes?" she stammered, caught completely off guard by this odd-looking stranger when she'd been expecting to see Joe.

"You're in my way." He nodded at the door. "You shouldn't be over here."

"What? Oh, sorry," she mumbled, and scurried off.

But instead of getting into her car, she found herself drawn to the gravesite with the basket of yellow chrysanthemums. She crept up on it, pushed her glasses up farther on her nose for a closer look.

An upright granite headstone. That had cost someone a nice chunk of change. The wind quickened, whistling through the leaves of the red oak tree standing sentinel over the grave. The tombstone read:

REBECCA ANNE BRACKEEN DANIELS

A carving of two entwined hearts followed the information, and underneath the engraved twin hearts was the epitaph:

ADORED WIFE OF JOSEPH
TWO HEARTS WHO BELONG TOGETHER FOREVER

Palm to her mouth, Mariah stepped back, her shoes sinking into the damp earth of the grave behind Rebecca's. Unnerved that she'd trod on someone's grave, she turned and fled to the safety of her car. She sat in the front seat, keys clutched in her hand, trying to make sense of what she'd just learned. Four things were clear.

One: Joe was a widower.

Two: His wife had been only twenty-six years old when she'd died. Younger than Mariah was now.

Three: Dutch, Joe's best friend, had died two years to the day after Rebecca's death.

Four: Joe had loved his wife very, very much.

Goose bumps rose on her skin. Sympathy pawed at her. Her heart softened. No wonder Joe had gotten drunk last night and fallen into the horse trough and slept it off in a stupor. He'd been in a great deal of emotional pain.

And she'd been so mean to him. Calling him a derelict. Acting rude.

That's what you get for making assumptions, for judging people.

Poor guy. She couldn't begin to imagine what he was going through. She owed him a big apology because Joe Daniels was a man still grieving the love of his life.

CHAPTER FIVE

Playing it safe means you're not even in the game.
　　　　　　　　　　　　　　—Dutch Callahan

Joe tromped to the Silver Horseshoe looking for something to take his mind off his sorrow. His head still ached from his go-round with Jose Cuervo, so he wasn't into that. He needed companionship more than anything else, a friendly face to keep him from dwelling on Becca and Dutch. He paused outside to scrape his boots on the welcome mat.

"Howdy, handsome," Clover greeted him from behind the bar the minute he opened the door. Her kindly face folded into a heartfelt smile. "What'll you have?"

"I'm not in a drinkin' mood."

"Well, honey, you did just walk into a bar." Her jovial tone darkened. "Is something bothering you?"

He sank down on the bar stool. "I guess I'll take a beer."

She poured up a mug and pushed it in front of him. Joe took a swig. Clover went off to fix a whiskey sour for another customer, and then came back, bar towel slung over one shoulder. "So that pebble in your boot got anything to do with Dutch's daughter?"

He took another sip of beer. "You know about her?"

"Saw her while I was on the way over to the Marin place this morning. She's cute."

"I suppose," he said.

"You don't like her?"

He shrugged. "I don't know her."

"But something's got you upset."

"She doesn't even seem to be mourning him." Joe rubbed the condensation off his mug with the pad of his thumb. "The man was her father and she doesn't give a damn."

"For one thing," Clover said, "everyone grieves in their own way. For another thing, she barely knew him."

"All the more reason to grieve. Knowing that you treated your own father like dirt and never had a chance to make amends."

"That's not like you, Joe," Clover chided gently.

"What?"

"Making snap judgments about people."

"Yeah, well, sometimes first impressions are the right ones."

"What's your impression of her?"

"Aloof. Cold." He thought of her soft lips, her golden hair, and immediately scrubbed the image from his mind.

"That wasn't the impression I had of her at all."

"No?"

"No. I thought she seemed . . ." Clover paused as if searching for the right word. "Lost. Vulnerable."

Joe snorted.

"Much like you."

"What?" He glared at Clover.

"You've been lost since Becca died and now with Dutch gone, you've lost your last anchor. I know you don't see it, Joe. Big tough cowboy can't admit he's fragile as peanut brittle, but you're projecting your guilt and shame onto Mariah."

"Projecting? Clover, have you been watching Dr. Phil?"

Clover straightened. "I saw a grief counselor after Carl died. I know things."

"Did it help?"

"Not much," she admitted. "You can talk about your feelings until you're blue in the face, but it doesn't change the fact the person you love is gone."

"Nope, it don't."

They looked at each other, two lost souls connected by grief.

Then Clover burst out laughing. "You want another beer?"

"Why not," Joe said joining her laughter. Sometimes things got so bad you just had to laugh or go insane.

Clover refilled his mug, then reached over and touched Joe's hand. "Lighten up on Mariah, Joe. It's not healthy to hold on to bad feelings. Try to make her feel welcome."

"Hey, I promised to give her a ride back to the ranch after she turns in her rental car. That's as neighborly as I'm gonna get." Already he regretted making that promise. Why had he made that promise?

"Try to see past Mariah's defenses. Yes, she's got big-city ways, but she could use a good friend."

"I'll leave that to you, Clover," he said, clinging to his resentment like a lifeline even though he really didn't know why, other than being around her made him think of Becca and Dutch, and that made his heart hurt. Too much pain. He'd had enough of it to last a lifetime. "Dutch was my best friend in the world, and getting chummy with his estranged daughter feels too much like consorting with the enemy. I'm just biding my time until I can buy back my land and send her packing."

The next morning, Joe followed Mariah into town. He barely spoke two words to her, just nodded and mumbled hello and then swung back into the cab of his pickup.

Fine. That was fine with her. She had nothing to say to him either.

She turned in the rental car. Joe led her to his pickup truck and opened up the passenger side door. Reluctantly, she climbed inside, not sure how to get out of this, equally unsure if she wanted to. Joe made her feel so mixed up inside on so many levels, she found it disconcerting. She found *him* disconcerting.

Tilting her head, she watched him scoot around the front of the truck. He was a commanding figure. Lean, hard-packed muscles poured into a pair of cowboy-cut denim jeans; broad, razor-sharp shoulders moving beneath a blue, yoke-style Western shirt. Although he stood six feet tall, there was a wiry compactness about him that was common to the limber men who wrangled horses and cattle for a living. Dutch had been built the same way.

"So," she said after several minutes, unable to stand the silence any longer. "I'm really surprised to see Jubilee has a good-sized airport and so many motels and three car rental chains. What's the draw? You'd think with Fort Worth being so close, everyone would just go there."

"We're the cutting horse capital of the world," he said.

"Seriously? I thought that was just some exaggerated brag for the welcome sign."

"Nope, it's true. People fly here from all corners of the world to trade, breed, and show cutting horses. Lots of celebrities own and train cutting horses— Christie Brinkley, Tanya Tucker, Linda Blair, Barry Corbin, just to name a few. It's a big deal. Plus, we host the Professional Rodeo Cowboys Association rodeo every July. Jubilee might be small, but we're influential," Joe said, the pride in his voice compelling.

At last, she'd found something that got him talking. "Have you always lived in Jubilee?"

"Born and raised."

That stopped the conversation, but luckily, they'd arrived at the law office of Art Bunting.

Bunting turned out to be fiftyish and slightly paunchy, and like most everyone in Jubilee, he wore Wranglers and cowboy boots to work. He had thick black eyebrows that belied his gray hair, and a pencil-thin mustache too small for his beefy face.

"I'm so sorry to hear about your father," Bunting murmured to Mariah as he took her hand in both of his. "He'll be sorely missed around here."

"Thank you," Mariah said. It felt weird to realize there were people who missed Dutch more than she did.

With a nod and a handshake to Joe as well, Bunting directed her to a chair. "Let's get down to work."

She sat and Joe stood at the back of the room, leaning against the wall with one shoulder, his hands tucked behind him.

Bunting took the chair opposite her, shuffled the papers on his desk, and cleared his throat. "I'm going to read to you what Dutch wrote. He was a cowboy through and through, so he didn't have an official will. The man didn't even keep a bank account. Talk about living off the grid. That was your dad. Anyway, he just wrote down his wishes on a piece of paper and brought them to me."

"When did he do this?" Joe asked.

"Right after you two swapped Miracle for the land. He wanted to make sure that if anything happened to him, Mariah would be taken care of. Other than planning for futurities, I think it was the most planning Dutch ever did."

Joe bowed his head. "Dutch was a true cowboy."

Emotion tugged at Mariah's chest but she couldn't really name it. Sadness, sure. Loss, yes. But there was another layer there she hadn't quite felt before. Her father had prepared a place for her. She had been on his mind. He did regret some of the choices he made in life.

"Would you like for me to read it to you?" Art offered.

Mariah nodded, knowing that if she were to read the letter, the tears she'd been holding back would start to fall, and the last thing she wanted was to break down in front of strangers. Destiny had taught her well. You couldn't let people see how you were feeling. You couldn't expose your tender underbelly if you didn't want to get attacked. Of course, she'd never expected her boss to turn out to be her primary attacker. "I'd appreciate that."

" 'Dear Art . . .' " Bunting began, then paused to editorialize. "I told you it was an informal letter." He cleared his throat again, adjusted his reading glasses, and continued to read. " 'In case something happens to me, I want to make sure my girl, Mariah, is taken care of. I couldn't take care of her in life. I didn't have it in me to be a good daddy. Horses are in my blood and I'm ashamed to say they took over. I left her and her mama high and dry 'cause I knew they'd be better off without me. But Mariah is the best thing I've ever done, not that I can claim any credit for raising her. I'm leaving her everything I own—the chunk of land that Joe Daniels traded me for Some Kind of Miracle. Stuffy, the first trophy I ever won, and my Dodge Ram dually. I'm sorry the house is a shack. I should fix it up and hopefully I will before I kick the bucket. If I don't then it won't be much good to her the shape it's in.' "

Art paused again, glanced at her to see how she was taking it. Mariah gave him a slight smile, nodded, encouraging him to continue. It was finally sinking in. Her father was dead. She'd never see him again. Never have a chance to reconcile. Unfair. The world was unfair. But she really had no one to blame but herself. She could have reached out to him, let go of her hurt feelings and resentment. But she hadn't and now it was too late.

" 'She'll probably sell the land,' " Art read. " 'I wouldn't blame her. She's grown up in the city, but part of me can't help hopin' she'll find her way back home to her roots. Her mama's feet are rooted as deep in Texas soil as mine are, even though Cassie would deny it. But that's neither here nor there, just explaining a bit. If Mariah does decide to sell the land, I hope she'll sell it back to Joe. If she doesn't . . . well, I have a dream. It's probably a stupid dream, but I can't get it out of my mind, so here goes. I pray she'll come back to Texas and that she and Joe will hook up to build an equine center for kids who ain't got much. I want to make cutting available to kids from all walks of life, not just for those who got a few coins to rub together. Joe and I have talked about such a project and more than likely we'll get around to it, but just in case something happens and we don't, I sure hope Mariah or Joe will make my dreams come true. Anyway, that's what I want, but I understand if Mariah can't give me that. Thanks, Art, for being a good friend and not acting too much like a damn lawyer.' "

Art stopped reading, put down the letter, took off his glasses, and rubbed them against his shirt to clear them of smudges. His eyes were misty. "Your father was a good man. I hope you see your way to making his dreams come true."

Mariah cast a glance over at Joe. His jaw was clenched as if he was trying to hold back his feelings.

So Dutch's last wish was for her to go into business with Joe and make an equine facility for underprivileged kids?

Sure it sounded good to Art and Joe. They were cowboys, horsemen. But to Mariah it showed Dutch's bone-deep selfishness. Everyone in town seemed to love and laud her father, but they didn't know what it was like to be abandoned by the man who was supposed to love and protect you no matter what.

Dutch had loved horses more than he'd loved her.

He all but admitted it in his letter. And yet, in the end, he wanted *her* to follow *his* dream. He hadn't known her. Hadn't known her at all. He'd had no real interest in her. In what she wanted. What *she* needed. There was that hurt again. She couldn't escape it no matter which way she turned.

Mariah pushed back the chair, got to her feet. "Thank you, Mr. Bunting."

"I suppose you need some time to think this all over, decide what you're going to do."

"No," she said. "I don't need any time at all. I already know what I want to do. I'm going to put the ranch up for sale. Rock-bottom price. I want out of Jubilee as fast as I can get out of here."

Steamed, Joe left the office ahead of Mariah. She had papers to sign, and he was so angry, he needed to walk it off before sharing the cab of his truck with her on the ride back to the ranch. Selfish, spoiled brat. Not even giving her dead father's request a second thought.

Well fine, that was her prerogative. He didn't care. He didn't want her hanging around here anyway, reminding him far too much of Becca, reminding him of how much she'd hurt Dutch. All he wanted was his land back and if she was inclined to sell it to him cheap, then so much the better.

He paced the sidewalk off the town square, trying to figure out how to get his hands on the money to buy her off and send her packing back to Chicago.

Fifteen minutes later, she came out of the office looking . . . well . . . to be honest, she looked like she'd been stirrup-dragged through a cactus patch. Immediately, his anger ebbed.

"Do you mind if I go grocery shopping?" she asked.

"Huh?"

"If I'm going to be stuck here for a while, I need supplies, and on the drive over, I spotted a small grocery on the block behind this one."

He wanted to say, *Hell no*. He didn't want to do any favors for her. She pissed him off royally. But the woman needed groceries, so what else was he supposed to do?

She started walking in the direction of the grocery store, leaving him not much of an option but to follow her, although he sure didn't care for looking like a lapdog. To keep from trailing behind, he took several long-legged steps and caught up with her.

"You got a grocery list?" he growled.

"I don't."

"You need a list. Being a wedding planner, I figured you keep lists."

She tapped her temple with a forefinger. "I keep it up here."

Why was he giving her crap about a grocery list? Was he just trying to punish her? Petty. Yeah, he'd admit it. He wasn't proud of it, but a guy couldn't help the way he felt—disappointed, irritated, snubbed.

At the door, a friendly young man with Down's syndrome greeted them and high-fived Joe. "Hello, Mr. Joe. We'come to Searcy's Gro'ery."

"Thank you, Rodney."

It was the exact same exchange Rodney had with every customer who entered the grocery store. Rodney had been in the same high school class as Joe's younger sister, Meg.

"Can I come riding at the ranch again?" Rodney asked.

"You're welcome anytime." Joe peeled off a cart from the row of carts before Mariah had a chance to commandeer one. He was running this show whether she liked it or not.

"Thank you, Mr. Joe. Will Mr. Dutch be there too?"

Joe shook his head. "Mr. Dutch died, remember? Your mama brought you to the funeral."

Rodney looked heartbreakingly sad. "Oh yeah." Tears misted his eyes. "Mr. Dutch, he gone to heaven."

"That's right, but you can still come riding at the ranch."

Rodney beamed and clapped his hands. "Yay!"

Then another customer came in behind them, and Rodney ran over to high-five the elderly man, who already had his hand raised in anticipation. "We'come to Searcy's Gro'ery."

"That," Joe said, once they were over by the produce aisle and out of Rodney's earshot, "is the kind of young person your dad wanted to help. Dutch gave Rodney free riding lessons."

"How noble of him to help other people's children," Mariah muttered.

Joe reached out to touch her shoulder, but regretted it the second he did it. He felt her stiffen beneath his grip and he immediately dropped his hand. "Don't be like that."

"Like what?" she snapped. "Honest?"

Lighten up on her. She's in pain whether she's admitting it or not. Joe softened. "Jealous. Grudge holding. I can tell that's not who you really are."

She glared at him anyway, tossed a sack of oranges into the cart, and stalked off to bag some green leaf lettuce.

"Dutch was very sorry for abandoning you."

"Really? Funny, I never heard that from him."

"He told me the story about how you were so ashamed of him that you ran off when he came to see you at your high school."

Mariah whirled on him, eyes blazing. "That was inappropriate coming to my school. I was fourteen. He was dressed up like a cowboy in one of the most exclusive high schools in Chicago. How did he think I was going to feel?"

Joe understood where she was coming from. Heck, his parents had embarrassed the fire out of him when he was a teen, but clearly Mariah had no idea how badly she'd hurt Dutch with her rejection. The old horseman had only told him about it when they'd gotten drunk together celebrating one of Miracle's wins. Otherwise, the taciturn Dutch would never have spoken of something so painful.

"Did you ever stop to consider how difficult it was for a lonely old cowpoke like him to walk into a place like that?" Joe asked. "Bunch of rich kids staring at him."

"Don't give me that baloney. He was the adult." She slung the lettuce into the cart, snatched up a prepack of cherry tomatoes. "He wasn't lonely. He had tons of friends, apparently all more important to him than his own daughter. Hell, he did more with Rodney than he ever did with me."

"You holdin' on to a lot of anger."

"You think?"

"Let it go."

"Yeah, well, you ought to let go of your dead wife. It's been two years, quit going on tequila benders."

The minute the words were out of her mouth, Mariah slapped a palm over her mouth and her eyes widened.

Joe took the emotional blow. Swallowed it. He'd provoked her, he was asking for it, but she played dirty.

Chagrin darkened her eyes. "Please forgive me. I'm sorry. I shouldn't have said that. I had no excuse to say that. I know nothing about you and your grief. It was rude and catty and none of my damn business."

"Who told you about Becca?" he asked coldly. He wanted to just walk off and leave her there, but he wasn't going to let her have control over his behavior.

"Look, could you forget I said that? I'm truly sorry I said it. I shouldn't have said that. I was way out of line."

"You're right," he said, his mildness of tone belying the hurt and anger punching hard against his throat, but he didn't want her to know how much she rattled his cage. "I should let go of Becca, but when you love someone as much as I loved her . . . well, I can tell that you've never loved someone that much, so you have no clue what I've been through."

Mariah caught her bottom lip up between her teeth. She looked as anxious to get away from him as he was to get away from her. She spun on her heels, headed for the condiments aisle.

Ah crap. Now he'd bruised her. He doffed his cowboy hat, shoved fingers through his hair. Why were they sniping at each other? Both of them with their emotions sticking out like spines.

He came up behind her as she studied the ingredients on the back of a bottle of salad dressing. "Mariah," he murmured.

She raised her head, an unexpectedly bright smile on her face.

Joe didn't know what to make of her. She had this sunny, optimistic get-'er-done attitude about her, but underneath was a darker, swifter current she struggled to mask. The deeper nuance was the part that drew him most. One wounded soul to another. They should stop slicing each other to ribbons.

"Could we declare a truce?" he asked.

Her hopeful, remorseful expression told him that she was ashamed of her dark current and sorry that she'd given him a glimpse. "You're forgiving me?"

Joe managed a slight smile; felt the gentleness slide down into his gut. No sense taking their individual aches out on each other. "In the interest of improving neighbor relationships, yeah. I forgive you."

"Thank you," she said. "I don't know why I'm being so mean."

"You're hurting." He wondered about her past, what had happened, who'd hurt her besides Dutch. Hey, wasn't that enough? How did a kid ever feel secure when their parents bailed on them.

"Yes, but that's not a good excuse. You're hurting too."

"You were just lashing out and I'm the handy target. You've been through a lot."

She nodded, ducked her head, grabbed for a bottle of ranch dressing. He thought he saw tears misting her eyes, but when she looked up again the tears were gone and her chin was set firm.

"Go ahead. Let me have it. I can take it." He moved closer until the tips of his boots were touching the toes of her shoes. "Speak your mind."

"No need," she said. "I've let it go."

"Are we going to talk about your father's last request?"

"What's there to discuss?" She plucked more supplies off the shelf—peanut butter and coffee, strawberry jam and a loaf of multigrain bread. Then she breezed past him and cornered the aisle. In the process, her shoulder lightly brushed his.

His head reeled from the unanticipated contact. His body stiffened. With resistance? Or something else? Something he didn't want to consider? Dammit. What was the matter with him? He hustled to keep up with her. "You made up your mind pretty quickly without giving it any real thought."

"What's to think about? I don't belong here and I want out as quickly as I can get out."

"I can accept that," he said. "Sell the ranch back to me."

"Sold," she said.

"That's mighty generous of you," he said, "but there's a hitch."

She paused in her foraging, turned back to look at him. "What's that?"

"I don't have the money, at least not that I can get my hands on. It's tied up in investments."

"Wrong answer. I want out of this place ASAP."

"Mariah," he said, "I do know you're hurting, but you don't seem like a heartless person. I promise I'll have the money by mid-December. Miracle is going to win the Triple Crown Futurity. That horse is special. If you can hold out until December, I'll have the two hundred thousand and can pay full market value for the place."

"Or I could slash the price and sell it within the next couple of weeks and be on my way."

"Please," he said. "I want to turn that part of the ranch into the equine center Dutch was hoping to start."

"You think that argument is going to sway me in your favor? Why should I make Dutch's dream come true? What did he ever do for me?"

"He left you a ranch."

"I've got dreams of my own."

"Which are?"

"Not that it's any of your business." She sank her hands on her hips, tilted her head, studied him a long moment. "I want to start my own wedding planning business."

"Here in Jubilee?"

She looked at him as if he was nutty as a pecan tree. "Of course not here in Jubilee. I just want to sell the land, get my money, and get back to Chicago."

"Can you just give me until Christmas?"

"That's over two months away."

"What's waiting for you in Chicago?"

The expression on her face told him the truth. That she had no ties in Chicago. It was just the place she'd lived for a long time.

She ran a graceful hand through her hair. She moved like a dancer, lithe and controlled. "I can't wait. I don't have any money."

"You've got a place to stay, rent-free."

"What about utilities and food?"

"Jubilee can be a cheap place to live if you're not keeping horses. Lots cheaper than Chicago."

She sighed. "I suppose I really don't have much of a choice."

Then she lifted her chin, squared her shoulders. He could see her struggling to push past her resistance, to accept the situation she was in and make the best of it. Joe knew how hard it was to get to acceptance, that final stage of grief. His grip on it was tenuous at best.

"Okay, all right. I'll give you until Christmas." She studied him with wide brown eyes, her top teeth worrying her bottom lip, blond hair curling around her shoulders, soft as morning sunshine.

He didn't like the way he was behaving. She'd needled him and he'd needled her, and now he felt badly about all of it. He wasn't usually such a jackass, and even though he didn't know why, Joe had a sudden urge for her to understand that.

"C'mon," he said. "Let's get these groceries bought and stowed. After that, I'm taking you to lunch."

CHAPTER SIX

You gotta let go of the old before you can grab on
to the new.

—Dutch Callahan

Y ou like barbecue?" Joe asked, inclining his head
toward the Mesquite Spit at the end of the block
as he loaded up her groceries into the backseat
of his extended cab pickup truck. The parking lot
was just as packed with cars today as it had been the
evening before; the smell of mesquite-roasted meat
hung thickly in the air.

Her stomach growled.

Joe chuckled. "I take that as a yes."

They entered the smoky barbecue joint. The clank
of dishes and the sound of country-and-western music
filled the air along with the mouthwatering aroma.

Heads turned. Feeling self-conscious, Mariah
glanced down to make sure she didn't have something on her clothes. In that moment, she wished she
was back at her old apartment in Chicago overlooking the lake, curled up under a blanket, eating chocolate chip cookies and watching *Gilmore Girls* on
DVD. Nothing cheered her up like the camaraderie

of Stars Hollow. Watching a small town on TV was a lot easier than trying to navigate one in real life.

"You look fine," Joe said, intuitively reading her thoughts. "It's just the locals wondering about the pretty new girl."

Mariah studied the floor. Concrete, stained a dark burgundy. She'd never thought of herself as particularly attractive. Yes, she knew how to dress the part. Destiny had taught her professional makeup tips and how to play up her assets. But it was all a ruse and she couldn't help feeling that someday someone was going to discover she was a fraud.

One look around told her that she didn't fit here in this quaint place made of rough-hewn cedar walls and crowded with rough-hewn people. Cowboy hats hung from the hat rack pegs along the far wall. The decor was wagon wheels and iron skillets, hay bales and taxidermied bobcats.

Another set of memories washed over her. Cowboy memories. Her father taking her to a rodeo. Putting her up on his shoulders and walking around to introduce her to other cowboys. A lump caught in her throat and she blinked.

Joe dipped his head so his mouth was close to her ear. "You okay?"

"Fine." She nodded.

"You're a good liar, Mariah Callahan." He put his hand to her elbow and guided her down the narrow walkway that felt more like a cattle chute, bordered as it was on both sides with metal signs advertising brands of horse feed. "Here we go."

The service was cafeteria-style. Grab a tray, help yourself to the fixings, place your meat order at the beginning of the line, and pick it up at the end. The other people in line greeted Joe and looked at her with curiosity.

"Who's this?" asked a red-haired man with a jovial face and weathered skin.

"Dutch's daughter."

"My Lord, is this Mariah?" The man stepped around Joe to envelop Mariah in a crushing hug. "I haven't seen you in a coon's age. I am so sorry about your daddy, little one."

"Um . . . thank you." Mariah had no clue who he was.

He let her go, stepped back. "Oops, where are my manners. I forgot to introduce myself. I'm Austin Flats. I run the tractor supply."

Mariah couldn't help smiling at his unusual name.

"I know, blame my daddy for not changing the family name. Could be worse, I suppose. Could be Austin Butts." He chortled at his own joke, but then quickly sobered. "We sure are gonna miss Dutch something fierce around here. He was one of a kind."

An arrow of pain pierced the tough armor she was trying to effect. Apparently, Dutch had been quite beloved in this town. She felt cheated. She'd wanted to love him too. Why hadn't he wanted to love her?

Joe paid for their order. When she tried to protest, he'd held up a hand. "My treat, no argument. An apology for acting like a horse's ass earlier."

Since she was broke, Mariah didn't argue. "Thank you."

They took their plates loaded with barbecue brisket to one of the picnic tables covered by red and white checkered tablecloths.

More people waved, nodded, and said, "Hello."

Joe said, "Give them a chance. They're ready to like you."

It was irritating the way the man could read her. She didn't much care for his skill.

An awkward silence fell. Mariah concentrated on the food, enjoying the sweet, smoky taste of the brisket more than she thought she would. The potato salad was the best she'd ever eaten. To keep from looking at Joe, she glanced at the pictures on the wall, all of them featuring rodeo or cutting horse events. One photo, on the wall over Joe's head, caught her eye. It was a snapshot of Joe holding up a huge gold belt buckle. He was surrounded by a group of women grinning at him like he'd created the cosmos. The caption underneath the photo read: "Glory Joe wins again."

Glory Joe? She remembered what her mother had told her. Joe had been a big deal rodeo champion.

"That was a long time ago," Joe said.

"What?" She startled.

"The photograph you're starting at. I'm not that guy anymore."

"It's irritating, you do know that."

"What is?"

"Your ability to know what I'm thinking."

"It's not my fault you're so easy to read."

Mariah scowled. She was *not* easy to read. She'd spent years affecting a noncommittal expression so she could successfully maneuver in the lives of the rich and famous. Many times, she'd been accused of being a sphinx. She'd considered it a compliment. Her ability to keep her mouth shut and her face impassive was one of the things Destiny had liked most about her. Now here was Joe telling her that he could read her like a first grade primer. She did not like this. Not at all.

"Lucky me," she sniped dryly, trying to regain her emotional equilibrium. "I got to see Glory Joe in the buff."

"I wasn't naked."

"Couldn't prove it by me."

"You have a dirty mind," he said, and she couldn't tell if he was teasing or not. "And you were trespassing."

"How was I to know I was on the wrong ranch? It's not like there were street signs."

"You think Dutch would own a house like mine? You think he would have that kind of money and not share it with you? Your father was a proud man, Mariah. He didn't make peace with you because he was ashamed of his circumstances. Don't you get that?" Joe stared at her like she was the dumbest woman on the face of the earth.

"Didn't he get that a kid doesn't care about money? A kid just wants her dad to hang around."

"Yeah, and the time he tries to make things up, you shun him for being exactly what he was. A poor cowpoke."

Guilt flamed her. She changed the hot potato topic. "So what happened to your admiring throng of women?"

"What?"

She nodded at the photograph. "The lineup of buckle bunnies. Your drinking chase them off?"

His face turned stony. "You don't know me. Stop acting like you do."

"I'm thinking maybe you're denying some hard truths about yourself."

"Can we just drop this entire line of conversation?"

"And just when we were getting so close."

"You're kind of a smart ass, huh?"

She smirked. "I can be, when the need arises."

"I can see why you're not married."

"How do you know I'm not married?"

"For one thing, no ring." He nodded at her hand. "For another thing, Dutch told me he was worried he'd turned you into a man hater."

"I don't hate men."

"You got a husband?"

"No."

"Boyfriend?"

"No."

"Why not?"

"What do you mean why not?"

"You're attractive, sexy, smart, and pushing thirty downhill, why aren't you married?"

She bristled. "I'm twenty-eight."

"And?"

"I've had boyfriends." She heard the defensiveness in her own voice.

"But none that stuck."

"No."

"Why not?"

Why not indeed? Secretly, was she afraid of getting hooked up with a guy who would walk out on her the way Dutch had walked out on Cassie? "I've been busy building my career."

"A career that has gone belly-up."

"Thank you for pointing that out."

"That was tacky. I'm sorry."

"Apparently, I bring out the worst in you."

"It's not you." He did look contrite. "You've caught me at a bad time in my life."

"Same here."

They looked at each other. Joe smiled. Mariah couldn't help smiling back.

"Let's talk about something neutral."

"Like Switzerland."

His smile widened, transforming his face. "Like Switzerland."

"Okay, here's the burning question about Switzerland. Why do they make army knives when they have no army?"

"It's just one of those paradoxes of nature."

The awkward silence was back. An uneasy image flashed in Mariah's head. She saw Joe as he'd looked in the horse trough, bare muscled arms, exquisite naked chest, granite abs. She closed her eyes and forced the picture from her mind.

"Mariah?"

She opened her eyes halfway and stole a surreptitious glance at him. He had long, extravagant black eyelashes that contrasted with the rest of his decidedly masculine features. The lashes softened his rugged looks, brought a bit of tenderness to his angular face. Her gaze dangled there and she could not make herself look away. A dreamy languidness rolled over her. It bothered her, this physical pull. "Uh-huh?"

"What are your plans for the rest of the day?" Joe asked.

Dragged back from fantasyland, Mariah shrugged, wiped the sticky barbecue sauce from her fingers with wet wipes provided on the table. "Clean up the cabin, I suppose. What about you?"

"Training Miracle. I'm already behind for the day."

"I'm sorry, I didn't mean to upset your schedule."

"You didn't. Dutch's dying upset my schedule."

Mariah let that go because she didn't know what to say.

"Would you like to meet him?" Joe asked.

"Who? The horse?"

"Yeah, the horse."

She shrugged. "I'm not much of a horse person."

"How do you know?"

"I'm a city girl."

"Just because you live in the city doesn't make you a city girl."

"No? I thought that was the definition of city girl."

"You can take the girl out of the country . . ." He left the cliché unfinished.

"I'm not a country girl. I like noise and hustle and bustle. I like the symphony and crowds and shopping on Magnificent Mile. The closest I've come to livestock is the bronze cow on parade at Michigan Avenue and Washington. City girl to the bone. That's me. If I had any choice, I would be so out of here."

"Hey there," he said. His tone was smooth, but his flinty eyes flashed a warning. *No one messes with me and mine.* "That's my hometown you're maligning."

He was sitting right across from her and when she shifted, her knees brushed his. Quickly, she moved her legs away.

A sultry look came into his eyes. Today, he wore a blue flannel button-down shirt over a white T-shirt. His jeans were starched. In spite of their arguing, or maybe even because of it, things felt too intimate sitting here with him, as if they made a habit of taking their lunches together every day. She didn't really know what to say, so she said, "The food is really good."

"You doubted my taste?"

"I doubted the decor."

"Looks can be deceiving."

She certainly knew that. "Tell me about it."

"Seems like you should be the one telling me about it."

"About what?"

"Whatever or whoever's got your face screwed up like that."

Mariah ironed out her expression, putting on her best noncommittal stare. It came in very handy when working with bridezillas of questionable tastes. "It's not important."

"Uh-huh."

"What's that supposed to mean?"

He raised his palms. "Nothing, nothing, it's just—"

"What?"

"You've got a burr under your saddle and you can buck all you want, but it isn't coming out. You've got to have help to remove it."

"And I suppose you're an expert on burr extraction."

He suppressed a grin. "I am at that."

"Lucky me."

"Yep."

"Yep what?"

"I'd say you're pretty darned lucky to have landed in Jubilee, Mariah Callahan. It's been a long time since I've seen a woman so in need of true friends."

Affronted, she said, "I have friends."

"Yeah?"

Yes, and except for Abby, who'd let Mariah crash on her couch when she lost her apartment, they'd all abandoned her after Destiny gave her the boot. She purposefully ignored Joe and took a bite of the beans. She'd assumed they were baked beans but they had a completely different taste. Pinto beans cooked in some kind of zesty sauce and spiced to perfection. "Mmm, what kind of beans are these?"

"Cowboy beans."

"Be serious."

"I am serious. That's what they're called." He pointed to the grease board menu mounted behind the checkout counter. Sure enough, they were cowboy beans. Mariah slid him a sidelong glance. This man was not at all like what he initially seemed. Yes, he was a good-looking, swaggering cowboy, but upon closer examination, she discovered he had unexpected layers. Smooth on the surface, but complicated beneath. She could almost feel the conflict radiating off him. His wanted to do good things like start an equine facility for underprivileged kids, versus the self-destructive streak that had driven him to down a bottle of tequila and end up in a horse trough.

The silence was back and it wasn't the good kind. Conversation buzzed around them, most of it related to horses.

Mariah concentrated on the meal, and when she was finished, wiped her sticky fingers with the wet wipes while she waited for Joe to finish eating. He seemed to be taking his time, savoring the food, in no rush. Did he normally eat so slowly? Did he do everything this slowly?

The creak of leather shoes on hardwood floor had

her looking up. The female sheriff's deputy from the day before loomed over their table.

"Hello again," Mariah said, and extended her hand to the formidable woman. "I apologize for not introducing myself yesterday morning. I'm Mariah Callahan."

"I know who you are," the deputy said, and sat down on the picnic bench beside Joe.

She made no move to give her name, so Mariah said, "And you are . . ."

"Ila Brackeen," she answered in a begrudging tone.

"Nice to meet you, Ila."

The woman just stared at her, then reached into her pocket, pulled out a hundred-dollar bill, and tucked it under Joe's plate.

Joe pushed it back to her. "Keep your money."

"A bet's a bet."

"It was a silly bet."

"I pay my debts." Ila put an arm around Joe's shoulder, leaned in, and whispered something.

"Yeah, okay," Joe said.

Mariah squirmed, feeling out of sync with these two and their familiarity. She wondered if they were sleeping together.

"Will I see you tomorrow night at the billiards tournament?" Ila asked him.

"Maybe. I've got a lot of work to do," Joe said.

"C'mon, you've got to give me a chance to earn my money back."

"I'll see what I can do."

Ila got up, tipped her cowboy hat to Mariah, and strolled away.

"What was that all about?" Mariah asked.

Joe shrugged, tucked the hundred-dollar bill into his wallet. "Nothing."

Fine. Great. Okay. Be secretive. Have an affair with the Amazon deputy. She didn't care.

She might be stuck in Jubilee, but that didn't mean she had to get sucked into small-town drama, politics, and gossip. She'd view this as simply marking time and keep from getting close to anyone.

It was safer that way. The few times she'd ignored that policy and let herself get deeply involved with someone, she'd gotten hurt. Keeping an emotional distance had always kept her safe. It was the one truth she'd been able to rely on.

She wasn't about to change now.

Ila sat in her cruiser and watched Joe and Mariah leave the Mesquite Spit. They were keeping their distance from each other—Joe on the outside of the sidewalk, Dutch's daughter nearly hugging the old stone buildings—a good three feet of space between them. Even so, Ila could almost see the sexual chemistry jumping from Joe to Mariah and back again. That's why they were staying so far apart. The current was too strong to cross.

She gritted her teeth against the anxiety knotting her stomach, resisted the urge to spring from the car and take Joe's arm, claim him as her man and make it clear to Mariah that he belonged to her. Ila narrowed her eyes at the interloper—petite, blond, vulnerable. Sweet little waif. She was a damsel in distress, and the last thing Joe needed was to get saddled with some helpless female. Especially a city girl who was bound to break his heart.

A knock at her window made Ila jump. Irritated, she jerked her head around to see Joe's foreman, Cordy Whiteside, grinning at her. She rolled down her window. "What?"

"How you doin', Ila?" His earnest eyes searched her face.

But Ila wasn't looking at Cordy. She was watching Joe hold the door of his truck open for Mariah. "What do you want, Cordy?"

"You."

"What?" That got her attention. Cordy was good-looking. Not Joe handsome, by any means, but certainly attractive. He was an honest guy. She'd never known him to lie. He was a volunteer fireman and ran a side business as a farrier. Too bad he was so short.

"As my billiards partner," Cordy said quickly. "For the tournament tomorrow night. You're the best pool player I know."

"Maybe."

"Ila? You okay?"

She shook her head. "Just got a lot on my mind. I haven't been sleeping well."

"It's Joe, isn't it?"

"Joe?" She made a dismissive noise. What did Cordy know? Had he picked up on her feelings for Joe? Was she that transparent? God, she was going to have to be more careful. She couldn't let her love flag fly. Not until Joe felt the same for her as she did for him. " 'Course not. We're just friends."

Cordy looked skeptical. "What is it then? You've been distracted for the last two days."

"Possums."

"Huh?"

"It's possums," she said, grasping at any excuse. Lame. Truly lame. Why had she thought of possums?

"Possums?"

"Yeah."

"The marsupial possum?"

"Yes."

"What about possums?"

"They're ugly."

"What's your point?"

"They're just big rats who hang upside down from trees and carry their babies around in a pouch. The females have two wombs and the males have bifurcated penises. It's unnatural."

"Not to the female possum. Can you imagine if he showed up with a regular penis? She'd be all like, 'Freak,'" Cordy said.

Ila pressed her lips together to keep from laughing. "Possums are obnoxious. A family of them lives in the oak tree above my roof. They scamper around all hours of the night keeping me awake."

"So this has got nothing to do with Joe?"

"Maybe. If I named one of the possums Joe."

"That's all your moodiness is about? Possums?"

"Yep."

"I could come over," Cordy offered. "Get rid of them for you."

"Cordy, I'm an officer of the law. I carry a gun. If I really wanted to get rid of them I'd shoot them."

"So you don't want to get rid of them?" Cordy sounded confused.

"If I got rid of them, what excuse would I have for being bitchy?"

"Good point." Cordy's soulful eyes met her. Those eyes said, *I get you, Ila Brackeen.* "So . . . um . . . possums, huh?"

A hard shiver gripped Ila. Shit. Was it true? Could Cordy see straight through her? Well, she wasn't about to let him know it. "Yep. Possums."

CHAPTER SEVEN

Tug on enough reins, eventually one of them will give.

—Dutch Callahan

Following her lunch with Joe, Mariah spent the rest of the day scrubbing and dusting, sweeping and mopping the disheveled cabin. She made room in the dresser drawers and unpacked her clothes with more than a smidge of reluctance. Unpacking her things felt like she was moving in, and moving in felt like resignation.

It felt like defeat.

To drown out her feelings, she turned on the old transistor radio she'd found on the windowsill in Dutch's bedroom. She'd sold her iPod on eBay weeks ago—along with most of her other extraneous possessions—when she was desperate for rent money. It was tuned to a country-and-western station, not Mariah's cup of tea, but when she went to turn the dial, the worn-out old plastic knob broke off in her hand. She tossed the knob in the trash. She was stuck listening to WBAP.

Stuck.

That seemed to be her current life theme.

Dolly Parton came over the airwaves, singing "I Will Always Love You."

She remembered that Dolly had been one of Dutch's favorites. She reached out to the picture on the wall of Dutch and Joe. She traced an index finger over her father's face and listened to Dolly singing about lost love and her heart hurt so badly she couldn't breathe. She couldn't cry. She wanted to cry. Wanted to fully mourn her lost father, but the tears refused to fall.

Resolutely, she turned from the picture, closed her eyes against the pain, and mentally shook herself.

Okay then. She was here. This was the situation. No more wallowing in self-pity. She needed to accept things as they were, get any job she could land, and just ride it out until Joe had the money to purchase the ranch from her. After that, after that . . .

After that, what?

One step at a time.

She'd seen the help wanted sign in the window of the Silver Horseshoe when they drove past it. Clover, the woman on horseback she'd met the day before, said she owned the place.

Why not start there?

The next morning, Mariah got up, showered, and started to dress in the one decent interview suit she still owned, but thought better of it. Talk about standing out like a sore thumb. The Chanel suit might have worked in Chicago, but what closed a deal here in Jubilee were cowboy clothes. Of which she had none.

She stood peering into the closet, wrapped in a thin cotton towel, her damp hair curling over her shoulders, as if something would materialize if she simply stared long enough. Finally, she put on the clothes she'd worn to lunch with Joe the day before. Black slacks and simple sweater. As the one concession to her true self, she put on the one indulgent item of clothing she had left. A pair of Manolo Blahniks.

As Mariah drove into Jubilee, past all the horse-oriented businesses, it occurred to her that she already had a connection here whether she wanted it or not. That she wasn't absolutely alone.

Because of who her father had been, everyone made assumptions about her. They saw her as an extension of him, even though she and Dutch had nothing in common. The thought was both comforting and worrisome.

Mariah parked Dutch's dually in the empty parking lot of the Silver Horseshoe that sat parallel to the interstate. This hour of the morning, the place wasn't open for business, but there was an old green pickup parked near the side exit door and she was hoping to find Clover here, or at least talk to someone who could tell her where to find the woman.

Her heels clicked against the asphalt. It was a big place, at least ten thousand square feet, part honky-tonk, part restaurant. Posters of upcoming bands adorned the walls along with a menu advertising the daily specials, an announcement that the Silver Horseshoe was closed on Sundays, and the help wanted sign.

She walked around to the exit door and knocked. Waited. Then knocked again. Just when she was about to leave, the door creaked open and Clover poked her head out. "Yes?"

"Do you remember me, Mrs. Dempsey?"

" 'Course I do, Flaxey. I'm old but my mind's still pumping on all cylinders."

"I didn't mean to suggest otherwise, but I do prefer to be called Mariah."

"Sure you do."

Somehow that sounded like an indictment, but maybe she was just being sensitive.

"Well, c'mon in." Clover motioned her inside the darkened building and led her down a narrow corridor to a cluttered office with deer heads mounted on the wall.

"Do you hunt?" Mariah asked to make small talk, and stared at a glassy-eyed buck.

"Carl did. They're his trophies." Clover waved a hand at a brown leather sofa that had seen more prosperous days. "Have a seat. Just push that horse tack over."

She was getting accustomed to furniture that served as a clearinghouse for horse supplies. She eased the bridles and bits aside and perched on the edge of the sofa.

Clover sat on the corner of her desk, one leg on the ground, the other dangling over the edge. She rested one hand on her thigh, braced the other hand against the desktop to stabilize herself. "What's up?"

"I need a job," Mariah said. "I saw your help wanted sign."

Clover gave her the once-over, narrowing her eyes. "You ever wait tables?"

"In college. And for a few weeks a couple of months ago."

"Let me guess. You waited tables at one of those high-class joints in downtown Chicago."

Mariah widened her eyes. "How did you know?"

Clover shook her gray head. "Honey, it's written

all over your face. You might have been born to a cutter, but you were raised around luxury."

"Not my luxury," she said. "I picked rich people's clothes up off the floor and did their laundry. I swept their floors and washed their dishes and scrubbed their toilets."

"But along the way you did learn how to appreciate nice things."

"What's wrong with that?"

Clover studied Mariah for a long moment. "Nothing. Absolutely nothing wrong with that."

"So you'll hire me?"

"You ever wait tables in a honky-tonk?"

"No," she admitted.

"We're packed every single night that we're open from five until two in the morning. You'll be on your feet the whole time, carrying heavy trays, getting sloshed with beer, getting thrown up on, getting your ass pinched."

The picture Clover painted wasn't pretty, but Mariah was desperate. And although she might not look it, she was tough. Besides, she'd had Destiny for a boss. After that, the Silver Horseshoe would be a stroll through the garden. "I'm a hard worker."

"It's a long sight from Hyde Park. If you don't want to get razzed by every cowboy in town, you're going to have to change your look." Clover swept a hand at Mariah's clothes. "Get you some cowboy boots, and Wranglers, the tighter the better. That is if you're angling for tips."

Hope fluttered. "You'll give me a job?"

"Maybe." Clover narrowed her eyes. "How long you planning on staying in town?"

"Just until Christmas," she confessed.

Clover folded her arms over her chest. "So why should I bother training a waitress who's only planning on hanging around for two and a half months?"

"I need money."

"That's really not my problem."

"But you knew my parents. You used to babysit for me."

Suddenly, Clover smiled. "You're just like your dad. You'll tug on any rein to see if it gives."

"Is that bad?"

"Tell you what," Clover said, "come back tonight just as a visitor. Have the blue-plate special, play a game of pool, take in the clientele, and then you come tell me if you still think you can handle the job."

Mariah didn't have much money left and she really didn't want to rack up debt on her one and only credit card. Normally, she kept it strictly for emergencies. But what was more urgent than buying clothes that would help her fit in and land a job? A uniform of sorts, if you will.

She remembered the Western wear store she passed on the way into town and headed there. The cowbell over the door clanged when she walked in. Dazed at the array of cowboy apparel options stretched out before her, Mariah stood there a moment, taking it all in.

From the circular racks of Western wear attire a red-haired, pigtailed woman a few years younger than Mariah materialized. An acre of freckles carpeted her nose, and her lips glistened with a fresh sheen of gloss. Mariah could smell the heavy strawberry scent from where she stood.

The woman possessed a round happy face, a button nose, and almond-shaped eyes the color of unripe olives. She wore an orange denim skirt that skimmed the top of her cowboy boots, a black turtleneck pullover sweater, and a pink suede vest trimmed with white faux fur.

"Howdy!" she exclaimed, "Welcome to Western Wear Palooza. Name's Prissy Purdue at your service."

"Um . . . hello, Prissy."

Prissy advanced on her, the bracelet at her wrist adorned with silver cowboy-theme charms jangling merrily. She grabbed Mariah by the arm and tugged in the direction she wanted her to go. "C'mon, c'mon, you gotta see the new stuff we just got in."

Swept along by Prissy, the force of nature, Mariah found herself pulled into the depths of the store.

"Look at this. I just opened the box." Prissy let go of Mariah's arm and lifted the flaps on a big cardboard box sitting in the middle of the floor. "Will you get a load of these?"

Pigtails bobbing, Prissy started yanking out cowprint purses and leather belts and rubber rain boots with horses printed on them. "Aren't they adorable. You can seriously get your cowgirl on with accessories like these. Which do you like best?"

Prissy held up two belt buckles. One was silver, embossed with the words: "Texas to the Bone." The other was gold and had the raised three-dimensional image of a man riding a cutting horse. "I know, I know, the cutter belt buckle is obligatory in Jubilee and gold is shinier than silver, but the Texas to the Bone is just so *badass*."

The other woman was yammering so fast that Mariah wondered if she was ever going to take a breath.

Prissy glanced down. "OMG!"

Startled, Mariah followed her gaze, saw a snake-skin belt on the floor, and for a horrifying second thought it was an actual snake. She jumped sideways.

"Are those Manolo Blahniks?"

"Huh?"

"Your shoes." Prissy said the words like she was exhaling a prayer and sank to her knees to inspect Mariah's shoes. "Manolo Blahniks."

She pronounced them *Man-ooo-loo Block-niks*, but Mariah didn't correct her. "Yes."

"Can I touch them?" Prissy's eyes had taken on a rapturous glaze.

"Um . . . I guess." Mariah slipped off the stilettos and handed them over.

Prissy petted them like they were cats. "We're the same size. Seven medium. You," she announced with conviction, "are not from Jubilee."

"No, I'm not."

"You're from a big city."

"I am," Mariah admitted, wondering what she'd walked into.

"I was born and raised in Jubilee, but I have dreams."

"Big-city dreams?"

"Oh no," Prissy said. "I love Jubilee. I just want to wear a pair of Manolo Blahniks at my wedding. I mean I love Western wear and all. As you can see it's my life." She waved a hand at the store. "But sometimes a girl just wants something sexy. Am I right?"

"You're getting married?" Mariah asked.

"I am." Prissy flashed a one-quarter-carat diamond engagement ring and grinned. "Paul asked me last night. He took me out to eat at the Mesquite Spit and he had them put it in my banana pudding. It was the most romantic thing ever." Prissy sighed dreamily. "We're planning to get married the first weekend in December."

At the mention of a wedding, Mariah's ears had pricked up. "Why so fast? You hardly have time to plan."

"Oh, I'm not pregnant or anything if that's what you're thinking. Paul's getting deployed to Afghanistan after Christmas and we want to be married before he goes."

"Sounds like a great reason to fast-track the ceremony."

"Fast-track." Prissy beamed. "That sounds so *in the know*."

"I am . . . *was* . . . a wedding planner."

"You quit?"

"I was let go."

Prissy made a noise of distress, shook her head. "Times are tough all over. I'm guessing more people are planning their own weddings on a shoestring budget, huh?"

"They are," Mariah said, happy that Prissy didn't ask more questions about why she'd gotten fired.

"So, what in the heck are you doin' in Jubilee?"

"My father passed away and left me Stone Creek Ranch."

Prissy gasped, splayed a palm across her chest. "You're Dutch's daughter?"

Mariah nodded.

"Oh my Lord, honey, let me give you a hug. You poor thing. It must have tore you right up that you couldn't make the funeral. Paul and I were there. It was really nice. Half the town got up and said kind words."

The next thing she knew, Prissy was enveloping her in a strawberry-scented hug. Mariah wasn't much of a hugger, but Prissy sure was. She squeezed her tight. Awkwardly, Mariah patted Prissy's shoulder blades.

Prissy pulled back, dabbed at the tears in her eyes. "It's Mariah, right?"

"Yes."

"Your daddy, he talked about you every time he came into the store. I know he'd be so proud that you came home."

"Jubilee's not my home."

Prissy waved a hand. " 'Course it is. Now that you own Stone Creek."

"I'm selling it back to Joe Daniels." She didn't know why she was telling Prissy this.

"Oh that Joe." Prissy sighed. "Isn't he gorgeous? Like Jubilee's version of a black-haired Brad Pitt. Except younger and sexier. It's so sad about his wife. He and Becca were a dream couple. They looked like figurines on top of a wedding cake. They were so cute together you could just eat 'em up with a long-handled spoon."

"Sounds . . . cannibalistic."

Prissy's high-pitched laugh resembled squealing bus brakes. "You're so funny. Seriously though, before he hooked up with Becca, that rascally Joe was a real ladies' man. But once he was with her, he never even looked at another woman. She was his world. And then Becca goes and gets herself killed."

Morbid curiosity took hold of her and Mariah couldn't stop herself from asking, "How did it happen?"

"It was so sad. She was barrel racing at PRCA rodeo in Duncan, Oklahoma. She'd been burning up the circuit, was all set to win the finals again like she'd done the year before, when her horse stumbled at top speed and threw her out of the saddle. She landed—*boom*." Prissy smacked her palms together. "Right on the top of her head. Broke her spine like Christopher Reeve, but she died on the way to the hospital. Just one of those horrible freak accidents."

Mariah felt as if all the blood had drained from her head to her feet. She thought of Joe and what he'd suffered, and her heart wrenched. She couldn't begin to imagine the level of his grief. "That's so awful."

"A bunch of us thought he might do something stupid."

"Like suicide?" Mariah whispered.

Prissy nodded solemnly. "They were so in love. It was that special kind of magic, you know," Prissy said. "Like me and Paul. First time we laid eyes on each other, we both just *knew*. It's killing me that Paul's going to the Middle East, but he keeps telling me that freedom isn't free. Somebody has to fight for it. I just don't know why it has to be him."

The cowbell over the front door tinkled.

"'Scuse me a minute," Prissy said, and bounded for the front door.

Mariah looked at the purses and belts and buckles strewn across the counter where Prissy had been stacking them.

"Well, speak of the devil," Prissy boomed to the new customer. "We were just talkin' 'bout you."

"We?" Joe said.

The sound of Joe's rich, dark voice sent an excited shiver over her skin, and Mariah had an impulse to run right out the back door. She just might have done it too, if Prissy hadn't shown up, trolling Joe behind her much as she'd done with Mariah earlier.

"Ta-da," Prissy said. "Your new neighbor is on a shopping spree too."

"Hello," Joe said, his gaze meeting Mariah's.

She raised a hand, smiled faintly.

"What were you looking for?" Prissy asked him.

"I need some new chaps. She Devil got me with her horn and split my old chaps right up the leg."

"She Devil?" Mariah arched an eyebrow.

"An ornery Brahma I own," Joe explained. "She doesn't take well to being cut by Miracle. Those two get along like Tom and Jerry."

"Miracle bested her I'm sure," Prissy said.

"He did, but She Devil took it out on me."

"Let me just go find those chaps. Same kind as before?"

"Yep."

"Be right back." Prissy disappeared.

"So," Joe said, resting his arm on a support column that was very close to where Mariah stood. She could feel his radiating body heat, his mouth crooked like a question mark. "You decided to go country."

"It was an issue of survival. Conform or be mocked."

He tilted his cowboy hat down lower on his brow and leveled her a cocky stare. "You need any help?"

"Prissy's taking care of me."

Joe lowered his voice. "About that, you might want to reconsider. Prissy's taste can be a bit . . ."

"Over the top?"

"I wasn't going to say it, but yeah." His grin could drop a buckle bunny at fifty paces. Cassie used to say the same thing about Dutch. Mariah wondered for the first time if her mother had been a buckle bunny in her youth.

Joe was standing too close. That alpha man thing. Closing in. Mariah hugged herself, putting her arms up for protection.

Against what? An outrageous smile?

But what got to her, what really screwed with her equilibrium, was that on the other side of the teasing smile, she knew the pain he struggled so hard to hide. Two sentences scrolled through her mind. One was sympathetic: *Hands off he's a widower*—the other was pure selfishness: *Wonder what he tastes like.* That last thought gave her an electrical jolt.

Joe leaned over, and for one crazy moment, she thought he was going to kiss her. Her breath made a rattling sound in her lungs.

He didn't kiss her, just reached overhand to pluck a black, broad-brimmed Stetson off the rack behind her. Her limbs went liquid as his sexy scent surrounded her. Now why was she wanting him to kiss her?

Because he's a hottie.

So what? She'd never been so bowled over by a man's looks before. Why him? Why now?

It was the widower mystique. Had to be. Blame it on her all-time favorite movie, *Sleepless in Seattle*.

"Here," Joe said, and settled the cowboy hat on her head. "Try this."

Mariah felt like a giant dork and reached to doff the hat, but Joe's words stopped her.

"You look good."

She swallowed against the heat of his gaze. The man had the uncanny ability to steal every rational thought in her head with a single glance. Nervously, she ran her tongue over her bottom lip. "You're not just saying that to flatter me?"

"Look." He took her by the shoulders and turned her to face an oval mirror hung on the wall beside the hat shelf.

The weight of his hands felt solid. Real. Honest.

Mariah thought of the men she'd dated in Chicago. Businessmen more concerned with their bottom line than anything else. She realized she'd never dated a man who was good with his hands. For the most part, she'd gone from cerebral types, drawn to the kind of man that was the antithesis to Dutch.

But Joe . . . Joe was just like her father. Passionate about horses. Good with his hands. Easy to be with. Was he as equally unreliable as Dutch? That thought put the brakes on her runaway fantasies.

"See," Joe murmured, his lips right next to her ear. His breath warmed her skin. She felt so many things she shouldn't be feeling. Desire, need, hope. Joe Daniels wasn't the answer to her problems, but damn if she couldn't help wondering if he could be the answer to her long, lonely nights. He took her chin in his palm and raised her head.

Mariah met her own gaze in the mirror, startled at the cowgirl who looked back at her. Dressed in the black Stetson, she looked the part. That made her feel immeasurably better. She'd always been good at playing the part. Accomplished at donning the costume of whatever role she assumed. But somehow this was . . .

What?

Staring at her reflection she experienced an oddly puzzling sensation, as if she'd been digging through an old trunk and run across some family keepsakes she'd known nothing about. Familiar yet foreign, like a once beloved friend, not seen for decades, changed beyond recognition. Had Cassie and Dutch once dressed her like this as a little girl? She couldn't remember, but it was likely.

"And these," Joe said, walking over to where the ladies' boots were shelved and retrieving a pair of exotic cowgirl boots. "You'd look sharp in Old Gringo."

She was still barefooted from when she'd taken off her Manolos to show Prissy.

Joe tossed her a pair of socks and the boots. "Try them on."

She had to admit, for cowgirl boots, they were very chic. Full-grain leather with a fashionably worn look. Leopard print with red piping details. Joe had excellent taste.

Mariah sat down on a stool that Joe brought over for her and slipped on the socks, and then the boots. They were surprisingly comfortable. She'd never had a pair of shoes that fit instantly, without any break-in period. But the Old Gringos seemed cobbled especially for her. Like Cinderella and the glass slipper.

Joe studied her feet, echoed her thoughts. "They're made for you."

"I'll take it," Mariah said to Prissy, who came floating back over with the chaps for Joe.

"The hat or the boots?" Prissy asked.

The price tag on the boots was a bit hefty, but if she had to wear cowgirl boots, she might as well go with the comfortable snazzy ones. When looking the part, Destiny had drilled into her, go all the way.

"Both. And let's throw in some Wrangler jeans and a half-dozen blouses."

"Dang, look at you." Prissy beamed and sank her hands on her hips. "Fittin' right in. Go ahead and pick out some shirts and jeans while I ring Joe up."

Joe followed Prissy to the cash register.

Mariah watched him go. The man possessed a magnificent butt.

Yes, so what? A magnificent butt did not a relationship make. Not that she wanted a relationship with him. She didn't. He was damaged. She was damaged. She didn't want a relationship with anyone. Not now. Not for a long, long time.

Still wearing the Stetson and the Old Gringo boots and lugging an armful of Western-style shirts and jeans, her Manolo Blahniks looped around two fingers, Mariah wandered to the cash register just as Joe was completing his purchase.

"See ya back at the ranch," Joe said, lifted a hand good-bye to Mariah, and left the store, cowbell clanging merrily in his wake.

"Joe likes you," Prissy said.

"How can you tell?"

"How can you not?" Prissy giggled. "You know, you look kinda like Becca."

She found that disconcerting. "In what way?"

"She was small like you and blond."

"But prettier?"

Prissy waved a hand. "Becca was prettier than everyone. Don't let that throw you off the hunt."

"I'm not hunting him."

Prissy's eyes rounded. "I sure would be if I didn't have Paul."

"I'm not interested."

"You like guys don't you?"

"Yes," she reassured Prissy, "I like guys."

"Then what's got you scared?"

Mariah blew a raspberry. "I'm not scared."

Prissy bagged up her purchases. "If you say so."

"I'm just not interested. We have nothing in common. He's country, I'm city."

"You look pretty country to me in that outfit." Prissy winked.

"All for show. Besides, he drinks too much."

"Where'd you hear that?"

Mariah shrugged. "Something I deduced on my own."

"You're wrong about that. Joe doesn't have a drinking problem. He hardly ever goes on a bender."

"But he does. Sometimes."

"He never did before Becca died."

"I don't need a guy who's still hung up on his dead wife. That's just asking for heartache." Mariah handed Prissy her credit card.

Prissy held up her palm. "No charge."

"What do you mean, no charge?"

"Joe already paid for you, purchases."

"No, no." Mariah shook her head. "He can't pay for my things."

"Honey, why not? If he wants to pay, let him."

"I don't even know the man. He can't buy me things."

Prissy looked confused. "Too late. It's already been taken care of."

Mariah grabbed the packages and went running out of the store, to chase him down. Joe was at the corner about to step into his pickup.

"Cowboy!" she hollered.

Every man on the street turned to stare at her.

"Not you," Mariah said. "Him." She pointed

at Joe and with bags bumping against her, hurried down the sidewalk. "Just what do you think you're doing?"

Joe tipped his hat back. "Just helping you on your quest to fit in."

"Well . . . well . . ." she sputtered. "I don't need your help."

"Wanna tell me why you're so mad?"

"I don't need you to buy my clothes."

"Never said you did."

"You paid for them."

"You were sleeping in your car. You're out of a job. You don't need to run up credit card debt. I was just looking out for you the way Dutch would have wanted me to."

"You mean the way that he didn't?"

Joe shrugged. "You could try saying, 'Thank you, Joe.'"

Mariah realized they were drawing a crowd. She shook a finger at him, the sacks sliding down her arm to her wrists. "You, Joe Daniels, are the most arrogant . . . cocky . . . show-off . . ."

"Yes, ma'am," he said, tipped his hat, got into his truck, and drove away, leaving her standing on the sidewalk amid snickers and curious stares.

It was going to be a very long two and a half months.

CHAPTER EIGHT

Even the Lone Ranger had Tonto.
—Dutch Callahan

Joe hadn't intended on going to the pool tournament at the Silver Horseshoe. The Fort Worth Triple Crown Futurity started at the end of November, and with Dutch out of the picture, he and his best hand, Cordy Whiteside, needed to work extra hard getting Miracle ready.

He thought he'd worn himself out with work, fixing the busted corral fence again and putting Miracle through his paces, so the horse would be too worn out to plan another corral breakout. That animal missed Dutch something fierce.

Joe did too.

But come nightfall, after he'd rubbed down the stallion and stabled him for the night, Joe found himself at loose ends and feeling bone lonely. He'd walked to the liquor cabinet, reached for a bottle of tequila, and then thought about the last time he and Jose Cuervo had done the tango.

Joe hesitated, hand wrapped around the neck of the bottle. For no good reason, he thought of Mariah

Callahan. How pissed off she'd been at him. He chuckled, thinking of the sparks in her eyes when she'd come chasing after him, berating him for paying for her clothes.

If he was being honest, he'd been thinking about her all day. While he'd been bumping the bit, directing Miracle to cut a particular calf from the herd, Mariah had been creeping around the edges of his mind like a shadow. He didn't want her there, not at all, but she wouldn't go away.

Just before dusk, he'd taken Miracle for a full run more to outrace his thoughts of her than anything else. To eradicate the vision of how lovely and exasperated Mariah had looked standing on the street corner with packages looped over her arm. By the time he returned from the gallop, twilight stars dotted the sky and the sun was nothing but a wan streak of orange, a shroud of evening clouds drawing closed the day.

He knotted his fist, felt a ferocious urge to wipe the trouble from Mariah's eyes. That's why he'd paid for her clothes. False sense of chivalry. The cowboy code. It had been a long time since he'd thought of someone else's troubles.

Selfish.

He'd been damn selfish. Wallowing in sorrow, then throwing himself into cutting as if no one or nothing else mattered. He bought her clothes to assuage his guilt.

Jose tempted, golden and destructive. *Drown it all out. C'mon, forget.*

He played the game of love once and lost. Lost so badly, his tale was a town legend. He wanted to blank it out. He licked his lips, then purposefully took the tequila to the sink, twisted off the lid, and poured it down the drain. Proud of his choice, he drove into Jubilee.

Now, he sat at the end of the bar; nursing a Lone Star, cracking open peanuts roasted in the hull, waiting for the pool tournament to start and watching Ila play darts with Cordy.

Joe noticed that whenever Ila wasn't looking, Cordy stared at her as if she was the sun and he was a seedling. While Ila, at five-foot-eleven towered over lovesick Cordy, who stood five-foot-eight in his cowboy boots.

Willie and Waylon wailed from the jukebox, beseeching mamas not to let their babies grow up to be cowboys. Ceiling fans whirled overhead. On the flat-screen television set mounted on the wall over the bar, the Dallas Mavericks were trouncing the Lakers.

Clover climbed up on the stool beside him. "Dutch wouldn't have wanted you to waste time mourning, Joe."

"It's not just Dutch," he said, picking at the label of his beer bottle.

"I know," Clover murmured. "But it's time to let Becca go. It's been two years."

"I never would have known that if you hadn't pointed it out to me."

"Sorry if I put my two cents in where it didn't belong." Clover held up her palms in a gesture of surrender.

"How easy was it for you to let go of Carl?"

"I still haven't let go of him," she said earnestly. "But I'm seventy. You're not even thirty. You've got your whole life ahead of you. Me? I'm just killing time until I can see Carl again."

Joe took a swig of his beer. Said nothing. What was there to say?

Clover clucked her tongue. "I miss the old Joe— wisecracking, hardworking, but always up for some mischievous fun. Why don't you ask out Julianne Fletcher?" Clover nodded at a shapely, dark-haired woman playing electronic trivia at the other end of the bar with a group of friends. Julianne was a cutter and a member of the Jubilee Cutters Co-op. "Her divorce just came through."

"Nah, she's still too wounded."

"Like you aren't? I'm not sayin' marry her. Just go out and have some fun."

Joe cocked his head and pretended to give it some thought so Clover would leave him alone. Then the door opened and Mariah Callahan strutted in.

All eyes in the place swiveled to take her in.

She hesitated on the edge of the threshold, looking as if she wanted to turn tail and run. A spurt of sympathy shot through him. Couldn't be easy being the new city slicker in a close-knit cutting horse town. She wore Wrangler blue jeans, a long-sleeved, white cotton cowgirl-style blouse, and the snazzy leopard-print Old Gringo boots he'd bought for her.

His lips parted. His eyes were glued to her sleek curves and he couldn't wait for her to turn around so he could check out her butt in those jeans.

Her chin went up and her shoulders straightened and she let go of the door and strode forward, a resolute expression on her face.

His skin heated up. Just the beer. It was just the beer making him feel flushed. Not the girl. Not the girl at all.

"How about that one?" Clover nudged him in the ribs with her elbow and nodded at Mariah.

He pulled his gaze from Mariah, studied the neon Michelob sign on the wall in front of him, took a pull from his warm beer. "C'mon, Dutch's daughter?"

"Don't say it like it's impossible."

"It *is* impossible."

"Why's that?"

Joe shrugged, wiped the condensation from the outside of his beer bottle. "I'm not interested."

"Liar."

"She didn't treat Dutch right," Joe brooded. "He loved her so much and she never once came to see him."

"You don't know the whole story," Clover said.

"And you do?"

"Dutch took off on her and her mama when Mariah was little."

"He was a great guy."

"To us, yeah. But to Mariah . . ." Clover shrugged, hopped off the stool, and went back around the other side of the bar. "Life is complicated. Ask her out. Give her a chance."

He shook his head, took another swig of beer. It was getting warm. "She's out of her element here. She'll be gone as soon as I can scrape up the money to buy the place back from her."

"I don't know about that," Clover said. "If she's got an ounce of Dutch's stubbornness, she just might surprise you."

Mariah edged up to the bar.

"Hello," Clover greeted her. "What'll you have?"

Joe busied himself with staring at the TV but he couldn't help watching Mariah from his peripheral vision. She *was* a curiosity. And she smelled really good too.

"I'd like a Riesling, please," she said.

"Sorry," Clover said. "It's Chardonnay or Merlot."

"Seriously?"

"Not many wine drinkers come to the Silver Horse-shoe."

"Chardonnay then."

Clover poured up the Chardonnay, set it on a napkin, and passed it across the bar.

Mariah stood there holding her wineglass by the stem, looking a little lost.

"Have a seat," Clover invited, canting her head at the bar stool beside Joe.

Mariah cast him a glance. He felt it rather than saw it because he was pretending to concentrate on the Mavericks forward who'd just made a shot from midcourt.

"Do you mind?" she asked.

"Free country." He waved, wondering why he was feeling so tense, and finally made himself look at her.

She put her glass back up on the bar, tucked a strand of hair behind one delicate ear, and scaled the bar stool. She was so petite that her feet didn't even reach the top rung.

A primal protectiveness that he didn't want to feel toward her stole over him.

"You gettin' settled in at Dutch's cabin?" Clover asked, wiping the bar with a towel.

"Yes." Mariah smiled faintly.

"Smoked 'im," Ila crowed, striding up to the bar as Cordy wandered off to the jukebox where Neil Young was singing "Are There Any More Real Cowboys?" "A celebratory beer, please, Clover."

Ila stood beside Joe, twisting her long, dark hair up on her head, and fanned her neck with her other hand. "Whew. I'm steamin' hot. Who knew victory could make you sweat?"

"Cordy let you win," Joe observed.

"What?" Ila looked startled. "No, he didn't."

"Yes, he did."

Flabbergasted, she sank her hands on her hips. "Why would he do that?"

"He's got a crush on you."

Ila wrinkled her nose. "No way. We're just friends."

"You tell Cordy that?"

"He's Jack and I'm the beanstalk."

"And he wants to climb you," Joe teased.

"Shut up!"

"I'm serious."

"Like your judgment counts for anything."

"What do you mean?" Joe asked.

"Oh hey," Ila said to Mariah. Apparently she didn't want to talk about Cordy's crush anymore. "I didn't see you there."

"And I didn't recognize you out of uniform," Mariah said. "You look very pretty in a dress."

Ila struggled not to look flattered. "You like my dress, Joe?"

"Pretty," he said. Why was Ila wearing a dress? She never wore a dress.

"The tournament's starting. Who all's up for a game of pool?" Cordy asked, rubbing his palms as he came over to stand between Ila and Joe. He had to reach up in order to lay a hand on Ila's shoulders.

Ila shrugged off Cordy's hand, downed half the beer Clover set in front of her in one long chug. "Me and Joe against you and Mariah."

"Who?" Cordy asked, his gaze fixed on Ila.

"Dutch's daughter." Ila waved in Mariah's direction.

"You're Dutch's daughter?" Cordy stopped drooling over Ila long enough to pump Mariah's hand like a water tap. "Welcome to Jubilee."

"Thank you." Mariah smiled at him.

Joe felt a draft of jealousy pass through him. Nah, it wasn't jealousy. He had nothing to feel jealous about. He had no relationship with her. More importantly, he didn't want one. He knew what was bothering him. Not jealousy for sure, just that one minute Cordy was drooling over Ila and the next he was spreading his grin over Mariah. He was trying to hog all the pretty women.

"Can you shoot pool?" Cordy asked Mariah.

"I've played a time or two."

"Don't worry," Cordy said. "I'm ace enough for the both of us."

"No way," Joe said, not knowing why he was letting himself get sucked into this. "Ila and I are beating the pants off you."

"Ha!" Cordy said, leading the way to the back room.

Mariah got off the bar stool to follow Cordy, and as she passed by Joe, he could have sworn he heard her murmur, "What the heck is it with you and the lack of pants?"

That made him grin.

On the jukebox, John Denver was singing "Rocky Mountain High," and Joe was trying hard not to stare at Mariah's cute little butt. But she was bent over the pool table. What was he supposed to stare at? There it was, looking all perfect and nicely rounded cupped in the sling of her blue jeans.

It didn't look like Becca's butt. Becca's butt had been sort of flat. But not in a bad way. He'd loved Becca's butt. It's just that Mariah's butt . . . well, there was nothing flat about it.

He hitched in a lungful of air and tried to force himself to glance away. But nothing doing, her butt was a magnet and his eyes were steel. She sank her shot, straightened, and grinned at the room, her blond hair floating around her face.

Little Bit of dynamite, he thought. *Comes in small packages. Simple but deadly.*

"Uh-oh, someone's been sandbagging," Ila said.

"I think we've been scammed," Joe agreed.

"Who me?" Mariah said innocently, and lined up to take her shot. She sank two balls on that one.

"Will you look at that?" Cordy beamed.

Joe looked. Mariah's butt was over the pool table again as she reached for a difficult shot. His libido cleaved a cleft of longing straight through the middle of him. No one had turned him on like this since Becca. His sex drive had come roaring back to life, and in a major way.

While he was happy to be feeling something below the belt again, he was very disturbed to discover Mariah was the one doing the arousing. Why couldn't it have been Julianne Fletcher? Hell, why couldn't it have been just about anyone else? He did not want this.

"Your turn." Cordy nudged Joe with his elbow.

"Huh? What? Oh yeah." He hadn't realized Mariah had missed her shot. He took his time chalking his cue.

When he looked up and found her smiling at him,

a wild sensation beat through his chest. He was a grizzly bear staggering from a dark cave after a long hibernation—fuzzy-headed, a little confused, and a lot ravenous.

No. Just no. This was not a good thing.

Joe moved down the table, looking for the best shot, and ended up near where Mariah stood with her back against the paneled wall, pool cue gripped in her hand. A narrow wooden pole the only thing between them besides air.

"Let's take this up a notch," Ila said. "Joe, show Ms. Callahan how it's done."

"My pleasure." Joe sank three balls and then scratched.

Cordy took his turn. Then Ila was up. For the most part, they were all evenly matched.

Or so it appeared.

Joe was enjoying himself. He'd played pool since grade school. Mostly with Ila on the billiards table in her family's rec room. He'd won more tournaments than he lost. As a teen, he'd been good enough at the game to hustle horse money from other cowboys. He had a mathematical mind. Angles and pattern of trajectory easily popped into his head. He could see the shots sinking before he ever put hand to cue. He was patient. He was controlled. He was good at taking advantage of other people's weaknesses. The same qualities he brought to cutting horses, he brought to pool. It made him difficult to beat.

Mariah was even harder to best.

When he finally figured out that she was better at the game than he, Joe ached ruefully . . . shame-facedly. It was like finding out she was a better cutter. Indignation welled up in him, painful as a stubbed toe, and he struggled to tamp it down. He'd underestimated her, and she used it to trounce his pride.

Cordy stood to one side grinning his fool head off, while Mariah sank another shot and then another and another with cool, deliberate movements. Each time a ball went in, Ila snorted, until soon she sounded like a pawing bull rushing a matador.

Mariah was controlling them all.

You better watch this one, Daniels, or you're going to lose everything to her.

The other tables in the back room filled up as other tournament players drifted it. The games weren't anything official. Just cutters who wandered into the bar after a hard day's work for camaraderie, a meal, a game, and a beer or two. Although the grand prize was two hundred dollars. Definitely worth playing for.

Clover came over. "You all want a pitcher?"

They ordered a pitcher of beer and kept playing. Cordy and Mariah won the first game.

"Rematch?" Ila asked eagerly.

"Yes," Joe said.

"How about you?" Ila nodded at Mariah.

Mariah glanced at her watch, "Actually there was something I wanted to talk to Clover about."

"She's here until closing time," Ila said. "It's not even late yet."

Mariah shrugged. "Okay, but just one more round."

"I say we switch partners," Cordy said, eyeing Ila like she was a big slab of filet mignon.

"Okay," Ila said. "Guys against girls. We'll stomp you."

"I was thinking more like you and me take Joe and Mariah." Cordy looked hopeful.

"They'll stomp us!" Ila exclaimed.

Mariah reached for her wineglass resting on the small table next to the pool table, unwittingly exposing her cleavage.

Joe wasn't paying much attention to Cordy and Ila. His gaze was fixed on Mariah's chest.

She set her glass down, turned back, and caught him staring. Frowning, she straightened, pulled her shoulders back.

He grinned. It felt good, having his sexual desire back. *Not that good, considering who's causing it.* "Mariah and me against you and Cordy," he said to Ila. "Or I'm out."

"Fine," Ila said, but she sounded testy. "Have it your way."

Ila broke, smacking the balls hard and sending them scattering. They played for a while. Then Ila said, "So Mariah, how long you planning on staying in Jubilee?"

"Until Christmas, after Joe wins the futurity and can afford to buy Dutch's place from me."

"Good thing," Ila said. "I don't see you as a cutter."

"You don't think I can be a cutter?" Mariah sounded annoyed.

"Hell no. It's either in your blood or it's not."

"I've got Dutch's blood running through my veins."

"Wouldn't know it by looking at you." Ila leveled her an unfriendly stare.

Mariah's chin hardened. "I just might fool you."

"Being a good cutter takes patience," Ila said.

"I'm patient," Cordy said.

"You have to know when to make a move and when to hold back." Ila smacked the ball so hard it bounced off the table, but Cordy caught it in his palm. Ila looked over at Joe.

"I know how to do that." Cordy sidled close to her.

"We know, Cordy," Ila said. "You're a born cutter. It's Mariah that's in question."

"Why does everyone in your universe have to be a cutter?"

"Have you ever been on the back of a cutting horse?" Ila asked.

"Not that I know of, but seeing how Dutch was my father, I'm sure he put me on the back of one at some point in my childhood."

"But you don't remember it?"

"No."

"Then you haven't been on the back of a cutting horse. Not when it counts."

"So it's that memorable?"

Ila leaned in close, lowered her voice, slid Joe a look. "Like the best sex you've ever had."

"That's a big promise." Mariah wasn't letting Ila intimidate her even though she was almost a foot taller. That impressed Joe. Ila intimidated ninety percent of the people who met her.

"You try it, you'll find out why everyone around here is hung up on cutting horses."

"Now you've got me wanting to give it a shot."

Ila leveled a glance at Joe. "Why don't you put her on Miracle?"

"She doesn't even know how to ride, Ila."

"I know how to ride," Mariah disputed.

Joe studied her. "Do a lot of riding in Chicago, did you?"

"Just because I haven't ridden in a long time doesn't mean I don't know how."

"Sounds like a dare to me," Ila said. "Let's put her on a cutting horse."

"What do we do with her if the bug bites?" Joe asked.

"Then she'll be like the rest of us. Out of balance, out of whack, out of our heads over cutting horses."

"You make it sound so righteously unpleasant," Mariah commented.

"Isn't that the way of things that are beautifully difficult?" Ila asked.

"You want to ride Miracle?" Joe set down his pool cue and assessed Mariah.

"I'd give it a try."

"Miracle's not just any horse."

"I know, he's the second coming of horsedom."

"He is." Cordy breathed. "In a manner of speaking. If Miracle was a quarterback, he'd be Roger Staubach."

"If he was a president, he'd be JFK," Ila threw in.

"If he was a lover, he'd be Casanova," Clover said, wandering over to see if they wanted another pitcher.

"You people are besotted over a horse." Mariah shook her head.

"We are," Ila, Clover, and Cordy chorused.

But Joe suddenly found himself seeing the Silver Horseshoe through Mariah's eyes. Men dressed in Wranglers, cowboy shirts, hats and boots, shooting pool, watching the basketball game, and talking about horses. Single women sitting at tables with their girlfriends, giggling and watching the cowboys and talking about cutting horses. Couples and families in the dining area of the Silver Horseshoe, eating the blue-plate special, talking Little Britches rodeo and cutting horses.

He supposed that to Mariah it was an alien culture,

even though her early beginnings were steeped in it. Having been abandoned by her father, she spurned this life as Dutch had spurned her, and Joe couldn't blame her. It was enlightening, seeing his home turf through her eyes, and it softened him toward her. A little.

Besides, she was trying. She deserved some credit for that.

Yes, yes, give her credit, but do not let down your guard. She's not the right one for you. She'll hurt you. Dammit all. He didn't want to be here feeling the things he was feeling.

"Where'd you learn to play pool?" Joe asked.

"When the rich people are away, the hired help will play," she said.

He arched an eyebrow. "Meaning?"

"Meaning the people my mother worked for had a billiards room and they were always jetting around to someplace or the other. As long as we cleaned up afterward, my mother would let me bring a friend or two over."

"You grew up as the hired help in rich folks' homes?" Cordy asked.

Mariah nodded.

"Explains a lot." Ila sank another ball.

"Ooh, who's that?" Mariah asked, and nudged Joe in the side with her elbow.

He followed her gaze. The people near the entrance parted and a man strolled in, cock of the walk, wearing a rodeo belt buckle the size of a hubcap. Trust Mariah to hone in on the biggest tool in Jubilee. Joe's ribs tingled where her elbow had grazed him, and he caught a whiff of her hair. She smelled like chocolate chip cookies.

"That's Lee Turpin. His daddy is the richest man in Jubilee," Ila said.

"He used to ride bulls in the PRCA during the same time as Joe," Cordy supplied. "Turpin always came up second place. He also dated Becca in high school before she started going out with Joe."

"Turpin and his horse Dancer are up against Joe and Miracle in the Fort Worth Futurity," Ila said, and sank another ball. "They're his stiffest competition."

Mariah shot Joe a look. "I take that to mean he's not a fan of yours?"

"And vice versa." Joe glowered at Turpin. The scuzzball.

"Turpin was really pissed at Dutch because he wouldn't sell Miracle to him," Cordy told Mariah. "There's some bad blood over that too."

"I have a feeling I'm sitting in the middle of a turf war," Mariah said.

"Uh-oh," Ila said, setting down her pool cue. "Turpin looks drunk."

"Ignore him," Cordy said. "It's your shot, Joe."

Joe turned his back on Turpin, picked up his cue. "The guy's a show-off, blowhard."

"Sounds like a lot of cowboys I've known," Mariah said.

"He's not a real cowboy," Joe said. "He lives in a condo, for hell's sake, and drives a Corvette."

"But he's a cutter, right?" Mariah asked, angling her head at Turpin.

He wished she would quit looking at the guy. Why did he care who she looked at? "After a fashion."

"What does that mean?"

"He doesn't know how to treat horses. Which is one reason Dutch would never sell a horse to him.

He's rough, runs 'em hard. I can't stand a man who mistreats animals." Joe heard the hatred in his voice, saw the startled expression on Mariah's face.

Back off. You're coming on too strong.

His mother used to tell him his strong passions would get him into trouble one day. He'd never been the kind of guy to sit on the sidelines. He threw himself into whatever venture he undertook. Rodeoing, cutting horses, grieving, making love.

Lazily, he flicked a gaze over Mariah's body. The woman could surely fill out a pair of jeans. His pulse jumped. Not good. Not good at all.

But the thing of it was, whenever he was around Mariah he felt alive again. For two years, he'd had a passion for only two things—cutting horses and nursing his grief like sustenance. He wasn't inclined to let either one of them go.

He turned away from her, felt the heat of her gaze on him as he smacked the ball with his cue, scratched, and then put his stick aside.

"You're losing your edge, cowboy," Ila crowed.

"Well, hello there, beautiful, where have you been all my life?" The sound of Lee Turpin's voice cut through Joe like a saw blade.

A tingle ran up the back of his hands and he curled his fingers into his palms. Tension fisted his shoulder muscles. Slowly, Joe pivoted.

Turpin loomed over Mariah, his stance wide. He stuck his hand out to her, cast Joe a sly glance from the corner of his eye. "Lee Turpin, sweet thing, and you are . . . ?"

"Mariah Callahan." She took his hand.

Joe gritted his teeth.

"Dutch's daughter. I am so very sorry for your

loss." Aggressively, Turpin hauled her to her feet, pulled her to his chest on the pretext of giving her a sympathetic hug.

Mariah's eyes rounded.

In disbelief? Surprise? Or was it delight? Some women liked pushy guys.

"You know, darlin'," Turpin drawled. "Just let me know when you're ready to sell your daddy's land. I've got two hundred grand sitting in the bank earmarked for that property."

Over the top of Mariah's head, Turpin's gaze smashed into Joe's, smacking him like a physical blow.

Once upon a time, when Joe and Becca were first dating, not long after she'd broken up with Turpin, Joe had caught them together in a pasture at a rodeo, standing between two horse trailers in an identical embrace. Except Becca's arms had been around Turpin's neck and Turpin's hand had been on Becca's ass. That memory was a shard of glass in his heart. Even though, as he stood there in the shadows, and he heard Becca tell Turpin it was over for good, that she was with Joe now, he couldn't erase the image from his mind of the woman he loved cradled in the arms of his nemesis.

Turpin stared at Joe over a river of bitterness, rivalry, and distrust, and then he reached out and planted a meaty palm over Mariah's shapely rump.

She gasped, grabbed for Turpin's hand.

Turpin hung on, his eyes stabbing Joe's, a dangerous smirk on his face.

"Let go of me!" Mariah demanded.

Turpin yanked her closer, just daring Joe to make something out of it. Instigating a brawl.

Joe had had enough. If Turpin wanted a fight, he'd give it to him. In an instant, he was climbing over the pool table, his anger scaling up to spill from dizzying heights. He body-slammed Turpin.

Everything happened at once.

Spectators surrounded their corner of the room, the air filled with commentary, egging on the fight.

Cordy grabbed for the back of Joe's shirt, attempting to restrain him. Joe barely heard it rip, hardly felt the rush of air against his skin.

"Stop it," Ila hollered, and he didn't know if she was talking to him or Turpin or both of them. All he knew was that if he had to, he'd dismantle Turpin's arm from its socket to get it off Mariah's behind.

Mariah shoved at Turpin's chest, just as Turpin thrust her aside. She went flying into the wall. The air left her lungs with an audible *oomph* and she landed on her butt on the floor.

The asshole had hurt her!

Joe snarled with rage.

Turpin raised his fists.

Joe charged him, headbutting Turpin in the bread-basket.

They went down slugging. Years of pent-up animosity coming to a head. They were pretty evenly matched. Both the same size, both lean and hard-muscled. But Joe had righteous rage on his side and he was winning, sitting on top of Turpin, smacking him in a bare-knuckled free-for-all.

But as he was doing it he kept thinking, *Here I am, back at the first stage of grief all over again.*

"Becca wouldn't have died if she hadn't married you," Turpin howled. "If she'd stayed with me she wouldn't have died. I wouldn't have let her keep

barrel racing. I would have made her stay home and
be a good wife."

Turpin's cheekbone sliced Joe's fist, but his words
were an arrow, going straight to the truth.

"Becca was her own woman. No man could con-
tain her. Not you. Not me. She lived. She died. She's
gone. It's over."

It's over.

The words echoed in his head and that's when Joe
felt it. True acceptance. Becca was gone, and he was
finally ready to let her go, even if Turpin wasn't. He
had options. He could start again. Could feel alive
again.

With Mariah?

No, no, not her. But with someone.

"Your fault," Turpin accused.

Joe grunted, glanced over and saw Mariah sitting
on the floor, watching him with frightened eyes. He'd
scared her. She was scared of him. Shame burned a
brushfire in his heart. What the hell was he doing?
What was wrong with him? Bully. Brute. Hooligan.

His moment of hesitation was all that Turpin
needed. He plowed a fist squarely into Joe's left eye,
knocked him back.

"Enough!" Ila commanded, simultaneously grabbing both Joe and Turpin by the scruffs of their
necks. "If you don't stop it right now, both of you are
going to spend the night in the county jail."

Joe and Turpin chuffed in simultaneous breaths,
both their hands flexed in a boxer's stance, Ila standing between them.

"If I let you go, will you stop it?" she asked.

Joe nodded begrudgingly, felt the anger drain
away. Stupid. He'd been stupid to let Turpin get to

him. He'd embarrassed himself in front of Mariah.
Dutch would have kicked his ass.

Turpin shrugged. "He attacked me. I want to press
charges."

"Shut up," Ila snapped. "You had it coming and you
know it. Now both of you, clean up this mess and give
Clover enough money to cover the damages."

Sheepish, Joe swiped the sweat from his brow,
turned to Mariah, offered his hand to help her up.

She looked into his eyes, shook her head.

He dropped his hand to his side. He couldn't really
blame her for not wanting to touch him. He'd gone
off his rocker, acted berserk. He'd terrified her.

Clover came toward them, stepped over the mess
of spilled beer and scattered pool cues. Cocked her
head at Mariah. "Well, what do you think? If you
still want the job, it's yours."

CHAPTER NINE

Timing has a lot to do with the outcome of the rain
dance.

—Dutch Callahan

Mariah's head spun. She'd never been in a place
like this. Seen a brawl like this. Felt quite like
this.

Excited. Alive. Real. On fire with desire.

How freaking bizarre was that? She should feel
shocked or alarmed or something appropriate. Instead, the sight of Joe defending her honor in the most
primal way a man could defend a woman turned her
on as she'd never before been turned on.

No man had ever fought for her. Over her.

It was wrong. So wrong, and yet all she wanted to
do was draw him into her arms and kiss him until she
couldn't breathe. Why couldn't she stop thinking like
this? She didn't want to think like this.

When he reached down a palm to help her up
the first time, she'd been so overwhelmed she'd just
stared at it. But this time, when he offered it again,
she eagerly placed her small hand in his big one.

Trembling.

She was trembling. His touch made her tremble.

Oh, this was serious trouble. Resist. Resist at all costs. *He is not the man for you. He's a cowboy in love with horses. Just like Dutch. Just like the first man who walked out on you.*

"You okay?" he murmured huskily, his left eye quickly swelling shut.

"I'm fine." She giggled. She giggled when she got really nervous. Unfortunate habit. "You're the one who looks like you've been run through a blender."

"Ha!" Turpin said from the other side of the room where Ila had pushed him. "The Turpin blender." He pantomimed punching a speed bag.

"Outta here." Ila ushered Turpin toward the exit.

"You're on Daniels's side because you've got the hots for him," Turpin accused Ila.

Ila planted both palms on his chest and shoved him out through the side door. The door slammed shut behind them. Mariah noticed Cordy got up and trotted after the duo. What was that all about?

"Well?" Clover held the empty beer pitcher balanced on a serving platter. "Do you need some time to think about it?"

"I'll let you know tomorrow," Mariah said. She did want some time to think through her options. She wasn't sure she could handle this. *Yeah? What choice do you have? You need money.*

"You seriously considering working at the Horseshoe?" Joe picked his cowboy hat up from the floor, dusted it off.

"Tossing the idea around."

They stood there staring at each other, undercurrents of energy flowing between them.

So what? You could ignore it.

"Thanks," she said. "For the rescue, but I could have handled it. You didn't need to get beat up on my account."

"I have no doubt." Joe settled his hat back onto his head. "But a man's gotta do what a man's gotta do."

"Even if that means acting like a fool?"

A wide grin split his face. "Even if."

The grin churned her knees into butter. *Dangerous. Proceed with extreme caution.*

"I gotta be up early in the morning," he said.

"Oh." What had she been expecting from him? An invitation to a make-out session in the parking lot?

"Past my bedtime."

"You've got to hit the mattress. Right, right. Nighty-night. Sleep tight."

Crap! She was idiot-babbling. And why had she said the word "mattress"? It sounded like she'd been thinking about mattresses in conjunction with Joe. She wasn't thinking about mattresses. Well, now she *was* thinking about mattresses.

His gaze roved over her as if he too was thinking about the comfort of mattresses. Then just before he turned to go out the door, he said, "Sweet dreams, Little Bit."

"When are you going to stop pining for Joe?"

"What?" Ila's head came up.

She'd just deposited Lee Turpin in the passenger seat of his girlfriend's car, after the woman had promised to drive him straight home to sleep off his drunk. Cordy had been hanging around throughout the whole process. They were in the back parking lot of the Silver Horseshoe, the October night wind cutting through her cotton dress like a razor. Joe hadn't even noticed she'd worn a dress for his benefit.

"When are you going to stop pining for Joe?" Cordy repeated.

His statement caught her unaware, but Ila wasn't about to let him see that. She snorted indelicately, went to put her hand on the butt of her pistol that wasn't there. It was an unconscious gesture she performed when she was feeling insecure. "What the hell are you talkin' about?"

"Joe's never gonna love you the way you deserve to be loved." Cordy's voice was low, dark.

Ila schooled her features not to give herself away. "You're nuts."

"Nuts over you."

Startled, Ila sucked in her breath, took a step back. Cordy was her buddy. Nothing more. Never anything more than that. She loved Joe.

"It must have killed you. Loving him when he was married to your baby sister. My heart breaks when I think about it."

"Shut up," she snapped.

But Cordy did not shut up. He just kept talking and moving closer. "I know it strikes a nerve and I know you can't help who you love, but Ila, if you'd stop moondogging Joe Daniels for half a second, you could see what's standing right in front of you."

A lump formed in Ila's throat. She thought she'd been so cool, so unobtrusive, hiding her unrequited love for Joe under the guise of friendship. But here was Cordy Whiteside, of all people, calling her on it. "I have no idea what you're yammering on about."

"Sure you do."

She held up a palm. "Back off, short stuff."

"Insult me all you want. It's not chasing me off."

Goose bumps rose on her forearms. The wind. That's all it was. The wind.

But Cordy was saying everything she'd ever wanted Joe to say to her. It was unsettling. She tilted her chin down and stared him straight in the eye, hardened her jaw, determined to let nothing, absolutely nothing show in her eyes. "What do you know about anything?"

"You're not the only one who loves someone who doesn't love them back." Boldly, Cordy held her stare.

He wasn't a bad-looking man. In fact, some women might even find him handsome. He had curly brown hair and winsome green eyes, and she *had* noticed his butt could rival Bruce Springsteen's in his prime butt days. But Cordy was slight. Compact. A dinky little guy.

"You mean you?" she said.

He reached out, took her hand. "Ila, let go of Joe and give me a chance. He'll never feel for you the way I do."

Panic flared through her like wildfire. Ila yanked her hand back, tucked it underneath her arm to keep it away from him. "B-but . . . you're shorter than me."

"You're almost six feet tall, Ila. Most men are shorter than you. Did you know the average height of a man in North America is five-foot-nine?" Cordy straightened. "I'm five-eight and a half."

"In your cowboy boots."

"If you discount any man under six-foot, you're already limiting your dating pool."

He was right. She automatically discounted any male under six-foot tall.

"You're prejudiced," Cordy accused.

"What?"

"Heightism. You're a heightist."

"There's no such thing as a heightist."

"You have a bias against people who aren't as tall as you."

"I don't have a bias." She bristled. "I just want to dance cheek-to-cheek with the man I love."

"Like you dance cheek-to-cheek with Joe?"

"You're a pain in the ass, Cordy."

"I'm what you need, Ila. A man who challenges you. Not one who cries on your shoulder, then goes off with some other woman."

"I'm not listening to this."

"Joe's interested in Mariah." Cordy swallowed hard; his Adam's apple bobbed visibly.

"Only because she looks like Becca."

"So you noticed it too."

Ila waved a hand. "She'll be gone quickly enough. I'm here for good. Joe's my best friend."

"And that's all he'll ever be."

"How do you know?"

"You're not a good fit."

"Says you. Joe and I are so much alike. We love to fish and hunt and we love the Dallas Cowboys and the Texas Rangers and the TCU Horned Frogs and—"

"That's the problem."

"That we're compatible?"

"That you're too much alike. It makes for a great friendship, sure, but where's the spark? The fire? The chemistry?"

"We've got chemistry," she insisted, knowing in her heart it was a lie. Cordy was making her face things she did not want to face.

"You don't or you would have hooked up before now. Have you ever slept with him?"

"That is none of your business."

"I'll take that as a no."

"You don't know anything about me."

"That's where you're wrong." Cordy stepped closer, chin up so he was looking her square in the eyes. The moon glinted off his earnest face. He was drawing aside her curtain of self-deceit and she resented him for it. "Your favorite color is blue. Your favorite meal is enchiladas with refried beans and Spanish rice. When you were six you had a crash on your bicycle and you have a moon-shaped scar on your shoulder and—"

Feeling as if she'd been stripped naked, Ila reached up to touch her shoulder.

"You got a hardship license to drive when you were fifteen because your daddy was working out in the Gulf of Mexico on an oil rig and your stepmother refused to drive you where you needed to go. You could have made straight A's in high school, but you didn't want to look smarter than everyone else so you purposely missed questions on your exams. Your favorite singer is Toby Keith and you lost your virginity to Ryan Tumley when you were twenty-one on your daddy's pontoon boot on Lake Twilight," Cordy said.

Ila's mouth dropped open. "How . . . how do you know all that?"

"The same way you know all those same kind of details about Joe."

She'd suspected Cordy had a bit of a crush on her. But she'd never imagined it was more than infatuation.

"I want you, Ila Brackeen. I've wanted you since I was eighteen years old. I can't get you out of my head."

"You're shorter than me," she said, clinging to the only objection she could grab at.

"So?"

"How would that look, you asking me to reach up and fetch something for you at the top of the cabinet?"

"It would look like a tall person helping out a shorter person."

"It doesn't bother you?"

"Why would being with the most honest, good-hearted woman I've ever had the pleasure to know bother me just because she was a couple of inches taller?"

"Three inches," she corrected, "and that's when you've got your boots on."

"Big damn deal."

"Wouldn't it be weird kissing me?"

"Why don't we try it and find out?"

Ila was still stunned at everything he'd just confessed. "Because I love Joe."

"Of course you love him, but not in the way that you think you do. Joe's a good guy, but you don't fit. You and him together? It's like two left shoes. You need a right shoe, Ila. Someone who'll challenge you, call you on it when you're fooling yourself. Someone who can't wait to get home to you. Someone who gives thanks to God every night that he's so lucky to have found you."

"That's you?" she whispered.

"If you let me be the one. Give me a chance," Cordy said. "Let me prove it to you. Let me show you that I can be far better for you than Joe ever could.

Let me wipe him right out of your memory. Let me do for you everything he never could."

Her stomach went all shaky. "Well shit, Cordy, why didn't you say something before now?"

"I was waiting for you to let go of Joe, but I'm almost thirty. I can't wait around any longer. I've got to speak my piece. Here it is. I'm putting my heart on the line."

Just then Joe came out of the Silver Horseshoe, headed for his pickup truck, his ripped shirt flapping in the breeze. Music spilled out after him. Etta James on the jukebox, wailing "At Last!" Joe raised his hand in greeting.

Cordy muttered an oath, scowled. "Worst timing ever."

Head reeling with the sentiment Cordy had just professed, Ila broke from him, ran toward Joe. "Hey," she breathed, looking into his face. "You okay?"

"Yeah."

"Oh, your poor eye." Ila reached a hand to his forehead.

Joe pulled back from her touch, stared at her oddly. "You're giving me sympathy and not flack? What's up, Il?"

Ila stood there, her hand still raised, her heart quivering with the fear that Cordy was right, that Joe could never love her as anything more than a good friend. A sister-in-law.

"Il?"

She felt the pain like a broken bone snapping. All this time she'd been waiting, waiting, waiting for something that would never happen. She'd had chances, boyfriends, lovers, men who wanted to marry her. But she'd never sunk deep into any of them because she'd been holding out for Joe. After he'd married Becca, she'd tried to move on. Tried and failed. Stumbled, fallen, lost.

But this, this was the camel-back-breaking straw. She could love him forever and he would never love her the way she ached to be loved. Never touch her with the passion she deserved.

Joe. Her heart wailed.

"Was there something you needed?" he asked softly, kindly, without a trace of desire. He did not look at her the way he'd been looking at Mariah Callahan.

You! I want you. Can't you see me? Don't you know? I've loved you since I was six years old.

Grief flooded her, a fountain of loss. Everything she'd clung to was dust in her hands. She couldn't let him see it in her face. Couldn't let him know her pain. She was too proud.

"Just . . ." She paused, her lungs banded too tight to breathe.

"Yeah?"

"Be careful on the way home."

"Have a good night, Il." Joe waved at the man standing behind her. "Cordy."

She turned, hand to her eyes, willing herself not to cry. Couldn't speak. The weight in her chest was so heavy she thought it might pull her clear into the center of the earth.

Cordy stood in the shadows watching.

Was he hurting as much as she was? Knowing that she loved Joe the way he loved her? Talk about FUBAR.

She felt as if she were standing on the edge of a bleak chasm. How easy just to step into it. Freefall.

Choices. Bad ones made. Wrong paths taken. Time wasted. Dreams shattered.

Here she stood in the parking lot of a honky-tonk, the sky filled with stars, her hopes eviscerated in a messy spill. Caught between moonlight and pain. A ship wrecked on rocky shoals. Staring down a narrow tunnel. Waiting for the oncoming train.

Could she ever wash away the stain of loving him?

Joe climbed into his truck and drove off.

Cordy was still there. Still waiting.

She couldn't deal with him. Not now. Without a word, Ila fled to her pickup.

Cordy didn't call to her. He just let her go.

Ila didn't even remember driving home. She staggered into the house. Stripped off her dress. The dress she'd worn for Joe's sake. In her underwear, she scissored the dress. Cut it to ribbons. A madwoman running with scissors.

Then she turned the scissors on herself, hacking at her long, dark hair. Cutting and snipping until she was completely winded. Then she sank to the floor, sobbing her heart out. Tossed the scissors into the pile of her hair.

After a time, she became aware of a soft knocking at her door.

Joe? leaped her crazy heart.

She got up, answered the door in her bra and panties.

It wasn't Joe standing on her porch, but Cordy.

He looked at her with such empathy it hurt her teeth. His eyes took in her savaged haircut, but he didn't flinch, didn't blink.

"Can I come in?" he murmured.

A paraphrased version of Mick Jagger wisdom whispered in her head. *Hey, if you can't get what you want, maybe you could accept what you need.*

Ila didn't hesitate. She reached out, took Cordy by the wrist, and led him to her bed.

CHAPTER TEN

You love what you love.
—Dutch Callahan

Mariah awoke at dawn the following morning with one thought in her mind. Those feelings she'd had last night for Joe Daniels were nothing more than the tipsy legacy of a couple of glasses of wine and a rush of adrenaline. She'd been right about him the first time. He was a cynical reprobate with a hair-trigger temper, given to explosive fistfights in bars. She didn't need that kind of headache in her life.

Scared much?

She batted away that thought. Last night, she'd received two offers. She had options now that she hadn't had a few days ago and she pondered them as she took her shower.

She could take Clover's offer of a cocktail waitress job at the Silver Horseshoe. Or she could sell the land to Lee Turpin right now and leave Jubilee forever.

On the surface, it looked like a no-brainer. Take the money and run.

But although she didn't condone Joe's behavior

at the honky-tonk, Lee Turpin gave her the creeps. Dutch hadn't liked him and he wouldn't have wanted him to have the property. A sense of loyalty she hadn't suspected she possessed welled up inside her. Some might say she was stupid for such loyalty and if she was going that far, why not turn the ranch into the equine facility for disadvantaged children per Dutch's last wishes?

She didn't owe her father anything. Or Joe for that matter, yet she couldn't in good conscience turn Stone Creek over to a jerk like Turpin. From the looks of it, she had a job waiting for her tonight at the Silver Horseshoe or she'd face the firing squad of her own conscience.

After getting dressed, she padded barefooted into the kitchen and put a kettle of water on to boil for tea. She stuck two pieces of bread in the toaster and turned to get strawberry jam out of the refrigerator. From her peripheral vision she saw something whizz past the window. A blur headed in the direction of her barn.

Curious, she turned off the stove, slipped her feet into slippers, grabbed a sweater, and ambled outside. She hadn't had time to really check out the horse barn since she'd moved in. She heard a whinny, walked around the side of the house, and found the stallion.

Mariah inhaled sharply.

He was the most beautiful creature she'd ever seen. He possessed a small, refined head with a straight, regal profile, strong muscular chest, and forceful hindquarters. His coat was sorrel, his mane jet black. His eyes were as dark as his hair.

He tossed his head, looked Mariah squarely in the face, and pushed straight toward her.

Mesmerized, she held out a hand. "Hello there, handsome."

Mariah's heart melted. She fell instantly, magically in love. "Oh my goodness," she whispered, and reached up to scratch him behind the ears. "You are a charming boy."

The past was a hook, pulling her headlong into memory. She'd forgotten that she knew things about horses. Indigenous things that had escaped her notice. Horses were in her blood, in her sinew, in the very marrow of her bones. She'd simply misplaced this easy truth.

One look into Miracle's eyes and she was catapulted into a joyous reunion with the girl she used to be.

Mariah recalled being very young, three or four, and breaking free from her mother's hand to fly across a pasture, hair streaming out behind her, skirt molding against her legs as she ran, her little red cowgirl boots sinking into the sand. Laughing, Dutch had snagged her around the waist, picked her up, and swung her onto a horse much like this one.

She recollected Dutch holding her little hand in his big one at a horse auction. The auctioneer jabbering so fast it made Mariah a little dizzy. The dusty air smelling of horses. Her daddy smelling of leather. He'd bought her pink cotton candy earlier, and some of it stuck to her pinafore.

Another memory spliced into that one. A dance hall. With Dutch and Cassie. Her parents doing the "Cotton-Eyed Joe"; Mariah balanced on Dutch's shoulders, clapping her hands in time to the music. On the table where they'd been sitting before sliding onto the dance floor sat Stuffy. Dutch had just won him in his first cutting competition in an unsanctioned match.

For one amazing moment, the entire world made sense. It was as if she understood the meaning of everything. And love was all that there was.

Splendor filled her lungs, expanded her heart. She remembered how connected her father had been to horses, how he'd shared his love with her. The memory, the realization was so heartbreakingly sweet her body felt suspended, as if by an invisible guy wire, connecting the past to the present.

"Dad," she whispered, and wrapped her arms around Miracle's neck. "I miss you so much."

She stood for a long time, her face buried in the horse's mane, feeling the throb of the pulse in his neck, tasting the salty flavor of sadness and regret thick on her tongue, her feet grounded solidly into the earth. This place that now belonged to her.

Then without warning, Miracle's heart rate picked up, his pulse quickening beneath her fingers. He flicked his ears, let loose with a snort, his eyes rolled wild, and he lurched sidewise, throwing Mariah off balance.

"What is it?" she cried, sensing something was terribly wrong with the stallion. "What's wrong?"

Miracle yanked away, pulling against her restraining hand, pawed the ground, chuffed out a lungful of air, and then turned and galloped off.

Mariah glanced down. A snake, as big around as a quarter and at least three feet long, sat curled up on a rock with its mouth wide open.

Snake!

Sheer terror drowned her.

The snake shook its tail, making a rough rattling

sound. For one horrifying second, her heart stopped beating.

Rattlesnake! Move! Run!

Her stomach pitched like a boat on class-four rapids spilling over a waterfall. Another memory sprang into her mind so vividly clear she could taste the coppery flavor of her own fear. A memory she'd completely blocked out until this moment. It played through her head in freakish slow motion as the snake swayed back and forth hypnotically.

It was the day Dutch had let her ride on her own pony all by herself. He'd ridden with her, cooing to her mount in a gentle tone, leading the way. They traversed a pasture much like this one. She remembered the sunlight had caught the metal of the bridle, reflected a prism of light. She'd been enthralled with the light and the fact that she was such a big girl, riding a horse all by herself. Sparkly light, sparkly little-girl happiness.

Then she'd heard the deadly rattling, just as it now echoed in the dewy dawn.

The horse had reared up in terror, bucking her off.

Mariah had hit the ground with a jarring thud, falling within inches of the rattlesnake. She knew it was going to kill her.

Then the bone-chilling crack of pistol shattered the air, along with the acrid smell of smoke. Dutch had shot the rattlesnake just as it coiled to strike.

But Dutch wasn't here to save her.

Not this time.

The snake struck. Hit her ankle. Sank its teeth into her tender skin.

Mariah shrieked, jerked back, felt her flesh tear

as tiny needles of pain shot up through her leg. Blood, hot and sticky, tracked down her ankle into her slipper.

Her pulse pumped hard and fierce, booming in her ears, a terrible drumming so loud she couldn't collect her thoughts. A rattlesnake had bitten her!

The snake danced back and forth. Taunting. Its tongue slithering from its atrocious mouth.

This was it. She was going to die. She was out here alone without a weapon. If she ran back to the house, she'd send the venom shooting through her blood. She couldn't move, couldn't speak. This was it. Her last day on earth. There was so much she regretted. So many things she'd done wrong. Was this how Dutch had felt just before he died? Had he known the pneumonia was killing him? Why hadn't he sought treatment? He'd written that letter and given it to Art Bunting. Made his last intentions known. Why?

The snake slithered away, its evil work done, leaving a foul odor behind it.

Thank God, it was gone. With the lessening pain in her ankle, she was able to hobble toward the metal horse fence and brace herself against it.

Don't panic. Stay calm.

She'd always been good at staying calm. It was one of the things Destiny had admired most about her.

Yes, but it wasn't easy to be calm when your darkest fear had come to pass.

Sweat coated her body. Was excessive sweating a symptom of a snakebite? Was her heart going to explode? Her mouth was dry. Her mind in chaos. She tried to yell, to holler for help, but when she opened her mouth no words came out.

She was too afraid to examine the bite. Her cheeks were cold, her hands hot. Was this normal? She had to shake it off. Get to a phone. Why hadn't she brought her cell phone with her?

The sound of a truck engine rumbled in the distance.

Joe?

Relief washed over her. Joe had come looking for Miracle. But what if he found the horse without coming to the barn?

She heard the truck approach, the engine stop, the door close. "Joe!"

"Mariah?"

"I'm here, out back. Near the barn."

"What's wrong?" he hollered.

"I've been bitten by a rattlesnake."

Almost instantly, Joe appeared around the corner of the house, running at full tilt. His face blanched pale. He rushed to where she stood. "Where were you bitten? How long ago?"

"My right ankle. It just happened."

Immediately, he bent at the waist, his hands going to her ankle. He yanked the slipper from her foot, his hands probing the bite. It was sore, but not terribly painful.

Suddenly, a hearty laugh of urgent relief rolled out of him and she felt the tension ease from his grip.

"What's so funny?" she snapped.

"This isn't a rattlesnake bite."

"It's not?" She leaned over, pushing her hair from her eyes, and tried to peer around him to get a good look at her ankle. "But I saw the snake."

"Did it rattle?"

"Yes."

"Did it sound like this?" He thumped a crunch of autumn leaves on the ground and produced a rattling noise.

"Yes."

"Certain nonvenomous snakes will shake their tails against something, trying to make you think they're rattlesnakes so you'll be warned off and leave them alone."

"Stupid defense mechanism if you ask me. People tend to kill venomous snakes. Are you sure it's not a rattlesnake bite?"

"How bad does it hurt?"

"Not much," she admitted. "Now that I've calmed down."

"See here." He moved aside to give her a view of her ankle. The blood had stopped and was already drying.

"It looks almost like a human bite, except with more teeth," she observed.

"Those are bite marks, not fang marks. Plus the wound site isn't inflamed. If you'd been bitten by a venomous snake, the area would be red and throbbing. From your description, it sounds like a rat snake. They can be pretty aggressive. Did it emit a foul-smelling odor after it bit you?"

"It did!"

"Rat snake," Joe confirmed. "They're really testy and they stink to high heaven when they bite."

"You've been bitten by a rat snake before?"

"Yep. When I was a kid, my brothers and I used to catch them."

"Eww."

"Boys will be boys. But look at it this way, we've got something in common now, we've both been bitten by a rat snake."

"Be still my heart."

"You know what this means, don't you?"

"No, what does it mean?"

"It means you're a bona fide Texan now. You can't claim to be a bona fide Texan until you've had some kind of run-in with a snake."

For some reason, the thought of being a bona fide Texan made her ridiculously proud. "I assume we're talking about the reptile species."

He grinned. "For the most part."

"Sorry for getting all theatrical on you," she said, feeling sheepish.

"Hey, it's nothing to be ashamed of. There are plenty of rattlesnakes around here. It's not something to take lightly. And while a rat snake bite isn't serious, it can get infected. Hang on," he said. "Dutch keeps a first aid kit in the barn. I'll get you fixed right up."

He disappeared into the barn and returned a few minutes later. That's when she got her first good look at his face. His left eye sported a vividly purple bruise from his fight with Lee Turpin.

"Does it hurt?"

He looked startled. "What? Oh, the eye." He shrugged. "I've had worse."

"You get into fistfights often?"

"Not in years."

"What was different about last night?"

Joe's face clouded. "Turpin grabbed your ass."

"How was that your problem? I'm perfectly capable of taking care of myself."

"I don't doubt it for a minute," he said. "It was just my misguided chivalry kicking in."

"There's old history between you and Turpin."

"Nothing worth talking about."

"That shiner tells a different story.

"Sit down on that rock." He indicated a large, flat river rock rising up from the ground.

"You're bossy."

"And?"

"It's rude."

"I'm a boss. I run a ranch. I'm supposed to be bossy. It's an admirable trait in the self-employed. Now sit."

She sat.

He knelt in front of her, opened the first aid kit. "Put your foot here." He patted his lower thigh.

"Would it kill you to say please?"

"Quite possibly."

She stared at him a long moment.

He patted his leg again, turned on the charm with a killer smile. Combined with the black eye, it made him look like a raggedy tomcat dragging home after a long night as king of the alley.

"C'mon," he drawled, "pretty please with sugar on it."

She tried not to smile at his cajoling, but she couldn't help herself, relented, and eased her bare foot down on his blue-jeaned knee. His thigh muscles were as tight and corded as his biceps.

"You said you have brothers," she said while he took a package of antiseptic swabs from the first aid kit. She tried not to notice how warm his leg was. "How many?"

"Two brothers and two sisters."

"Big family."

"Yep."

"Where did you fall in the birth order?"

"Second. My oldest brother, Chase, is a trauma surgeon. He lives in Dallas. There's me, then Kimber, my sister. We're just eighteen months apart. She's an attorney in Houston. Then there's Rick, he's in grad school at the University of Oklahoma. He's studying meteorology. He's one of those crazy storm chasers. Then there's my baby sister, Meg. She's finishing her last year at TCU in the nursing program."

"Did you go to college?"

"Nope."

"Why not?"

"No college courses on how to be a cowboy. It's in your blood. The only preparation is on-the-job training. Every one of my siblings went against the ranching life. I'm the only one who took to it."

"Do your parents own a ranch?"

"That's where we all grew up. Right here on this ranch. Green Ridge's been in the Daniels family for five generations. I bought it from my parents when I won my last rodeo purse. My dad has arthritis and he just couldn't do the physical labor anymore. He and Mom bought a place on Lake Twilight in Hood County. They run a little antique store in town just to keep busy."

Joe tore open a package of the antiseptic wipes and with his head bent over her foot, swiped the brown Betadine solution over the bite marks. Suddenly, he laughed.

"What is it?"

"Will you look at that." He looked up from his handiwork.

"What is it?"

She peered at her ankle. He'd connected the teeth patterns and it formed the letter D.

"That rat snake marked you with my brand." His dark eyes met hers. "D for Daniels."

Mariah gulped. There was something so utterly compelling about this man, so sexy and elemental. That's when she knew she was toeing a highline wire of pure trouble. He was a cowboy. The antithesis of the kind of man she wanted, the kind of life she wanted to lead.

His head was so close to hers and all she could do was stare at his full, angular mouth. She saw what was in his eyes, felt a corresponding desire grab hold of her.

It was strange, this casual intimacy. Partially, it was an emotion she'd never experienced before, at least not quite in this way. An awed closeness that made her diffidently aware of the fact that they were, for the most part, strangers. Another part of her felt a heedless sense of ease. Why did she feel so comfortable here? She should feel awkward, displaced, but she did not.

Autumn leaves flurried on the breeze, scattered and clattered dryly across the ground. A solitary red oak leaf landed on Joe's shoulder, adding vibrant weight to his right side. He tilted his head in the same direction, unaware of how the gesture furthered the illusion of lopsidedness. He studied her as if he was trying to guess the contents of a brightly colored envelope addressed to someone else.

I'm not that much of an enigma. I just know how to put on a good show.

"Still scared?" he asked, nodding toward where the rat snake had once coiled.

"Kind of," she admitted, but only if she looked down. If she kept her gaze on his face, she forgot about the butterflies in her stomach. Forgot about most everything but the expression in his eyes, the smile tugging at the corners of his mouth. There was something about the way he looked at her that calmed Mariah, slowed her down, made her feel . . . *welcomed*.

She caught a whiff of his fragrance. Delicious. Spicy. All man. She had a sudden urge to lick him to see if he tasted as good as he smelled.

His smile drew her closer.

"You are not going to kiss me," Mariah declared, and leaned forward.

"Who me?" Joe murmured.

"We make about as much sense as a pair of three-legged jeans."

"Not even that much sense." His voice went husky.

"We're not that stupid."

He moved closed. "Too smart to get involved."

"We barely know each other."

"Even though we're neighbors."

"But only for a couple of months. I'll be leaving before Christmas."

"Hardly worth the effort," he murmured, his hand on her shoulder.

"The timing is off."

"Yep."

"So nothing is happening." She dared to inch closer.

"Nada, zip, zero."

"Kissing would be disastrous."

"Mistake of the highest order." Joe twirled a lock of her hair around his index finger.

"I mean it's not like we can take this anywhere."

"Nope."

"We're certainly not going to bed together."

"Not even just to sleep."

"We'll forget all about this sexual chemistry."

"What sexual chemistry?" His palm cradled the back of her head.

Get up, move, cool off. Put some distance between you and this so-sexy-he-should-be-outlawed cowboy.

It sounded good. She should listen to her own advice, but Joe was so damn enticing all she could think about was *I wonder what he tastes like.*

Why was she suddenly so hot? Like a Maine lobster in a cooking pot, hot.

Their noses were almost touching. Their gazes cemented. Her body thermostat was completely out of whack, blazing, boiling, burning. Joe's pupils dilated, his cheeks pinked. Mariah knew hers did too.

"You're going to get up and walk away," she said. "Like you'd just come across a grizzly bear cub."

"I am."

He didn't flinch.

Neither did she.

Her bare foot was on his thigh. He was on his knees before her. One of his hands was pressed against the nape of her neck, the other around her ankle.

Mariah's nipples hardened. "I thought you were backing off."

"I'm gone."

"You're not moving."

"I'm vapor." He stayed put.

Her breath whistled faintly as it slipped over her teeth. She'd been waiting so long to exhale. "Thanks for the first aid."

"You're welcome."
"So long."
"See ya around."
"Bye."
The next thing Mariah knew, Joe was pulling her savagely into his arms.

CHAPTER ELEVEN

There are three ways to argue with a woman. None of them work.

—Dutch Callahan

Kissing Mariah felt meant to be. Right there in the pasture just outside the horse paddock, behind her father's cabin, he cradled either side of her face in his palms and looked deeply into her eyes.

She didn't blink. Didn't glance away.

In his years as a professional bull rider, Joe had kissed a lot of women, and each had held her own special thrill. Becca had been the best kisser of the bunch, but this kiss, ah, this kiss with Mariah . . . *well* . . . there was just something about it that transcended any other kiss he'd ever experienced. Something about Mariah that transcended any other woman.

Even Becca.

And that thought made Joe feel disloyal and guilty as sin, but it didn't stop him from following his instincts and he despised himself for his weakness.

She tasted like honeyed mead, thick and sweet and

potent. Kissing her made him think of golden sunsets and sleepy sunrises. Of long, hot, steamy nights.

Mariah sank against him, her hands knotted into fists at his shoulders, her head tilted back, her mouth slack and willing. Her body language showed her conflict. Closed-off hands, open lips.

Joe kissed her harder than he should have, branding her mouth with his. Damn, he was lost, and for a man who prided himself on being in control, it unhinged him.

She chose that moment to dart her sly little tongue between his teeth. Delighted, he laughed out loud and she laughed with him. Mariah. The daughter of his best friend. It was scary, yep, but he wanted more.

With a start, Joe realized he was ready to heal.

But Mariah? She was leery of men. Leery of *him*. If he pushed too hard too soon for more than she was ready to give, the whole thing could blow up in his face. Honestly, he was still pretty damn shaky himself.

Mariah pulled away and broke the kiss and he didn't try to stop her. She blinked at him, her full lips still parted. "What," she whispered, "was that all about?"

"Impulse."

"A bad one!"

"So the kiss was no good, huh?" he teased.

Her eyes widened and she drew in a deep breath. "It was way more than good. It was over-the-top awesome. *That's* the problem. There's always a catch when something is too good to be true."

"It was special for me too," he murmured. His hand was on her ankle again, her foot still on his thigh. She was squirming like a trap-snared critter. "So where do we go from here?"

Mariah held up both palms like a stop sign. "There's no 'we.' There's you and there's me, but there is definitely no 'we'. It was just a kiss. One that shouldn't have happened. But it did, and the best thing is to put it behind us and forget it ever happened."

"Best thing, huh?"

"Yes." She tugged her foot from his grasp, hopped off the rock, backed away.

His gaze drifted to her ankle. To the D etched in Betadine. D for Daniels. He grinned and let his eyes track a path up her compact, curvy figure to her face. A golden spiral of soft curls fell across slender shoulders. In the early morning sunlight, the grass spiked with dew, she looked like a Druid princess rooted in nature. She'd laugh if he told her that. She considered herself thoroughly cosmopolitan.

He enjoyed looking at her, sheet creases on her cheek, sans makeup and with glasses on.

"You wear glasses," he said.

She snatched them off her face, hid them behind her back.

"Put them back on. They make you look all smart and scholarly."

"They make me look like Harry Potter."

"I like them." He stood up, tried to reach around behind her to go for the glasses.

She clung to them. "I don't usually let people see me in them."

"Why?"

She shrugged. "It makes me feel vulnerable."

"If it bothers you so much, why don't you have laser eye surgery?"

"Too chicken," she admitted.

"Fear trumps vanity."

"I'm not vain," she denied.

"Then put your glasses back on."

"Okay," she said, "maybe a little vain."

"Here." He took the glasses from her hand, opened them up, set them gently on her face. "There now." He brushed a lock of hair from her forehead, felt her shiver beneath his touch. "Isn't it better to see what you're looking at?"

Slowly, she shook her head. She took a step back and then another. "It's safer when you're all fuzzy and far away."

"Don't go," he surprised himself by saying. Without even trying, she'd bewitched him and he had no idea why or how.

She was already halfway across the distance between the barn and the cabin.

"You don't have to run away," he said. "I won't kiss you again." He paused. "Until you ask me to."

Soft laughter rolled out of her like music. She sank her hands on her hips, causing her shoulders to open wide and her breasts to lift perkily. "You've got a pretty big ego on you, Joe Daniels. To think you have the power to chase me off."

The kiss had already inflamed him, but one look at those proud nipples outlined through the material of her shirt sent sizzling heat straight to his groin. Instantly, he hardened. The speed of his body's reaction to Mariah knocked all rational thought from his brain. In a desperate attempt to hide it from her, he picked up the first aid kit, held it strategically in front of him.

He couldn't keep his eyes off her. He traced his

gaze over the length of her long neck, wished it was his mouth doing the traveling. Wished he could nibble her sensitive skin, make her moan with pleasure.

She studied him.

He held her stare, but it was all he could do not to slink away. She'd turned the tables on him and he felt like a young whippersnapper—randy as hell and out of control. Once upon a time, he'd been a pretty smooth operator. But all that vanished under the intensity of Mariah's gaze.

"This could never work."

"What?"

"Us."

"Why not?"

"I'm not staying in Jubilee."

"Right."

"So let's just leave things alone."

"Makes perfect sense." He shook his head, completely disagreeing with his agreement.

"No sense starting something we can't finish."

"None at all."

"No matter how pleasurable it might be."

"Don't even bring it up."

"The kiss is forgotten."

"What kiss?"

Mariah took a few steps toward the house, then stopped. "Joe?"

"Uh-huh?"

"It's not you. It's me."

"You don't have to lie."

"It's true though. You're ready for a fresh start, but I'm not. I want to go back to my old life just as soon as I can. But you're a good guy. I know that. I can tell by the way everyone in town looks at you, talks about you. There's someone wonderful out there just waiting for you."

"You're pretty wonderful yourself, Little Bit." Then before he lost all reason, gave in to his primal urges and kissed her again, Joe turned and walked away.

Ila woke up with a bad haircut and a man in her bed who was not Joe. At first she panicked, drawing the sheet to her chin, staring up at the ceiling. Wondering how she was going to get out of this. Then she remembered exactly how good Cordy had been in bed. And how unexpectedly well endowed he was. God might have shaved a few inches from his height, but he made up for it in other places.

She smiled. Just a little bit.

"Happy?"

Crap! Cordy was awake, propped up on one elbow staring down at her.

"You have to go," she said.

"How about I make us some breakfast?" He got out of bed as if she hadn't said anything. "I make a mean omelet and you need to eat. You're too skinny."

"I don't eat breakfast."

Cordy clucked his tongue. "Breakfast is the most important meal of the day."

She was so busy staring at his exquisite bare butt that the smart retort almost didn't roll off her tongue. "Tell me, Whiteside, have you ever been mistaken for a Jewish mother?"

His grin was irritating as sunshine. "If anything about me resembles a Jewish mother, I didn't do as good a job last night as I thought I did. Move over and let me try again."

Ila held up a restraining hand as he made a move to slide in on her side of the bed. "Overachiever."

"I would have let you be on top. All you had to do was ask." He chortled.

Ila rolled her eyes and sat up, pillow cradled to her chest. "You've got to go. You're simply too damn cheerful."

"Another reason we're perfect for each other." He leaned over to kiss her cheek. "I'm perky, you're bleak."

Ila got the pillow up just in the nick of time. Holy doughnut, what in the hell had she gotten herself into? "Dial it down a notch, skippy."

"I'm making you breakfast while you dial the hairdresser." He pointed at her head.

She'd totally forgotten about her desperation haircut. She ran a hand through her hair, gasped. "Oh my God!"

"Hey, I think you look kinda cute with that punk rocker thing going on, but you might want to get someone to even it up."

"This is horrible, this is a nightmare, this is—"

"Cathartic," Cordy said, slipping into his jeans and zipping them up. "That was one way to get Joe out of your hair. Get rid of the hair."

"Joe isn't out of my hair," Ila hollered as he walked out the door. She threw the pillow after him, collapsed back onto the bed. "Just because you and I had sex, don't start thinking it means anything."

Cordy stalked back into the room, his sunbeam face suddenly eclipsed with a cloudy frown. "I'm gonna let that crack about Joe go because I know you've been nursing that love a long time and it's going to take you a while to come to terms that it's time to let go of your fantasies and accept real life, but there's one thing I do promise you, Ila Desiree Brackeen."

"Yeah?" she said truculently, folded her arms over her chest, glared at him.

He crawled up on the bed, cradled her chin in his palm, stared her straight in the eyes. "Listen to me and don't you forget it. Make no mistake. What we did last night means *everything*. From here on out, *I'm* your man."

For the next week, Mariah kept busy waiting tables at the Silver Horseshoe and tried her best to stay out of Joe's way. It was easy enough. She worked nights and he spent his days training Miracle for the futurity and running his ranch and he never once set foot inside the bar. At least not during Mariah's shifts.

Whenever they passed on the road into town, he'd honk and she'd wave or vice versa, and they'd both paste polite smiles on their faces and quickly drive on. Thankfully, Joe must have solved the problem of Miracle's Houdini-like skills because the stallion did not return to her barn.

Unfortunately, Lee Turpin did show up at the Silver Horseshoe. He was there every night, giving Mariah the eye and flirting with her outrageously, but he didn't touch her again. She owed Joe for that.

She struggled to stop thinking about Joe, and the kiss they'd shared behind her house, but time and time again, she found her thoughts straying to him. She would be serving a pitcher of beer, see a young man kiss his wife or girlfriend, and her knees would melt as she remembered exactly how Joe's lips had felt against hers.

No matter how many times she told herself to stop thinking about him, she couldn't seem to stop poking at the idea of them doing far more than kissing. Joe's wicked tongue had roused something disturbingly unpredictable inside her.

"Can you work Sunday night?" Clover asked her on Friday.

"We're closed on Sundays."

"To the public yes, but we've got a private wedding reception and I want to make sure we have enough waitstaff. It's a big party. Couple hundred guests. We host a lot of wedding receptions. Thirty or forty a year. The Silver Horseshoe is one of the few places in town that can accommodate big wedding parties."

"Oh, okay, sure. I'll work Sunday." Better to be working than rambling around the empty cabin alone. Without a television set or the Internet, there wasn't much to do there anyway. Her cell phone had 3G service, but surfing the Internet on that tiny screen was frustrating. "No problem."

But a wedding reception in a roadhouse just felt . . . *wrong*. It grated against Mariah's belief that weddings should be magical. Special. Hopefully, a once-in-a-lifetime event. Weddings were about memories. The best possible memories, and they shouldn't be shortchanged. But here in Jubilee, no one seemed to care about magic unless it was in relationship to a horse.

On Sunday, she arrived at the Silver Horseshoe to find Clover in the dining room moving tables around with the bartender, Bobby Jim Spears.

Mariah took in the setting. Neon beer signs on the wall. The stained paisley carpeting. The suede curtains trailing fringe. The saloon-style doors that led into the big room. It was fine for a cowboy nightclub, but for a wedding reception? The decor made her feel sad for the couple.

"What do you need for me to do?" she asked Clover.

"Set up the tiered cake tray and put out the Twinkies and Ding Dongs."

Mariah blinked, thinking it must be some kind of odd Jubilee code. "I'm not following you."

"See those boxes of Twinkies and Ding Dongs stacked up on the bar?"

"Yes."

"The Twinkies are the bride's cake, the Ding Dongs are the groom's cake."

"You're serious?"

"This is Jubilee, not Chicago. People are on a budget. They don't spend a lot on fluff stuff."

Yeah, because they spend all their money on cutting horses. "They could have gotten cakes from Wal-Mart just as cheaply," she said.

"These were free. The groom's mother works at Mrs. Baird's day-old bakery and they were about to throw them out," Clover said.

Too stale for the day-old bakery, so serve them to the wedding guests. Gotcha. My Big Fat Redneck Wedding.

Okay, that was snotty. But there were tasteful ways to do a wedding on a budget and still be true to the bride and groom's roots.

"We're simple people here," Clover said. "It doesn't take much to make us happy."

"I'm not saying people should change who they are, just that, well, that a wedding should be special. Something you can think back on fondly with pride instead of embarrassment."

"That's one point of view. Some people figure, just get hitched and then throw a party and invite all your friends."

"It's supposed to be a once-in-a-lifetime event."

Was she being narrow-minded? She tried out the concept of a wedding being no more special than any other party. She turned the idea around in her head, and then rejected it. Most likely it was simply a matter of a tight pocketbook. All the brides she'd ever known wanted their wedding day to be special; they might settle for less, but they wanted more. They wanted the dream of lifetime love launched by a magical wedding day. The key was showing a bride how she could make that happen on a tight budget.

Trying her best not to cringe, she set up the cake tier and began arranging the Twinkies and Ding Dongs as artfully as she could. "What now?" she asked Clover when she finished.

"Beer fountain."

"Excuse me?"

"In place of a champagne fountain. No one around here drinks champagne."

She forced a smile. "I'm on it."

Mariah had to keep reminding herself she wasn't in Chicago anymore. That she was no longer involved with high-society wedding planning. It was hard letting go of something she'd done her entire adult life. She'd gone to work for Destiny Simon when she was sixteen, her first real job besides helping her mother clean houses.

She'd met Destiny through the Willowbrands, the family she and Cassie had been living with at the time, when the Willowbrands' oldest daughter, Felicity, had gotten married. Mariah had been fascinated by the elaborate process, leafing through the bride's magazines Felicity left scattered about, and she found herself dreaming wedding bell dreams. Eavesdropping at the door whenever Destiny came to the Willowbrands' house loaded with sample books. Volunteering to go shopping with Mrs. Willowbrand and carry packages.

Destiny had taken note of her eagerness to get involved. "Would you like to earn a little spending money?" Destiny asked her.

Mariah felt like she'd been offered the keys to heaven. She became Destiny's gofer. It turned out she had not only a passion for wedding planning, but a flair as well, and since she'd grown up in households of the rich, she knew how to blend into the background, how to hold her temper and her tongue, how to seemingly do what she was told, but still manage to convince people to do what she wanted.

Destiny took note of her skills, used them to her advantage. She took Mariah under her wing, mentored her in the wedding planning business. When Mariah graduated high school, Destiny told her she'd put her through college if she'd continue to work for her. Destiny was the face of Elegant Weddings, but Mariah became the engine.

And then had come Mariah's ultimate downfall.

"Honey?" Clover asked, coming to put a hand on Mariah's shoulder. "Are you all right?"

Mariah shrugged, forced a smile. "Just homesick."

Clover looked suddenly sad.

"What is it?"

"Just thinking about Dutch and how disappointing it is that you two never reconciled. Family is important."

Mariah swallowed, looked away, and changed the subject. "What else do you need for me to do?"

Clover said nothing. Mariah glanced up and saw a deep sadness reflected in her eyes. But Clover quickly shook her head and put a smile on her face. "Help me hang the decorations."

They decorated the back room of the nightclub with paper streamers, trying to make it look as festive as possible. Mariah put her judgment aside and went at the task with the fervor she'd always thrown into planning any wedding. By the time the guests arrived, the place had been transformed. While it might not be a ballroom at the Four Seasons, apparently it suited this bride and groom, who marveled slack-jawed when they came into the room.

"Wow," exclaimed the bride, who was clearly six months' pregnant, her low-cut, skin-tight wedding dress pulled snugly over her extended belly and revealing far more cleavage than Mariah wanted to see. She curled her fingers around her new husband's forearm. "Don't it look pretty, Junior?"

"Nothing looks as pretty as you," Junior said, his eyes glued on his bride.

A Lynyrd Skynyrd cover band took the stage and refrains of "Gimme Three Steps" had the guests, the majority of whom were dressed in jeans, boots, and cowboy hats, hopping and jumping. The crowd hooted as the groom spun the bride around the dance floor.

Then everyone shouted the three-step chorus, clapping hands raised in the air over their heads, creating a mosh pit atmosphere.

Mariah had to admit that it was one of the liveliest wedding receptions she'd ever been to and the married couple's joie de vivre was infectious. Hmm, how come it was that the more elegant the wedding, the more staid the reception?

The night melted into a mad mosaic of food, drink, and song. She was so busy, she didn't even recognize Prissy Purdue as she bused tables until Prissy said, "Howdy!"

No one could mistake Prissy's ebullient greeting.

"Oh, hello." Mariah smiled at the redhead. Today her hair was done up in a flattering French twist.

Prissy looked puzzled. "You're working for Clover?"

"I am."

"But you're a wedding planner."

"Not a lot of job opportunities for unemployed wedding planners in Jubilee. People here seem to go for freestyle weddings." Mariah waved her hand at the room. "Looks like waiting tables at a wedding reception is as close as I'm going to get."

"Can I talk to you in private," Prissy hollered over the noise of "Sweet Home Alabama."

Mariah glanced around at the maddening throng. "I can spare a couple of minutes. Let's duck outside."

They slipped out the exit door. The temperature was cool but not cold, and there was no wind. A fat yellow harvest moon sat just above the horizon. The smell of pumpkins from the pumpkin patch across the highway scented the night. Mariah breathed it in. A welcoming contrast to Chicago in mid-October.

"What's up?" Mariah asked.

Prissy folded her arms around her, lifted her chin in the direction of the room they'd just left. "I don't want my wedding to be like that."

"Like what?"

"Tacky. Redneck." Prissy shook her head. "But

our budget is so small I'm afraid that's exactly what's going to happen. Besides, my mama says my taste is all in my mouth."

"What are you asking of me?"

Prissy brought her hands up, pressed her palms together like a prayer. "Paul's got some wealthy relatives from Chicago and I don't want to be shamed in front of them. Since you did fancy weddings in Chicago . . . could you please help us have a special wedding? Affordable but still classy?"

Here was someone asking her to ply the trade she loved. Hope lifted her heart.

"Keep in mind we can't pay much," Prissy said.

She could do it for free. Help Prissy out and at the same time, get her reputation. Why not launch a wedding planning business right here in Jubilee?

With what? She was broker than broke. And even if she could do that, it would mean getting stuck in Jubilee forever, and while she liked most of the people she'd met here, this just wasn't her kind of place. She'd never get back to the city where she belonged.

Once upon a time, before Destiny had raked her over the coals, she'd wanted so badly to believe that love and marriage could last. But the stars had been permanently wiped from her eyes.

Most of the time when people were talking about love, they meant infatuation. Real love came from sticking with your partner through thick and thin— the bad times, the illnesses, the babies, the in-laws, the money trouble. The rest was all smoke and mirrors, and she'd been damn good at her job providing that smoke and those mirrors. She didn't know if she wanted to keep perpetuating the myth, but the truth was, she didn't know how to do anything else, or who she would be if she stopped doing those things.

"Please," Prissy begged. "I don't want to end up with pull-tab boutonnieres and beer koozies as party favors. Help!"

"Sure, I'll help any way I can." In the back of Mariah's mind, a germ of an idea began to form.

CHAPTER TWELVE

Bloom where you're planted and if you can't do
that, plant where you bloom.

— Dutch Callahan

J oe fought to keep from thinking about Mariah.
Too much was at stake to be distracted by a pretty
face and a fabulous set of lips. This was Miracle's
chance to take the Fort Worth Futurity. To win the
golden prize that belonged to Dutch. Success required
Joe's full attention.

But he couldn't seem to go two minutes without
thinking about her. Thought. Obsessed. Yearned. It
bothered him, this inability to concentrate. The last
time he'd felt so overcome had been . . . well . . . when
he'd fallen in love with Becca.

Joe gritted his teeth. He wasn't falling in love with
her. He liked her. Admired her. Enjoyed looking at
her. And he certainly enjoyed kissing her. Wanted to
make love to her so badly it made him hurt.

But that was it. Nothing more. No matter then
that she'd been heating up his dreams, twisting his
nights with hot longing. He would not allow emotion to derail him from his goal. When Miracle won

the futurity, he was going to take the winnings, buy his land back from Mariah, and build that equine facility for disadvantaged kids and call it the Dutch Callahan Center. Mariah might not care about her father's legacy, but Joe sure did.

Ignoring the visceral tug that made him want to go to the Silver Horseshoe as an excuse to see Mariah, he worked extra hard, putting Miracle through his paces. The horse, who lived for cutting cattle, rose to exceed Joe's expectation.

Then one evening, when he just had to see her or go mad but didn't want her to know it, he finally drove to the Silver Horseshoe.

"Haven't seen you around in a while," Clover said. "Something you want to talk about?"

"Not really."

"Her name wouldn't be Mariah Callahan would it?"

"Why do you say that?"

"Doesn't take a rocket scientist. It's written all over your face. You've got it bad, boy."

Joe snorted. "Don't be ridiculous."

Clover just arched an eyebrow.

"Is she here?"

"Actually, no, she took off early."

"Oh." Joe stared into his full beer, felt stupid as hell.

"You look like you have something to say."

"I don't."

Someone put Bonnie Raitt on the jukebox. She was singing "Thing Called Love." Clover stared at him.

"What?"

"I never took you for a coward, Joe Daniels," Clover said.

Joe scowled. "I'm not a coward."

"You're running away from Mariah."

"I'm not running away," he denied. "I'm just . . ." Ah hell, he was running away and everyone could see it but him.

Clover sank her hands on her hips. "You're scared."

"I wouldn't call it scared."

"Chickenshit a better term?"

Joe laughed. "Don't hold back on my account, Clover."

"You know, if Becca was here she'd kick your ass for not moving on. Becca might have had her faults, but she wasn't one to hold on to the past. She's gone, Joe, and she's never coming back. That part of your life is over."

"I know," he admitted.

"Then what's the problem?"

"I don't ever want to hurt like that again."

"Aw, poor baby. He got one helluva bruise and now he never wants to ride another horse again."

"It's not the same and you know it."

"Isn't it? So you had your heart broken. Any of us that have been around for any length of time have had our hearts broken. That's life. That's all it is. Loving, getting hurt, but daring to love again, even though you know you're probably going to get hurt again. That's the triumph of the human spirit. The infinite capacity to love."

"That's quite a speech."

"Thank you. Now get over yourself."

"Oh yeah, just like you moved on after Carl died."

Pain flashed in Clover's eyes but she quickly shut it down. "That's how come I'm entitled to give you this advice. No one ever took me aside and told me what I needed to hear. That my life wasn't over at fifty-five just because my man up and died on me. I loved Carl with every breath in my body, loved him since I was sixteen years old, but I couldn't put my grief aside. I couldn't see that there was still love for me if I only had the courage to reach out and take it."

"You could have found a new love and that person could have died too."

"Joe, none of us are getting out this world unscathed. You're only thirty years old. Are you telling me you're not ready to try again? To love again?"

Was he ready? He lusted after Mariah. He couldn't deny that. And he respected her. She was something else indeed. But part of him felt that she was out of his league. That she was going to open her eyes one day and realize she didn't want to be in Jubilee. That she missed the big city and then she would be gone, taking his heart with her. Nah, much better to never go there in the first place.

"It's not that simple," Joe said. "Mariah and I, we're nothing alike. Have nothing in common."

"No, you're making it harder than it has to be."

"What are you saying?"

"If you want someone to challenge you, keep you on your toes, then marry someone who's not like you are. It's too easy to get complacent when you're too much alike."

"So you advocate fighting in a relationship?"

"Of course I do. It clears the air. And the makeup sex—"

"Don't need details about that."

Clover smiled. "Joe, don't let her get away. Go to Mariah, tell her how you feel."

How did he feel? When he thought about losing Mariah, his heart froze up. That's why he was scared. Because he wanted her so badly he couldn't entertain the idea of losing her. So he pretended he didn't want her.

"Don't be like me," Clover said. "Spending the rest of your life regretting not taking a chance. It's no way to live. It's time for a fresh start."

Nine days after he'd kissed Mariah, Joe was out exercising Miracle when a white pickup truck with "Cutter Construction" stenciled on the door drove up the road.

What in the hell was Lee Turpin doing out here?

Joe narrowed his eyes, watched as Turpin motored past his house. Turpin rolled his window down and stuck out his left hand with his middle finger extended.

The asshole was going to see Mariah.

Was she dating him? Turpin hung out at the Silver Horseshoe, and with Mariah working there, he'd had time to start up a flirtation.

A distant humming buzzed Joe's ears, angry as swarming bees. He clenched his teeth, knotted his fist, jealousy pushing against him, as demanding as a petulant child.

An urgent, uncontrollable command filled his head. *Go get her. Claim her.*

Joe snorted, tugged on Miracle's reins, and galloped after Turpin's pickup. Mariah had no clue what she was getting into. Lee Turpin was as slick as a used car salesman, with a reputation for charming the panties off young women.

Um, once upon a time, you had the same reputation.

Yeah, but that was a long time ago. Before Becca. Before he'd settled down.

By the time Joe reached Mariah's place, Turpin

was already out of his truck, up on the porch, talking to Mariah. His hound dog eyes hooked on her breasts. Joe fought off an overwhelming urge to sock him in the jaw.

"Joe." Mariah raised a hand. "Hi, hello, good morning."

Was it his imagination, or was she thankful to see him? Feeling edgy, he reined Miracle in beside the porch. "Morning, Mariah. What's up?"

Turpin leveled him a cold stare. Joe returned it full volley.

"I called Cutter Construction and, um . . . Lee showed up."

He could tell by the way she said it and her body language—hands folded across her chest, shoulders tilted away from Turpin—that she hadn't known Cutter Construction was owned by Turpin's father or that Lee worked for him as a contractor. Relief snuffed out Joe's jealousy. She wasn't dating Turpin. In fact, she didn't even like the man.

"You need help buildin' something?" Joe drawled, trying to act casual.

"I'm interesting in having a cowboy wedding chapel built along the property line between my place and yours." She waved a hand, indicating the area. "That spot's got the best road access."

"A cowboy wedding chapel?" he repeated like a lunkhead.

"I can't really host cowboy weddings without a cowboy wedding chapel, now can I?"

That statement gave him pause. "Wait a minute. You've decided to stay in Jubilee?"

"You said it yourself. You can't afford to buy me out and the real estate market is in a slump. But you know what's not in a slump?" Her brown eyes sparkled with excitement.

"Weddings?"

"Exactly. Did you know the filings for marriage licenses are up ten percent in Parker County?"

"I did not."

"It's true." She nodded.

Joe tipped his cowboy hat. So she was here to stay? He wanted to believe it, but he didn't see it. She didn't belong here. Not in the long run. Not this intelligent, well-dressed, smart-as-a-whip city woman. "Running your own business isn't easy," he cautioned.

"Don't listen to him," Turpin said. "He's just trying to scare you off."

"Who asked you?" Joe glowered, wondering why he was discouraging her. Dutch would have loved the idea of Mariah making Jubilee her home.

"Mr. Turpin, your estimate is too high," Mariah said to Lee. "I appreciate you coming all the way out here, but I think I'm going to have to go with a more economical plan."

"I could go lower," Turpin stroked his gaze down her body. "For *you*."

The sexual innuendo in the other man's tone had Joe's hands springing into fists again.

"How much lower?" she asked, tightening her arms under her chest.

Turpin's stare hung to the smooth curve of her breasts covered in a bright red sweater. "What are you willing to pay?"

"You're not honestly considering hiring him," Joe interjected.

"I need this done on a shoestring budget." Mariah shrugged. "If Lee can help me . . ."

"I can do that," Turpin said.

Joe drew in a slow breath. He wanted her to stay. One look at those soft lips, and messy desire rolled through him sizzling hot, molten fried. "You're serious about this?"

Mariah's chin notched up. "Yes, yes, I am. I've always been the kind of woman to bloom where I'm planted. I ended up here, it's time for me to blossom."

He liked her philosophy, even if he didn't like the way she was going about it. He felt torn in two directions. Part of him ached for her to stay, but another part of him was scared as hell that she'd be the ruin of him. "You're going to have people traipsing through my property all hours of the day and night consulting about wedding plans, disrupting my horses," he grumbled, his contrariness fretting him.

"I've been meaning to talk to you about that," she said. "I want to build a real road out here so my clients don't have to bump through your cow pasture to get here."

"You want to pave my land?"

"Not your land," she corrected. "The easement."

"He's just pissy because things have changed," Turpin said. "Joe doesn't handle change well. Now about that price—"

"Shut up, Turpin. This is between me and Miss Callahan." Joe muttered, his gaze pinning Mariah to the spot.

She notched her chin upward, clearly not going to back down, but her tongue flicked out to touch her top lip with uncertainty. She had a right to pave the easement for improved access to her place, but he wasn't about to admit that. "I can do it without your permission."

Joe glared, at a disadvantage. What was wrong with him?

Turpin moved a few steps toward Mariah, met Joe's eyes with a taunting dare.

Don't rise to the bait.

Turpin leaned in closer. So close that he was almost touching her. Aligning himself with her, and Joe knew Lee had nothing good on his mind.

She looked so tiny standing beside him and yet so fierce. Life could run her down. People could betray her. And still, she'd fight. But she looked so vulnerable that he felt his heart melt into a puddle of chocolate. He could no more hurt her than he could hurt a kitten abandoned on the roadside.

"I'll do it," Joe said. "Me and my ranch hands, we'll build your chapel for free."

Mariah floated into Jubilee, an indelible smile on her lips. Joe had offered to build the chapel for free. She knew it was partially due to Lee Turpin standing on her front porch, but part of her hoped it was because he wanted an excuse to be around her. She'd seen the way he looked at her. Knew the way he made her feel.

It was both scary and exhilarating.

But now she'd made a commitment to stay in Jubilee, and while Joe might be offering his labor up for free, she still had to pay for supplies, and that wouldn't come cheap. Plus the road needed to be paved and the horse barn transformed into a venue for wedding receptions. So she'd made an appointment with a banker at the First Horseman's Bank of Jubilee. She planned on putting the property up for collateral.

Her own wedding planning business.

Mariah's pulse quickened at the thought. She'd always wanted to do this, but she'd been too comfortable working for Destiny. For the first time, she considered that getting fired had been a blessing. That gave her a shivery feeling of fate.

Now, she was positively euphoric. Joe was going to help. Her dream was within her grasp. She walked into the bank, marveling at the smell of money, at the gleam of the golden fixtures, at the slow, lazy turn of the overhead ceiling fan, at the photographs of horses on the wall. In her mind's eye, she could see the chapel filled with wedding guests, a cowboy groom and cowgirl bride exchanging vows.

It felt good. It felt real. It felt right.

The receptionist greeted her, told her to take a seat, and gave her a loan form to fill out. A few minutes later, she called Mariah in to meet with one of the loan officers.

"Come on in, Ms. Callahan." The woman behind the cherrywood desk waved her inside. She had a thick mane of black hair with a ruler-wide stripe of pure white surfing the right side of her midpart, making her head look a bit like a lopsided skunk. "I'm Nancy Hickok. Yes." She laughed. "I'm distant kin to Wild Bill."

"Nice to meet you."

"You're Dutch Callahan's daughter."

"I am."

"I'm so sorry to hear of his passing. Dutch was quite the character."

"Thank you."

"Please take a seat."

Mariah sat.

"May I?" Nancy held out her hand for the loan form.

Mariah passed it over to her, suddenly feeling nervous and self-delusional.

Nancy studied the form for a long moment. "You're employed as a waitress at the Silver Horseshoe."

"I am."

"You've been working there for less than two weeks."

"I have."

Ms. Hickok frowned. "You want to start a wedding planning business."

"I do."

"Do you have a business plan?"

"Yes." She reached in her purse and drew it out. She'd written up the business plan the night before.

"Very good." A smile replaced Hickok's frown. She read the plan. "Oh, this is excellent. You have experience in the field of wedding planning."

"I worked for the best wedding planner in Chicago, Destiny Simon."

Hickok blinked at her; a few strands of the white streak broke loose from the pack and trailed across her eyebrow. "If you worked for the best, then why did you leave?"

Hot seat question. Mariah rubbed her palms against her thighs. *Great, show her just how nervous you are*. How best to answer? "I . . . um . . ." She cleared her throat, scrambling for a good response. Briefly, Mariah closed her eyes. She was sunk. "I was fired," she admitted, her earlier euphoria gone like air from a balloon.

"I see."

"Will that affect my ability to get a loan?"

"No."

Mariah let out a pent-up breath.

"But I simply can't give you a hundred thousand dollars."

"I'm putting the cabin up for collateral."

Nancy's laugh rolled off the office wall. "Dutch's cabin?"

"Yes."

"Honey, that thing is termite-riddled and falling in, and that paltry land isn't worth much either."

"How much could I get?"

"Ten thousand tops."

Poof! There went her dreams. That's what she got for getting her hopes up.

"There's nothing else I could do? What if I throw in Dutch's truck too?"

"I'm afraid not."

"I have no recourse at all?"

Nancy settled back in her chair, stroked her pencil between her two fingers. "Have an upstanding member of the community cosign the loan for you and maybe I could go fifty thousand."

Okay, all right, this was the universe's way of telling her that she wasn't supposed to stay in Jubilee and start a wedding planning business. Ultimately, this wasn't what she really wanted anyway. Planning cowboy weddings. She belonged in the city. Everything was settled. Joe planned on buying the land back from her and she could let him off the hook about building the wedding chapel on her property. The man had enough on his plate getting ready for the upcoming Triple Crown Futurity without adding her to the mix. Besides, she knew he only agreed to do it to keep Lee Turpin from coming around.

Yes, it was a sign. Wait things out. Pursue her

dream later. It made the most sense. If it made the most sense, then why did she feel so disappointed?

She started Dutch's truck, planning on heading back to Stone Creek, when her cell phone rang. "Hello?"

"What are you doing right now?" Clover asked.

"Nothing."

"Great, could you come by the bar? I've got something I need to show you."

"What is it?"

"Just swing by," Clover said, and then hung up the phone.

The bar didn't open until five P.M. so Mariah wasn't expecting to see a conglomeration of vehicles in the parking lot. Her curiosity piqued, she parked, got out, and went inside.

"Surprise!" chorused a dozen voices.

Mariah startled. Blinked at the people assembled. A banner strung over the bar said: "Welcome to Jubilee, Mariah." "What is this?"

"It's a surprise party, welcoming you into the fold." Clover grinned and gave her a hug. "You're part of our community now and we were hoping you'd join the Jubilee Cutters Co-op. Let me introduce you to some of our members."

With a hand around Mariah's waist like she was family, Clover guided her around the room, introducing her to everyone. A lot of them she'd met waiting tables at the bar, and effervescent Prissy, she already knew.

"I'm so happy you decided to stay here and build a cowboy wedding chapel I could bust." Prissy hugged her hard. "You won't regret it."

"How did you find out about that?" Mariah asked.

"It's Jubilee. It's hard to keep a secret around here. And FYI, Lee Turpin is a huge gossip."

"Thanks for the heads-up." Yeah, so much for that. She'd be gone soon enough now that the loan had fallen through.

Someone pressed a glass of punch into her hand. Someone else herded her toward the hors d'oeuvres. The entire group was bubbling about the upcoming futurity and the chances of Joe's Miracle winning it. Most felt confident he was going to beat Lee Turpin and Dancer.

They talked to Mariah about Dutch. Sang his praises. Told her how wonderful her father had been. Mariah pasted a smile on her face, nodded. It was nice of them to throw her a party, but she felt out of step with the crowd. She was an exile in the land of cutting horse people. The talk swirled and swayed over her head. Cutter's cross, cutter's slump, cutting for shape. Deep cut, draw, dry work. Hot quit, herd holder, leak. Sticky, time line, turn-back horse. Stay hooked.

"Cool boots," said a pregnant woman sitting at the end of the buffet table. She had hair the color of gingersnaps.

"Thanks." Mariah wriggled her toes.

"I can't wear boots anymore. My feet swell. These puppies could out sponge a sponge." She lifted her feet, revealing that she was wearing a pair of decorative flip-flops.

"I'm still getting used to the feel of cowboy boots. They're . . . um . . . different."

"You're adapting quickly. It took me a lot longer to get accustomed to the cowboy way of life. My name is Lissette Moncrief, by the way." The woman patted the bottom of the chair beside her. "Have a seat."

Mariah liked her instantly and settled into the chair. "You're not from Jubilee?"

"Dallas," she said, and gave Mariah a little wink. "I understand the culture shock of coming from a big city to Cutterville. It's like stepping back in time."

Mariah laughed. "How'd you end up here?"

Lissette placed a hand around her rounded belly. "My husband, Jake. He convinced me Jubilee was a better place to raise kids. He's from here."

"What does Jake do?" Mariah asked.

"Once upon a time, he was a cutter." Lissette's face clouded, her mouth thinned, and her blue eyes took on a faraway expression. "But now he's a soldier. He's in Afghanistan."

"Will he be home in time for the baby's birth?"

A small smile played at the corners of Lissette's mouth. "That's the plan."

"Do you know what you are having?"

"A boy. Jake is so proud."

"It must be tough on you with Jake being out of the country."

Lissette nodded. "But at least I have the co-op." She waved at the people gathered around them. "They've all been so good to me. I feel like I'm never alone. They keep me sane."

"That must be a nice feeling."

"But this bunch does take some getting used to," Lissette admitted. "They're a town of eccentrics."

"Eccentrics?" Mariah raked her gaze over a cowboy who had two fingers pressed to the side of his head and was leaning over, pawing the ground, imitating a bull as he expounded on the cutting horse story he was telling.

"Okay." Lissette smiled. "Cutting-horse-obsessed

kooks. But goodhearted cutting-horse-obsessed kooks."

"Do you work outside the home?" Mariah asked.

"I used to," Lissette said. "I'm a pastry chef and I worked for the largest wedding caterer in Dallas."

"Really?" Excitement shot through her. At last. Someone in Jubilee she had something in common with. She almost asked Lissette if she'd be interested in a job working for her as a caterer, but then she remembered Nancy Hickok had put a quietus on that dream.

"Now all I do is sit around and watch my feet swell. Doctor's orders."

"Sounds very weighty."

Lissette groaned, laughed. "You have no idea, but I made the petits fours. What do you think?"

Mariah bit into one of the little cakes on her plate, moaned with pleasure at the taste of rich dark chocolate with raspberry frosting. "Divine."

"I think it's why Jake married me. Key to a man's heart is through his stomach and all that."

"If that's the key to a man's heart, then I'm in trouble," Mariah confessed. "I burn water."

"So what do you do?" Lissette asked.

Mariah told her.

"Wedding planner, hmm. We could use one of those around here."

"My thoughts exactly, but I can't get a small business loan," Mariah said glumly, and gave her the details of her meeting with the loan officer.

"Who needs a small business loan?" Clover asked, coming over to plop down in the chair across from Lissette.

"Mariah," Lissette said. "She wants to start a

wedding planning business but Nancy Hickok won't give her one without a cosigner."

Clover looked at Mariah. "I'll cosign the loan for you."

"I can't let you do that," Mariah protested.

"Why not?" Clover waved her hand at the room. "I have no one to leave my vast empire to."

Mariah gulped. "I just realized that if I started a wedding planning business, it will be taking money out of your pocket. I can't do that."

"Honey, you'd be doing me a favor. I'm getting too old to host these wedding receptions. I was looking to get out from under the responsibility."

Mariah's heart picked up a restless rhythm. "You're serious?"

"Serious? No. I'm only serious about cutting. But sincere, yes, I'm sincere."

"No. I can't accept it." Mariah shook her head. "What if I fail and cause you to lose your money?"

"Here's a thought. What if you succeed and cause me to make money?"

"How would that work?'

"I bet on you and you don't let me down."

"So no pressure, huh?"

Clover grinned. "Not at all."

"Why would you do that for me?" Mariah asked, incredulous.

"Honey, I changed your dirty diapers. We're like family. Now let's go see Nancy Hickok."

CHAPTER THIRTEEN

There's magic and then there's miracles, they ain't the same thing.

—Dutch Callahan

Mariah drove back to the ranch on a celebratory high. It was her day off from the Silver Horseshoe, she had fifty thousand dollars in the bank, she was within weeks of making all her dreams come true, and the first person she wanted to tell about it was Joe. He hadn't been at Clover's party because he was too busy training Miracle.

Her life had been a series of disappointments, but this time she wasn't going to let anything stop her. She'd found herself unwillingly plunked down into a lemon grove, but that meant she had all the tools she needed to open a lemonade stand, and that's exactly what she intended on doing.

Bloom where you're planted.

Something Dutch used to say to Cassie when he'd drag them to yet another dead-end spot. "Bloom where you're planted."

So now you're living by the gospel of Dutch?

Hey, the man must have done something right. Everyone in Jubilee loved him.

She pulled to a stop outside the ranch house at Green Ridge and got out of the truck.

Joe was in the corral sitting in a cutter's slump on Miracle's back and they were playing a game of can't-get-past-me with a curly-haired Hereford calf.

The calf dodged left, so did Miracle. Then the calf would dart right, but Miracle was a step ahead of it. Back and forth, over and over. Frustrated, the calf bawled for its mama.

She walked toward the corral fence. Joe hadn't seen her yet. His attention was glued to the calf. He wore a blue chambray shirt open at the collar, and the sleeves were rolled up to his elbows, revealing those ropy forearms thick with dark black hair. Chaps covered his strong legs, and his black cowboy hat was cocked back on his head. Watching the man and horse move as one sent a wave of emotion swimming through her. It was like the most beautiful dance in the world.

Joe Daniels was the sexiest thing she'd ever seen. She couldn't tear her eyes off him. As if he could feel her staring, Joe glanced up, met her gaze, grinned, and sent Mariah's heart reeling sideways.

Don't. Watch out. He's just like your dad. So wrapped up in cutting horses that there is no space in his life for anything else.

He reined in Miracle, allowing the calf to cross the corral to its mother, and slipped from the stallion's back. Doffing his hat, he crossed the distance from the middle of the ring to the fence where she stood watching.

"Hi," he said, sounding breathless.

"Hey."

"What's got you looking so smiley?"

"It's a go."

"A go?" He ran a hand through his rumpled hair, then pushed open the corral fence, and came out to join her.

"The wedding chapel, transforming the barn into a reception hall, my wedding planning business, all of it. I got the loan. Well . . . after Clover cosigned the note for me."

"So it's official. You're staying in Jubilee?" Did his voice sound hopeful or was it merely her imagination?

"I'm staying in Jubilee," she confirmed.

Joe let out a whoop, and to Mariah's shocked surprise, he scooped her up in his arms and spun her in a circle.

Now she was breathless too. "What was that for?"

"I'm just . . . Dutch . . . your dad would be so happy you finally came home."

She wanted to tell him that Jubilee wasn't her home, but she had to admit she'd never felt as welcomed anywhere as she did right here. He sat her on the ground and she stepped back to get some perspective. When she was too close to him, she lost all reasoning power.

"So," she said, "I'd like to start construction as soon as possible. I've called an architect. I know you're really busy getting Miracle ready for the futurity so I'm letting you off the hook. I—"

"You'll need help cleaning the place up. I'll be there with my hands tomorrow morning. Is seven too early?"

"Seven is perfect."

They beamed at each other.

Watch it. Watch it. You don't want to get involved with a cutting horse cowboy. Especially one who is still hung up on his dead wife. Nothing but heartache down that road.

Good advice. Smart advice. But that didn't stop her from falling into the depths of his dark eyes.

"Hey," he said, "would you like to try your hand at cutting?"

"What?"

"Just to see what it feels like."

"I . . ." Shivery excitement shimmered through her. "Okay, sure, but I have no idea what I'm doing."

"That's what I'm here for," he said.

"It's been years since I've ridden a horse."

"It's not something you forget."

Pulse thumping, she eased up to Miracle. The beautiful horse sniffed her when she held out her hand and then she climbed into the saddle.

"See that brindle cow in the middle of the herd?" Joe nodded at the small herd of cattle in the corral.

"Uh-huh."

"Just ease into the herd and drive her out." He stood on the ground, hands on his hips.

"Okay," she murmured. "Here goes nothing." Gently, she nudged Miracle's flank with her boot heels and he walked forward into the herd. "Um, this isn't She Devil, is it?"

"No," Joe assured her. "This little heifer is polled. She Devil has horns."

The stallion parted the herd and the brindle cow backed away from Miracle.

"Once you're clear of the rest of the cows, drop your rein hand. Relax now. Sit easy and never take your eyes off the heifer."

"Got it," Mariah said.

"Trust Miracle and just let him work on his own. He knows what to do."

The brindle cow broke away. With her gaze fixed on the animal, Mariah dropped the rein to signal to Miracle that he was on his own.

And then, holy cow, what a ride!

Miracle immediately moved to block the cow from returning to the herd. Back and forth they went, the cow trying to get back to its group, Miracle standing in its way with an intensity Mariah had never experienced. It was like riding a bouncing yo-yo. Back and forth, back and forth. Miracle never gave an inch. Joe kept encouraging Mariah to stay relaxed and let the horse have his head. Finally, the calf bellowed, spun, and ran in the opposite direction from the herd.

"What do I do now?" Mariah asked, feeling a little panicky.

Joe let out a whoop of joy and doffed his cowboy hat. "Nothing, darlin', you just cut your first cow. It's official. You're a cutter."

Mariah couldn't help grinning. It had been fun. No, not just fun, *exhilarating*. Her blood sang and her cheeks heated and she couldn't wait to do it again. "Can I cut another one?"

Joe burst out laughing. "You're hooked. Clearly the apple does not fall far from the tree. Sure, go ahead. Cut another one."

An hour later, the sun was almost gone and Mariah had a profound appreciation for the thing her father had loved more than his own family.

"You wanna help me put Miracle to bed?" Joe asked. "We could talk about your plans for the wedding chapel."

"Yes, sure."

"C'mon." He put his arm to the small of her back—she had to admit it felt pretty damn good there, but at the same time, wished it didn't—and ushered her into the corral. He whistled and the horse came trotting over.

Miracle looked at her with his seductive brown eyes and lowered his head.

"You can touch him." Joe nudged her forward.

Mariah took a step toward the horse. Her father's love of horses, and they way he'd thrown her over for them, had prejudiced her against the animals. Unlike most young girls, she'd shunned horses while her friends had been enamored of them.

Cassie had been part of that as well, discouraging her from any horse-related activities. As a result, she hadn't been around them since . . . well . . . since Dutch had left. But the sweet tugging she'd felt in her heart the first day she laid eyes on the stallion was back, drawing her toward him. Her father's DNA ran through her veins after all.

Joe led Miracle to the barn. Mariah tracked after them. He went to a shelf, took down an airtight jar, opened it up, removed two sugar cubes, and passed them to her.

Mariah placed one in her palm and stretched it out to Miracle. Gentle as a lamb, he reached out and delicately took the cube from her hand, his lips lightly grazing her skin. She was jettisoned back to the past, remembering another horse, another sugar cube, and her father.

"You can catch more horses with sugar than vinegar, Flaxey," Dutch had said.

With Dutch, all his sayings had had something to do with cowboys and horses. There hadn't been room in his life for anything more. Even if she hadn't been part of his world, she had to admire his single-minded focus. He'd loved horses with all his heart and soul. Rather than resent the animals, wouldn't it make more sense for her to embrace them? Try to find out what it was that her father had loved so much. See if she could discover why they'd meant more to him than she had.

"He never meant to neglect you," Joe said.

"What?" Mariah looked up.

"Whenever you think about Dutch, you pull your bottom lip up between your teeth and get a faraway hurt look in your eyes."

"How do you know it's about Dutch?"

" 'Cause usually after you get that look in your eyes you say something derogatory about him and get all huffy."

Did she? "I thought I hid it better than that."

"You try," he conceded. "I'll give you that. And you've probably got most people fooled. But I see through all that bluff and bluster. I know your dad hurt you. I also know Dutch didn't mean to."

"I hate that you know so much more about him than I do. I resent that."

"I know that too."

Miracle's cool nose touched her hand again, looking for more sugar. Then the stallion nuzzled her neck.

"What's he doing?" she asked, alarmed.

"I'll be danged," Joe said.

"What is it?" She rounded her eyes wide, the smell of horse filling her nostrils as Miracle seemingly kissed her cheek.

"He likes you."

"Oh please, he's just a horse."

"I wonder if you don't smell a bit like Dutch."

"Of course I don't."

"Same DNA. You can wear perfume and lotion, but underneath it all, you smell like your chemistry."

"Are you saying this stallion is getting amorous with me?"

"Not at all," Joe said, "just that something about you attracts him."

"Right."

"The same way you attract me."

"What?" she whispered, not sure she'd heard him correctly.

Joe took Miracle by the bridle, tugged the horse back from her neck, and captured Mariah's gaze. They were standing very close. The pupils of his eyes dilated dark and hot like some fierce volcano on the verge of eruption. "You heard me."

"You're attracted to me?"

"Do you really have to ask?"

"Why are you attracted to me?" she had to ask, risking ruining the chemistry cooking between them. "Is it because I remind you a little of your dead wife? People in town tell me I resemble her."

Instantly, a shadow descended over Joe's face. Why had she said that?

"You look a little bit like her," he conceded. "But the resemblance stops with the petite stature and blond hair. In personality, you're nothing like her."

They studied each other. She wished she knew

what he was thinking. Wished she possessed mind-reading skills.

"Have you dated anyone since she died?" Mariah asked.

"Dated?"

"Okay." She took a deep breath. She had to know if she was simply the rebound woman here or if there was a chance for something more. "Have you had sex with anyone since she died?"

At first, he didn't say anything, and for the longest time, she thought he wasn't going to answer, that she'd upset him. Finally, he spoke in a low, soft voice. "No on both counts."

"So in other words, you're horny and I'm handy."

Joe looked affronted. "That belittles us both."

Now she really did feel like an ass, but she had to know where she stood. What was this thing they were playing at?

"I get that you're scared," Joe murmured, stepping closer. "I'm scared too."

"What do I have to be scared of?" she denied, notching up her chin.

"This," he said, and lowered his head.

He wanted her. His body ached for hers. He had to have her or go mad with need.

But taking her meant putting himself in a position he wasn't sure he wanted to be in. He didn't want to hurt her, but he couldn't offer her any promises. He was a mess and he knew it. Ravaged by Becca's and Dutch's deaths. Obsessed with cutting horses. The only reason no one had called him on his obsession was that he lived in a town of people who were just as obsessed with cutting horses as he was. Part of him knew it wasn't normal to be so consumed and another part of him was surprised to find that anything had broken his focus.

Mariah had taken his mind off Miracle and the futurity and put it squarely on sex. Whenever he was around her, his brain fogged and all he could think about was the sway and dip of her hips when she walked, the smell of her that obliterated all common sense.

And the need. Damn, the sharp, stinging need to have her, possess her, be with her and only her.

That scared the living shit out of him.

So to combat it, he buried himself in work, hiding behind his horse, avoiding her as much as he could. That had worked for a while. But it wasn't working any longer. Joe lowered his head, feeling like a randy stallion.

There she stood. In jeans and a fluffy white sweater as soft as a spring lamb. She wore the sassy, leopard-print cowboy boots he'd bought her.

His tongue welded to the roof of his mouth. All the hairs on his arms stood at attention. His muscles coiled, waiting.

She smiled, clearly not realizing just how much she turned him on. She was studying him as intently as he was studying her. Joe swallowed. Mariah mirrored his movements.

He forced himself to smile when what he wanted to do was throw her over his shoulder, carry her up to the hayloft, strip off her clothes, and make love to her right here, right now. He moistened his lips.

Mariah moistened hers.

What the hell are you playing at, Daniels?

The thought ate at his brain as his mouth took

possession of Mariah's. One taste and he thought no more.

He inhaled her, unable to get enough. He craved more. More of her vanilla scent. More of her sugared lips. More of her soft skin.

He wrapped his arms around her, pulled her up off her feet, pressed her against the wall of the barn. Her legs wrapped around his waist, her arms tangled around his neck. She tossed back her head, and he buried his face against her long, sweet throat. Breasts and chest collided, melded.

Her fingers found their way to his hair, sliding silkily through the strands, setting his scalp tingling. Her touch fired the most peculiar awareness, filling him with wonder.

She touched his face as if she was committing the bones of his cheek and jaw, the texture of his skin to memory. He touched her too, using his fingertips to imprint her on his brain.

"Joe," she whispered huskily, "Joe."

"Mariah." He breathed.

"What does this mean?" she whispered.

"I don't know," he answered honestly. "I just know that I want you."

She worked the buttons on his shirt.

"What are you doing?" A sly tickle of delightful alarm passed through him.

"I want you too." She nipped at his bottom lip as her hot little hands slid into the opening she'd made in his shirt.

Everything about her inflamed him. The hungry look in her eyes. The softness of her curvy body. The heat of her.

He took possession of her mouth once more. Kissed

her harder. Longer. Her tongue responded, tentative and exploring. Her movements roused the barely leashed beast in him. His muscles tensed, rippled beneath her palms. It was all he could do to check his passion, hold himself back.

Never, in all his thirty years on earth, had he ever felt anything so perfect, so right. It felt like the highest disloyalty to Becca. To want another woman more than he'd ever wanted her. That shook him to his core. Put the brakes on the runaway passion he'd hitched a ride on.

He pulled his mouth from Mariah's. "We . . . I . . ."

"Shh." She placed her index fingers over his mouth. "Shh. No need to say anything." She dropped her legs, lowered herself to the ground.

His erection was so stiff he could barely draw in a breath. He said nothing.

"You need time," she said, stepping back, stepping away. "I get it. So do I. Let's just . . . let's just . . ."

"Put Miracle to bed for the night?"

"Yes." Her voice quivered. "Yes. What do we do first?"

"He needs to be combed out. I'll get the curry-comb." Baffled, Joe stepped away from her, both bereaved and relieved. He'd never experienced anything like this crazed, desperate need, and that's why he could not lose himself to it. Loss of control. Control was the only defense he had, and she broke it like a hammer on fragile glass.

Joe handed her the comb. Their fingers brushed. He broke out in a sweat. Stepped away. Held Miracle's bridle while she began combing him out.

In spite of his best intentions to stomp on the attraction—although calling it attraction was putting it mildly—Joe studied Mariah in the dying light fading from the window.

Her head was down as she groomed Miracle, brushing his flank and cooing softly to the stallion, her long blond hair pulled back in a ponytail that swished across the side of her face. His gaze got tangled in her rhythmic movements. She had such pretty hands. Unusually long fingers for a woman so petite, but slender and smooth. Mesmerized, he felt his breathing sync to hers.

"All done," she said after several minutes. "He's ready for his oats and bed."

She glanced over at Joe, and when their eyes met it was like being shot in the chest with an arrow. The shock of impact, followed by a stunning vibration that echoed up his chest, down his shoulders to set his arms tingling and his pulse racing.

What was this? What was this?

He didn't trust it. This feeling was too hard, too soon. It felt righteously wrong.

Mariah smiled and set the currycomb on the shelf running along the wall. A long silence stretched between them. The air cooled as dusk gathered in shadowy blue whispers.

"How did you get that scar?" she asked.

It was only then that he realized his shirt was still open from where she'd unbuttoned it earlier. "This?" He touched his chest.

"You've got other scars?"

"Oh yeah. Lots of them."

"From what?"

"Mostly my rodeo days."

"Can I see them?"

"What?"

"Your scars."

As if he wanted to show her his bunged-up knee. It was a weakness he didn't want to dwell on.

She came closer, crossing the hay-strewn ground. He caught a whiff of her again—that intoxicating vanilla scent.

"It's on your left side, correct?"

He nodded.

"Over your heart." She reached up to touch his chest, ran her fingers over his shirt in search of the scar.

Goose bumps spread over Joe's arm. He was accustomed to being in control. Doing the exploring. But here was Little Bit, turning the tables on him.

"Joe," she beguiled.

Not knowing why he obeyed, Joe's hands wrested off his shirt, giving her a full view of his bare chest. Why the interest?

Sympathy flared in her eyes. "You're marked."

"Yeah, so what?"

"I need to see what life's done to you." Mariah's hot little hands skipped over his ribs. Why were her hands so warm? They should be cold with the temperature outside, but her fingers were as toasty as socks fresh from the dryer.

His breath expelled in short, raspy pants.

Then she leaned down and pressed her lips to the jagged, erratic scar and lit him up inside.

She raised her head, met his eyes. "Does it ever hurt?"

"Not anymore."

"What happened?"

He told her as simply and straightforwardly as he could. "I was trying to saddle break a wild horse and he threw me onto a barbwire fence. My foot got caught in the stirrup and the horse dragged me down the fence."

She hissed in her breath as if she'd been burned. "I'm so sorry."

"Hey, it wasn't your fault."

"I know, but I hate the thought of how much you've suffered."

He shrugged. "All part of life. Everyone suffers."

Joe knew he should put his shirt back on, but he didn't. He looked at her and she looked at him. In the enclosed confines of the barn, alone with her, all he could think of was how much he wanted— *needed*—to be with her.

If Cordy hadn't picked that moment to open the barn door, Joe might have very well lifted her into his arms and carried her up into the hayloft and done what he'd been dreaming to do to her from the moment he'd first seen her standing over him at the horse trough.

"What's up?" Cordy asked, eyeing Joe's bare chest and the red flush on Mariah's cheeks. "Oh, um . . . am I interrupting something?"

"No!" Mariah and Joe said in tandem and jumped apart.

"Just cleaning up," Cordy said. "Putting the tack back in its place."

Mariah mumbled something and dashed through the open door. Joe put on his shirt.

"Sorry," Cordy said. "I didn't mean to kill the moment."

"You're fine. Good. Nothing was happening."

"That's not what it looked like to me."

"Forget what you saw, all right? There's nothing going on between me and Mariah."

"Maybe not yet . . . but you're barreling downhill on a black diamond slope."

"I know," Joe said. "That's why nothing's happening."

"Yeah," Cordy snickered. "Keep telling yourself that. If you do it long enough, maybe you'll eventually believe it."

Mariah sped to her cabin, her mind in turmoil. What in heaven's name had she thought she was doing? Asking Joe to let her see his scar? Clumsy attempt at seduction. Surely, she could do better than that.

But it hadn't been planned. One minute she'd been there brushing Miracle and the next she'd been staring at Joe as a sudden heat flooded her body, and all she could think about was getting the man undressed and upstairs in that hayloft. She'd long harbored hayloft fantasies. She and some hunky guy going at it in the barn. Even thinking about it now made her go all hot and tingly.

What a mess.

Joe was everything she never wanted in a man. He was a cowboy and obsessed with cutting horses. She didn't trust obsessive men. If Dutch had broken her of that, growing up in the homes of rich and powerful men had echoed that lesson. Besides, Joe had already had his one great love, and she wasn't going to sell herself short by playing second fiddle to a woman with whom she could never compete.

It doesn't have to be some great love affair, whispered a rabble-rousing voice at the back of her head. *Just great sex.*

But she had a feeling it wouldn't be so easy to separate her emotions from her physical needs. Not where Joe was concerned. She wanted him, but she was so afraid of that desire. Terrified she was going to get burned.

Joe would be here at seven in the morning to begin clearing off the land. Thankfully, he'd have a crew with him and they wouldn't be alone. To think she needed chaperones in order to keep her hands off a man. This acute need was very new to her. New and disturbing.

She climbed into the shower, hoping to scald the desire right out of her skin. It didn't work. Instead, touching herself only seemed to imprint Joe into her brain. She fingered her lips, the taste of him embedded on her tongue.

And when she dried herself off and crawled naked between the sheets, she did more touching, and in the end, it was Joe's name she cried out in the darkness.

Agitated, confused, guilty, sad, and hopeful, Joe paced the stables. He didn't know what to do with these feelings and he had no one to talk to about it. The two people whose opinion mattered to him most were buried in Oak Hill Cemetery.

He thought of Ila, but she'd been acting really weird lately, as if she was mad at him for something, although he had no idea why. He thought of his parents, but didn't want them to worry about him. He'd caused them enough distress during those dark days after Becca died.

Becca's horse Pickles was awake, watching through the slats in her stall. His wife had been riding Pickles when she'd been killed. Joe hadn't blamed the horse.

Becca wouldn't have blamed her either. But he hadn't done anything with the mare in two years. The ranch hands rode her, worked her out, but for the most part, Joe had kept his distance. He'd considered selling her, but he hadn't had the heart for that either.

He walked over. Pickles's soulful eyes met his, and he wondered where in the hell his life had gone.

"I know you miss her too, girl," he murmured, and scratched in a swirl pattern behind the quarter horse's ears.

It was just really beginning to sink in that Dutch was dead too. That he'd never again see his mentor and best friend. A deep sense of longing and regret tugged at him. The same emotions he'd been feeling for the past two years multiplied. Longing for what had been. For what could never be. Dutch would never see Miracle win the futurity. Would never reconcile with his daughter. Would never have grandchildren or remarry.

It soured his stomach. Hurt his heart. And then there was the thing that was really eating at him.

Mariah.

His attraction to her unsettled him because he hadn't felt one whit of desire for anyone since Becca. And he'd gone and told Mariah that he and his hands would build her wedding chapel. He'd be around her every single day.

Dumb. He was dumb as a stump.

He shook his head. Maybe he could backtrack. Retract the offer. Why had he made the offer in the first place?

Maybe it was because of his loyalty to Dutch. Take care of his daughter for him. Maybe it was because Mariah seemed so alone and vulnerable even as she struggled so hard not to show it. Or maybe, just maybe, some small part of him hoped that he'd been wrong. That lightning could strike twice. That a man could get lucky enough to have two great loves in one lifetime.

His chest tightened at the thought. At the hope.

Risky, risky, allowing himself to believe that he could be that lucky. Because his luck had been pretty damn rotten so far.

CHAPTER FOURTEEN

Never pull a fast one on someone who can out-draw you.

—Dutch Callahan

During the next four weeks, Joe, his six ranch hands, and Mariah worked on constructing the wedding chapel.

Mariah's schedule was packed. She got up at seven and did whatever needed to be done on the chapel, setting the forms for the cement foundation, raising walls, running errands, making phone calls. In between, she worked on planning Prissy and Paul's wedding. Then she worked from six P.M. to two A.M. at the Silver Horseshoe. She didn't get much sleep, but keeping busy and exhausted was a good thing. It kept her from dwelling too much on Joe. Which was another good thing. No repeat performances of that night in the barn.

Except for the times they were working together on the chapel and she'd glance over to watch him wielding some kind of tool, the muscles in his arms bunching with a free-swinging ease that took her breath. Then, to keep from thinking things she shouldn't be thinking, she'd snatch her gaze away and work even harder.

She still couldn't believe Joe was doing this for her for free. Paying his ranch hands from his pocket to spend time on *her* project. Why was he doing it? What did it mean? She wasn't accustomed to people who did things without ulterior motives. Every time she tried to thank him, he'd shrug it off and say, "That's what friends are for."

Somewhere along the way, they *had* become friends. Probably transference of his friendship with her father onto her, but for the first time in her life, Mariah understood the meaning of true friendship. She thought of the old joke. A good friend will help you move. A really good friend will help you move a body. She could add to that, the best of friends will help you build a wedding chapel out in the middle of nowhere.

Luckily, they got the foundation poured, the walls up, and the roof on before the autumn rains hit. That just left inside work, most of which she could do by herself and let Joe off the hook somewhat so he could concentrate on gearing up for the futurity that started near the end of November. Unluckily, the cabin wasn't in nearly as good shape as the wedding chapel. When the first rainstorm blew through, it was suddenly clear why there were so many metal feed buckets in the laundry room.

The roof leaked.

A lot.

And not just over the sink.

She should have done something about the cabin's roof before the rain hit. But she didn't have time to worry about it now. All her focus was on getting the wedding chapel built and the barn converted into a reception hall before Prissy and Paul's wedding the first weekend in December. So she stuck buckets under the drips, and kept to her rigid schedule.

Work.

Her salvation. Work was the one thing Mariah knew how to do well, and honestly, even though every night she fell into bed bone-tired, she was having the time of her life. She had no boss to displease. No one to tell her where she messed up or to crack the whip. She didn't need overseeing. The freedom made her wonder why she'd waited so long to start her own business.

On the Sunday before Thanksgiving, Mariah worked inside the chapel alone. She'd developed an irritating cough that had kept her up most of the night. She hadn't bothered to put in her contact lenses, and paint speckled her glasses. She wore a ratty pair of jeans, a flannel shirt, sneakers, and an old peacoat she'd found in Dutch's closet.

It was late afternoon and she was at the front of the chapel up on the top of a ladder, rolling sand-colored suede paint just below the ceiling, when she heard the door open. She turned her head, expecting to see Cordy. He'd gone into town to pick up the cowboy artwork that Mariah had ordered for the walls.

Instead, Joe's tall, lanky frame filled the doorway. He looked like the sweetest kind of trouble in scuffed cowboy boots and holey Wranglers, carrying several four-by-fours balanced on his shoulder. Water clung to his hair like a halo and his jacket was dappled with rain.

Her pulse spiked at the sight of him, and she curled her fingers tight around the top of the ladder to hold her balance.

"Where do you want this?" Joe asked, his boots making a slinky sound against the bare cement floor as he sauntered toward her.

She squinted in the light from the open door, a trickle of sweat sluicing down her spine. "What is it?"

"Wood for the altar."

"I already ordered the altar from a builder in Fort Worth."

"Deal fell through," he said. "The builder is going out of business."

"What? No!"

"Yep."

"How do you know that?"

He held up her cell phone. "Text message. You left your phone at the Silver Horseshoe last night. Clover asked me to bring it to you."

Mariah let loose with a colorful swearword.

Joe grinned. "Don't worry. I've got you covered."

"You can build an altar?"

"Don't look so skeptical. These hands are good for more than just reining in horses and . . ." His mischievous gaze raked over her.

"Don't say it."

"Say what?" he asked, appearing all innocence and setting the boards near the bottom of the ladder. He cocked his head, glanced up at her.

Seriously, was she the only one who was having erotic midnight fantasies about getting naked and rolling around together? Dangerous fantasies she couldn't keep from thinking about.

"Come down," he said.

"Why?"

"So we can have a civilized conversation where I don't have to crane my neck."

"Welcome to my world. I spend my life craning my neck."

"You need to take a break," he scolded. "You push yourself too hard."

Her legs were wobbly. From his proximity, no doubt. Why did he affect her like this? She set the paint roller in the tray, and then eased down the ladder and stepped to the ground with a little sigh.

Joe stepped closer. It was all she could do not to back up.

"What?" she whispered.

He reached out a finger.

Mariah sucked in her breath. He was going to touch her. For the first time in four weeks. Her pulse sprinted. She felt hot all over.

Joe lightly swiped a finger over the tip of her nose. "Paint."

"Oh."

"More here." His finger wiped at the little indention between her nose and her upper lip.

"What do you think?" Mariah said in a rush, waving a hand at the walls. She felt dizzy. Standing so near Joe unbalanced her equilibrium.

"You've accomplished a lot in a short amount of time," he said, sinking his hands on his hips.

"*We've* accomplished a lot." She paused, raised her chin, and lowered her voice. "I could not have done it without your help."

"Everyone needs help now and again, Little Bit."

She canted her head. "Why do you call me that?"

He shrugged. "You don't want me to?"

"I've never considered my stature a handicap."

"I don't mean to offend. It's a cowboy thing," Joe explained.

"Ah," she said, not knowing what else to say. The man was too distracting with raindrops on his lashes and those dark bedroom eyes assessing her. "Break over. I gotta get back to work."

"Mariah, you have to stop pushing yourself so hard."

"Like you don't push yourself?" She cleared her throat to suppress the tickle at the back of her throat. A coughing fit would be so unattractive.

"Guilty as charged. But just because I have bad habits doesn't mean you have to be stupid too."

"Look, it's not that much longer," she protested, trying not to let him see just how exhausted she was. She tried to smile, but she couldn't force her lips to go all the way up. "Another day and a half and I'll have the whole chapel painted and we'll be ready to put in the maple hardwood floor."

"What's the rush?"

"I promised Prissy and Paul I'd have the chapel ready in time for their wedding."

"It's still three weeks away. No one is going to get upset if you don't have everything perfect."

"I'll be upset," she said. "I'll know. It will bother me."

"No matter how hard you work, or what you do, nothing is ever perfect."

It was a simple statement and yet so profound. It was the dark side of being a perfectionist. No matter how hard you tried, you could never make everything perfect. She knew that. Hated it.

"Honestly," he said. "It takes a lot of hubris to assume you have the power to make anything perfect."

"You're saying I have a big ego?"

"No, sweetheart, I'm saying you're running your-self into the ground."

Sweetheart.

Mariah started up the ladder, but paused to push aside a lock of hair that had fallen over her forehead. She was surprised to find sweat beading her brow. She shivered, suddenly cold. Her knees trembled.

Come on. Snap out of it. You'll be okay. You'll just need to . . .

She swayed.

"Mariah!" Joe's exclamation made her blink.

He reached for her just as her knees buckled and she pitched backward from the ladder. One arm went around her waist, the other to her forehead. "My God, you're burning up, woman. How long have you had a fever?"

She shook her head. "I'm okay."

"Stop being so stubborn."

She planted a palm against his chest, intending on pushing him away and standing on her own two feet, but her stupid legs wouldn't obey and her vision blurred. There seemed to be two Joes holding her, scolding her.

"That's it. You're going to bed."

"No," she protested weakly.

"Yes," he said firmly.

He scooped her into his arms and trod from the chapel. She tried to protest, but the words stuck to the roof of her mouth. It felt good to let go of the reins, to let Joe take over. Other than her mother, she'd never had someone she could depend on.

Stop this. You can't depend on Joe. He's Dutch all over again. Cutter to the bone.

"You look dehydrated. When was the last time you had something to drink?"

She frowned, unable to remember.

"If it's been that long, then it's too long. People die of dehydration, dammit. Do you want to be like Dutch and keel over from working yourself to death?"

Like father, like daughter, she thought dizzily.

Joe smelled so good. Like soap and leather and outdoor man. His shoulder was firm beneath her cheek, his arms tight around her. She felt as if she'd downed a glass of wine too quickly. Her perception was altered, her mind a mosaic of images. Her pulse raced. She felt helpless.

"Please," she whispered. "Please."

"I'm here, Mariah. I'm going to take care of you. Everything is going to be all right."

He carried her to the cabin, but once he was inside, he let out a strong curse. "What is this?"

"What?" She blinked. Her head hurt. "Oh, the buckets? Gotta leaky roof."

"No kidding. Why didn't you tell me?"

"No need. I've got plenty of buckets."

"If you get pneumonia from sleeping in a damp house, I swear, Mariah Callahan, that I'm gonna spank you."

"Sounds kinda interesting."

"You're out of your head from the fever. And you can't stay here. You're coming home with me."

She didn't protest. She was feeling too rotten and he made good sense. He pivoted on his heel and carried her out to his pickup truck. They bumped across the pasture, headed for Green Ridge.

By the time he got her into his house, into his bed,

everything was a blur. She'd never been in his house before, but the surroundings didn't register. Leather furniture. Hardwood floors. Dark colors. Her impression didn't go much deeper than that.

He carried her to a bedroom. To a rustic bedstead made of polished, rough-hewn hickory and sporting a luxurious pillow-top mattress. The comforter had horses on it. But of course, in Jubilee, horses were comforting.

Joe stripped off her shoes, dropped them to the floor—*thump, thump*. Then he reached for the zipper on her jeans.

"Well, I've dreamed about you getting me naked." She giggled, on her back, staring at the ceiling. A ceiling without water stains or rain dripping in. "But I never thought it would be like this."

"Me either," he said grimly, grabbing hold of the hem of her jeans. "Hips up."

She rose up, startled to discover how difficult that was, and he tugged the pants off her body. Mariah lay there in flannel top, T-shirt, and underwear, not feeling the least bit shy. Why wasn't she feeling shy? She should be feeling shy. Shouldn't she?

Joe sank down on the edge of the mattress beside her and cast a glance over her. It was a worried look, nothing sexual about it.

Too bad. She reached up with an index finger, smoothed the line between his eyebrows. "Don't look so frowny."

"You're out of your head. I'm calling Doc Freeman. He's old as dirt but he still makes house calls."

"I'm not. I'm . . ." She paused, unable to remember what she was thinking. "Hey." She patted the bed beside her. "Why don't you join me?"

"In a minute. I've got to get some fluids and aspirin down you. Lower that fever."

She wrapped her arms around his neck. "C'mon, stay."

"You have no idea just how much I'd like to crawl under those covers with you, sweetheart, but not right now. Not like this. You just lie back against the pillow and take it easy."

"Spoilsport." She pouted and flopped back on the pillow, then shivered, suddenly cold.

Joe disappeared, but he returned a few minutes later with a glass of ice water and two aspirins. He leaned over, handed her first the aspirin, then the water. "Take these and drink all the water."

She obeyed, mainly because he stood there with his arms folded over his chest, until she'd downed it.

He took the empty glass, set it on the bedside table. "Are you cold?"

"Nope."

"Hot?"

She grinned, reached for him. "Hot for you."

"You're out of your head, darlin'."

She seemed to have lost all filter control over her tongue. "Out of my head over you."

He chuckled. "Shh, close your eyes. Try to get some sleep."

Mariah stifled a yawn. "Just for a minute. Just until the aspirins kick in. Then I've got to go back to work."

Joe snorted. "Over my dead body."

She clicked her tongue. "No way. I want that body fully alive."

"Don't worry about that." He left again and came back with a cool, damp cloth. As he bathed her forehead, Mariah had a flash of memory. Dutch. Bathing her forehead in a similar manner when she'd been sick. She'd never recalled the memory before and it twisted inside her. Had Dutch taken care of her the way a daddy should? Or was this a false memory, conjured up by the fever and a desperate need to believe her father had indeed loved her.

She shivered. "Cold."

Joe stopped bathing her forehead and heaped blankets on her.

She shivered harder, her teeth chattering. "So cold."

"Scoot over," he said.

"What?"

"Scoot over," he repeated. "I'm going to get in bed with you to warm you up. Transference of body heat."

"'Kay." She scooted.

He reached out and wrapped his arms around her, tugging her against his body. He was in his underwear and shirt too. When had he taken his jeans off? She didn't remember him taking his jeans off. Oh well. This was nice.

"How's that?" he asked, tucking the covers up under her chin.

"What if I'm contagious? What if I make you sick?"

"I'm healthy as a horse."

"That's an odd saying," she mused.

"What do you mean?"

"Well, from my limited knowledge of horses, it seems like they're always sick with something. Colic, stone bruises, pyoderma."

"You have a point. Then I'm much healthier than a horse."

"Good to hear. I'd feel terrible if I made you sick."

"You're not going to make me sick. Now go to sleep."

"Yes, sir," she said, her eyelids already half closed.

"Mariah?"

"Uh-huh," she murmured.

"Did you mean it or was it just the fever talking?"

"Mean what?"

"That you'd been dreaming of getting naked with me?"

Mariah never answered his question. She was already fast asleep.

Joe crawled out of bed and got dressed. He'd called Doc Freeman when he'd gone to get her some aspirin and the elderly physician promised to come out within the hour. While he waited, Joe went to make sure his ranch hands had everything under control. The rain had picked up and was coming down in steady sheets. More heavy rains were predicted for the next few days. Bad timing, considering that first rounds of the Fort Worth Futurity started the day after Thanksgiving.

Doc Freeman arrived and went in to examine his patient. Joe paced the hallway. All he could think about was how Dutch had died from pneumonia and the sorry state of the cabin. He could kick his own butt for not paying more attention to the condition of the place. Here he'd been helping Mariah build a chapel, when the first thing he should have done was put a roof on her home.

"Forgive me, Dutch. I should have taken better care of your girl."

Doc Freeman emerged from the bedroom a few

minutes later. "Bronchitis," he diagnosed. "She just needs rest, lots of liquids, and these antibiotics." He took a handful of pharmaceutical samples from his bag and passed them to Joe. "Give her one twice a day. I just gave her a tablet for tonight."

"Thanks, Doc. How much do I owe you?"

The stooped old man held up a hand. "I'll send you a bill."

He saw the doctor out, and then went to make a pot of homemade chicken soup in the Crock-Pot in case Mariah woke up hungry. When he finished that task, he went back to the bedroom.

At one point she woke, thrashing and turning, throwing off the covers. She babbled about being hot. He checked her temperature. It was a hundred and three. Alarmed, he gave her more aspirin and sponged her skin with cool water.

"Hot," she said, "so hot." She tore at her clothes, whipping off her shirt, her bra, her panties.

Stunned, Joe stared at her beautiful body and instantly he was hard. So hard it took his breath. He closed his eyes against the shocking tingle arrowing through him. He opened his eyes again and his gaze met hers. He studied her lips, her breasts, her belly, her . . .

Need seized him by the throat. Throttled him. Razor-sharp sensations sliced through his loins, and images of him and Mariah having sex peppered his mind.

Disgusted with himself, he drew back. She'd already dropped back against the mattress, her eyes shuttered closed. He tugged the sheet up over her, more for his sake than hers.

Breathing hard and heavy, he stumbled back to the chair in the corner. Sat in the darkness watching over her.

After that, Mariah slept soundly, her breath slow and raspy. At some point, he fell asleep too.

Several hours later, Mariah stirred, coughed.

Joe jerked awake. The room was totally dark.

"Joe?" she whispered.

"I'm here."

"I can't see you."

He got up, moved to the dresser, fumbled through the top drawer in the darkness for the candles and matches kept there in case of power failure. Finally, he found what he was looking for, struck the match, lit the candle, and settled it onto the dresser. The scent of pineapple and cilantro filled the air. His nose twitched. One of Becca's kitchen candles.

"How are you feeling?" he asked, moving over to perch on the edge of the mattress beside her.

"Better. Thank you for staying with me."

He looked into her eyes, felt a thrust of emotion so strong he couldn't name it.

She touched his chest, and all the breath stilled in his lungs. With tentative fingers, she traced her way up to his neck, trailing her fingertips over his face in the dim light.

"Joe," she murmured. "Joe."

His name on her tongue sounded like the holiest of music. The soft contact of her hand burned through his skin, seeped into his blood.

Damn his hide. He was a total bastard for feeling anything sexual. She was sick and weak, but he couldn't stop his body from reacting. Especially when her delicate little fingers came back to trace the jagged scar on his chest through the fabric of his shirt.

She wriggled closer and his erection stiffened. He opened his mouth, his breath coming out in raspy gasps. It was all he could do not to drag her into his arms and squeeze her tight. Not because he wanted sex, although he had to admit his body was desperate for her, but simply to reassure himself that her fever had truly broken and she was on the mend.

He kissed her forehead. It was tepid, cool. "Fever's gone."

"Thanks to you." She smiled at him, reached up to touch his chin. Then she frowned. "I don't remember what happened. One minute I was painting the chapel and the next . . ."

"You collapsed."

"And you carried me into the cabin?"

"We're not at the cabin," he said. "You're here. At Green Ridge. In my bed. I couldn't leave you in that leaky cabin alone, and besides, that twin bed was just too damn small for the both of us."

"I'm naked." Her eyes widened. "How did I get naked?"

"You were burning up with a fever."

"And you . . ." Her voice got husky. "Took my clothes off?"

Joe closed his eyes, thinking about the graceful lines of her body. If he lived to be a hundred he'd never forget. "You undressed yourself. You were just trying to cool off."

"I'm cool now. In fact, I could do with a little heating up." An inviting expression slipped over her face. She reached out, traced her fingertips over his bare arm.

Joe froze, his pent-up breath an ache in his chest. His body yearned to join with hers, but he was caught between the past and the present. Between what had been and what could be. Part of him wanted to take her and let the consequences be damned. Hell, from the moment he'd laid eyes on her, he'd dreamed of a moment like this. But did he want Mariah? Or was he simply trying to recapture what he'd lost with Becca?

It was a disturbing question.

And what the hell was she doing to him with those wicked fingers of hers? Dammit, he desperately wanted to let her keep exploring. He wanted to explore *her*.

Incredible, unbelievable sensations ran through him. Sudden insight blinded him. She was the best thing that had happened to him in a long, long time.

She shifted, propping herself up on the pillows, holding the sheet up to cover her bare breasts.

Joe studied her in the candlelight. He loved the sound of her voice, low and melodious. Loved her smell, like a kitchen at Christmas. And he loved the way she moved, graceful as a doe, lithe and swift.

Mariah looked so heartbreakingly beautiful, tangled up in his sheets. He hungered to make love to her, but he didn't dare. He was terrified of being with her, terrified he couldn't give her what she needed, terrified of hurting her. Terrified of investing too much into a relationship with her and ending up hurt himself.

He couldn't make her any promises. He'd been down this road before, seen it end tragically. Plain and simple, he was afraid to love her. She was a city girl at heart, and in spite of the wedding chapel project, he knew it was just a matter of time before she left Jubilee.

Left him.

Coward.

Maybe so. But he was damaged goods, fundamentally broken, and he couldn't love her the way she deserved to be loved.

She wriggled closer, rose up, splayed a hand over his chest. Then she touched her lips to his, softly, gently.

"No," he said, pulling back. "This isn't happening."

Her eyes widened but her voice was certain, clear. "You like kissing me. I can feel your heart thumping fast against my palm."

"I'm not denying that I want you."

She reached down and touched his shaft through his jeans. "You're hard."

"And getting harder by the second," he said, his voice coming out as if he were speaking through a wad of cotton. "But I don't have to act on animal impulse. I'm in control of myself."

"Are you?" She purred, devilishly.

He drew on every bit of strength he possessed. "Yes."

"Then why did you sit down here beside me? Especially when you knew I was naked?"

Why indeed? He had no answer to that.

"I want you, Joe. I want you to make love to—"

"No, Mariah."

"I'm not asking for promises. I don't *want* promises. I just want us to make each other feel good. Is that so wrong?"

No. Not wrong. Not wrong in the least.

"I don't want to lead you on. I don't want to hurt you," he said.

"You're not leading me on. I'm a big girl. I know what—"

"You say that now, but—"

"Stop interrupting and just listen to me a damn minute, cowboy," she said.

Joe's eyes widened. No one spoke to him in that tone of voice, not even his willful Becca. Not when he put his foot down. Becca never challenged him directly. She just slipped around behind his back. Such sass from anyone would have grabbed his notice, but coming from Mariah, it was a sucker punch to the gut.

Mariah sat up straight, her beautiful bosom popping free of the covers, revealing two perfect breasts in the flickering candlelight. "Look, if you don't want to have sex with me, then just say so. But stop pretending it's because you don't want to hurt me. Be honest. You're still hung up on your ex-wife. That's fine. I get it. I'll never compare to the sainted Becca."

"Becca was no saint," he growled, totally surprised that he said it.

He hadn't known he was going to say it.

"Tell that to the entire town of Jubilee. Everywhere I go, it's Becca this and Becca that. Becca hung the moon. I get it. She's a goddess and I'm a mere mortal. That doesn't mean that you and I can't have some fun together."

"Becca was far more mortal than you'll ever be."

"I know. Because she died. I can't compete with that, Joe," Mariah murmured.

"I'm not asking you to."

"Then what's the holdup? What am I doing wrong? I've been waiting for weeks for you to make a move, and nothing. I thought we connected. I thought after that night in the barn—"

"Because," he said, finally admitting the full truth to himself as he was admitting it to her, "I've been living so long in the dark that I've forgotten how to see the light. I don't want you to get lost in my darkness, Mariah. I care about you too much to let that happen."

CHAPTER FIFTEEN

If you come to a fork in the road, take it.
—Dutch Callahan

Mariah awoke just before dawn feeling better than she'd felt in days. She sat up, stretched, yawned and looked around the room. For a moment, she'd forgotten where she was, until she saw Joe asleep in the chair at the foot of the bed. Her memory blurred fuzzy, but she remembered bits and pieces of the night before.

He brought her to his house. Put her in his bed. Sat with her until her fever broke. His kindness and concern touched her in a place no man had ever touched. She awakened naked. She was still naked. Quietly, she searched around in the depths of the covers and found her clothes. She slipped on her underwear, her T-shirt, the soft blue flannel shirt she'd worn over the tee. She needed a shower, fresh clothes. She needed to get out of here.

Joe lay slumped down in the overstuffed chair, his legs extended out in front of him, his head resting off to one side on the plump cushion. She took in the snug fit of his T-shirt and the fact he was still in his blue jeans. But he'd shucked his belt and boots. Beard stubble ringed his hard jaw and a lock of jet black hair had fallen over his forehead, reminding her of the first day they'd met when he'd seemed so dark and mysterious.

She itched to touch him, to smooth back his hair, run her fingers over that scratchy beard, press her lips to his. Thank him for taking care of her.

The air smelled faintly of pineapple and cilantro and she spotted the scented candle on the dresser, recalled that he'd lighted it during the night. The bedroom was decorated just as she imagined it might be. Cowboy all the way. It occurred to her that she was lying here in the queen-sized bed Joe had shared with his late wife. That made her feel a hundred different things, none of them comfortable.

"Mornin'," Joe said. He sat up and stretched his arms toward the ceiling. His T-shirt went up with the movement, giving her a peek at his awesome abs.

"Morning," she echoed.

"How you feelin'?"

"Much better," she said. "Do you think I could take a shower?"

"Sure, sure." He got up. "I'll see if I can find some clean clothes for you to put on."

"Becca's clothes," she said.

"Yeah," he admitted. "She was about your size."

"You know," she said, the idea of wearing his dead wife's clothes making her feel weird, "I think I'm well enough to go back to the cabin."

"No. That roof is a sieve. You'll never heal in that damp environment. Besides, it's been raining in solid sheets all night, the road to the cabin could easily wash out. Even if I could get you back there, I'm not leaving you somewhere you could get stuck alone for days until this bad weather passes."

She started to argue, but when she threw back the covers and went to swing her legs off the bed, sudden dizziness took her breath away. He was right. She wasn't strong enough to be alone yet.

"Easy," Joe said, his hand going around her back. "Light-headed?"

Mariah heard a soft catch in his voice. He smelled good—masculine and hearty. His scent hooked her so surely that she didn't want him to ever let go of her. But his proximity was dangerous within the parameters of a bed. Being so near him, so vulnerable to him, caused a strange unraveling inside her. She wanted him, but she wasn't ready for him, and she suspected he wasn't ready for her either. If he had been, he wouldn't have kept his distance this past month.

So she lied, slipped from his grip. "It's passed."

But Joe wasn't easily fooled. He took hold of her elbow. "I'll help you to the bathroom."

She turned her head to look at him, to argue, but got trapped by the hypnotic lure of his coffee-colored eyes. The irises were almost as dark as his pupils, dilated wide in the bedroom's dimness. That made her dizzier than the residual fever weakness.

Thankfully, he left her at the door of the bathroom. She took her time with showering, letting the hot water wash over her. By the time she finished, and padded back into the bedroom with a thick bath towel wrapped around her, she found stylish pink lounging pajamas spread out for her on the bed, along with pink crew socks and pink slippers. The bed had been made but the covers were turned down in case she wanted to crawl back in. She smiled at the efforts Joe had taken to make her comfortable.

She and Becca had been close to the same size, although Mariah had never been a pink person. She put on the clothes, and then opened the bedroom door.

The smell of cooking chicken curled down the hallway, calling her name. It might be morning, but she was ravenous to eat anything for breakfast. Running a hand along the wall to keep her steady, she followed the scent into the kitchen.

Joe had just come in from outside. He was scuffling his boots on the mat at the door and shaking off a black rain slicker. He glanced up, saw her standing there, and simply stopped everything he was doing to stare at her.

Feeling self-conscious, she reached up to run a hand through her hair. She was in his wife's clothes. Was he seeing Becca in her? That made her stomach dive. The last thing she wanted was to be a substitute.

"I . . . I . . ." Joe stammered. "I've been out checking on the livestock. I listened to the weather report. Another line of fierce storms is moving through. This might go on for a couple of days."

"So . . ." Mariah gulped. "It's just you and me."

"Yes."

"Alone."

Their gazes locked.

Unnerved, Mariah was the first to break the stare. "What is that heavenly smell?"

"Chicken soup. I put it in the Crock-Pot last night."

"I'm starving."

"How about oatmeal and cinnamon toast for breakfast? We can have the soup for lunch."

"You can cook?"

"My mother believed a man should be able to make his own meals. She taught all us kids to cook. My dad taught my sisters how to change the oil in their cars."

"Smart parents." Mariah weaved on her feet.

"Hey." Joe rushed to cover the distance between them. "You're still shaky as a newborn fawn. C'mon, I'll get you set up on the couch."

He took her by the hand, guided her into the living room, and installed her on the wide leather couch. He covered her with a lap blanket decorated with stampeding horses, turned on the TV, put the remote control and a box of tissues within her reach. "Now, you snuggle in while I tend to breakfast."

After breakfast, Joe built a fire in the fireplace. Outside, heavy rains lashed against the windows. He paced back and forth in front of the window, a caged lion anxious for escape.

She had to wonder if he was restless because of being stuck here with her.

"Relax. Come sit." She patted the spot on the sofa beside her.

He eased down, keeping a cushion between them.

"Got any games we could play?" she asked.

"We've got dominoes. It was Bec—" He stopped.

"Dominoes would be great," Mariah said brightly, putting a big smile on her face. He should be able to say Becca's name without feeling awkward. The woman had been his wife. Nothing would ever change that fact. Still, it made Mariah feel . . . *lonely.* Joe's heart was still twined up with his dead wife. She didn't know what to say about it, so she didn't say anything.

They played dominoes with the smell of chicken soup in the air and the warm crackle of mesquite wood burning in the fireplace and the sound of relentless wind and driving rain pounding against the house. Lightning flashed. Thunder snapped like gunfire.

After ten games, they were tied five to five. Evenly matched.

"Do you feel up for hot chocolate?" he asked.

"Hot chocolate sounds great. You keep spoiling me like this and I'll never want to go back to my cabin."

"I could make us some popcorn too. See if there's any good movies on TV."

"You are the host with the most," she said.

A few minutes later, Joe was back on the couch with her, two mugs of hot chocolate and a big bowl of popcorn on the coffee table in front of them. Joe took over the remote control, flipping from channel to channel.

He zoomed past Tom Hanks standing at a gravesite.

"*Sleepless in Seattle*! My favorite movie. Go back, go back."

Joe flipped the channel back to the opening credits of *Sleepless in Seattle*.

It was only when Tom Hanks's character told his son, Jonah, that they didn't ask why, that it fully dawned on Mariah that the movie was about a man who'd lost his beloved wife.

To Mariah, this quintessential romance was a tale of fate, destiny, two people who were meant to be together. She'd never given the fact that Hanks's character, Sam, was a widower much thought. Yes, widower status was what made Sam so appealing, but now, here with Joe, all Mariah could think about was that Joe had suffered the way the Tom Hanks character was suffering. When Becca had died, he had lost his true north, his romantic compass, and now here was this movie rubbing his nose in it.

Mariah gulped. "That's okay. You can change the channel. I've seen this show a hundred times."

"Does it make you uncomfortable?" Joe asked. "Watching this show with me because it's about a widower?"

"I don't want to make you uncomfortable. Does it make *you* uncomfortable?"

Joe drew in a breath so deep she heard it from her side of the couch. "This movie is about a widower's struggle to come to terms with his wife's death?"

"You've never seen it?"

"Bits and pieces. Not the whole thing."

"That's partially what it's about. It's also about acceptance and how you never really know where you belong until you accept circumstances for the way they are rather than what you wish they were."

"Then let's watch it."

"Are you sure?"

"Hey, maybe Tom can give me some tips."

"Okay," she said. "But feel free to change the channel if anything bothers you."

At first, the tension in the room was palpable, but as the movie went along, Mariah could feel Joe relaxing. Maybe when the show was over he would be able to talk to her about Becca. The trouble was she didn't really want to hear about her, but if talking could help Joe move on with his life, she'd listen.

Finally, they fell into a companionable silence, watching the Tom Hanks character keep himself walled off, watching Meg Ryan become engaged to the wrong man simply because she was so desperate for love.

Am I that desperate? Was she trying to make herself fall in love with Joe?

Mariah slid a glance over at him, and she was surprised to find him glancing back. Their gazes hit, sparked, shot away like marbles bouncing off each other.

She wondered what he was feeling. Heck, she wondered what *she* was feeling. Joe was a special guy and she enjoyed being with him, but he'd been cut to the bone by the loss of his wife. Was it stupid to think he could ever love anyone as much as he'd loved Becca? She couldn't replace his wife, didn't want to replace her. But she couldn't deny her growing feelings for him.

They both reached for a handful of popcorn at the same time, their knuckles grazing as they dug in. Instantly, the tension was back, but it was a different kind of tension this time.

Sexual tension. Blistering and tight.

Mariah quickly moved her hand, focused on the TV screen. It was the part where Annie walked right past Sam in the airport and he feels *something*, even though he doesn't know her. When Sam mutters to himself, "God, she's beautiful," and tries to follow Annie, it was one of those magical movie moments that took Mariah's breath.

But no matter how hard she tried to concentrate on the story, every nerve ending of her body sang with awareness of the man sitting beside her. The sexy man who compelled her the same way Sam compelled Annie. He'd suffered so much. All she wanted to do was take the pain away.

She fisted her hands against her thighs clad in the pink lounging pajamas that had once belonged to his wife. Her throat constricted. Her shoulders tightened. Restlessly, she wriggled her toes inside the thick woolen socks. She could feel the heat radiating off Joe's body. Or maybe her fever was back. She certainly felt . . . unlike herself.

The television station cut to commercial. Joe muted the noise.

"They could have gotten together much sooner if Annie had just realized that she was settling instead of holding out for the magic of true love. And if Sam would have let go of the idea that it wasn't possible to have two great loves in one lifetime," Mariah babbled, simply to fill the silence, punctuated only by the sound of driving rain.

"Then there wouldn't have been a movie," Joe pointed out.

Mariah sighed. "Such pain they both suffered."

"Foolish Annie," he said. "Blind Sam. Luckily they had Jonah or they would never have met."

"All great matches need a Jonah to facilitate things I suppose," Mariah said. "How did you and Becca meet?"

Joe shrugged. "We knew each other all our lives. We both grew up right here in Jubilee. But it wasn't until I saw her competing at an out-of-town rodeo that she really caught my eye. Before that, I had my head so deep into bull riding that I didn't pay any attention to anything else. The men were all over Becca and I thought, *I've got to make her mine or lose out forever.*"

"How long were you married?"

"Just two years. She's been gone as long as we were married."

"We don't have to talk about her . . ." Mariah paused. "Unless you want to."

"You don't want to hear about my heartbreak."

"I do," she said, and reached out to put a hand on his forearm. "But only if you're comfortable talking about her with me."

"Sam had an advantage," Joe said, nodding at the actors on the television screen and turning the volume back up. "He got to tell Annie his history over a radio call-in show. It's much harder face-to-face."

They fell silent again.

Later in the movie when Annie and Sam looked across the road at each other in that moment of recognition, Joe reached across the couch and took Mariah's hand.

The gesture stilled her breathing.

"This is a good movie," he said softly when it was over. "Gives a lonely guy hope."

Her heart jumped. *Thump-thump.*

He squeezed her fingers. "Sam hung on to his grief for too long."

"Everyone grieves at their own pace."

"Yes," he said, "but if you keep holding on to what's gone, you miss out on what's right in front of you."

She tilted her head, afraid to hope, but wanting to so badly.

Joe leaned in closer.

Mariah held her breath.

His lips brushed hers, soft and sweet. It was a

languid kiss with no expectations or promises. Just pure and simple. His lips against hers. Then he pulled back, said nothing else, but kept holding her hand.

"You know," she said, feeling the need to say something, anything to center the sudden dizziness spinning her head. "The fictional call-in show featured in the movie really does exist in Chicago."

"No kidding?"

"I used to listen to it when I'd get down about my own life. It helped me feel like I wasn't alone. That other people were out there who felt the same way I did."

"Is the show still on the air?"

"Yes. It's called *Midnight with Dr. Dana*. It's only satellite radio now."

"I'm assuming it comes on at midnight."

"That's when most people need to talk. In the middle of the night. Alone and hurting, having a crisis of faith."

"Did you ever call in?"

"No, but I wanted to. After I lost my job."

"Do you think it was odd the way Annie fell for Sam simply over what he said on the radio? I mean she'd never seen him. He could have been a toad."

"I don't think that it would have mattered to Annie. She fell in love with who Sam was inside, not what he looked like. They shared the same values, even if they had opposing beliefs about love."

"Opposing beliefs? I didn't pick up on that."

"Sure, Sam believed you only got one shot at happiness. Annie loved everyone. Even people that didn't deserve her love like Walter. She had a tendency to sell herself short. Sam on the other hand, wanted lightning to strike. He believed in grand love or nothing at all."

"I hadn't thought of it that way."

"I've seen the movie a lot. It really resonates with me."

"Why is that?" He rubbed his thumb over the backs of her knuckles.

"I think it's the message of hope. That you truly can have a second chance at happiness."

He snorted.

"There you go. Disbelieving, just like Sam."

"I'm not saying I don't believe in love. Just that it's hard to put your heart back in the vise again when you already had it cracked like a walnut."

Mariah smiled. "But cracks are how the light gets in."

He looked startled. "That's insightful."

"Can't take credit. I heard it in a song somewhere."

"But you remembered it. Points for that."

She touched his shoulder. "Tell me about her."

Joe clenched his fists, his face was unreadable but he couldn't hide the tension in his jaw. Mariah had always been able to read people easily. She'd grown up watching for cues, looking for signs from others that told her how to behave in order to get along in a world that wasn't her own. She'd learned well. Excelled at pretending to be something she wasn't. Toe the line. Do what's expected of you if you want to be of value.

Mariah swallowed against the emotions pushing inside her. Emotions she didn't quite understand. Her impulse was to wrap her arms around Joe and tell him that she was so sorry he'd lost his beloved.

"I . . . I have trouble talking about her."

"Maybe that's the problem," she ventured, even though the cautious side of her that had shot her to success was screaming at her to just let things lie. It was none of her business. And yet, as impossible as it might seem, she couldn't just leave well enough alone. "You're keeping all your emotions jammed up inside you. If you talked, let them out, maybe you could let go."

If she wanted to understand Joe, she had to hear what he had to say whether she wanted to or not. His history was what had made him. Ignorance was not an option. Not if she wanted something more.

And she did want something more.

It had been gathering for a while. These feelings.

Joe's eyes flared darkly. Had she pushed too hard? Why was she pushing? A smart woman would just walk away. Once upon a time she would have just walked away. Why didn't she just walk away?

She knew the answer before she even thought it—rhetorical question of the highest order. Joe was in pain and all she wanted was to ease his suffering, and if pushing and prodding would do that, then that's what she would do. He'd pushed her when she'd been in physical pain, forcing her to go to bed when she'd stubbornly clung to her goal of painting the chapel. He'd been right then and she was right now.

Joe stood up, splayed his hands to the small of his back, and paced the floor. The sound of his feet on the hardwood filled the silence. "Becca was a pistol."

"Excuse me?"

"Sorry." He offered a small smile. "Cowboy term. She was a spitfire. Half the men in town were in love with her. She was tempestuous. Impossible to please, and I was crazy for her."

Jealousy sucker-punched her. *You started this. You asked for it.* "Sounds like she wasn't good enough for you."

"You've got me up on some pedestal. I was no saint either. Don't get me wrong. I never cheated on Becca. I might have been a hell-raiser in my day, but once I'm committed to a woman, I'm committed to her. But I've done things I'm not proud of."

"We all have."

He walked over, sat down, took her hand again, squeezed it. "You're not built for Jubilee."

"What makes you say that?"

"You've got big dreams."

"So do you."

"But we've got different kinds of dreams."

I can dream your dreams with you, she wanted to say, but she didn't dare. It would kill her soul if she let herself fully love Joe the way he deserved to be loved and then things didn't work out between them.

"Becca had a way of making you feel more alive than you'd ever felt in your life," he went on, "but it came with the danger of a downed power line. She was moody and driven. The only person I've ever known who was more driven than my wife was your father." He flicked a gaze over her. "And you. I know you had your issues with Dutch, but like it or not, Mariah, the apple doesn't fall far from the tree."

Mariah drew herself up. "I'm nothing like my father."

"You're exactly like him. Same dogged pigheadedness. Same need to believe in something bigger than yourself."

"And you're not?"

He shook his head. "I didn't used to be. Not until,

well, Dutch was my lifeline after Becca's death, and without him and cutting horses"—Joe shrugged—"I don't know where I'd be."

"You're healing."

"I miss Becca," he murmured.

Mariah's hopeful heart frosted over. She tried not to feel jealous. How petty was that? Feeling jealous over a dead woman. "I can't imagine."

He stopped pacing, exhaled. "But I know it's time to let go."

Mariah held her breath.

"I want to move on."

"That's . . ." She trailed off. Anything she said could easily be misconstrued. She didn't know what to say, so she just let the word lie there, exposed and orphaned.

"I loved Becca, but my wife was far from perfect. I think that you think she was perfect."

"I haven't made any assumptions."

"The town has already done it for you. They've canonized Becca because she died young and beautiful and in tragic fashion."

"It does make a good sad tale."

"She was pregnant when she died," he blurted.

Mariah brought her palm to her mouth. "Oh Joe, no!"

"I lost not only my wife, but the unborn child I didn't even know she was carrying."

"How did she die?" Mariah came right out and asked it. There was no easy way.

"You haven't heard from the town grapevine?"

"I want to hear it from you. Things get embellished when they're passed around."

He drew in a breath so heavy his rib cage shuddered.

"She died in a barrel racing accident. Championship-quality barrel racer. She was on her way to winning top honors." He paused.

Mariah waited, understanding that he needed time to tell this story in his own way.

"It's the main thing we had in common. Love of rodeo. We were on the road much of the year. Going from town to town, rodeo to rodeo. Most of the time she was in one place, I was in another."

"I know how the circuit works," Mariah said.

She thought of all the places they'd lived in when she was a child. How she'd always felt displaced. The odd kid out. To make up for her displacement, she tried to excel at everything—school, sports, social clubs. She was always wearing masks. Putting on the costume of whatever group she was affiliated with. Doing whatever she could to fit in. No, not just to fit in, but to be the best at whatever she tried, even if she didn't enjoy it.

"It was an exciting life, an interesting life, but after a while, I wanted more." Joe rubbed a hand over his thigh.

"More?"

"I felt . . . *insubstantial*. After you win a few tournaments, get several brass belt buckles, what else is there to prove? The glory fades pretty quickly."

Mariah thought of Dutch. Cutting horses had not only been in his blood, they'd been his drug. It sounded like the same had been true of Becca. But what about Joe? On the surface, he seemed to be as consumed by cutting horses as her father had been. But on deeper inspection, was there much more to the man? Hope lurched, staggered, then picked up momentum.

"I wanted to settle down. Buy a ranch, start a family. But Becca was younger. She wasn't ready." He stared down at his hands. "I don't think she would ever have been ready. Becca's life force couldn't be contained. Then I got injured, bought Green Ridge from my parents, but Becca wasn't happy with that."

"Joe, you don't have to say any more. I shouldn't have pushed you to talk about her. There's no—"

"No," he interrupted. "You're right. I haven't spoken about her to anyone since it happened. Not even to Ila. When she comes over, we just drink and tell each other jokes and cry."

"What *is* your situation with Ila?"

"She's my oldest friend."

"Have you two ever . . . um . . . hooked up?"

"No!" he said. "She's like a sister, hell, a brother, to me."

"Does Ila know that?"

"What do you mean?"

"I think Ila's in love with you, Joe."

"Nah." He shook his head. Denial. "She's not."

"Are you sure she's not just been biding her time, waiting for your grief to abate? Waiting for you to notice her?"

He looked startled. "I don't feel that way about Ila. She's just a good buddy."

"But Ila feels that way about you."

"How do you know this?"

"The look on Ila's face whenever she's watching you and she knows that you're not looking."

"Crap." He blew out his breath, looked unsettled. "I had no idea."

"You have to tell her that you're not interested. You can't keep stringing her along."

"I didn't even know I was stringing her along. Shit, Mariah." He ran a hand through his hair. "Really?"

She nodded. "That's why she's so rude to me."

"Because she knows you and I . . ." He let his words trail off, not defining what was going on between them.

You and I what? What were they? Mariah's mind spun, but she said nothing.

"Anyway," Joe said. "After Becca died we learned she was six weeks' pregnant." His voice cracked and he blinked rapidly.

Mariah's heart constricted. "Oh, Joe. You lost two loved ones that day."

"Here's the kicker," he said in a husky tone. "She had a pregnancy kit in her purse. As if she knew she was pregnant, but she didn't want to take the test until after the rodeo. She knew it would be her last chance to win. Knew that a pregnancy would sideline her for a long time. So she waited. If she'd just taken the test first, I know she wouldn't have ridden. I'd still have her. We'd have a baby by now."

The anguish on his face broke her heart into two pieces. Realization clawed at her. The man wasn't ready to love again.

He might never be.

CHAPTER SIXTEEN

When you're scared, there's only one cure; cowboy up.

—Dutch Callahan

S o that's my sad story," Joe said. "What about you?"

"What about me?"

"Any long-term relationships in your past? Boyfriends, lovers, husbands?"

"No husbands. I haven't had many boyfriends. I'm not the most gorgeous woman in the world and I do work a lot."

"There are all kinds of beauty, Mariah. Sure, some women might be supermodel-gorgeous, but you know what? They intimidate guys. I know. I was married to one."

"Yeah," she mumbled.

"But when I look at you, I see so much more than just a pretty face. I see the kindness in those brown eyes. I see warmth and compassion in your smile."

She opened her mouth to protest, but he held up his hand to stop her.

"You *are* pretty. And I bet there were a lot of guys just waiting to date you."

"There were a few guys," she admitted. "But I didn't want to get serious with any of them. I was so focused on my career. I was young and not really thinking about anything except making a mark for myself in the wedding planning business. I always wanted my own business someday."

"And now you've got it."

"Not hardly." She grimaced. "I've booked one wedding and I'm doing that for free."

"You have to start somewhere."

"I've made a start," she echoed.

"So tell me about Chicago."

She pushed the round, wire-frame glasses up on her nose. He liked when she wore her glasses. It made her less intimidating, more approachable. A tattered, beat-up guy like him needed a woman who was a bit myopic.

While he was staring at her, she snagged the right corner of her bottom lip up between her teeth. He liked that too. The vulnerable, girlish gesture unleashed the protective guardian in him. He leaned toward her because the closer he got, the more stable she made him feel.

Her delightful smell addled his brain and it was all he could do not to sidle even closer.

"You loved your job. Didn't you?" Joe asked.

"Yeah." She breathed.

The wistful note in her voice muscled up his chest. She missed Chicago. Missed her home. Missed her career. She didn't belong here. He knew it. She knew it, and yet here she was trying to make the best of the situation. He admired that about her. Adaptability.

"What did you love about it?" he asked.

"Making the fantasy real. Making people's dream come true. If only for a day."

"So what happened with the dream job?"

Mariah's face colored. "I made a huge mistake."

"What kind of mistake?"

She waved a hand. She had such pretty hands— long and slender, competent and strong. Joe had never thought of hands as sexy before, but Mariah's hands turned him on. Hell, everything about her turned him on. That was the problem.

It's just sex. And she reminds you a little of Becca.

Physically, maybe a little. She was petite and blond, agile and compact, but there the resemblance ended. He wasn't projecting his feelings for his dead wife on her.

Was he?

It was a confounding thought.

"Hey," he said. "You don't get away with that. I opened up to you, it's time you opened up to me."

"And tell you about my greatest failure?"

"We all fail."

"I don't. Not usually." She bit her bottom lip again. "But it's because I'm always wondering what people think of me. How I'm perceived, and I act accordingly. It's worked well for me until, well . . . it didn't."

Joe waited for her to elaborate. When she didn't speak, he feared the iceberg was never going to thaw. Did she realize how she held herself apart from others, a little aloof, unobtainable in her perfection?

If only he could get her to talk. Discover who she really was beneath that smooth veneer. Find out the nature of the heart beating within her. But did he really want to do that? If she told him about herself, it would increase the bond between them. A bond that scared him. She had so much potential to hurt him. Wouldn't it be better to leave the mask in place? Let things lie? Keep these feelings light and high?

"I'm listening," he prodded.

She shrugged. "I have trouble opening up."

"Trust issues," Joe said. "I suppose you can lay those at Dutch's feet."

"I can and I have, but you know what? I understand now that I can't blame everything on Dutch. He did what he did. I am who I am. This is the way my life happened. I can't change any of it. So I've decided I'm going to accept it and let it go and move forward."

Joe leaned back, but kept his hand on hers. "You've made a lot of progress since you got to Jubilee."

"I have?" she said, sounding both surprised and pleased. She drew her knees to her chest. She looked so vulnerable in those pink pajamas, her hair mussed, her glasses perched on the bridge of her nose.

"So you shouldn't have any problem telling me what happened. You're safe here."

Safe? What was he doing? What was he saying? Did he really want to offer her safety? Was he actually taking that step?

Hey, you just spilled your guts to her about Becca.

Yes, and he had no idea why he'd done so.

The movie. It was that sappy movie. Becca used to tease him for being sentimental. He'd been the romantic in the family. Not his wife.

Mariah wrapped her arms around her knees, hugging herself. In all honesty, they were finally getting to know each other, dig deeper beyond the surface attraction, and that set his heart thumping hard.

Did he really want to take that step? He could turn the television back on, change the subject, make an excuse and go check on the horses.

"It was at the wedding of one of the wealthiest old money families in Chicago," she said. "Everyone who's anyone was there."

"Oprah?"

Mariah nodded.

Joe whistled. "I'm impressed."

"Lots of heavy hitters. Tension like you wouldn't believe. My boss, who I've never seen frazzled, was high-wire tense. But for some weird reason I was totally calm. I'd spent my life preparing for an event like this. I wasn't going to screw up."

"I don't like the way this is going."

"I was in charge of the wedding reception. It was at the aquarium. Pretty venue, but a logistical nightmare of wedding reception planning," she continued.

"Sounds nice."

"It was. No money was spared. We're talking a quarter of a million dollars here."

Joe whistled.

"Pocket change to these people."

"So what happened?" he repeated.

"Everything was going smoothly until Mayor Krimpholder cornered me behind a tank filled with clown fish. It's weird the things you remember. He pushed his hand up the hem of my dress and cupped my ass, and all I could think about was the clown fish."

"I wish I'd been there," Joe said. "I'd have decked him."

"I did deck him." Mariah smiled sweetly.

Joe hooted.

"I think it was the first time in my life I ever acted on pure instinct. Usually, I evaluate everything I do, decide whether it's the right move or not. But there I was staring at a clown fish, this fifty-something-year-old, married man's hand on my butt cheek, and it just hit me what a cliché I would be if I allowed this to happen."

Joe growled low in his throat, fisted his hands on his thighs.

"Here I'd been working eighty hours a week to put on this wedding. I put up with a load of crap from the client, but hey, that was okay. It's my job to please. I take pride in the fact that whatever I do, I do it well. And then, here's this man, who has a daughter close to my age, fumbling inside my panties, breathing garlic from the canapés on the back of my neck, and I just snapped."

Joe laughed. "Okay, it's not funny, but I am so in love with the image of you smacking this dude that I can't help it."

Love.

Had he actually said the word "love"? Joe swallowed, watched Mariah's face. But she was accomplished at hiding her emotions. He saw nothing more than the flick of her eyelashes.

"I slapped him and told him to keep his hands to himself. You'd think people would be on my side. But no, that's not how it went down. He put a hand to his cheek and hollered out that I'd assaulted him because he'd dared to complain about the quality of the service."

"Asshole."

"You can say that twice and not be wrong. My boss, who I thought would back me up, just threw me to the wolves. She fired me on the spot and then blackballed me in Chicago. I couldn't get a job with any wedding planning firms in the area."

"That is so wrong."

"It happened. I took a job waiting tables at a four-star restaurant in downtown. Then one evening the wealthy old money clients whose daughter's wedding reception I'd wrecked came into the restaurant for dinner. The next day, I lost that job too. After that, I couldn't get a job scooping cat litter at a pet store."

"Bullshit," Joe exclaimed.

"Yes, but I was expected to be a good girl. Tolerate the groping. Smile and go about my business. My boss actually told me that was the reason why I was paid such a high salary. It was my job to please the clients and I should have just made a joke of the mayor fondling me. When she said that, I felt like a prostitute."

He realized now why she hadn't wanted to talk about it. Not because she wasn't ready to open up to him, but simply because she hadn't wanted to relive the painful memory. He felt guilty for pushing her. "You're out of there now. You're here and you've started your own business, and by gum, if anyone tries to lay a hand on you, I'll do to them what I did to Lee Turpin. You were with the wrong people, Mariah. You didn't belong in Chicago."

"I thought I did," she whispered. "I needed to belong somewhere."

"Inheriting Dutch's cabin saved you."

"It was the answer to my prayers," she admitted. "Except it was nothing that I would ever have expected. And I'd much rather have Dutch alive. I wish I could turn back time, build a relationship with him."

"We all have regrets," he said. "I suppose all we can do is try to do better in the future."

He could see the reflection of the flickering firelight in her eyes. Knew she suffered just as he suffered. It was a different kind of pain, but hurt was hurt and loss was loss. They could make each other feel better if they weren't so damn scared of getting hurt again.

"C'mon," he said, and tugged her into his arms.

They sat there for the longest time, snuggled up on the couch together, listening to the rain drum and the wood in the fireplace snap and crack.

"I wear a mask," she said after a long while.

That puzzled him. "What?"

"I put on whatever face I think people want to see. It's how I've managed to survive in the world."

"We all do that from time to time. Fake it till you make it."

"But with me, it's more than that. I want to try to explain it to you so you can understand why I treated Dutch the way I did when I was fourteen and he came to my high school to see me."

Joe understood that it wasn't him she needed to convince. He let her talk, reaching out to gently stroke the silky strands of her hair. He liked that she was confiding in him. Trusting him. It was a big step for them both.

"Because my mom and I lived in other people's houses, we never had a home of our own. I learned how to adapt to meet other people's expectations. Whenever I'd enter a new situation, I'd immediately start figuring out how to blend in. Just as I did when I got to Jubilee and bought—well, you bought me— cowboy clothes. I have a sixth sense about what a group will accept and I start behaving that way. So when I was in high school at Hyde Park, I was one of those rich kids. I wasn't a displaced cowgirl as Dutch saw me. And I was so afraid that if people knew he was my father that I'd be ostracized from the group. In high school, fitting in is so important."

"It's okay," Joe said.

"It's not. Because in trying to fit in with everyone, I ended up fitting in with no one. I didn't know my real place."

"And now?"

She smiled. "This cowboy wedding planning business, it's becoming real. I'm beginning to think this is where I belong. Then again, maybe I'm just deceiving myself again. I mean, why risk rejection when acceptance can be bought by simply wearing a mask?"

"Do you feel like you're wearing a mask now? Do you feel that way with me?" he dared to ask.

"No," she said. "And that's what scares me about you."

He brushed her cheek with the pad of his thumb. "Why should being your true self scare you?"

"Because," Mariah whispered, "I don't know who that woman is."

"You might not know," he said, "but I do. She's self-confident and efficient, energetic and practical. She's smart and adaptable. And do you want to know what I like best about her?"

"What?"

"I like how she bounces back so quickly. How balanced she is. How she can take life on the chin and keep going full steam ahead."

"I just try to stay busy to keep from thinking too much," she confessed.

He trailed his fingertips over her forearm—gently,

lightly, just to let her know how much he appreciated her. "You know what else I like about you?"

"No."

"The way your lips taste." He leaned over, looked into her eyes. He was treading on treacherous ground. One wrong move and he'd lose his footing. If he were smart, he'd get up, run away.

But at that moment, fleeing was the last thing on his mind.

Joe's distracting thumb kept moving over her skin, kneading, massaging. He didn't say anything; his quietness, the security of him wormed into her heart. His patience surprised her. He was a powerful man, a man accustomed to being in charge and getting his way and taming wild bulls and cutting horses.

In her experience, powerful men weren't quiet and patient. But there was a deeper side to Joe. Had it emerged after his wife's death? Had his loss taught him quietness and patience? Whatever the cause, his silence had the effect that words or actions never could have. It made Mariah want to share everything with him.

Then he leaned over and kissed her—softly, sweetly, gently.

Mariah did not pull away.

"How does that feel?" he asked.

"Nice. Very nice."

"Just nice?"

"You're holding back."

"I am. You sure you want more?"

She stared into his eyes, got lost in the abyss of those dark pupils. "I've wanted more from the moment I first laid eyes on you in that horse trough."

"Naked cowboys are your thing, huh?" He chuckled.
"Apparently."

"Come closer, woman," he said, and pulled her into his lap.

She fit neatly against him, as if she'd been made for sitting in his lap.

Joe turned her around so they were facing each other. He ran his hand up the nape of her neck, splayed his fingers through her hair, and tugged her head down to meet his lips.

She kissed him right back with all the passion that had been building inside her for the past several weeks. Kissed and kissed and kissed.

Joe was the one to take it past the kissing, as she knew he would be; her alpha cowboy, strong and in control, but never inconsiderate, never out solely for his own pleasure. His palm slid up underneath her shirt, skimming hotly over her bare belly to her breasts, and her world cracked open.

She clung to him. Outside, the rain beat on the tile roof. Inside, they were snug in the cozy womb of his living room, the firelight throwing long shadows over them. His bold tongue teased her teeth apart and she loosened her jaw to let him all the way in.

You shouldn't be doing this.

But for the life of her, she couldn't think of a single reason why not.

Then he found a sweet spot between her ear and her chin. An erogenous zone that turned her to putty. She moaned softly, curled into him. She was straddling his lap, her hands wrapped around his neck, her raised knees pressed into the back of the couch. Beneath her bottom, she could feel his erection growing increasingly stiffer.

Strong, confident, decisive, he boldly conquered her mouth again, kissing her hard and long as his hand brushed lightly over first one nipple and then the other, taking control as only an alpha man could.

An ancient, burgeoning need melded her to him, stoking her hunger, cementing their connection.

"You can say stop at any time," he said. "I just want you to know that."

"You have the same right, but I don't want to stop."

"Me either, I just want you to know that this is the first time since . . ."

Becca died.

The words hung unspoken in the air between them.

He shifted, sliding her off his lap, then moved down to the rug on the floor in front of the fire, taking her with him. Then when he reached to untie the string at the waistband of her pajamas, her heart started pounding an unruly rhythm.

"Wh—"

He closed off her words with another kiss, then pulled back and whispered, "Trust me."

He blazed a trail like his pioneer ancestors, kissing a heated path from her mouth to that sweet spot under her chin to the hollow of her throat to . . . *oh my!*

While his mouth was kissing her, his fingers unbuttoned her pajama top, pushing it aside, and now his wicked mouth was on her tender, aching nipple and it was the most exquisite sensation.

Butter. Hot melted butter.

Then while his tongue teased her nipple, that naughty hand slipped beneath the waistband of her pajamas.

Helplessly, she arched her hips, felt the pajama bottoms being tugged off her. The draft of cool air, the pressure of his palm, the tingles racing over her skin made her shiver.

"Woman," he whispered, and kissed her again, but while he was doing that, those evil fingers were sliding beneath the silky material of her panties.

"Man," she said, and nipped his lip.

He laughed and eased his finger between her legs and into a spot that sent her mind skidding off the deep end.

She swallowed against the sensation, closed her eyes, rode it like a magic carpet to the stars.

"Yes?" his voice whispered in her ear.

"Yes." She should have been embarrassed. She would have been embarrassed. This was so intimate. It felt as if they'd skipped some steps, but it felt so very, very good that she didn't care.

When the second finger slid in to join the first, her entire body tensed, quivered.

"Oooh." She sighed and draped the back of her hand over her eyes. She was so hot! Was her fever back?

She felt tight everywhere. Tight and sensitive and so aware, and when his thumb hit her trigger button she was almost jolted straight out of her skin.

Joe chuckled and then did some crazy, amazing, unbelievable things with his fingers.

But the pleasure didn't end there. As his fingers played her, his mouth was surfing down her belly, lower and lower, until she was stiff as a plank, waiting in anticipation for where she prayed he was headed.

Then there he was.

His sweet, sweet lips. On her inner lips. Licking.

Baffled. She was baffled that anything could feel this good.

He toyed with her, prolonging the agonizing pleasure. Holding her at bay.

She made a noise of frustration low in her throat, then pushed her pelvis against him. She toed the rim of a dark peak, surrounded by the heat and pressure of his madding mouth, the smell of mesquite, the sound of her own soft moans.

This wasn't right. She wanted him too much. No one should be this out of control with desire. It was too dangerous. Anything could happen. She'd gone too far. Lost too much of herself.

Then just like that, she broke.

A whimper tore from her throat. She grasped for him, threaded her fingers through his hair, and held on tight as wave after wave rolled over her. By the end she was trembling and sobbing with joyous release.

"Mariah? Are you okay? Did I hurt you?" Alarm tinged his words as he scooped her into his arms and held her cradled against his chest. "Mariah, sweetheart, speak to me."

"I'm . . . fine . . ." she whispered weakly.

"It was too much. You're recovering from a fever. I should never have started this," he berated himself.

"I'm so much more than fine," she reassured him.

"You could have a relapse." He was buttoning her shirt, pulling her panties up. Searching for the pajama bottoms.

"Joe, you're not listening. I'm speechless from the incredible orgasm you just gave me. I've never . . . come that way."

"Really?" He grinned from ear to ear.

"Now don't let it go to your head, but yes."

He smiled, shook his head. "You look so damn beautiful right now."

"We're not going to do anything more?"

"Not now. Not tonight."

"Why not?" she asked, feeling petulant. "You didn't get anything out of it."

"That's where you're completely wrong. Your pleasure . . . feeling you come . . . you were so hot. You made me feel so good. I haven't felt this good in a long time."

"If you think that was good . . ." She strayed a hand to his zipper, but he blocked her hand.

"No," he whispered. "I don't have a condom. We'll wait. I can wait. Let's just take this one step at a time."

"What's the next step?" she asked tentatively.

"Meet the parents."

"What?" she said, feeling alarmed. She didn't know if she was ready for *that*.

"You'll come with me to my parents' house for Thanksgiving dinner."

CHAPTER SEVENTEEN

> The biggest troublemaker you'll ever meet stares
> you in the face when you brush your teeth.
> —Dutch Callahan

The rain quit the next day, but Joe wouldn't let Mariah go home. He put her in the guest bedroom and told her to rest and then he disappeared. Bored, but still feeling a little weak after her bout with the fever, she spent the morning on the phone and on the Internet riding herd on the wedding preparations for Prissy and Paul's wedding.

In between the calls and the Googling, Mariah thought about Joe and what had happened between them the previous evening. Things had changed, shifted. The distance evaporated. Intimacy loomed. Her mind pinballed from emotion to emotion, bouncing off the bumpers of delight, fear, excitement, and worry.

They were working toward something. She was building a life here in Jubilee and Joe was rapidly becoming part of it.

Oh gosh. Did she want this? Was she ready for their friendship to move to the next level? She'd kept men at a distance for so long as she built her career, she honestly didn't know how to stop doing that. But she wanted to. Oh yeah, she wanted what most everyone wanted. A home. A family. She was due. It was time. Why not just embrace what was happening and hold on for the ride? Her stomach dipped, tingled.

A smile curled over her lips. Dating Joe would be like riding a cutting horse. Thrilling. Exhilarating. Addicting.

And that was where the fear set in.

The thought of losing all control went against everything inside her. Still, there was some part of her that yearned to give in, yield, succumb.

Hope budded.

Maybe, maybe. She hugged herself. *Joe.*

Around noon she grew hungry. Mariah left the guest room intent on finding something to eat for lunch and paused to go into what she thought was the downstairs bathroom. When she opened the door, she immediately realized her mistake.

Polished trophies gleamed from a row of shelves. Numerous trophies featuring cowgirls on wild-maned horses.

Belt buckles too. Silver, gold. Big and imposing buckles mounted on the paneled wall.

Photographs of Becca. Zipping around barrels. Galloping full-out. Or in the winner's circle holding up one of the polished trophies. The woman had been an incredible beauty. A younger version of Michelle Pfeiffer. Sleek, cool, perfect.

On display in the middle of the room, positioned on a stand, was the *pièce de résistance*. A championship barrel racing saddle. Becca had won the national rodeo title the year before her death.

The room was a shrine. To Becca.

The floor dropped out from under Mariah's feet.

So much for budding dreams.

Joe finally came in around midnight. She lay in the guest room listening to him, remembering what he'd done to her the night before, thinking about the Becca shrine she'd found. She hoped he'd come to her so they could talk.

He did not.

The next morning, she got up before he did, determined to see him before he went off to work. She cracked eggs and started making omelets.

What are you doing?" Joe demanded.

Mariah jumped. She hadn't heard him come into the kitchen. "Hi!"

He stared at her with astonishment, his gaze drifting from her hand confidently flipping the omelet to his blue and white striped, button-down shirt that she'd found in the guest room closet and slipped on over her T-shirt and panties. She hadn't wanted to wear any more of Becca's clothes and she'd just put her own clothes into the washing machine.

The shirt was so long, and she was so petite, that the hem of it hit her just above the knees. The material was thin, the sleeves rolled up to her elbows, and several top buttons were undone.

She thought she was fully covered but the lusty expression on his face pushed the air from her lungs, and in her mind's eye she saw herself as he saw her. Mussed hair, bare feet, naked under a thin film of cloth. Full-on seductive.

She didn't mean to look that way, so she lightly, breezily said, "Cooking breakfast for you."

"You've been ill. Go back to bed," he commanded, pointing a finger toward the bedroom.

"I'm fine. I'm feeling much better. In fact, I'm ravenous."

He watched her through languid, half-lidded eyes, a lazy grin tugging at the corners of his mouth, as if the sight of her cooking his breakfast was the source of great amusement.

She slid the omelet onto a plate and carried it to the kitchen table. "Here, eat up."

He sat down, but before she could move away, he grabbed her arm and pulled her to him. "It's dangerous, woman, to go around dressed like that."

She melted against him. She wasn't alone in this. He was feeling it too. Still, there was that room filled with Becca.

She wriggled in his grasp. "I'll go change."

Joe released her, raised both palms. "No, it's okay. I can keep my hands to myself."

I don't want you to keep your hands to yourself. I want you to take me right here on this table, erase the ghost of your wife, she longed to say. But instead, she said, "When can I go back to my cabin?"

"You can go back today if you want. I'll take you over after breakfast."

"Oh yeah, I have so much to do on the wedding chapel and—"

"And you're going to take it easy, right? The futurity starts next Tuesday and I'm going to be busy."

"I understand."

"We'll have more time together when it's over."

"I'm busy too," she reminded him. "Prissy and Paul's wedding is less than three weeks away."

They finished breakfast and Joe drove her back to

the cabin. The minute she arrived, she knew something was different.

"The roof!" she exclaimed. "It's new!"

"I couldn't let you stay in that place without a roof. I called the co-op. We put it on yesterday."

"In one day?"

"There were twenty of us."

"Oh Joe." Gratitude lifted her up. "This is . . . this is beyond the pale."

"Don't you get it, Little Bit? That's what people do here in Jubilee. They help each other. You're one of us. We take care of our own."

She placed a palm across her heart. "I feel so welcomed."

"You are," he said, and kissed the tip of her nose. "Now just wait until you get to meet my family. You might start having second thoughts about me."

Joe hadn't brought a woman home for Thanksgiving dinner with his family since Becca. He had to admit to feeling a bit skittish about thrusting Mariah so forcefully into the oversized bosom of the Daniels clan. Especially on Thanksgiving, which was always such an intense time because of the Fort Worth Futurity that took place right in the big middle of the festivities.

He was also worried his family might read more into their relationship than was there. Yet.

What was this relationship all about?

Hell if he could define it. He wanted her something fierce, but he was afraid to let his emotions off their chain. The last time he'd done that, he'd been flattened. But the truth was, he wanted her here with him. Couldn't picture spending the holiday without her, and he wasn't about to leave her in her cabin alone eating turkey dinner from a microwaved carton.

They now stood on his parents' doorstep of their Cape Cod–style cottage overlooking the lake just out-side the neighboring town of Twilight. He'd brought a bouquet of flowers for his mother. Mariah had a fruitcake.

"Ready?" Joe asked.

"As I'll ever be." Mariah smiled at him.

His heart zinged and he raised a hand to knock.

"Wait, wait."

"What is it?"

"How do I look?" She twirled for him, her little red wool skirt flaring out around her legs encased in the cowboy boots he'd bought for her. She wore matching red tights and a red and white striped shirt. She looked like a red-hot candy cane. Lickable and delicious.

"Gorgeous."

"Be honest."

"Like a red oak in autumn. You'll steal the show."

"Is my hem too short?"

"It's perfect. You're perfect. Don't worry."

"Easy for you to say. You're not walking into a roomful of strangers."

He reached out to take her hand. "Just be yourself. Never fear, I've got your back, Little Bit."

That's when Joe realized he meant it. He'd protect her, no matter what.

Joe had her back.

There was no time to process what he'd said. The door opened. Joe introduced her to the two smiling, gray-haired people welcoming her in, ushering her over the threshold, pulling her into hearty hugs. First Frank Daniels, and then his wife, Margo.

"Come in, come in."

"Nice to meet you."

"Let me take your coat."

"Can I get you something to drink?"

"Fruitcake, how lovely. Frank, look, Corsicana fruitcake, my favorite. Thank you, Mariah."

The odd familiarity of Thanksgiving dinner with strangers enveloped her in a sharp-edged embrace. She'd spent her childhood watching other families' celebrations as her mother waited on them. It had been an unusual upbringing that made her easily adaptable, but at the same time made her feel peculiarly unreal. As if everything was staged, an act for show. The ability had served her well, but she couldn't shake the sensation that other people experienced the world in a more honest and complete way.

The living room was filled with people she didn't know. Joe took her by the hand and introduced her around the cozy room. A fire crackled in the fireplace. On the flat-screen TV mounted over the mantel, the Dallas Cowboys tussled with the Washington Redskins.

She met Joe's oldest brother, Chase, the surgeon, and his wife, Zoey, who was also a doctor. Chase was taller than Joe and stockier. Zoey was exotic, with almond eyes, a French accent, and fabulous collarbones shown off in a scoop-neck sweater. They had a toddler son named Garrett. Someone mentioned that Joe's other brother, Rick, was out in the backyard.

Mariah shook hands with Kimber, Joe's sister, and her boyfriend, Dane, who was a cutter like Joe. There was also Meg, the youngest Daniels. Both sisters were fine-boned, with chestnut hair and crooked grins that made Mariah feel especially welcomed.

Next, Joe took her to the kitchen, where she saw Ila Brackeen leaning against the counter talking with an elderly woman who was even shorter than Mariah. The woman stood stirring a pan of something on the stove.

"You know Ila." Joe nodded.

Ila raised a hand, gave a curt "Hey."

"And this," Joe said, putting his arm around the elderly woman, "is my grandmother Daisy Daniels, but we all just call her Gamma."

The tiny woman eyed Mariah speculatively as if she could see straight through her. She might be in her eighties, but her black eyes were razor sharp. She looked from Joe to Mariah and back again. Mariah fancied the little old lady knew exactly what she'd done with her grandson.

"Joe," Ila said, snagging his elbow. "Your brother Rick needs help outside frying the turkey. C'mon."

Joe opened his mouth to respond, but before he got anything out, Ila dragged him out the back door, leaving Mariah to fend for herself with Gamma.

"Taste this," Gamma Daniels said, extending a spoon toward Mariah's mouth.

"What is it?"

"Just taste it."

Mariah eyed the concoction. It looked like cranberry sauce. Innocent enough. Right?

"What? You afraid it's poisoned?" Gamma narrowed her eyes.

"No, no." Mariah took a bit. Mmm, it was the best cranberry— Suddenly, her mouth ignited, it was all she could do to swallow it down instead of spitting it out. "What is that?"

"My specialty, hellfire cranberry sauce," Gamma bragged. "Here you go." She extended a glass of water to Mariah that apparently she had at the ready. "Cranberries, orange zest, and habanero peppers. It was my husband's favorite thing about Thanksgiving, God rest Lloyd's soul."

Eyes watering, mouth aflame, Mariah gulped the glass of water. "What did he die from? A seared esophagus?"

The sadistic senior citizen chuckled, nodded to herself. "Yep, it's a good batch."

"Great." Mariah coughed.

"So," Gamma said, turning to eye her. "You're the one who's put a smile back on my grandson's face. Good for you."

Mariah didn't know how to respond so she simply nodded, smiled. "Joe's a nice guy, Mrs. Daniels."

"Call me Gamma." She reached over to squeeze Mariah's hand. "From what Joe has said about you, I feel as if I know you already."

"Uh-oh," Mariah teased. "That sounds ominous."

"It's all good, I assure you. Even when he's grumbling about you."

"He grumbles about me?"

"In the same breath that he's singing your praises. You've impressed him."

He'd talked about her to his grandmother? She wasn't accustomed to being knocked off balance, but everything about Joe had her careening from one emotion to another. Luckily, she was adept at schooling her features. She took another sip of water to calm her blistering tongue.

"I can see I've embarrassed you," Gamma said. "That wasn't my intention. We're an unruly gang, so jump right in and don't let anyone run you over. Especially Ila."

"Thanks for the warning." Mariah smiled.

"You're going to be just fine." Gamma slipped an arm around her waist. "As long as you don't break Joey's heart."

Suddenly, the warm welcome turned slippery. Fitting in here was conditional. Love Joe or get out. Mariah cleared her throat. "You don't have to worry about that, Mrs. Daniels. Joe and I are just friends."

"Does Joe know that?"

"Absolutely." Okay, maybe she wasn't being totally honest.

Gamma looked skeptical. "He may look all tough and blustery, our Joey, but he's got a fragile heart. He loves so easily and so deeply. He's a one-woman man. If he loves you, it's for keeps. Trouble is, he believes you only get one shot at love."

Yes, she knew that. She'd seen the Becca shrine. "Admirable," she said, because she didn't know what else to say.

Gamma gave her an odd look. "You've never been loved like that, have you?"

Considering that her own father had run out on her, was it any wonder she kept men at arm's length? "No," Mariah murmured.

"Well, hold on with both hands. When a Daniels man loves you, you're one hundred percent loved. Just make damn sure you love him back."

"Joe's not in love with me." She laughed. It was a shaky sound.

"Hmm," Gamma said.

"Hmm what?"

"I guess it's for the best that you're not in love with him then."

Fear winnowed through her veins. She wasn't prepared for this. These feelings. Her reaction. She might not be in love with him, but she was falling fast, and here was Gamma telling her she better slam on the brakes. "Why's that?"

"Cutting, horses, his work means everything to him. If you can't share that with him the way Becca did, well . . ." Gamma trailed off. "Let's just say you both deserve to be happy, and Joe shouldn't have to choose between the woman he loves and the work that burns in his blood."

Ila pulled Joe around the side of the house before he even got a chance to say hello to his brother Rick, who was lounging in a chaise beside the turkey fryer, with a beer in his hand and a fire extinguisher by his side. "I've got to talk to you."

"There's not a problem with the turkey?"

"No." Ila frowned. "Keep up. It was a ploy to get you outside."

"Okay, I'm outside. What's the matter?"

Ila paced in front of him. "I've got to ask you something important."

"Shoot."

She wrung her hands. Which wasn't like Ila at all. She wasn't a hand wringer. Something was different about her. "Hey, you cut your hair."

She stopped pacing and stared at him with such sadness that it hurt. "Over a month ago, Joe."

"I'm sorry I didn't notice," he said. Becca used to get really irritated if he didn't notice when she changed her hair or bought new clothes. "That was selfish of me."

She gnawed at her thumbnail.

He reached out, took her by the shoulders. "Hey, what's up? You know you can tell me anything."

Ila stared him in the eyes, steely as always. At least that was normal. "Can I really?"

"Sure. Of course. You know that. We've been friends forever."

She paused. "Do you remember that time when we were sixteen and I kissed you under the bleachers at the Fourth of July rodeo?"

Joe paused. He'd totally put that out of his mind. They'd been drinking Boone's Farm Wild Raspberry and he'd assumed the kiss had been nothing more than a product of too much cheap wine.

"Do you?" she pushed.

Joe had a feeling he was about to fail some important test. "Vaguely."

She swallowed so loud he could hear it. Her pupils constricted. "That's what I thought," she whispered.

"Ila, what is this all about?"

"You're *with her*, with her, aren't you?"

"Mariah?"

"No, Mrs. Santa Claus." Ila's breathing came in short rasps. "Of course Mariah."

"If you think I'm trying to replace Becca, don't worry. Becca will always have a special place in my heart. She was my wife and I loved her, but Mariah . . ." His voice softened as he thought about Mariah. The woman who'd made his torn-up, dormant soul bloom again. A smile tilted his lips. "Mariah makes me feel whole in a way I've never felt before. Not even when I was married to Becca. Me and Becca . . . well . . . we were a lot alike and that's not a bad thing, but I've discovered—"

"You're in love with her," Ila said flatly.

Joe splayed a hand to the back of his neck. "I—"

"No." Ila cut him off, plastered her palms over her ears. "Don't answer that. I don't want to hear that."

Just then the back door snapped shut and they both looked up to see Cordy striding across the yard toward them, looking like one of storm-chasing Rick's tornado-brewing clouds.

"Ila," Cordy hollered, "could I have a word with you?"

"No," Ila said.

"What's going on?" Joe asked.

"Clueless," Ila muttered.

"None of your damn business," Cordy snapped.

Joe stepped back. His easygoing employee had never spoken to him like that. "I just wanted to help."

"You can't help," Ila and Cordy yelled at him in unison.

"Okay." Joe raised his palms in a gesture of surrender.

"You better go check on the woman you came with," Cordy said. "I think Mariah's losing ground with your Gamma."

"Don't tell me she gave Mariah hellfire cranberry sauce."

"She's your Gamma, you figure it out," Cordy said.

He should never have left Mariah alone with Gamma. "I hope you two get things sorted out," Joe said, and then hightailed it to the kitchen to save Mariah while she still had her taste buds intact.

* * *

Ila would never have imagined that five-foot-eight-with-his-cowboy-boots-on Cordy could look like a ten-foot, fire-breathing dragon.

"What were you doing out here with him?" Cordy challenged.

"He's my brother-in-law, I can talk to him if I want to talk to him."

Cordy clenched his jaw so tight the muscles under his ear twitched. "I thought we had this settled."

"You can't go busting into jealousy every time I talk to Joe."

"It's been over a month, Ila. I thought we were building something—"

"We've been sleeping together. That's all."

Cordy looked as if he'd been slapped hard across the face. "You still haven't accepted the fact that I'm your destiny, not Joe."

Ila rolled her eyes. "I don't believe in that destiny crap."

"You don't believe in us?" His voice cracked and he looked like she'd shot an arrow straight through his heart.

"As a couple?" Ila shook her head, felt mean and selfish and guilty. "Not really."

"I see I've got my work cut out for me." Cordy hardened his chin.

"Cordy, you can't make me love you."

"And *you* can't make Joe love you."

Ila stared at him. Cordy looked so earnest. Her gut lurched. She knew Joe was lost to her. He was in love with Mariah. She could see it on him even if he wasn't ready to admit it. She had to let go of her unrequited love. It wasn't fair to anyone. Not to Joe, not to Mariah, not to Cordy. Not to her.

"But you know what?" Cordy said. "I deserve better than being your rebound guy. I'm not settling for second best. I love you, Ila, but I'm not going to beg. I've got too much dignity for that. You want Joe? Go get him."

"You're breaking up with me?" Ila was surprised by the sharp pinprick to her gut.

"I am."

"Cordy," she said, sudden panic rising inside her.

But he'd already gone, slamming back into the house and leaving Ila feeling more confused than she'd ever felt in her life.

The Daniels clan sat around the dinner table, and immediately after Joe's father said grace over the meal, the conversation went to the futurity as everyone dived into the food. They passed plates around the table family-style.

Mariah had watched big extended families having Thanksgiving dinner over the years, but she'd never belonged to such a group. She'd always been the outsider trying to fit in. Everyone was warm and friendly. Joe, who was sitting across the table, winked at her.

How nice it would be to fit in here. It was something she'd always longed for, but feared could never exist for her. A place where she belonged.

The whole time Joe was talking horses and cutting and the futurity with his father and Dane.

He sounded so much like her father. Love of horses shone in his eyes, and she thought about what Gamma had said. She wanted to let herself go, to follow her heart, but she was so afraid of ending up with a younger version of her dad. Unable to love anyone as much as he loved horses.

"Where's Ila?" Margo asked.

"She left," Rick said. "Pass the potatoes, Gamma."

"Want some hellfire sauce?" Gamma asked to the room at large.

"No!" everyone chorused.

"Why did Ila leave?" Margo asked, taking the hellfire sauce off the table.

"She and Cordy had a fight," Rick supplied.

"Ila's seeing Cordy?"

"Not anymore. Their fight was as interesting as a thunderstorm."

"They'll get back together," Gamma predicted. "Ila's in love with him, she just doesn't know it yet."

"Gamma claims to be psychic," Kimber explained to Mariah.

"No claiming to it. I am psychic. Didn't I predict there was a new woman coming into Joe's life? Who knew it was gonna be Dutch's little Flaxey."

Flaxey.

It felt strange that these people knew more about her father than she did. Knew that he'd called her Flaxey.

Then Gamma was off, talking about Dutch and how much she missed him, and the rest of the family was soon chiming in. She knew they were trying to make her feel welcome, but hearing all these things she never knew about her father only made her feel more distant from him than ever.

But she smiled and ate turkey and pretended to fit in, and all she could feel was the fear that none of this wonderful life, this wonderful family could be real.

CHAPTER EIGHTEEN

A cutter's gotta do what a cutter's gotta do.
—Dutch Callahan

The futurity took up all of Joe's time, and while he wanted to be with Mariah, planning Prissy and Paul's wedding took up all her time. In spite of Joe being distracted by Mariah, Dutch's horse was smoking the competition, winning event after event. Joe was more certain than ever that the stallion *was* going to take the Triple Crown Futurity. The only other horse and rider who came close were Lee Turpin and his horse Dancer.

He wished Mariah didn't have to work so hard. That she could be there to watch him. To see her father's horse excel time and time again. She'd promised to go to the remaining events after the wedding was over. Part of him hated being away from her for so much time, but another part of him was relieved. It gave him some cooling-off time. He'd been rattled by his growing feelings ever since they'd watched *Sleepless in Seattle*.

He was falling in love with her, but he still had the fear that it was simply because she reminded him of Becca. Especially after she'd confessed to him that she wore a mask whenever she was around people, doing whatever it took to fit in. Was she just trying to fit in here in Jubilee? Or did her heart really belong in Chicago? He didn't want her to settle for anything less than what she truly deserved.

In the end, he decided to put it out of his mind and just ride Miracle to the win. Once the Triple Crown Futurity was behind him, once the wedding was behind Mariah, they'd both have a chance to examine things more closely and see if they truly had what it took to make their relationship work.

On the day of Prissy and Paul's wedding, Mariah was surprised by how calm she felt. She'd never been this calm about a wedding, but everything seemed to fall into place.

Thanks to Joe, his hands, and the Jubilee Cutters Co-op, the chapel was finished on time and looked resplendent in simple elegance with a cowboy stained-glass window. The barn had been converted into a reception hall large enough to hold two hundred guests comfortably.

Nothing went missing. No one was late. The crowd was jovial. The weather was perfect. The bride glowed in her Western-cut bridal gown and cowgirl boots. The groom showed off in his Texas tuxedo (tuxedo jacket with tails and new black jeans with razor sharp creases down the legs). Pastor Penney performed a traditional ceremony.

The decorations were understated but stylish. The bride's and groom's cakes, made by Lissette Moncrief, were intricately beautiful. Prissy's colorful wildflower bouquet carried out the inexpensive but tasteful cowboy theme. The Mesquite Spit catered the barbecue meal.

After the ceremony was over and the reception was in full swing, and everyone was dancing to "Cotton-Eyed Joe," a well-dressed older woman came up to Mariah. Mariah knew the woman had money. She'd learned to spot wealth a long time ago.

"Hello, I'm Grace Bettingfield, Paul's aunt from Chicago. I understand you're from Chicago as well."

"Yes," Mariah said, and shook her hand. "I'm pleased to meet you."

"Well, I simply have to tell you that I never imagined it was possible."

"What's that?"

"An elegant cowboy wedding. When my sister told me that the reception was being held in a horse barn . . ." She paused. "Well, you can imagine my dismay. I thought, *Shades of* Green Acres. *What is my nephew marrying into?*"

"There is a bit of a culture difference from Chicago to Jubilee," Mariah admitted.

"But this . . ." The woman swept a hand at the reception hall. "It's beautiful. Even if they do insist on playing that music."

"They're having fun," Mariah pointed out. "Cotton-Eyed Joe" was as obligatory at a cowboy wedding reception as "Y.M.C.A." was to an L.A. bash. "Wait until they do the hokey-pokey."

The aunt groaned good-naturedly. "Thank you for making this experience memorable in a good way."

"It was my pleasure."

"Where did you learn to put on such a well-oiled affair?"

"I used to work for Elegant Weddings in down-town Chicago."

"You worked for Destiny Simon?" Grace Betting-field sounded awed.

"I did. Do you know her?"

"I am acquainted with Destiny, and I must say she's been having some business trouble lately. Now I wonder if it's because her right-hand woman was wooed to Texas."

"I never said I was her right-hand woman."

"You didn't have to." Grace winked. "It's obvious. Do you have a card?"

Mariah pulled one of the cards she'd had printed up from her pocket and passed it to Grace. It would have been human nature to gloat at the news that things weren't all peaches and sunshine for Destiny, but instead, Mariah found herself feeling sorry for her old boss. She was just happy that everything had turned out well for Prissy and Paul.

Grace Bettingfield wasn't the only one to pay com-pliments on the wedding. By the end of the night, more than a dozen people had asked for her business card. Satisfaction over a job well done settled in her stomach along with the Texas-grown sparkling wine that had turned out to be as tasty as champagne—and a whole lot cheaper. She didn't for one second regret following her own dream instead of Dutch's and turning the place into a wedding venue instead of an equine facility.

Ah, Joe. Just thinking of him made her smile.

When had Joe become such a bright spot in her life? Every time he walked into a room, her gaze went straight to him. When he smiled at her, Mariah's heart skipped. Whenever she was alone in bed, she'd reach across to the cool, empty spot beside her and imagine him in it.

Joe Daniels had slipped under her skin in a way she'd never thought possible. She'd tried not to fall in love with him because she knew he was still holding on to Becca. Knew also that they didn't have much in common beyond chemistry.

Joe.

The bride and groom had ridden away on the groom's cutting horse and most of the guests had already gone, but here was Joe, helping out. He grabbed hold of a big plastic trash bucket and was busy busing tables.

She kicked off her high heels and padded over in bare feet. "You don't have to do this."

"And leave the whole thing to you? No way."

"I'm a businesswoman, I can handle it."

Joe surveyed the mess. "It'll take you until three in the morning by yourself."

"It's my job, it's what I get paid for."

"There's that independent streak again. Do I have to give you another lecture on the virtues of accepting help? Just say, 'Thank you, Joe.'"

She smiled. "Thank you, Joe."

"You're welcome, Little Bit."

She grabbed a plastic tub for the dishes and started loading them up. The barn door opened, and Ila and Cordy wandered in.

"Are they back together?" she murmured to Joe.

"Yep. Ila and I had a long talk. We got some things straightened between us. She decided to stop overlooking Cordy because he's not as tall as she is, and Cordy's so crazy for her he can forgive her anything."

"Hi guys," she called out to them. "What's up?"

"We came to help," Ila said.

Now that surprised her.

"Say, 'Thank you, Ila,'" Joe whispered.

Mariah grinned. "Thank you, Ila and Cordy. I do appreciate the help."

"See there," Joe said. "You're getting the hang of this. Before you know it, you'll be one of the gang."

One of the gang. It had a nice ring to it, but she was still afraid to get too invested in that thought. She'd turned the place into a wedding chapel because she needed money, and planning weddings was the only skill she possessed. It wasn't the way she'd imagined her life going, but she had to admit, she loved being in charge. Loved running her own wedding planning business rather than working for someone else. All those years she'd worked for Destiny Simon, never daring to dream that one day she could be just as successful if she found her own milieu.

Was Jubilee her milieu?

She looked around. She hadn't wanted it to be her milieu. Not when she'd first arrived. She'd been resistant to the cowboy way of life. In her mind, the cowboy lifestyle had stolen her father from her. But there was something to be said for living close to land, for taking pride in the small things, for not showing off, for appreciating what you had.

Ila and Cordy worked together like they'd been training for an Olympic event. They were so much in unison, a true team. Watching them together, anyone would think they'd been a couple for years.

She wished she and Joe were more like that. More in sync instead of still feeling each other out.

"They're good together, huh?" Joe said, coming over to slide his arm around her shoulder.

"They are."

"I'm happy for them. Ila's the best and Cordy's a great guy."

"Ila wasn't too taken with me in the beginning."

"But she accepts you now, and that's a big step in my book. Ila doesn't let you into her inner circle unless she trusts you with her life."

"I'm not in her inner circle."

"She's here, isn't she? You gotta remember that people in small towns can get stuck in a rut. Sometimes we need an infusion of new blood to blow us out of our comfort zone."

"And here I thought everyone believed I was the Unabomber."

"A few people did." He grinned. "Cooter Johnston, for instance. But then he's a conspiracy theorist and paranoid to the bone. 'Course, getting hit by lightning three times might have something to do with it."

"He's been hit by lightning three times?"

"He golfs in the rain."

"I can see why he might be paranoid. Maybe someone *is* out to get him."

Joe laughed, and Mariah realized that, oddly enough, she was having fun.

In less than an hour, Joe, Ila, Cordy, and Mariah had cleaned up the barn. It would have taken her three times longer on her own. Maybe Joe was right. Maybe asking for help wasn't such a bad thing. A warm, sentimental feeling crept up on her.

"Night." Cordy tipped his hat as he and Ila made for the exit.

"Good night, Ila, Cordy. Thank you so much."

"You'd do the same for us," Ila said.

And that's when Mariah realized it was absolutely true.

Joe turned out the lights in the barn, took Mariah's hand, and led her out into the silvery moonlight. "You're done with the wedding planning for now."

"Yes," she said, "but I received a handful of business cards. Hopefully, there are more weddings in my future." She pulled other people's business cards from her pocket, fanned them out in front of him.

"Put those away for now. I want your complete attention."

"Yes, sir." She stuffed the cards back into her pocket.

He took both of her hands in his. "We've both been so busy we haven't had a chance to talk since Thanksgiving."

Her heart fluttered. Finally. They were going to talk. Thank heavens she'd been so busy she'd had no time to dwell on his silence. He'd been just as busy. She knew how much the futurity meant to him so she hadn't said anything either.

"Tomorrow is Sunday, you don't have to work at the Silver Horseshoe."

"No," she agreed.

"And I have a day off from the futurity."

"Oh?"

"Imagine that," he said, drawing her closer to him. "We both have a day off at the same time."

"Imagine that," she echoed.

"I was hoping, if you weren't too tired from the wedding planning, that maybe we could pick up where we left off after the rainstorm."

"Oh, were you?"

"Yes." He smiled, dipped his head. "I was."

She tilted her face up to accept his kiss. "I think that's an excellent idea."

Then she took him by the hand and led him to her cabin.

Once inside the house, once inside the circle of Joe's arms, Mariah grew nervous. She was afraid of losing this precious moment, of never getting it back again. She wanted so much to hope for happily-ever-after but she was afraid to believe in it.

She couldn't wait for him to kiss her. To do more than kiss her. The somnolent way he looked at her, the way his fingers moved up her arm felt so intimate. He dipped his head.

The floorboards creaked under their feet.

Mariah's breath hung in her lungs.

He brushed his lips over hers, soft as a sigh. His fingers played up the back of her neck, angling her head, raising her face up so he could extend the kiss.

She was falling, deep into an endless sea of sensation.

His dark eyes ensnared hers. She leaned into him. She'd been hungering for this—*for him*—for weeks.

He kissed her for what could have been hours or minutes. The experience was that riveting. His mouth took her higher and hotter until nothing mattered but the two of them. All doubt evaporated. Nothing had ever felt so right, so perfect.

Joe scooped her into his arms and she wrapped her hands around his neck, holding on tight. His grip was strong, his muscles bunched around her body. His warm breath feathered the fine hairs at her temple.

He pressed his lips to her cheek. It felt nice. Sweet. Like a gentle wind on a hot summer day.

Sexual desire hummed across her nerve endings,

heating her body from top to bottom. He laid her gently on the bed, stepped back, and gazed down at her, his eyes shimmering in the moonlight slanting through the crack in the curtains.

Mariah's throat tightened at his expression. He looked at her as if she was the most beautiful thing he'd ever seen. She felt wanted, cherished. Tears pushed at the backs of her eyelids.

"Make love to me, Joe," she whispered.

"Are you sure?" he asked. "Is this what you really want? Once we make love, there's no going back."

"I've never been more certain of anything in my life."

"Me either." He breathed.

He sank down on the bed beside her, his hand reaching for the zipper at the side of her dress. Slowly, he tugged the zipper down. His knuckles rubbed against her skin bared by the parting teeth. He leaned over and, with lips hotter than a branding iron, kissed the fluttering pulse in the hollow of her throat.

He stretched out beside her, all shirt and skin, man and heat, smelling of leather and spicy cologne and pure essence of Joe. He tasted of wedding cake and champagne. Promise. He tasted of promise.

His mouth explored her neck, finding all kinds of spots to lick and nuzzle until he had her squirming, then he pulled back and lay on his side beside her, stacking his palms under his chin while he studied her in the darkness.

She stared back. Mesmerized.

"Wh-why did you stop?"

"I want to take my time. Enjoy this. Enjoy you."

They spent the next several minutes undressing each other. Taking their time, never rushing. Once they were completely naked and he'd put on a condom, he trailed an incredibly light caress over her collarbone. "You are so perfect."

Mariah trembled.

He kissed her breasts, the flat of her belly. Used his hand to excite her nipples, send her blood thrusting through her veins.

"Joe . . ." She whispered his name on a sigh. He made her feel so good. No, good didn't begin to describe it. Nor did any of the other superlatives that sprang to mind. It was beyond great, super, terrific, awesome . . .

Okay, she had one. *Splendid*. Being with him felt splendid.

His masculine scent surrounded her. His eyes darkened. His hand tightened around her wrist.

Her body burned from her heart to her stomach straight down to her sex. Burned and ached and craved.

His mouth claimed hers again.

All her senses were altered—sound, sight, taste, smell, touch. She existed in an uncharted but delicious land. She was total awareness. Barbed strands of fevered sensation pricked her.

He whispered her name, and his beautiful hands were busy making her feel alive in a hundred different ways. Frenzy fired every nerve ending.

"What do you want? What can I do for you?" she asked.

"You're doing it."

"No, really. Do you like it when I touch you here?"

He groaned. "Yeah. I like that."

"How about this?"

"You don't have to work so hard. I'm pretty easy to please."

"It's just that . . . well . . . I want to do this right."

"Honey, you can't go wrong when you put your hand *there*."

She laughed, but that didn't stop the insecurity. It had been a very long time since she'd been with a man and she'd never been with one who made her feel like this. Part of her wanted to pull on her clothes and rush away until she could figure out what all this meant, if, indeed, it meant anything more than sex.

It does and you know it.

That's what had her so nervous. This meant something. Did she really want to take the plunge? Yes, her body wanted him, but was she ready?

Mariah touched the tip of her tongue to her upper lip and thought about where they were. In the cabin that had belonged to her father. With a new roof put on by the Jubilee Co-op. The small, cozy room felt like a cocoon. A cocoon where she didn't really belong.

"Hey." Joe rubbed a palm up her arm to her shoulder. "What's wrong?"

"Nothing's wrong."

"You're tensing up."

She shrugged.

"Talk to me."

"Nothing's wrong, it's just that . . ."

He waited. When she didn't continue, he whispered, "Let go." His breath was a warm brush against her ear. "Let down your guard. Drop the mask. You don't have to pretend with me. Be you, Mariah. One hundred percent."

That startled her. Both because he'd read her mind

and because he was right. She was still trying to fit in. If you spent your life being a chameleon, how did you know what was really you and what was merely the milieu you'd adapted to?

"What are you so afraid of?" He tickled her belly with his fingertips.

"I'm afraid . . ."

"Yes?"

"That I'm simply trying to be what you want me to be."

"And what is that?"

She waved her hand at the room around them. "A cowgirl. Dutch's daughter." *Your late wife.* "I'm afraid that if you knew the real me you wouldn't want me anymore."

"You underestimate me and your own appeal. You let me see your naked body, now let me see your naked mind."

Mariah drew in a deep breath. "I'm scared."

Joe intertwined his fingers with hers. "I've got your back . . . and your front." Then he grinned, pressed his lips to her belly, and blew a raspberry against her skin.

Mariah giggled and Joe kissed her again. Then under his tender, thrusting strokes, her body eclipsed her brain, she forgot her anxiety, and simply let go.

"I never expect . . . well, I knew you'd be . . . but wow . . . never this," Mariah said after they made love a second time.

"Never what?" Joe asked, lazily toying with her nipple.

She shivered, curled against him. "I never expected you to be so incredible."

He chuckled.

"What's so funny?"

"You. You're so earnest."

"What's wrong with that?"

"Nothing's wrong with that. It's just you leave yourself open to a lot of hurt."

She pulled back, looked up into his face. "What do you mean by that?"

"Some things aren't meant to be taken seriously."

"Like Slinkys and Silly Putty."

"Yeah."

"Like unicorns and rainbows."

"Pretty much."

"As if this thing is going anywhere beyond a quick roll in the hay?"

"I didn't say that." His voice deepened and his eyes darkened.

"You didn't have to. I know this is hard for you."

"What do you mean? Being with you is easy."

"I meant . . . Becca."

"Oh." He was silent a long time.

Why had she brought up his wife? What was wrong with her? Things had been going so well and here she'd brought up his dead wife.

"I am . . ." He cleared his throat. "Was something of a mess."

"I know that too. On my first day here, I found you drunk and naked in a horse trough."

"I wasn't naked."

"Almost."

He smiled lightly. Kissed her forehead. "Mariah, I want to offer you the moon and the stars."

"But you've been there before and you've realized the moon and stars aren't yours to give."

"Something like that," he acknowledged. "Right now, I'm just living in the moment. It's all any of us really have."

"That's okay." She snuggled closer. "I don't need the moon and the stars."

"You're not like Annie in *Sleepless in Seattle*? Looking for magic?"

She shrugged, not sure what to say. "I suppose a lot of women are looking for magic. Most of them settle for far less."

"Don't settle, Mariah. You deserve to have your dreams come true."

"So do you," she whispered.

"I'm close," he said. "If Miracle wins the futurity, not only do my dreams come true, but so do Dutch's. He spent his life chasing this dream, only to never see it realized. Since you're staying, I'm going to use the winnings to open the equine center on another part of my land."

Ah, there was the rub. Joe could devote himself to cutting, but when it came to relationships, was he a lot like his hero Dutch? Untrustworthy. She thought of what his Gamma had told her at Thanksgiving. *Cutting, horses, his work means everything to him. If you can't share that with him the way Becca did, well . . .*

That thought squeezed her heart. She couldn't be falling in love with a man who was just like her father. A man who would inevitably put horses before his family.

"My father's dream lives on," she whispered, not knowing what else to say. "Through you. I'm sure he thought of you as a son."

"Does that bother you?"

"Some," she admitted. "It hurts that you knew my father better than I did. I don't want to be like my mother, pining for a guy who was too in love with horses to pay much attention to her. It's better to never have loved than to be so strung up by it that you can't see reality."

"Reality is overrated."

"Says the man who's never had to live in it. You were raised in a loving family. You got to follow your dreams. You had life handed to you on a silver platter."

"Until Becca died." The teasing look vanished from his gaze.

Mariah didn't rush to fill the silence because she didn't know what to say to make things right again.

He bent his head to kiss her, but she could tell things were different. His muscles were tense, his eyes muted. "Mariah," he started, "I don't mean to make you feel—" He broke off, cleared his throat.

"It's fine." She held up a palm. She didn't want to hear any more. "I get it. Live in the moment. Be free. No expectations."

"That's not . . . you're okay with that? It's what you want for now?"

"Sure," she lied, slipping the mask back into place. "In fact, that's how I prefer to keep things. Light and easy. No commitments, no promises, no expectations."

She told him what she thought he wanted to hear. It was all right. They'd had a good time. She was cool as ice. Chameleons were adaptable that way. Then she wrapped her arms around his neck and pulled him to her, kissed him until she forgot once more who she was and what she really wanted.

CHAPTER NINETEEN

Old cutters never die, they just join the riders in the sky.

—Dutch Callahan

Joe lay in the darkness listening to Mariah breathe, his heart filled with a dozen different emotions. He was so lucky to be with her. So happy. He wanted to tell her what he was feeling. Wanted to let her know how much he loved her. He'd done his best to show her, but in the end, that hadn't been enough. He needed to say the words.

He'd been about to tell her that he loved her when his throat had seized up. He wanted to say the words so badly, but all he could think was *If I tell her I love her, if I admit it out loud, I could lose her the way I lost Becca.*

Rationally, he knew that saying he loved her wouldn't jinx her to an early death, but his battered, old, superstitious heart needed a running start. He'd cleared his throat, working up the courage to say what was on his mind, when she'd told him she preferred to keep things light and casual.

A kick to the gut.

She wasn't as invested in him as he was in her.

It hurt. That realization. So he closed his mouth, folded up his feelings, and kissed her right back. There was no rush. He could take things slow. Spend his time and win her over fully. Once her wedding planning business really took off and she could see herself carving out a forever life in Jubilee, then he'd tell her how he felt.

But for now? It was best to turn off his mind, bury his feelings, and the only way he knew how to do that was to focus on cutting. Miracle had saved his sanity once. Now, he had to trust that the horse could save his new love.

In the meantime, he'd do his damnedest to please her.

Sometime later, Joe and Mariah were pulled from their dreamy tangle of arms and legs by the shrieking wail of sirens and the acrid smell of smoke.

Dazed, Joe sat up, his hair falling into his face.

"What is it?" Mariah whispered.

"Fire," he said, springing from the bed. "Somewhere close by."

"The chapel!" she exclaimed.

They scrambled for their clothes, shimmying into jeans, pulling on shirts, jamming feet into boots. Within seconds, rumpled and bleary-eyed, they were tumbling out into the heaviness of predawn.

Layers of smoke clouded the sky. The sirens shrieked closer. They raced toward the chapel that butted up against the back of Joe's property. Only a thick growth of underbrush and cedar trees separated his barn and corral from the chapel. But the chapel wasn't on fire.

They spun on their heels. The wind carried a sharp crackling noise along with the smoldering scent of singed cedar. Just above the tree line, in the direction of Joe's house, deadly fingers of flames grasped for the sky.

In one dark breath, they both said, "Green Ridge."

They moved like one person, one mind, going for Joe's truck parked at the side of her cabin. Once they were inside, seat belts on, Joe revved the engine, spun the truck around, then reached out with his right hand and took Mariah's left. She squeezed it. Giving him comfort. Letting him know that he wasn't alone. She was here with him.

The sound of sirens screamed, almost upon them.

Mariah hissed in her breath and prayed hard. Every part of her body tensed. The sweet euphoria of lovemaking that she and Joe had shared vanished into the dark night.

The closer they got, the thicker the smoke grew and the brighter the flames danced. Fear twined tight around Mariah's heart. Two fire trucks and an ambulance sprinted up the road at the same time Joe's King Ranch bounced around the corner of the pasture. A sheriff's cruiser was already parked in front of the house.

"It's the barn!" she gasped. "And the fire is out of control, headed for the cedar break."

"Miracle," Joe said, his voice coming out in a barely audible gasp.

Mariah's heart stopped.

Joe couldn't believe his barn was on fire. Couldn't comprehend that his horses' lives were in danger and the rampaging fire was moving fast through the cedar breaks headed straight for Mariah's chapel. Couldn't even begin to accept that something tragic could have happened to Miracle.

He didn't remember stopping the truck or getting out. He could barely see. Smoke stung his eyes. Dazed, he started running toward the barn. He might have run right *into* the barn if Ila hadn't suddenly appeared from the smoke, a bandana over her nose and mouth.

She raised a hand, planted it on his chest. "Joe! Stop!"

Then he felt Mariah's fingers go through his belt loop as she tried to tug him backward.

Ila's eyes were somber and red-rimmed. Soot streaked her cheek.

A horse whinnied. Miracle? Joe jerked his head around. Saw instead Clover's mare Juliet tied to the hitching post in front of his house. What was Clover's horse doing here?

Clover often took predawn shortcuts through his ranch when she was making the rounds on her co-op duties. Had she been the first to see the fire? Had she sounded the alarm? Had she—

His stomach churned and his thoughts fractured as through the smoke he saw a fireman performing CPR on a prone form.

Jesus, was it Clover?

He plowed a hand through his hair, shifted his gaze back to Ila. Her expression was grim. He felt the tight pressure of Mariah's hands on him. No, no. This had to be a nightmare. This couldn't be happening. To lose Becca and Dutch and now Clover within the short span of two years. No. This was not happening. He had to wake up. He was going to wake up.

But the heat and the noise and the choking smoke

invading his lungs told him this was no nightmare he could shake off.

A battalion of firefighters ran to and fro, dragging a tangle of equipment. His ranch hands were in the mix, grabbing for fleeing horses. The lights from the rescue vehicles dimmed in the oblivious sunrise. Emergency medical technicians carrying a stretcher hustled toward the body on the ground.

"Clover?" he yelled over the noise and chaos.

Tears misted Ila's eyes and she shook her head.

Joe's whole body sagged. "Is she . . . ?"

"It's bad," Ila said.

"And Miracle?"

"The barn's empty. It looks like Clover saw the fire, came over to get your horses out, and in the process, she was . . . overcome." Ila's voice cracked. She liked to play tough, but Joe knew what a soft touch she really was. This was ripping her apart.

Fear and remorse kicked up a tornado in Joe's gut. He should have been home. If he'd been home, none of this would have happened. Instead, he'd been with Mariah having sex. Clover might die and Miracle was missing because of his damn lust.

He didn't even realize he'd let out a cry of anger and anguish until Ila put a hand on his shoulder. "Don't go to pieces on me, Joe, not now. Just let the professionals do their job."

Dumbstruck, he watched them load Clover's motionless body into the ambulance. His ranch hands coughed through the smoke, leading horses to safety. He searched each animal that passed, looking for Miracle. Each time he was disappointed. If Ila and Mariah hadn't been hanging on to him, he would have rushed into the burning barn.

Meanwhile, the blaze had reached the cedar breaks. The firefighters were focused on controlling the barn fire and keeping the blaze from getting to his house. They were undermanned and outgunned. The fire leaped to the tips of the cedars, rolling at a furious rampage toward Mariah's wedding chapel.

Mariah's fingers bit into his upper arm and he knew she'd realized it as soon as he did. There would be no saving the chapel, even as extra fire trucks from the neighboring county came screaming onto the property.

Joe stood there hung on the horns of helplessness, watching everything he loved slip through his fingers.

"Miracle could be at my barn," Mariah whispered. "Maybe somehow he survived, and ran to the place he felt safest. C'mon, I'll drive."

In a daze, he followed her to the truck, his heart a hard knot in his chest. He couldn't believe how calm she was. So cool and in control. Becca, the drama queen, would have flipped out. But here was Mariah, sliding behind the wheel, slipping her seat belt on. Calm did not mean she was without emotion. When she turned to glance at him, the look in her eyes was one of abject sorrow and deep empathy, but quickly she hardened her chin and the expression disappeared. She wheeled the pickup in a U-turn, zigzagging around the emergency vehicles, and started up the dirt road to her cabin.

Fire trucks lined the area from the cedar breaks to Mariah's cabin. The firefighters had soaked the ground around the cabin and the barn to keep the blaze at bay from those structures and they were valiantly shooting water at the fire crisping through the cedars, but there was no saving the chapel. Its proximity to the trees precluded all hope of salvation.

Mariah skirted around the fire engines and pulled up beside the barn. Simultaneously, they got out and turned to watch the fire swallow the chapel they'd worked so hard to build. Joe came around the side of the truck, pulled her against his chest. "I'm so sorry, Little Bit."

Her body was tense, rigid. "No matter," she said. "What's done is done. The chapel is gone, but that doesn't mean we can't pray for a miracle."

They found Miracle pacing inside the barn that Mariah had turned into a reception hall. The horse had knocked over tables. Chewed on the bandstand. Left horseshoe prints on the floor.

Unbridled joy filled Joe and he ran to the stallion. Miracle was alive! Exuberant as a kid, he threw his arms around the horse's neck. Miracle nickered a greeting. Joe glanced over and saw tears misting the corners of Mariah's eyes.

"It is truly a miracle," she whispered. "Dutch was looking out for him."

"And Clover," Joe added.

At the mention of Clover's name, a dark pall dissolved their elation.

"Well, I'll be damned," Cordy said from the doorway. "He's alive."

"Thanks to Clover."

Silence fell.

"All the rest of the horses are accounted for. The co-op started showing up and we loaded them up in trailers. Various people have offered to take them until this all settles down," Cordy said.

Joe nodded, clasped Cordy on the shoulder. "Thank you."

"I'll look after Miracle," Cordy offered, "if you want to go on to the hospital to check on Clover."

"Aren't you going?" Joe asked, not really wanting to leave Miracle, but anxious to go see about the dear woman who'd put her life on the line to save his horses.

"Not until Ila can cut loose and go with me."

"Okay," he said reluctantly. "Thanks."

Joe reached out, took Mariah's hand, and guided her back to his pickup truck. The sun was fully up now, casting a hard yellow glow over the smoldering chapel. The grass around the cedar breaks was charred and mini fires still burned, but it was under control now. Safe enough to leave the protection of the cabin in the capable hands of the Jubilee Fire Department and the county volunteers.

They didn't talk on the way to the hospital, just held hands, their fingers fiercely joined.

The small ER waiting room at Jubilee General was packed with cutters. They muttered greetings clapped one another on the shoulder, but mostly they were silent, sitting glumly, waiting for news of one of their own. Mariah guided Joe to an empty chair in the corner. Her strength and courage amazed him. When this was over, he was going to tell her what he should have told her last night. He loved her. Completely and unequivocally.

Thirty minutes later, a doctor came into the waiting room. "Who is with Mrs. Dempsey?"

"We all are," Austin Flats said.

"Who's her closet relative?"

"She didn't have any kin left." Art Bunting got on his feet. "We're it."

The doctor took a deep breath. The wary flick in his eyes slammed a fist of fear into Joe's gut, and he knew what the doctor was going to say before the words left the man's mouth. "I'm very sorry to have to inform you that Mrs. Dempsey didn't make it."

"What?" Lissette Moncrief stood, wrapped an arm around her pregnant belly.

Nancy Hickok blinked, put a hand to her chest. "Are you saying Clover's dead?"

"I'm afraid so."

"What did she die of?" Joe asked.

"She suffered a massive myocardial infarction, probably brought on by the stress and exertion."

Guilt robbed Joe of speech. It still wasn't real. Clover was gone?

"No," Bobby Jim Spears denied. "Not possible. We were going to the final day of the Triple Crown Futurity on Saturday. Clover is riding the flag into the ring for the opening event."

The people in the room took a collective breath. A few burst into audible sobs. Lissette's knees buckled, and Austin Flats reached out to guide her back down to a chair.

Someone murmured, "She finally gets to see Carl again. If there was ever anyone in love, it was those two."

Joe sat numb. Mariah reached up to put an arm around his shoulder. He looked over at her, saw tears streaming down her face.

"Oh, Joe," she whispered.

He pulled her into his arms and held on to her for dear life.

The pneumatic door opened and everyone turned

to see who was coming into the ER waiting room.

It was Ila. She took one look at everyone and started shaking her head.

"Clover's dead," someone told her.

Ila's jaw hardened and her eyes turned to flint. "Then someone is sure as hell going to jail for manslaughter. Fire chief's been out. The blaze in Joe's barn looks like arson."

They buried Clover on Thursday.

The following morning, the day before the final futurity event, Ila and the fire chief arrested Lee Turpin for setting the fire to Joe's barn that had also burned down Mariah's wedding chapel. Official manslaughter charges were pending the autopsy results. Turpin confessed, breaking down in tears and admitting he'd been trying to harm Miracle so Joe wouldn't beat him out of the Triple Crown Futurity, but swearing he never meant to hurt Clover.

Mariah had been so wrapped up in mourning her boss and comforting Joe that she hadn't had time to fully process losing the wedding chapel. It seemed fate was mocking the fresh start she'd made, but the burning of the wedding chapel had simply been collateral damage that had nothing to do with her. It was bad luck. Not fate. She could start again. Still, in her current state of mind, the task felt daunting.

Immediately after the funeral, they held a wake at the Silver Horseshoe—Clover had left the place to her bartender Bobby Jim Spears—and all the drinks were on the house. Ila arranged for designated drivers to take the mourners home.

They were telling stories and toasting Clover

when Mariah's cell phone rang. It made her think about how another phone call, another death had brought her to Jubilee two and a half months earlier. Not so long ago the cutters had gathered in the exact same way to mourn her father and she'd missed out on all of it. He'd wanted her left out of his life, even at the end of it. She couldn't deny how much that hurt, no matter how hard she tried to pretend that it didn't.

"I'll be right back," she whispered to Joe, and stepped into the back room to take the call. She'd been expecting a call from her mother. The paneled office made her think of Clover. She blinked, unable to see the caller ID through a mist of tears. "Hello?"

"Mariah?" said the woman on the other end.

It wasn't her mother. "Yes?"

"This is Destiny . . . Destiny Simon."

"Um . . . hello." Mariah's stomach constricted. What did the woman want from her?

"Hi, how are you?" Destiny asked as if they were the best of friends. As if she hadn't fired Mariah for defending herself against sexual assault.

But then that was Destiny. Always going where opportunity existed. Never much caring whom she hurt on her way up the ladder. She'd given Mariah her start, but Mariah's fallacy had been in modeling herself after a woman who stood for nothing beyond the glossy image. Being in Jubilee, becoming part of the cutter community had taught Mariah what she truly valued, and that wasn't success at any price.

"I'm fine, Destiny, how are you?"

"I heard from Grace Bettingfield that you started your own wedding planning business."

Here it comes. She's going to accuse me of some-how stealing her techniques or something. It was precisely what Mariah would have expected from her ex-employer. "I did."

"In fact," Destiny said, "Grace said you're a stunning success."

"I wouldn't say stunning. Not in your terms."

A long silence stretched over the phone. Mariah toyed with the idea of just hanging up. But something—maybe it was that burned-down chapel—kept her hanging on.

Destiny cleared her throat. "Look, I'm going to lay my cards on the table."

"Please do."

"I made a big mistake."

"Thank you for having the courage to tell me that."

"I want you back. You're irreplaceable."

"Excuse me?"

"You heard me. Don't make me beg. I haven't been able to find anyone of your caliber since you left. No one works like you do. No one had your innate talent for staging. No one understands how important image is—"

"That's because image isn't all that important. Not really. Not when it counts. What counts are people you can count on to have your back."

"Is that a dig?"

"Not at all. I've just learned a few things since I've been in Jubilee. Things like honor and loyalty and trust."

"Okay, I'll admit, I was wrong to let you go. I know Mayor Krumpholder is a sexist pig. I should have backed you up."

It did feel good to hear Destiny admit she was wrong. "Let me ask you a question."

"All right."

"Would you be making this call if Grace Bettingfield hadn't been singing my praises?"

Destiny hesitated.

"That's what I thought. Good-bye."

"Wait. Listen. Don't hang up."

Mariah didn't hang up. She didn't know why she didn't hang up. Maybe it was the small part of her that still chafed over having been fired in such a dramatic way. Or maybe it was the fact she still wasn't certain what was going to happen between her and Joe. "What is it, Destiny?"

"What are you bringing in on those cowboy weddings? It can't be anything like what you were pulling down here."

"It's not, but you know what? I have peace of mind now that I didn't have back then."

"But you can't truly be happy. Not in that backwater town. You're a big-city woman. You thrive on pressure and being at the top of your game. I know you, Mariah Callahan. You're just like me."

Once upon a time, that might have been true, but she'd changed a lot in the past several weeks. "What is it you want?"

"Come back to work for me. I'll double your salary."

Mariah paused. If Destiny doubled her previous salary, she'd be pulling down over a hundred grand a year. But that was for an eighty-hour workweek. No private life. No Joe. No Jubilee. No community of co-op members ready to pitch in when you got in a pinch.

"I don't think so," she said.

"Triple it then. I need you back." Destiny sounded desperate. She must be desperate to offer Mariah triple her salary.

Mariah sucked in a deep breath. "Let me get this straight. You're offering me three times my old salary to come back to Chicago?"

"I've already sent you a contract. I got your address from Grace Bettingfield. It should be in your mailbox. Please, before you say no, just think about it. Everything you ever dreamed of is within your reach."

After Clover's wake, Joe and Mariah returned to the cabin. All his horses were now being stabled in her barn. So much for her reception hall. But she no longer had a wedding chapel. Her budding business had been wiped out. She started to feel a bit sorry for herself, but immediately squelched the thought. Clover had lost her life. Next to that, a business was inconsequential. But after Destiny's call, she couldn't help feeling that she was at a new crossroads.

What did the future hold?

"C'mere," Joe said, and held out his arms to her.

She went to him and he wrapped her in a comforting embrace. She rested her head against his shoulder, the crisp material of his funeral suit stiff against her cheek.

"Clover is in a better place," he whispered. "She's getting to see Dutch again and she's reunited with her Carl. She loved him so much. I got the impression she was just marking time until she could join him."

Tears leaked from Mariah's eyes. "Oh, Joe."

He tightened his grip around her. Held her tight. Held her close. "Mariah," he whispered.

She was the one who started the kissing. Going up on her toes, planting her lips against his throat, her fingers working the knot of his tie. "Joe."

When she reached his chin, he lowered his head to give her easier access to his mouth. His arms tightened and he pulled her up hard against him, his tongue slipping softly between her teeth.

They kissed for what seemed like hours, slow, languid kisses, designed to comfort, not inflame. But the taste of him, the heat of his body, the sound of his breathing in her ears revved her up anyway.

Desire coiled inside her, taut as a bedspring. She nibbled and sucked, kissed and licked, enjoyed his heady masculine flavor. Quickly, the hunger spread, shooting heat throughout her entire system. She had to have him or go mad. She didn't care if it was for all the wrong reasons.

Her body ached and throbbed, and only Joe could sate her. She reached up to thread her arms around his neck, shove her fingers through his hair, tug his head down farther as she intensified the kissing.

For a few minutes, he went along with it, but when she trailed a hand to his belt, tucked her fingers into his waistband, and tugged at the buckle, Joe shook his head, pulled back. "No, Mariah, no."

"Why not?" she asked in a plaintive whisper. "I want you. You want me. Let's just go for it."

"You're aching and raw. Sex isn't the answer. I just want to cuddle with you on the couch or snuggle on the bed with you. We've got plenty of time to have sex. There's no rush."

"But I need you," she insisted. "I need to feel you inside me." She reached down to touch his erection through his zipper. She could feel him growing harder. "You want me too."

"I do," he said hoarsely, "but I don't want to take advantage of our grief."

"We made love after Prissy and Paul's wedding."

"That was different. You weren't raw and vulnerable."

"Why is it so wrong to make love now?"

"You just want to feel better."

"That's true. I do."

"Sex isn't going to take away the pain."

"I know that. But I need to be close to someone. I need to feel you inside of me. Please, Joe, please."

"Oh God, Mariah."

"Please," she whimpered.

He scooped her up in his arms, carried her to her bedroom, kicked the door open with his boot, and then gently laid her out on the bed. He stepped back, looked down at her, his eyes full of sorrow and tenderness. "You are so beautiful."

She went up on her knees, reached out for him, her fingers undoing the buttons of his shirt.

"You want to make love?"

"Uh-huh."

"Fine, we'll make love." He stripped off his jacket, undid his buttons.

While he was undressing, she pulled her dress over her head, flung it over the doorknob. He made a noise, half pleasure, half pain, and joined her on the bed.

They finished undressing each other. Slowly, sweetly. Then when they were completely naked, Joe pressed her down into the mattress covered by a quilt Clover had given her. He dropped kisses all over her face. She wrapped her arms around his waist, pulling him close to her. His hard shaft rested against her thigh. He looked down at her with gentle eyes.

"Sweetheart," he murmured, "this isn't going to bring any of them back."

"I know, but maybe, just maybe it will bring *me* back."

Those must have been the magic words he was hoping to hear, because he groaned and slowly entered her.

She was hot and slick for him, hungry for his body. She spread her legs wider. He eased in deep. She whispered his name. He whispered hers right back.

Their previous joining had been playful, joyous. They'd enjoyed themselves. This lovemaking was not joyful. It was not playful. It was somber and heavy, but laden with a meaning far deeper than sexual enjoyment. In this joining, a spiritual component locked them together. This was conviction. An exultation of the soul.

Clover was gone, reunited with her beloved Carl at last.

Dutch was gone too.

And Becca.

But Mariah and Joe were still here. Physical beings expressing their growing sentiment for each other the only way they knew how. Through kissing, touching, holding, melding.

This merging . . . this was . . . *precious*.

It was a moment she would remember always. The soothing of grief through love, a pure emotion of two spirits joined as one.

The circumstances surrounding their lovemaking were unhappy, but she could already feel the healing. The people they'd loved were dead, but they were still alive. Alive and with each other.

There was comfort to be extracted here. Comfort and a vast understanding that love couldn't be killed. They would always love the people they'd lost, but that didn't mean they couldn't love each other as well.

Love.

She did love Joe. Had suspected she'd been in love with him for many weeks. She'd just been afraid to admit it. Consummating their passion had assured her it was true—*but this*—this grief sex cemented everything. She wanted to tell him that she loved him. Loved him so much that her heart was overflowing with it, overflowing and mingling with her sorrow, a bittersweet balm for the dark things in the world. But she was still afraid. If she said it and he didn't say it back . . . well . . . she didn't think she could stand that.

So she said nothing, but she showed him how much she loved him. She used her tongue and fingers. Her body was an instrument of everything she felt, giving him full access to her.

Then a mighty rapture rolled through their bodies. A feeling of completeness so true and real it took possession of their minds, hearts, and souls.

She and Joe were one.

CHAPTER TWENTY

Good sense comes from experience, and a lotta
that comes from actin' like a damn fool.

—Dutch Callahan

The sun spilling through the window awoke
Mariah. For one brief moment, she smiled, her
body sweetly achy from the night she'd spent
with Joe, but then she remembered. The fire. Her
chapel. Clover. Everything.

Gone.

Her smile vanished and the sorrow seeped in again.

She reached for solace, throwing her arm across
the other side of the bed in search of Joe, but found
nothing except cool, empty sheets.

And a note.

Her hand fisted around the crinkle of notebook
paper. She sat up, pushed the hair from her eyes, and
squinted in the morning light.

*Gone to Will Rogers Coliseum with Cordy and
Miracle. Sleep in. The final event isn't until
noon. See you there. Later on, we have to talk.*

We have to talk.

That sounded ominous. Joe hadn't awakened her. Hadn't taken her with him. What did that mean? Was he going to tell her things were moving too fast? And here she'd been on the verge of professing her love for him. Thank God, she'd never actually said it. All the joy she'd experienced in his arms the night before evaporated, and doubt bombarded her.

Don't freak. It's probably nothing. He wants you at the event. That's a good thing.

What if he wanted to break up?

But why? What had she done? Last night had been so special. Maybe that was it. Maybe it had been too special and *he'd* freaked. Maybe he wasn't ready for this deeper step. Well, maybe she wasn't ready for it either. If he wanted to back off, take a break, then okay. She could go back to light and easy. That's the way she'd wanted it in the first place. But then, but then . . .

She'd fallen in love.

Oh God, she was in love with him and he didn't feel the same way about her. He still loved Becca. That's what he wanted to talk to her about. To let her down easy. He must have sensed she was feeling more for him than he was feeling for her and he wanted to untangle things before they got too knotted up.

Except the leaden weight in her stomach told her it was already way too late. She was in too deep.

Chill! Don't borrow trouble. Just go to the futurity, cheer him on, and let whatever happens be okay.

Easy to say, but so damn hard to do. She wanted him so much. It was scary how much she wanted him. She'd never ever wanted a man like this. She'd finally let down her guard and now here she was, naked to the world, waiting for the smack in the face.

It might not be a smack in the face. You might get lucky like Cassie did with Ignacio.

She got out of bed filled with tremulous hope. Got dressed in the cowgirl clothes she'd grown accustomed to wearing. This morning, however, the outfit felt as alien as it had the first day she'd put it on. She had an apple for breakfast. She shrugged into a jacket, went outside, and walked over to the charred husk of the chapel. The burned-out smell of sooty destruction curled in her nose. Gone. All gone.

Honestly, there was no longer anything for her here. She'd proved she could start her own wedding planning business. If she could do it in Jubilee, she could do it anywhere. This had been a steppingstone. A learning opportunity. Maybe it wasn't meant to be anything more than that.

If Joe didn't want her—if he was still too much in love with Becca to embrace what they could have together—she could start over. Start again. Even though the very idea made her sick to her stomach.

For a long time, she stood there, thinking about Joe, thinking about her options. Thinking about what she wanted. Mostly, she didn't want to get hurt.

Too late. Too late for that.

Finally, she wandered past Joe's place, headed toward the mailbox that sat beside his at the end of the road. She'd let the mail stack up since the fire. In the box, she found the contract from Destiny. On her walk back up the road, she opened it up.

Here it was. Her ticket out.

If she wanted out. Last night she would have said wild horses couldn't have dragged her back to Chicago, but now? Worry clutched her throat.

You're being silly, borrowing trouble. Do something to keep your mind occupied until it's time to leave for the futurity.

Determined to shake off the apprehension, she went back into the cabin, tossing Destiny's contract on the kitchen table as she passed by on her way to the bathroom. She pulled her makeup kit from the drawer, took out her mascara wand, and stared at herself in the mirror. Who was she now? City girl or country woman? Cowgirl or cosmopolitan? Dutch's daughter or Destiny's employee or Joe's . . . *what?*

She stroked on too much mascara. She blinked and it smeared underneath her left eye. It gave her a battered look. She reached for a sheet of toilet paper to blot it away.

Darn it. Out of toilet paper.

Sighing, she padded to the hallway closet for a new roll. When she opened the door, Stuffy fell from the top shelf where she'd stowed him the day she'd cleaned the cabin from top to bottom, barely missing striking her shoulder.

The snake hit the ground hard and the chunk of the shellacked wood that he was mounted on cracked open. A white envelope fluttered to the floor.

A secret compartment.

She hadn't known there was a secret compartment in the base of the snake. Bending at the waist, she picked up the letter. It had her name printed on it and the address of the place where she and her mother had lived when Mariah was fourteen. In the far left corner was her father's name and address.

On the far right was an uncanceled stamp. The edges of the envelope were yellowed with age.

Forgetting all about her smeared mascara and the

toilet paper, Mariah cradled the letter to her chest. Goose bumps lifted on her arms. A message from the past. Did she have the courage to open it after all these years?

She went into the small living area, plunked down on the couch. Drawing in a fortifying breath, she gently opened the letter, unfolded it, and began to read.

Dear Flaxey,

I'm sorry I came to your school today and embarrassed you. I shouldn't have done that. I just wanted to see you real bad and didn't stop to think that maybe you didn't want to see me. It was selfish of me to just show up like that. I got what I deserved. I'm so sorry for how I left you and your mama. I got no excuses. No reasons that'll make sense to you. I do love you so much. More than you can possibly know.

But I got a sickness inside of me I can't control. It gets in my blood the way alcohol or drugs eats up some folks. Horses are my addiction. They're a habit I can't shake. I can't think of anything but being a cutter. I live it, breathe it, want it with every cell in my body. I tried so hard to be a good daddy, but I failed you. I'm obsessed with horses. Most cutters are. It's why we clump together. The only ones who understand us are other crazy cutters.

I realized I couldn't be a husband and a father and a cutter. I made a choice. I abandoned you and your mama to save you from the burden of my sickness. I've regretted that choice every

*single day of my life, but I can't say I would
have the strength of character to make a different choice if I had a do-over. Anyway, I just
wanted to see you and try to explain in person,
but I know I don't have that right. I threw it
away when I threw away my family.*

*I'll go to my grave sorry. I hope that some-
day you'll find it in your heart to forgive me.
I loved you the only way I knew how. It's not
good enough, but it's all I've got. I love you,
Flaxey girl, and if there's one word of advice I
could give to you, it's never get tangled up with
a cutter. We're poison.*

*Be well. Have a happy life,
Dutch*

She had believed Dutch hadn't cared at all. She'd
been wrong. He'd cared so much that he'd stepped out
of her life. Not because he loved horses more, as she'd
imagined, but because his main concern had been
for her. He'd known he couldn't give her what she
needed. The horses had been his consolation prize.

Mariah's heart ripped. "Oh, Daddy, I wish I could
turn back time. I wish I could have truly known you."

A clot of hot tears dammed Mariah's throat. The
entire letter upset her. Smothered her with guilt.
Ripped her heart with regret. But the words on the
page that kept dancing up and down through the
mist of her tears were these: *If there's one word of
advice I could give to you, it's never get tangled up
with a cutter. We're poison.*

It might be wrong to lump Joe in with her father,

but she couldn't help thinking he was as obsessed with cutting horses as Dutch had been.

Shaking off her gloomy mood, Mariah put the letter back in the stuffed snake and then drove to Will Rogers Coliseum where the final day of the Triple Crown Futurity was being held. She arrived at the ticket counter only to discover the event was sold out, and she wouldn't have gotten in if she hadn't seen Cordy in the parking lot.

"Come with me," he said, and escorted her in through a side exit. "I'm so happy you got here. Joe's been a nervous wreck and that's not like him at all."

The place was packed. Everywhere she looked there were cowboy hats. The place smelled of horses, hay, leather, beer, and roasted peanuts. Cordy positioned her in reserved front-row seating. "Watch that door." He indicated with a nod of his head. "Joe will be coming through there any minute."

"Thanks."

"Gotta go now," Cordy said, and disappeared through the door.

Music played. The announcer got busy over the microphone, ticking off the names of the remaining contenders. From a white iron gate on the opposite side of the arena, cowboys let a herd of mooing cattle into the ring.

When Joe and Miracle cantered through the entrance, a cheer went up from the crowd. The announcer narrated the event, but Mariah didn't know enough about cutting to follow the scoring. It didn't matter, because the man on his horse in the middle of the ring riveted her.

Riveted everyone.

Joe and Miracle moved like poetry. The cattle were helpless against the pair. They moved as a perfect unit, complicated in their simplicity.

A thrill grabbed her and wouldn't let her go. Joe was the best at what he did. Watching him took her breath. The look on his face was part supreme concentration, part utter bliss.

Her heart soared. She was in love with him and she couldn't do anything to change it. But she loved him too much to ever put him in the position of having to choose between her and cutting. That had been her mother's mistake with her father, trying to get Dutch to be a family man when that kind of life just wasn't in him. Like it or not, you had to accept people for who they were.

What did the future hold for them? For her?

While Mariah fretted, Joe won the futurity. Won it on the horse trained by her father. Joe had achieved his goal. He'd honored Dutch by winning the Triple Crown Futurity.

Waves of emotion washed over her—pride, joy, sadness, fear, hope, loss, celebration. The spectators leaped up in the stands, shouting and cheering. Cowboys herded the cattle from the ring. Joe and Miracle entered the winner's circle, received the trophy, received a check for four hundred thousand dollars, had their picture taken.

Joe's eyes were alight as he gave a small speech, then he looked across the arena and met Mariah's gaze. His grin widened. He talked about Dutch and announced that Mariah was in the arena. Thundering applause followed.

Then Joe sobered and asked for a moment of silence for Dutch and Clover. Cowboys and cowgirls took off their hats, held them over their hearts. Silence fell over the entire gathering, and Mariah swore she felt Dutch's presence. Clover's too. Tears burned her eyes. She blinked hard, fighting them back.

Cordy led Miracle away and the crowd swooped down on Joe. Mariah tried to get to him, but found herself jostled aside. Whooping and shouting, the throng launched him on their shoulders, moving him along mosh pit–style toward the exit, the group chanting as one voice. "Party. Party. Party."

The grin swallowed his entire face. Joe was on top of the world and she wasn't with him.

They carried him past where Mariah stood wedged against the wall. Joe spied her, and as impossible as it seemed, smiled even bigger. "I'll meet you back at the cabin as soon as I can," he hollered over the noise.

And then he was gone, whisked away by a tide of victory, leaving Mariah standing in the wake, nothing more than a piece of flotsam on the current of a cutter's life.

Happiness over winning the futurity ebbed quickly. Joe was torn in a dozen different directions. Reporters, friends, officials for the National Cutting Horse Association all vied for his time. But all he could think about was how quickly he could get all this celebratory brouhaha over and go share his victory with Mariah.

He couldn't wait to wrap his arms around her and tell her how special she was. How much she meant to him.

It was two hours later before he was able to shake off all the hangers-on and make his way back to Stone Creek. Dutch's pickup truck was parked out front. He ambled up onto the porch, his heart thudding crazily. He knocked on the door.

Mariah opened it.

"Hi." He smiled.

"Come on in." She stood aside, brought her arms up to hug herself, raising her guard, shoring her defenses.

Were they back to that? He thought last night had changed everything between them. She probably felt left out. He couldn't blame her. He shouldn't have left this morning without waking her up. He thought he was doing a good thing letting her sleep in, now he saw how she could have misread his behavior. His mind had been on the futurity and he'd dropped the ball. Hell, he should have told her last night that he loved her, but he'd wanted to wait. Tell her in a non-sexual context.

"We did it," he said. "We won."

"I know. I'm so happy for you."

Okay, he must have really done something wrong. He could feel an arctic breeze blowing between them. "It wasn't just for me. It was for Dutch too."

"I know."

"Is something wrong?" He stepped closer.

"I found this inside of Stuffy." She handed him a letter.

Joe opened it up. Read it. He could feel Dutch's pain, could understand Mariah's. He raised his gaze, met her eyes. "I'm not your father."

"You're a cutter."

"You don't really believe that all cutters are poison. Clearly, Dutch was hurting when he wrote this, but he was smart enough not to mail it."

Mariah shrugged. "He kept it all these years. It must have meant something."

"Little Bit." He held out his arms. "Come here, we need to talk."

"This is your day to celebrate. I didn't mean to make this about me." She danced away from him, went into the kitchen. "Are you hungry? I'll make us some sandwiches."

"Mariah, talk to me."

She opened the refrigerator, started taking out packages of luncheon meat. "I've got turkey, ham, and bologna."

"I don't care."

"Do you prefer mustard or mayo?"

"Will you forget about the sandwiches?" He moved into the kitchen, went to drop Dutch's letter on the table, and that's when he saw it. Some kind of business contract. Quickly, he scanned the opening paragraph, realized it was from her old boss.

His spirits, which had been so lofty just minutes ago, nosedived. He felt as if he'd been body-slammed by an elephant. With a shaky hand, he picked up the contract. "What the hell is this?"

"My boss offered me my old job back at triple my salary," Mariah said.

"You're considering taking it." Joe's voice iced up.

"I've lost the chapel and with it, my wedding planning business. There's nothing really holding me here. Especially now that you've won the futurity and can buy your ranch back." She caught her breath, praying he would say that of course she had something holding him here. That *he* was the reason she should stay in Jubilee.

But he didn't say that. Instead, he said, "I see."

Okay then. This was what she'd feared. That he

didn't feel as invested in the relationship as she did. Or that he was still too hung up on Becca to move forward.

She was going to beat him to the punch. Act like their lovemaking had meant nothing more to her than great sex before he could do the same to her. Self-preservation springboarded the lie onto her tongue. "Don't get me wrong," she said. "We had a lot of fun. I really enjoyed being with you, Joe, but I get that I'm the rebound girl. Everyone has to go through that after a relationship ends."

"Is that what you think?"

She stood with her hands behind her back, pressed up against the counter, her gaze on the luncheon meat strewn across the table. "You and I, we could never work. Not really. Your marriage with Becca worked because she was just like you. She loved horses the way you do. You both put your careers before your marriage. And that's fine, but I can't settle for that kind of relationship. I need more."

Joe's jaw tightened and his eyes flashed anger. "You don't get to do that," he said. "You don't get to pass judgment on my marriage to Becca."

"I'm not passing judgment. It worked for you. I'm just giving you my observation."

"No," he said, "you're making excuses for why you're running back to Chicago just when things were starting to get real for us. Last night . . ." He trailed off. Fisted his hand.

"Last night was funeral sex. Grief creates a lot of emotions. We took comfort in each other. We—"

"Why are you doing your damnedest to torpedo us before we ever really got started?"

"I'm not—"

"You are!"

She hauled in a claustrophobic breath. "You want to know why?"

"I do."

"I can't be like my mother. I won't be like my mother. I won't play second fiddle to cutting. You're too much like my father. I can't live with the fear that my man will take off on me without a moment's notice."

Joe's eyes turned to flint. "I get that you have daddy issues. I understand Dutch screwed you up. But I'm not him. I want a family of my own."

"You say that, but I saw you in that ring. You were on a cutting horse high. I've seen that same look in Dutch's eyes."

Joe rounded the table, removing the barrier between them. She had nowhere to go. Her back was against the wall and he wasn't letting her get away. "Tell the truth," he said. "You're not really afraid that I'm like Dutch."

"You *are* like Dutch."

"I love cutting and horses, yes that's true, but be honest with yourself, Mariah, and you'll discover what you're really afraid of." Tension coiled his muscles but his voice was soft and gentle.

His gentleness unwound her. She hugged herself tight, warding him off with the only defense she had. "What's that?"

"That you're incapable of a long-term relationship."

"That's not true," she protested.

"Name your longest relationship, not counting your mother."

"I was with my boss Destiny for eleven years—"

"That's a work relationship. And you're accusing

me of being obsessed with my work? I've been married and happily monogamous. I've loved deep and held on tight. But you? You have no idea if *you* have what it takes to make a love relationship work. You tell yourself you don't want to be like Annie in *Sleepless in Seattle*, that you're not going to sell yourself short, you're not going to settle, but that's not the real truth, is it?"

Miserably, Mariah shook her head. He was right about everything.

"The truth is you're afraid that *you're* just like Dutch. That you can't be in a committed relationship because you have no idea how one works."

That was it. He'd unmasked her one hundred percent. He knew her better than she knew herself. Stunned by his insight, Mariah stared at him, openmouthed.

"Well, you know what? *I'm* not going to settle," Joe said. "I need a woman who's going to love *me* one hundred percent. So go on back to Chicago if you think that will make you happy. I'll have Art Bunting draw up the papers buying Stone Creek back from you and I'll write you a check for the full purchase price."

Then with that, he turned and walked out of her life.

For a week Joe wandered around in a daze. The morning after the night he broke up with her, Mariah packed up and moved back to Chicago.

The last time he'd had felt pain this bone-deep had been in the hospital emergency room two years ago when the doctor had come out to tell him and Ila that Becca hadn't made it. That moment had been horrible. The worst moment in his entire life. But this moment? This pain? He'd caused it. He'd broken up with Mariah for being scared when what he should have done was hold on to her for dear life until she realized he was never ever going to walk away from her the way Dutch had done.

But in the end, he'd been the one to send her away. It had the same results.

It's got to be this way. It's better for it to be like this. She didn't belong in Jubilee. She can have the world. All you've got to offer her is the cutter's way of life.

Except nothing felt logical or right about this decision. It felt wrong on so many levels.

It was all he could do not to book a flight to Chicago and tell her he was the world's biggest ass, that he loved her more than he loved breathing. That he'd give up everything. Sell everything to be with her. The ranch. Miracle. Everything.

Because she'd been right about his marriage to Becca. It hadn't been a true partnership. It had been two people merged in common interests. But he wanted more than that. With Mariah, he knew they could have more than that if they could both just get past their fears.

Crippled with emotional pain, he drove to Jubilee, to the Silver Horseshoe. Ila was there playing darts with Cordy. He wasn't letting her win. Joe ordered a tequila. He knocked it back.

Bobby Jim raised an eyebrow.

"Another," Joe said.

Ila frowned and came over. Cordy got a little twitchy, so she went back, bent over and gave him a kiss, then returned to sit on the bar stool beside Joe.

"You look like shit."

"Thanks."

"You should look good. You won the fricking Triple Crown Futurity."

"Yay for me." He downed the second tequila.

"What's wrong?"

"Mariah's gone back to Chicago."

"What the hell did you do to her?" Ila glared at him.

Joe shrugged. "I bought the ranch back from her."

"Why the hell did you do that?"

"It was the arrangement we'd made. Miracle and I win the futurity, I buy the land back."

"But she was building a wedding planning business here."

"The chapel burned down. Her ex-boss offered Mariah her old job back in Chicago. There was no reason for her to stay."

"I thought you two were an item."

"Yeah, well . . ." He shrugged. *So did I.*

Ila shook her head. "I don't get you."

"What?"

"You sent away the best thing that ever happened to you."

"Um . . ." Joe saluted Cordy. "I think you did the same thing with my ranch hand."

"I realized what a huge dumbass I was. That's why I get to call you on your dumbassedness."

"I'm just holding Mariah back. She can be so much more successful in Chicago."

"Bullshit!" Ila exploded. "Mariah is the best thing that ever happened to you, bar none. She was good for you too. She called you on your bullshit. Not like Becca, who just went on her way and did her own thing. You might have loved my sister, and God bless her, I loved her too, but we both know Becca could be pretty spoiled and selfish."

Joe glanced down at his hands. "Another one, Bobby Jim. He was working hard on numbing himself.

"You love Mariah."

"It's not love. It's just . . . she made me feel better."

"You love her and she loves you."

"She doesn't love me."

"Argh!" Ila threw her hands in the air. "You are the most stubborn man I have ever known. And dumb. And blind. You didn't even realize that I'd had a crush on you since grade school."

"You're pretty much a dumbass," Cordy called from across the room.

"Cordy helped me see how useless that crush was. But I had to let go of the idea of you before I could see the prize that was standing right in front of me." She stopped to blow Cordy a kiss. "Just waiting for me to notice him the way I'd been standing around waiting for you to notice me. Cordy opened my eyes and now I'm here to open yours. Whether you want to admit it or not, you're in love with Mariah, and I think you might love her even more than you loved Becca, which is what's really scaring the shit out of you. The thing you had for Becca was mostly sexual. Think about it, Joe. What was it you admired most about my sister?"

"She was beautiful."

"Right. And exciting. But that was about sex too."

Ila had a point.

"If you'd met her now, I doubt Becca would have caught your interest."

She was right about that too.

"Mariah's got something Becca never had. Something that you're sorely lacking."

"What's that?"

"Balance. You've always been out of balance. Just like Becca, just like Dutch. It's been all horses all the time. Horses are great, but dammit, Joe, they're not everything. And when you were with Mariah, you were beginning to realize that. She got you out of yourself. If you let her get away, then you are the dumbest cowboy on the face of the earth. And it's taken a lot for me to say this to you because not so very long ago, I would have stabbed her in the back if I thought it would get you to notice me."

"Ila," he said. "I'm sorry if I hurt you in any way."

"You're forgiven," she said. "As long as you go get Mariah back."

Mariah returned to Chicago, but she did not return to work for Destiny.

She'd been down that road. Knew all too well where it led. She'd had her own business once. She would have it again. And in the meantime, she had the money Joe had given her for the ranch as a cushion.

It had been ten miserable days since she'd left Jubilee. Ten days of trying to prop up her spirits and get her joy back. She'd been foolish to let down her guard with Joe. She'd known better. Had known what she was walking into, but she'd done it anyway.

Forget Joe. It's over. Focus on the here and now.

She leafed through the jobs on CareerBuilder, scrolled down the page on her computer, noting the possibilities. She took a sip of her freshly brewed coffee. Her stomach immediately roiled, the way it had been doing for the last few days. Just her luck, she was probably coming down with something.

The phone rang. She glanced over to see it was her mother. Cassie had been calling her every day since she'd told her about moving back to Chicago.

"How are you today, sweetie?"

"I'm fine, Mom. You don't have to keep calling me."

"You don't sound fine. Are you sure you're well?"

"I am a little queasy," she admitted. "But it'll pass."

There was a long silence on the other end of the line and then Cassie said, "Could you be pregnant?"

"No, there's no . . ." Mariah paused as she realized her period *was* late. Several days late. She'd been in such turmoil over Joe that time had slipped away from her.

"Is that a maybe?"

"I'm on the pill. Joe used protection. We used protection."

Panic wrapped fingers around her throat. She couldn't be pregnant. The thought of having a child, raising it without a daddy, was too unbearable to think about. She didn't want a little one growing up without a father the way she had.

"Birth control isn't infallible," Cassie said.

"I'm not going to panic until there's something to panic about." That's when she realized she couldn't remember if they'd used a condom when they'd had sex after Clover's funeral. They'd both been so caught up in grief they could very well have forgotten.

"Go out now, buy a pregnancy kit. Take the test. Call me back the minute you know something."

"I'm sure it's nothing but a stomach bug and my period is late because of stress and—"

"Pregnancy test. Now."

"Okay."

A half hour later, Mariah was in the bathroom willing the plastic stick not to turn pink. Pink meant pregnant. But at the same time she was praying not to be pregnant, another part of her was imagining a baby. Soft and sweet, with midnight black eyes just like Joe's.

Stop it!

Emotions ripped at her. Hope and joy, sadness and fear, worry and regret. So much emotion. What was she going to do?

Mariah looked at her watch. It had been three minutes. Tentatively, she peered at the stick, and in the moment her spirits soared. *Thank you, thank you, thank you.* The joy in her heart overflowed.

No matter how she might wish it otherwise, Mariah was happy, happy, happy.

Picking up the plastic stick with the bright pink plus sign, Mariah turned to go call her mother.

After she found out about the baby, Mariah started listening to *Midnight with Dr. Dana.* She didn't know why. It was torture really. Doing something that made her think of Joe. She still hadn't made up her mind how she was going to break the news to him. She didn't want him to be with her simply because she was pregnant with his baby.

She lay on her bed and stared at the ceiling, listening to the psychologist dish advice. Finally, she couldn't stand it any longer and she picked up the phone to call in.

"Hello, you're on *Midnight with Dr. Dana.* Who is this?"

"Sleepless in Chicago." Okay, so she wasn't terribly original.

"Hello, Sleepless." Dr. Dana chuckled. "What's your question?"

"You know, Dr. Dana, *Sleepless in Seattle* used to be my favorite movie."

"I take it that it's no longer your favorite movie."

"That's correct."

"And why is that?"

"I was dating a man like Sam, the Tom Hanks character in *Sleepless*."

"I'm guessing that it didn't turn out so well."

"That's what's wrong with *Sleepless in Seattle*. It never showed the actual relationship between Annie and Sam. It was all romantic hooey."

"Ah, Sleepless, I see your problem. Tell me more about your Sam and maybe I can help you make sense of what happened in that relationship."

On his way to DFW airport to take a redeye to O'Hare, Joe turned his satellite radio on with fumbling fingers, searching for the station Mariah had told him about. He found it, and the song that was playing punched him square in the gut.

It was "Hallelujah," sung by Jeff Buckley, a song about a love affair gone wrong. He sat in the truck listening, his heart a gaping chest wound. The lyrics twined around him, haunting and inescapable. Life was filled with sorrow and loss. He dropped his forehead to the dashboard, fisted his hand, and spurred by the ballad, ate the anguish like poison.

He thought of all the things that had slipped through his fingers. Becca, bull riding, Dutch, Clover, Mariah . . .

Mariah.

"And now listeners, it's *Midnight with Dr. Dana*."

Someone called in. Asked Dr. Dana if she was stupid for breaking up with a great guy who hated her parakeet.

Joe rolled his eyes and let his mind wander to Mariah. He was listening to the station to feel closer to her. He imagined she was listening at the same time he was listening and if he could reach out through the airwaves, he could touch her.

Of course, he was also working up the courage to call in on the show just in case she was listening. He was thinking there needed to be a really big, grand gesture to win her back, apologize for being such a stupid jackass.

"Hello, you're on *Midnight with Dr. Dana*. Who is this?" Dr. Dana said.

"Sleepless in Chicago."

When Joe heard Mariah's voice, he almost ran right off the road. He had to call in. He pulled off the highway, stopped in a Taco Bell parking lot, dug out his cell phone. He could scarcely breathe.

Dr. Dana hung up with Mariah after telling her to think about giving the guy more time if he truly was the man for her.

Joe finally got the phone out and the number dialed. It took several more minutes before he was connected to the switchboard.

"Hello, caller, who is this?"

"This is Sleepless in Jubilee."

"My, we have a lot of sleepless listeners tonight."

"Well, you are on at midnight," he couldn't resist saying.

"And we are cranky from our lack of sleep, aren't we?"

"Listen, I'm the guy."

"What guy is that?"

"I'm Sam."

"You're Tom Hanks?"

"No, I'm Sleepless in Chicago's Sam."

"You're the guy our previous caller was talking about? The one who lost his wife?"

"Yes, yes, that's me."

"Do you have something to say to our female Sleepless?"

"Yes. Don't give up on me, Little Bit. I love you. I love you with all my heart and to prove it, I want to sweep you off your feet with romance. I'm on my way to Chicago. Meet me tomorrow at midnight in the only place a cowboy would feel like he belonged in Chicago. If you still want me, be there. If not, I'll go back to Jubilee and never bother you again."

"Oh my goodness," Dr. Dana said. "We have our own Sleepless drama playing out tonight. "I hope you're still listening, Sleepless in Chicago."

Mariah was reaching over to turn off the knob on the radio when she heard Joe's voice say, "Sleepless in Jubilee."

She bolted upright in bed, turned the volume up, and sat there riveted. He was coming to Chicago and he wanted her to meet him tomorrow night. In a special place. Just as Annie had asked Sam to meet her at the Empire State Building.

"I'll be there, Joe, I'll be there."

At midnight the following evening, Joe waited by the bronze cow on parade outside the Chicago Cultural Center, praying that his attempt at being romantic wouldn't go horribly awry. The sky was crowded with clouds and it felt like at any moment rain would pour from the sky.

He paced back and forth, continually checking his watch. Chicago and Texas were on the same time zone, weren't they? He had on his boots and his Stetson. The streets were almost empty. How stupid had he been asking her to come out in the middle of the night. Dumbass, dumbass, dumb—

A taxi drove up. The back door opened.

Mariah stepped out.

They stood there staring at each other on either side of the bronze bull. But then Joe saw she had on the leopard cowboy boots and black Stetson he'd bought for her.

They drew a simultaneous breath.

"Annie," he said. "You came."

"But of course, Sam. You grovel well."

"You ain't seen nothing yet, sweetheart." He went down on one knee right there in the street. "I'm your man, Mariah. I'm putting my heart on the line. I told myself I was letting you go because you deserved better than Jubilee. But I was just lying to myself. I let you walk away because I was afraid. Afraid to love again, afraid to lose you the way I've lost so much."

"So you drew the gun and shot me before I had a chance to shoot you in a love duel?"

His eyes narrowed, his throat moved when he swallowed. "What can I say? I was a fool. A scared, lonely fool."

"Not a fool," she whispered, reaching out to brush a lock of hair from his forehead. "Human. I was stupid too. You were right. I wasn't scared you would walk out on me. I was scared I didn't have the staying power for a real relationship."

Her touch dissolved him.

Everything about her was warm. From the hue of her honeyed hair to the softness of her velvety eyes. Her rounded chin had a competency to it when she was intent on her work, absorbed in a task that took all her attention.

"I love you," he said. "I love you, I love you, I love you."

"Okay, okay, you can get up." She laughed. "I love you too."

He rose to his feet.

Lightning flashed. Thunder crashed. Lightning flashed again.

"Looks like lightning does strike twice," he said.

"Unless you're Cooter Johnston," she said, and stepped into his arms just as the heavens opened up to soak them both with rain.

Laughing, they held hands and ran to hail another taxi.

EPILOGUE

Home is where you hang your Stetson.
—Dutch Callahan

The two naked cowboys in the claw-footed bathtub presented a conundrum.

Which one did she hug first? Her sexy husband who was bathing their son. Or her six-month-old little cowboy named Jonah.

Jonah, squirming and cooing at the sight of his mother, won out. He was smaller and slipperier. Mariah grabbed a towel and wrapped it around their gorgeous baby boy.

While her equally gorgeous husband stepped from the bathtub and leaned down to kiss her.

"Hey, you're getting me wet."

"When did that ever bother you?" He laughed and swatted her bottom.

She giggled and took the baby to the nursery. She diapered him, dressed him in a onesie, and put him in his crib to play with his stuffed horse while she got changed.

"What time is it?" Joe asked, slipping his arm around her and drawing her into their bedroom.

"Six. We need to get a move on. The dedication is at seven."

They were dedicating the Dutch Callahan Equine Center for disadvantaged children, built on the site where the wedding chapel had once stood. Now there was a new chapel on a plot of land Joe had bought for her in Jubilee. All the cutters from the co-op would be there.

"Hmm, we have just enough time for some hanky-panky." Joe nuzzled her neck.

"Honey, eight seconds might be a great score for a bull rider, but for a lover, not so hot."

"Ha-ha." He danced her to the bed.

"The babysitter will be here at any minute."

"Too bad." He started unbuttoning her blouse.

She giggled. How could she refuse her man anything when he made her happier than she'd ever been in her life? She kissed him. Felt his erection stiffen.

With Joe and Jubilee, the ambivalence she'd always felt about her life, about where she belonged, disappeared. She opened herself to him. Not just her mind and her body and her heart, but the very soul of her emotions. She stopped resisting. Stopped being scared. Anxious to show him how she felt, she reached out to take his hand and led him to bed.

He kissed her gently, grazing her mouth.

Their kisses quickly escalated, and soon they were in a fevered rhythm.

Heaven. He was in heaven. Joe sank into his dear sweet wife, wondering how he could ever have been afraid of loving her. He'd never been so happy, and everything they'd gone through to get here was worth it.

Mariah impishly squeezed him tight with her love muscles, working him over as only she could. Her

soft moans drove him wilder. Then she came in soft,
sweet gasps.

Joe's body gave one last shudder and he lay gasping
against the mattress. He raised his head, glanced over
at Mariah. Her eyes were closed, an angelic smile on
her smooth face.

"Little Bit of dynamite," he murmured.

She trailed her fingers up his chest to his shoulder,
and then turned her face into the side of his neck with
a satisfied sigh. Only the sound of the ticking clock
and their harsh breathing interrupted the silence.

He felt great. No, not great. Alive. Mariah had
breathed life back into him. Resurrected his soul.
Mended his broken heart.

Joe ran his fingers across her cheek, slipping them
through the silk of her hair. She'd given him such
pleasure. Made him whole again.

"Miracle," he whispered. "You're the true miracle."

Mariah leaned over, sassily nipped his bottom lip
with her teeth, and whispered, "And don't you ever
forget it."

And now a sneak peek at
Lori Wilde's next book

THE COWBOY
AND THE PRINCESS

Coming in Summer 2012,
only from

**AVON
BOOKS**

You might be a princess if . . . you have to ditch
your bodyguards to get some "me" time.

Brady Talmadge had five unbreakable rules for
leading an uncomplicated life.

One stormy June night in Texas, he broke
them all. Starting with rule number five.

Never pick up a hitchhiker.

He'd honed the rules through twenty-nine years of
trial and error, most of them compiled while towing
his vagabond horse trailer from town to town, and as
long as he stuck to his edicts, life flowed as smooth
and simple as the Brazos River ambling to the Gulf.

In regard to the hitchhiker rule, he learned it the
hard way. He had a permanent whup-notch on the
back of his skull from a pistol-whipping meted out by
a wiry, goat-faced thief who'd taken him for thirteen
hundred dollars, his favorite belt buckle, and a pair
of ostrich-skin cowboy boots. Never mind the four-
day hospital stay that drained his savings account to
zero because he'd had no health insurance.

On the satellite radio, the weatherman warned of
the fierce line of unrelenting storms moving up from

Hurricane Betsy. "It's gonna be a wet night, folks. Find someplace warm and dry to hole up with someone you love."

Brady took the exit ramp off Interstate 30, heading for the parking lot of Toad's Big Rig Truck Stop on the outskirts of Dallas. His headlights caught a lone figure huddled on the road shoulder, thumb outstretched. Automatically, his hand went to his occipital bone.

No dice.

Lightning flashed. Thunder crashed. Rain slashed. The hitchhiker shivered violently.

Sorry about your luck, fella.

The eighteen-wheeler in front of Brady splashed a deluge of water over the skinny stranger. Small, vulnerable. Been there. Done that. Lived through it. The fella raised his face, and in a flash of fresh lightning, from underneath the hooded sweatshirt, he saw it wasn't a guy at all, but a woman.

No, a girl actually. Most likely a runaway.

Don't do it.

Trampas, his Heinz 57 mutt—who, come to think of it, was a hitchhiker of sorts as well—peered out the window at the dark night and whimpered from the backseat. A year ago, Brady had found the starving puppy, flea-bitten and tick-ridden, on a long stretch of empty road in the Sonoran desert.

He was already driving past her. He'd almost made it. Then hell, if he didn't glance back and meet the girl's eyes.

Please, she mouthed.

Aw, shit.

He didn't mean to do it. Hadn't planned on doing it, but the next thing he knew he was slowing down and pulling over. And that's when he broke rule number four.

Avoid damsels in distress.

That rule came to him courtesy of a short-skirted cowgirl broke down off Route 66 in Flagstaff. She thanked him for changing her flat by inviting him back to her place for a home-cooked fried chicken dinner and rocking hot sex, except she neglected to tell him she had a grizzly bear–sized husband with a high temper and a hammy fist.

Brady rubbed his jaw. He wasn't going to give the runaway a ride. Just get her inside the building and out of the storm. Maybe buy her a meal if she was hungry. He would toss her a few bucks for one of the cheap bunk-and-bath motels attached to the truck stop and advise her against hitchhiking.

Meddling. That's meddling in someone else's business.

Yeah, and where would he be if Dutch Callahan hadn't meddled in his life fourteen years ago?

Prison, most likely. Or the bone orchard.

He hit the unlock button, knowing it was a bad idea, but doing it anyway. The hitchhiker ran for his truck. She was short enough so that he couldn't see anything but the top of her head from his perch behind the wheel without peeping into the side view mirror, but he heard her fumble the door handle on the passenger side.

The howling wind snatched at the door, ripping it from her pale, trembling hand and throwing it wide open.

Brady glanced down.

The hitchhiker looked up.

Her eyes were a dusty gray, too large for her small,

narrow face, and she stared right into him as if she knew every thought that passed through his head, yet didn't hold it against him.

He tried to take a deep breath, but to his alarm, discovered that he couldn't.

For one brief moment, they dangled in suspended animation. Their gazes meshed, their futures strangely entwined.

Drive off!

Of course, he didn't, couldn't. Not with her standing there looking like a soaking wet fawn who just lost her mother to a hunter's gun. But the impulse to run, Brady's instinct to avoid complications at all costs, fisted around his spine and wouldn't let go.

"Thank you for stopping," she said in a voice as soft as lamb's wool. Looped around her shoulder she carried an oversized satchel. "Your kindness is much appreciated."

The breath he'd tried to draw finally filled his lungs with a swift *whoosh* of damp night air. He nodded.

Somehow, she managed to plant her feet on the running board, grab the door in her right hand, and then swing up into the seat in one long, smooth, ladylike movement. Her satchel rustled as she tugged the heavy door closed behind her, and with a solid click they were cocooned inside.

Alone.

Her scent, an intriguing combination of rain and talcum powder and honey, filled the cab, vanquishing his own leather, horse, and beef jerky smell. The sweatshirt hoodie was tied down tight under her chin so that he couldn't see her hair, but her eyebrows were starkly black in startling contrast to skin the color and texture of fresh cream. She possessed the cheekbones of a Swedish supermodel, as high and sharp and cool as the summit of Mount Everest, but in spite of that barrier of heartbreaking beauty, there was something about her that had him yearning to toss an arm around her shoulders and tell her everything was going to be okay. Maybe it was because she was so ethereal—pale and slender and wide-eyed.

She wore dark blue jeans. Plain, brown, round-toed cowboy boots shod her petite feet. In spite of being drenched, both the jeans and boots looked brand-new.

Trampas leaned over the seat, ran his nose along the back of her neck.

"Oh." She startled, laughed. "Hello." She reached out a hand to scratch the mutt behind his ear. He whimpered joyously. Attention hound.

"Down, Trampas," Brady commanded.

The dog snorted, but reluctantly settled, his tail thumping against the backseat.

The hitchhiker turned to snap her seat belt into place, the satchel now clutched in her lap.

"I'm not going anywhere," Brady said, his words hanging like a curtain in the air between them, not making a lick of sense coming from a traveling man who dragged his home behind him.

She raised her head and met his gaze again. "I beg your pardon, sir?"

Speech eloped. Just ran right off with his brain. On closer inspection, her eyes weren't simply gray, but loaded with tiny starbursts of sapphire blue. He motioned toward the gas pumps. "I was just . . ."

She canted her head and studied him as if every word that spilled from his mouth was golden. "Yes?"

"Gonna get some gas."

"That is acceptable." She folded her hands over the satchel.

Huh? As if she was giving her permission? "And supper. I was gonna have supper."

"Here?"

"Yes."

"Then why did you stop to pick me up?"

Beats the hell out of me. "You looked cold. And wet. You looked cold and wet."

"I am," she confirmed. "Wet and cold."

He reached over to turn on the heater, angling the air vents toward her. He had never turned on the heater in June in Texas. First time for everything. "Why didn't you go inside the truck stop?"

She shrugged as if the gesture said it all.

"No money?"

Her slight smile plucked at him.

"You hungry?"

The shrug again, accompanied by a shy head tilt. She licked lips the color of red honeysuckle, and for no good reason at all, he thought of caramel—sweet, thick, chewy. If he kissed her, she would taste like caramel. He just knew it.

You're not going to kiss her. Get that idea out of your head right now. You don't need the hassle.

But the more Brady tried not to think about kissing her, the more her lips beckoned.

"You got a name?" he asked.

"Do you?"

"Brady. Brady Talmadge." He put out a hand.

She looked at his palm as if shaking hands was an alien concept, then finally took it for a brief second, smirked like someone enjoying a private joke, and said, "Annie."

"No last name?"

She paused. "Coste."

"Well, Annie Coste, you can join me inside for a meal, my treat, or you can find yourself another ride and be on your way. It's up to you." Damn, he hoped she chose the latter option. She had trouble scribbled all over her. Yeah, so why had he broken his own rules? Because he was a sucker for doe-eyed damsels.

Sucker.

That was the operative word.

"I am hungry," she admitted.

"Great," he said.

Great as a busted axle. Why had he picked her up? Stupid. Glutton for punishment. Misguided sense of chivalry. Dumbass. What a total dumbass. What was wrong with him? But come on, how could he have left Bambi shivering by the roadside when some un-scrupulous son of a bitch could have given her a ride instead? Things had been humming along just dandy and now he was stuck with her. If he'd kept driving— which he couldn't have because he was almost out of gas—he would be in Jubilee within ninety min-utes. Jubilee. The closest thing he'd ever had to a real home. He didn't want to take her there.

She's not your problem. You can't save everyone, Talmadge. It's not like you're a paragon yourself.

The thoughts loped through his head as he fueled his truck underneath the protective awning and put Trampas into the trailer. The dog curled up on his bed in the air-conditioned living area and gave him a look that said, *I like her.*

"Only because she scratched your itch," Brady grumbled, and shut the door.

He climbed back inside, pulled the truck around

the rear of the building with the semis and looked over at Annie. Raindrops still clung to her long eyelashes and the hoodie of her sweatshirt. Was it weird that her eyebrows were dark, but her eyelashes were light?

As they walked into the restaurant, the big red digital clock on the wall over the door flashed 9:15. The place was rowdy busy. A port in the storm. Truckers in baseball caps and cowboy hats lined the red and chrome swivel stools at the counter up front.

Several men craned their necks for a better look at Annie. Brady took a step closer toward her, rigging himself up in that she's-with-me strut that came naturally to a cowboy in the company of a good-looking woman. The hum of voices and clang of silverware drifted to the vaulted rafters. The air smelled of diesel exhaust, chicken fried steak, and yeast rolls.

Brady stood back to let Annie go in front of him.

She hesitated, resistance in her eyes as if uncertain how to proceed. C'mon. Surely she'd been in a truck stop before.

"This way." He held out his arm as a guide and ushered her past the front counter on their left and the clear glass refrigeration units chock full of homemade pies, spread high with meringue, sitting on rotating shelves. She stopped to stare at the pies, as awestruck as a five-year-old.

"We'll get some for dessert," he said.

Her beaming smile heated him up like an electric blanket on a cold winter night. "Really?"

"You can have two slices if you like." Brady escorted her past the "Seat Yourself" sign to an empty booth in the back of the room situated underneath the head of a mule deer buck.

Eyeing the taxidermied animal, she slid across the red vinyl seat, untying the string of her hoodie as she went, and then she slipped the satchel from her shoulder. She cleaved to the thing like she had gold bars in it.

Brady secured the seat across from her.

She tugged off the hood, revealing black hair chopped short and spiky. It looked as if she'd taken a pair of jagged-teethed pruning shears and hacked it off herself, but he supposed it was probably some hip salon cut that cost a hundred bucks or more. The harsh hairstyle, paired with her wide gray-blue eyes and pale skin, gave her the appearance of an anime cartoon heroine—waifish and innocent—accentuating the whole damsel-in-distress thing.

Next, she wrestled out of the sweatshirt, revealing a simple white blouse with capped sleeves, showing off toned arms that knew their way around a biceps curl. She was not the typical truck stop hitchhiker. No piercings (not even her ears), no tats (at least none he could see), no skimpy, too-tight clothing flaunting too big breasts. She was like a daisy sprung fresh in the garden. No, that was too common. Not a garden daisy, but a rare buttercup growing on a mountaintop. Sunny, sweet, lustrous. Unexpected. Special.

Special?

What the hell? Where was that coming from?

If he was smart, he'd pass her twenty bucks, get up, and walk out. Clearly, he was not smart because instead of doing that, he took off his straw Stetson, settled it on the bench seat beside him, and ran a hand through his hair.

The right side of the booth butted up against a thick, rain-painted plate-glass window. Outside, the vapor lamps glowed ghostly in the rumbling storm. Inside, someone with a sense of humor set the juke-box playing "Let it Rain" by David Nail.

Annie harvested a napkin from the red and chrome dispenser on the table and started polishing the Formica surface, whisking away crumbs left behind from a slapdash busboy's one-swipe attempt at cleaning the tabletop.

A waitress, dressed in a retro pink dress with a white bib apron and battered sneakers, bopped over with two menus tucked under one arm and two glasses of water in her hands. "Here y'all go," she said. "I'm Heather and I'll be back in a minute to take your order." Then off she went.

Brady shifted his attention back to Annie. Her head was bowed over the menu. One dainty finger slid down the list of offerings.

"What is chili?" she asked, raising her head to meet his gaze.

He startled again, just as he had when she climbed into his truck. Something about those eyes unraveled him in a way he'd never been unraveled, and Brady was no stranger to peering into the eyes of gorgeous women. "You've never eaten chili?"

She shook her head.

"You're not from Texas."

"How do you know?"

"Texans cut their baby teeth on chili."

"I am not from Texas," she admitted.

"Where you from?"

She rested one hand on the satchel beside her. "What is chili exactly?"

"It's ground or shredded beef cooked in a tomato-based sauce."

"And served cold?"

"No. It's hot. Both temperature and spice wise."

She looked puzzled. "If it is hot, then why do they call it chili?"

Something was decidedly off about this one. "Dunno. Sarcasm maybe?"

"Sarcasm?"

"They don't have sarcasm where you're from?"

"May we get some?" she asked.

"Get what?" Brady asked, his mind rambling to all possible meanings of the phrase "get some." "Sarcasm?"

"Chili."

"Okay," he said, just like that. So much for rule number three.

Never order chili at a truck stop.

That rule was self-evident. No unsavory details needed, but when the waitress came back, Brady handed her the menus. "Two bowls of chili. I'll have a Coors and the lady wants . . ."

"Might I have a cup of tea?" Annie asked.

"You mean hot tea?" The waitress gave her a strange look. Probably not too many truckers ordered hot tea.

"Yes, please. Thank you." Annie sat like she had a ruler implanted in her spine. Straight. Proper. "Earl Grey if it is available."

"I'll see what we got." The waitress pivoted and scooted off.

Annie hugged herself, grinned. "This is so enjoyable."

Brady cocked his head, trying to detect some kind of accent, but her speech was as plain as a Midwest newscaster. Sometimes her word choice was a little formal, a little stiff, which didn't quite jibe. Who was she? Her inscrutable gray-blue eyes revealed no secrets. "What is?"

"Ordering chili in a truck stop with a real-life cowboy."

"Are you from another country?"

"Are you?"

"No," he said.

She spread her hands, delicate and smooth, against the Formica tabletop in a prim gesture. She wore no rings, no bracelets. No jewelry at all. Her nails were short and painted with clear polish. Simple. Understated. Elegant. No adornments needed. "And there you have it."

What was she talking about? He felt as if he'd missed a step or two in the conversation. She looked so young. Not a single wrinkle on her face. No blemishes either. Flawless complexion.

"How old are you?" he asked. What if she was underage? This could be the beginning of a major snafu.

"How old are you?"

"Twenty-nine."

"I'm twenty-four."

"Naw." He shook his head. "You can't be twenty-four. I'd say twenty at most."

She raised both palms out from her head, shrugged. "It is true."

"You have some great genetics."

She glanced around the room at the other diners. "This place is quite interesting."

Interesting? Furrowing his brow, Brady followed her gaze. Nothing special as far as he could see. Asking her where she was from wasn't getting him anywhere. Clearly, she didn't want to talk about her past or why she was on the run. He understood that impulse. He tried a different track. "Where are you going?"

"Where are *you* going?"

"Jubilee."

"Where is Jubilee?"

Dammit, here she was doing it again, running the conversation in circles. "About eighty miles southwest of here."

"Is that where you live?"

"No."

"Why are you going there?"

"A job."

"What kind of job?"

"I work with horses."

"You are an equine veterinarian?"

"Not exactly."

"What exactly?"

"You could be a reporter, you know, with all those questions. Are you a reporter?"

"No, I am just naturally curious about people," she said quickly. "What exactly?"

"I work with horses who've been emotionally traumatized."

"Oh!" She broke into a big smile. "Like the Horse Whisperer in that dramatic novel by Nicholas Evans."

"It's not as glamorous as Robert Redford made it out to be in the movie, but yes, I do rehabilitate horses who've been injured or harmed or developed phobias."

"How did you get started in that line of employment?"

"I just sort of fell into it."

"Is it a difficult job?"

"Not from my point of view. But horses are sensitive, highly intuitive animals. You have to know how to handle them."

"How is that?"

"With a gentle hand and a loving heart."

"I like that." She leaned forward. "What an exciting profession."

"It's just what I do." He paused. "But I do love it."

"Where do you live when you are not healing horses?"

"In my trailer."

Dejection flickered across her face. "You do not have a home? You are a homeless person? I have never met a homeless person. Is it truly terrible? Being without a home?"

Beam me up, Scotty. I don't know what planet I've landed on, but the hitchhikers in these parts are freaking nuts. "I live in my trailer. That's my home."

"Traveling from town to town?"

"Living on the road is the ultimate freedom. Footloose and fancy-free. I can go anywhere I want, anytime I want to go. No limitations. No expectations."

"I cannot imagine such circumstances."

"No roots, nothing holding me back."

Annie pressed the fingertips of both hands against her lips. "It sounds so sad."

Brady blinked. Something dark and uncomfortable slithered across the back of his mind. Something he couldn't capture or name, but it slithered all the same. Swift and heavy, scraping his brain. "What's so horrible about freedom?"

"It is lonely."

"No, no. Not lonely at all. I have my dog, Trampas, and friends all over the country, and there's the horses and . . ." He trailed off, trying to think of all the wonderful things about his life.

"No one special," she finished for him.

Brady snorted. "Hey, if you're so happy and your life is choked with special people, what are you doing hitchhiking in the rain on a Friday night?"

She pulled herself up on the edge of her seat and looked down her nose in a stately expression of the highborn. "I am out for an adventure."

"Yeah? Got away from the zookeeper, did you?" Now, that was tacky. He shouldn't have said it, but his gut poked at him.

"Pardon me?" The regal expression vanished and the vulnerable girlishness was back—hurt, disappointed.

Brady shook his head. "Never mind."

Thankfully, the waitress showed up, interrupting the weird conversation. "Toad's chili twice." She sat two blue bowls of steaming cinnamon-colored chili, swimming in the glistening grease of too much cheddar cheese, in front of them. She plunked down Brady's beer with barely any foam, and then she slid a small metal pitcher of hot water in front of Annie, along with a tea bag. "No Earl Grey. All we got is orange pekoe."

"Thank you." Annie graced the waitress with a smile as if bestowing a title upon her. "May I have an additional spoon, please?"

"Sure thing." The waitress grabbed an extra spoon for her.

Brady peered into his bowl and accepted his fate. That's what you got when you broke rules. He dug into the chili. Just as he feared, it was deceptively delicious.

He tried to blank his mind and focus on eating, but then the satchel on the seat beside Annie moved. Huh? Was he seeing things? He narrowed his eyes and noticed the sides of the satchel were made of braided mesh.

The satchel moved again.

"Whoa!" Brady jumped. Which wasn't like him. Usually he was laid back, not the least bit jumpy, but things just kept getting weirder.

Annie looked up. "What is it?"

He pointed. "Your bag moved. Twice."

"Oh." She put a dab of chili on the end of her spoon and reached for the satchel.

A little brown head popped from the side corner of the bag, and a tiny black button nose twitched.

"What the hell is . . . *that*?"

Annie laid a finger to her lips. "Shh, this is Lady Astor. My best friend in the whole world."

Shiny black eyes fixed on him.

"Seriously? That's a dog?"

"Lady Astor is a Yorkshire terrier. She is one year old and she weighs six pounds." The Yorkie lapped chili from Annie's spoon.

"You brought her with you on Annie's Big Adventure?"

"Of course, I could not, in all good conscience, leave her at the pal . . ." She trailed off, got a strange look on her face, and finished with ". . . leave her home alone."

"Ever heard of a kennel?" Did they have those in whatever la-la land she was from?

Annie glared as if he suggested she run the dog through a blender.

"Hey, you're the one who carries her around in a satchel."

A distraught furrow creased her brow. "She is comfortable in it. The mesh sides let air get in. It keeps her dry in the rain and I bought the most expensive one they had and—"

He raised a palm. "You don't have to justify it to me."

"Do you really think it is a bad thing that I keep her in a satchel?" She worried a paper napkin between her fingers.

"Why do you care what I think?"

"I am not—" She shut her mouth.

"You're not what?"

She tilted her head back, gave him that condescending glare again. "Disregard that."

"C'mon, you can tell me." Brady hated secrets. Had since he was a kid and he'd learned—well, there was no point going *there*—but whenever he was around someone who was obviously hiding something, he couldn't resist nudging for full disclosure. He'd discovered a lot of unexpected things about people that way. "It's not like you're ever going to see me again. Your secret is safe with me."

"I have no secret," she insisted, but her earlobes pinked and she did not meet his gaze.

"None? Nothing? Not even a tiny white lie you want to confess?"

Her eyes widened and she seemed even paler than before. Did the woman ever go out in the sun? "No."

Brady's lie-o-meter went off. Big time. He did not

know who or what Annie Coste was, but she spelled complication in capital letters.

Lady Astor finished licking the spoon, and then burrowed back into the satchel. She did seem to like it in there.

Annie picked up the second spoon that the waitress had brought her and daintily dipped it into the chili. Brady couldn't help watching her bring the curved stainless steel up to her full pink lips. When they finished their meal, they ordered banana cream pie, and Annie attacked it with gusto.

"I am not allowed to eat like this at home." She moaned a soft sound of pleasure and put a hand to her stomach.

"Allowed to?"

She ignored that, flicked her tongue out to lick a spot of frothy meringue from her upper lip, laughed. It was an airy sound that had real joy behind it, a gleeful laugh that embraced life in a hard hug. If he never saw her again, he would always remember the sound of her laughter, because it sounded like freedom.

For some reason, just hearing her laugh made him laugh and they both sat there underneath the mule deer, the smell of grease in the air, the taste of banana cream pie on their tongues, laughing and looking at each other and having a high old time together. It was the most fun he'd ever had at a truck stop, bar none.

Slowly, her laughter drained away.

So did his.

They were left with just the looking.

Mesmerized, he pulled a palm down over his mouth. He couldn't figure out what compelled him more, his attraction to her or his curiosity about her.

The healthy, masculine part of him was already

toying with the idea of seducing her. She was sexy in an unusual way and it had been months since he'd taken pleasure in the company of a willing woman. But his gut was saying, *Back off.* Something wasn't right. All was not as it seemed.

To distract himself, he turned and peered out the window. The rain was still washing down in angry torrents. Through the dark night, a long black limousine emerged and pulled up to the gas pumps.

"Now there's a sight you don't see every day at a truck stop in this neck of the woods unless it's prom night," Brady said. "But prom was two weeks ago. Unless it's a school with a late prom."

"What is that?" Annie asked in her slightly prissy, nondescript tone.

It drove him nuts that she had no birthplace-identifying accent. Who was she? Where was she from?

"Limo."

The chauffeur got out to fuel the vehicle. The rear door opened and two other men emerged. They were dressed in expensive suits tailored to perfectly fit their bodies. One man was tall, the other squat, and they both wore sunglasses at night and jaunty fedoras pulled down low over their foreheads.

Who were these guys? Mobsters? Secret Service? The Blues Brothers?

Then he remembered that former President Franklin Glover's daughter, Echo, was getting married this weekend and the president's ranch, where the nuptials were being held, wasn't far from here. It had been all over the radio for days.

Most likely they were Secret Service. But in a limo? He would have expected a black Cadillac Escalade with bulletproof glass.

Brady felt movement beside him, turned his head to see Annie had gotten up to come peer over his shoulder. He swung his gaze back to the window. Her warm breath tickled the hairs on the nape of his neck.

A fierce craving hammered down his spine and drove to his groin. He swallowed hard, fighting off the reaction. Yes, okay, she got a rise out of him, but he did not have to do anything about it. In fact, a smart guy would get the hell out of here as fast as possible. Unfortunately, Brady had never been particularly smart when it came to women. He always seemed to go for the troublesome ones.

The two guys from the limo broke into a trot, rushing to get out of the rain, and headed for the front door of the restaurant.

Annie made a noise of distress.

Brady jerked his head back in her direction.

She stood clutching his cowboy hat in her hands, her head raised expectantly. "May I sit here?"

"Um . . . sure."

She set his straw Stetson on the table and sank down beside him, her gaze coddling his. She did not look out the window. Did not glance around the room. Her eyes were on him and him alone.

Unnerved, he scooted as far across the seat as he could, his shoulder bumping up against the cool glass window.

At that moment, the Blues Brothers came into the seat-yourself dining area, scanning the room as if searching for someone.

Annie leaned in closer.

There was nowhere else for Brady to go. This development took him completely by surprise. He didn't know if he liked it or not.

"You are very handsome," she said.

"Um . . . okay."

"I want to kiss you."

Stunned, he blinked. "Huh?"

"Kiss me."

"What?" Had he heard her correctly?

"Kiss me."

The Blues Brothers were talking to Heather, the waitress.

Do not kiss her. Something is not right. Warning! Whatever you do, do not kiss her!

"Kiss me now!" she demanded, and puckered those honeysuckle lips.

He held up a palm like a stop sign. "I don't think so."

"Why not?"

"I don't like being bossed around."

"Please," she wheedled.

"Well, when you put it like that," he drawled. "No."

"You do not find me desirable." She reached out to stroke his chin with an index finger. He caught a whiff of her talcum powder scent.

"Quite the contrary."

"So why not?"

Brady peered into those big gray-blue eyes and he was a goner. Ah shit. What the hell? Why not? Illogically, he pulled her into his arms and proceeded to dismantle rule number two.

Always trust your gut.

Her lips were heated satin, melting Brady's self-control like cotton candy dunked in hot soda pop. She tangled her slender arms around his neck, tugging him closer, but she did not loosen her jaw.

Mystified, he lightly rested the tip of his tongue against her bottom lip. Was she going to let him in?

"Hmm, mmm." Annie increased the pressure of the kiss, but she did not part her teeth.

Okay, this was the first time he'd ever had a woman beg him to kiss her and then not let him fully do the job. Brady didn't like to brag, but he knew he was a good kisser. Many a woman had told him so.

Kissing was his second favorite part of lovemaking. He loved to taste things. Explore. Savor. Push limits. And he'd been right. Annie did taste like caramel. He wanted more.

She loosened her arms around his neck, broke the lip lock, rested her forehead on his. "Are they still there?" she whispered.

"Who?"

"The men in the suits and fedoras."

Once more, Brady shifted his gaze to the dining room. The Blues Brothers were gone. He glanced back at Annie. Took in her glistening lips. Inhaled her innocent fragrance. Heard her soft intake of breath.

Right then and there, he trifled with his number one rule for leading an uncomplicated life. The rule that had kept him safe, satisfied, and single for twenty-nine years. The rule he was about to shatter into a million little pieces.

Never tell a lie.

"They're still here," he said. "You better keep kissing me."